MESMERIZE

Also by Darlene Corbett

Visible

MESMERIZE

a novel

DARLENE CORBETT

WordCrafts

Mesmerize
Copyright © 2026
Darlene Corbett

Hardback ISBN: 978-1-967649-40-2
Paperback ISBN: 978-1-967649-41-9

Cover concept and design by Mike Parker.
Front cover art © Tabinda / Adobe Stock

Published by WordCrafts Press
Cody, Wyoming 82414
www.wordcrafts.net

"Good stories often introduce the marvelous or supernatural..."
~C.S. Lewis

In the beginning was the Word, and the Word was with God, and the Word was God.
~John 1:1

PART ONE
Meet & Match

Chapter One

Delphina

Delphina flicked her wrist, unfurling the delicate folds of her fan like a peacock spreading its plumage. Her lips curved into a smile as she aerated herself and strode down the sidewalk wearing her Jimmy Choo heels.

What tale might you weave about this weekend, Storyteller?

Hmm. Let's pretend.

Flecks of pastel watercolors splashed across her mind's landscape, streaming into random letters that connected into syllables, words, sentences, and paragraphs.

"Woah."

Stumbling on a crack in the concrete, Delphina swayed but steadied herself.

"Phew." Close call.

Delphina, pay attention. Stop contriving stories. You don't know what will happen. Nor will you be listening to anyone because you're just helping the organizer.

And about you?

Are you kidding?

Penning a tale about this chapter in your twenty-eight-year-old book of life would evoke a long yawn, causing the reader to discard it. So, relinquish any meanderings, concentrate on your career, and right now, focus on your steps, or you might be less lucky the second time.

After almost spraining her ankle last year, Delphina decreased her heel height to three inches. The near miss-encounter with a surgical boot forced her to choose health over height.

Determined to prevent that from happening again, she ended a long-term affair with her stilettos. As she departed from each pair, her hands glided over her beloved heels, stroking and kissing one shoe at a time.

"Goodbye, beautiful. Someone else will wear you well, giving you a chance to dazzle again."

With that, she placed each into a local charity bin, and to appease her petulant self, she purchased platform heels.

More comfortable and enough elevation.

Now, although beads of sweat trickled down her back, a sauna beat the steam room back home. But August in Sin City? Why did her mother want an event at the end of summer in 100-degree weather?

An image of a striking woman appeared. With silver threads draping her shoulders and arched, sable brows crowning her jade eyes, Lucia wagged a finger at her. "And why not? What holidays occur in August? None. And why not get the lesser rate for one of the most beautiful hotels in the world?"

Delphina frolicked toward the majestic fountain display. Water nymphs danced in splendor. A treat for her as she rushed toward the hotel. Frank Sinatra's ageless song, *Fly Me to The Moon*, played for all to hear, prompting her to close her eyes and sway. Droplets sprinkled on her face, and warmth infused her body as she rocked back and forth and hummed.

Closing her fan and dropping it into her bag, Delphina snapped her fingers and immersed herself in the tune.

Bam.

Out of nowhere, someone banged into her. A shudder reverberated throughout her body.

Her Louis Vuitton pocketbook tumbled from her arm. Lipstick, a compact, pens, the fan, and an iPhone spilled, clattered, and

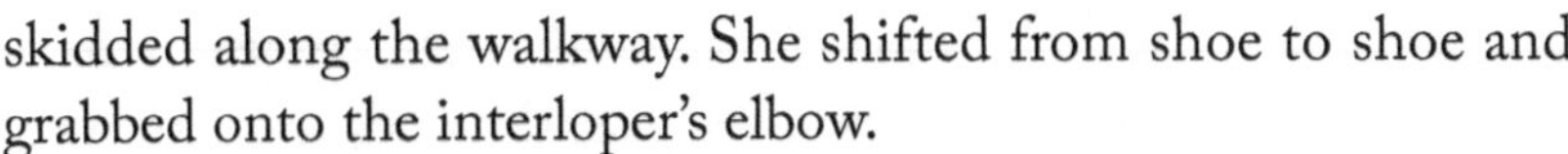

skidded along the walkway. She shifted from shoe to shoe and grabbed onto the interloper's elbow.

"Are you okay?" a gravelly voice asked.

"Yes." Delphina released her hand and stared at the surrounding clutter.

"So sorry." The man stooped down to collect the fallen items. "I'm in a hurry to get to the event."

Delphina frowned, shook her head, and bent down as endless feet clomped around them. "No problem."

She threw everything into the bag, raised her head, and gazed into the most unusual face she ever encountered.

A shock of gray-streaked, black hair fell over the man's eyes. He threaded his fingers through it and pushed the locks from his face. "So much for man-gel working, but…" He grinned, picked up the Louis, and offered his hand. "Again, I apologize for bumping into you. Let me help you up."

Delphina's mouth dropped open, and she stared, unable to prevent herself from drowning in azure eyes, crowned with long, black lashes. Her eyes remained cemented.

She shook her head, thrust her palms on the concrete, and propped herself up. "Thank you. I'm all set." She stood, wobbled, and almost lost her balance. The man reached for her arm to steady her.

Delphina drew her shoulders back, pulled away from him, and slapped the residue from her hands. She shifted her gaze.

"Will you attend the event tonight?"

"I'm assisting the organizer." Delphina glanced at her watch. "Oh, I must hurry." She turned on her heel and *clicked-clacked* as fast as she could.

The man strode alongside her.

"By the way, I'm Alex, short for Alexander, and you are?"

"What?"

"Just wanted to introduce myself. I know there are lots of creeps out there, so I understand if you'd prefer not to tell me your name."

"Delphina." She pushed her gaze straight ahead.

She reached the door of the hotel, and the man jumped in front of her. Alex grabbed the handle of the glass door. "Please allow me." He swept his hand for her. "Delphina. What a beautiful name."

She peeked at the lanky six-footer and caught a cleft chin, a lopsided smile, and one crystal blue eye. "Thank you and thank you." She stomped ahead of him.

"Are you named after the flower?"

Delphina headed to the Ladies Room, and words trailed her. "You can ask my mother who's running the event."

"Nice to meet you, Delphina. See you there."

Delphina didn't respond and entered the luxurious sitting room of the Bling Hotel. Signaling the comings and goings of a variety of visitors, a mix of beautiful aromas spritzed around her like a harmony of fragrant flowers. She took a deep breath of the delicious scents, settled into one of the velvet chairs in front of a mirror, and blinked at her reflection. Golden curls woven into a tight French braid with bangs and wisps of coils framed her oval face. She removed oversized, leopard-print, faux reading glasses and studied her brownish-gold eyes.

Yes, a bookish appearance.

Wrapped in a titanium bubble.

Safety. Safety from…

From what?

Hurt.

Delphina applied pink lipstick, rubbed her lips together, and placed her glasses snug on her face. She wanted to go unnoticed, unlike those who would attend the event in search of love and marriage.

But Delphina?

No thanks.

Not after what happened last year. A second and far-worse rupture. Not going for strike three.

Now, as they say, all work and no play for her. But the role as professional storyteller stimulated her as if it were playing.

Her mother's voice trickled into her ears. "Time for a change. Open yourself to love again."

Right before they flew to Las Vegas, Delphina's eyes probed her mother's. "Is that why you asked for my help?"

"No, but I'm hoping you'll see beyond… Well, I don't have to say it."

"Sorry, Mama. Not there yet. Maybe never."

How does she trust again after what happened? A double whammy.

Delphina glanced at her hands.

No jewelry adorned them except a watch on one wrist and a single gold bangle on the other, a gift from her Sito. She rubbed her left ring finger up and down. A naked fourth digit once again, almost glaring at her, insisting to keep it that way.

Delphina splayed the long fingers she inherited from Lucia. Her mother's words echoed in her mind. *Tsk, tsk. What happened to your French manicure? What about those gorgeous rings?* Yes, Lucia would throw her hands up before dropping them back. *Don't let him rob you. My darling, remember, God gifted us with these elegant branches, so dress them and dazzle others.* With two wide rings of mixed yellow and rose gold, and five twisted, jeweled bangles on her wrist, Lucia raised her hands. *Like me.*

Clink, clink.

Sure, Mama, sure. Good for you. But me? Not now. I want plain.

A stillness crawled into the suite, and she turned her head side to side. She sighed, leaned her chin under her palm, and stared at her reflection again.

"Okay, Delphina, no one is here, so allow yourself a moment with Alex." A dreamy glaze brushed over her face. "Those eyes, that chin."

A rustling interrupted her voice, and as she turned her head, crimson toasted her cheeks. A woman with short, spiky hair in a slinky, sequined dress pattered from the toilet area. "I was in the stall fixing my Spanx. I thought I was alone. Were you talking to me?"

Delphina shook her head and laughed. "To myself."

"Oh, honey. I do that all the time." The woman looked her up and down. "You're going casual, I see."

Delphina nodded. "Well, I…"

"No need to explain. You're a stunner, even in business chic." The woman's eyes jumped to the clock above, and as she ambled out of the suite, words dropped behind her. "Yikes, I'm late. You better hurry, girl."

Delphina returned her gaze to the mirror and allowed her chin to lean on her hands.

But before extinguishing him altogether, Alex looked more like an Alexander and should refer to himself by his given name.

What are you doing?

None of your business because he's not becoming a part of yours.

She closed her eyes, and a broom protruded into her mind, sweeping every part of his face away.

Delphina stood and inspected her designer short black jacket. She tugged at the collar of her white blouse and examined her sleek black pencil skirt. Her eyes moved to her shoes again.

In a very low voice, she said, "Don't let me fall, Jimmy Choo. I descended to this height on purpose."

She tapped her black leather sandals.

Yes, I moved along just fine until that overeager Alexander bumped into me.

Delphina smirked. Not his fault. Pay attention and no one will knock you over.

She glanced in the mirror again, raised her chin, and in a voice armored in a warrior's confidence, she said, "That's right. Be on the lookout for anyone who tries in more ways than one. Never, ever again."

She cocked her head, and an etching of shaggy salt and pepper hair barged into her thoughts.

Maybe again, but not right now.

Alex

The name crowning the Bling Hotel couldn't have been more suitable. The ambitious entrepreneur created something unforgettable and surpassed everyone's wildest expectations.

Alex shielded his eyes with his hands as his gaze moved upward. Bling darted across the chandeliers.

He placed his hands on his hips and grinned. Yup. Bling, bling above.

His gaze settled on the interior.

Muted pastel colors swirled together. Wow. The opposite. Comfortable. Almost, umm, mesmerizing—but not with the noise.

A buzz of different voices cluttered the atmosphere.

Taking a sip of his vodka martini, his bloodhound nose detected a subtle scent of spearmint puncturing the space.

Lucia's idea?

Splashing the atmosphere with invigoration?

Yup. She'd do that to keep everyone refreshed.

Alex's eyes scanned the room. What a setup for the evening's affair. Fifty round tables with woven wrought-iron bases topped with glass. They stood on display with satin-cushioned chairs and waited for their occupants. A single coral rose adorned each table and teased those who hoped to find love.

He waited with the others for Lucia to stand on the podium and announce the rules. His eyes settled on the attendees who bustled through the room. Ladies, in short dresses, sipped their Cosmos or glasses of wine. Several sauntered by and flashed smiles at him.

He and most of the other men held glasses of spirits or beers, wore jackets and trousers, and a few, like him, sported a tie.

He loved ties, and men and women complimented him on his choices.

Tonight, he chose a silk aqua tie embroidered with the figure of an elephant, one of his favorite animals. He noticed it today as he strolled by a window display. *Buy me*, it beckoned.

How could he resist?

When he returned to his room, Alex laid the tie against his clothes. Perfect. It brought out the darker shade from his shirt, which complemented his lightweight gray suit.

Now, all spruced up, Alex leaned against the bar. Many women told him that combining his cleft chin, unusual eye color, and streaked gray hair drove them wild.

Ever since childhood, women of all ages squeezed his chin with, "You're adorable," or "How can I stay mad at you."

How did he respond?

Laughed. And when puberty coated his voice with a deep, graveled tone, he created more of a stir.

Twenty-nine-year-old Alex shrugged off the attention. Although never consumed by his outward appearance, that dark episode a year ago reminded him of the tenuousness of life. His looks didn't rescue him. Instead, they might have worked against him, and only his parents' support, therapy, and faith in God salvaged him.

He winced any time he ventured down that dangerous path. Red pointy nails.

Ouch.

His fingers touched the area, still a reminder, even though the wounds healed. With the help of a skilled plastic surgeon, the scars became almost invisible.

But internal trauma remained.

Hey, don't go there, pal. Shut it down, like you do at work.

Alex concentrated on the cool, metal cross that touched his chest as he waited for the games to begin. No matter how decorative his outside appearance, the most important item lay beneath.

After the crisis, psychotherapy brought him back from the cliff of despair, but his faith saved him from a fatal leap. Faith and prayers, and he'd never forget how they helped, often gazing at the sky with a whisper of thank you.

Although he respected people's religious beliefs or lack of faith, he expected the same in return, and he didn't shy away if a challenge arose.

A potential partner? Different story. She needed to believe in God. Nonnegotiable.

Lucia headed his way and opened her arms.

With a Syrian background, her golden skin contributed to her looking good for a woman over fifty. Medium-height, slender, long white hair, and youthful. Tonight, she wore a black sleeveless dress.

"Lucia, you never age."

"Oh, Alex, you flatter me."

She hugged and kissed him hard on the cheek. "Mwah."

Her green eyes flashed. "I'm pleased you've come. Many of my Boston area clients accepted my invitation, but you," she said in a low tone, "are special."

Alex's eyes smiled at her. "Ah, I'm honored, but watch out. I might get an enormous head."

She cooed, "You, Alex? Never. But I can't say enough how happy I am that you're here."

"I see what I would've missed if I declined. Quite the spectacle, Lucia."

"Yes, a place, I hope, where people might find a potential partner, even if it's not the person sitting across from them."

"You never know." Alex laughed as his eyes roamed the room and landed on Delphina.

Lucia's gaze followed his. She jutted her chin. "Alex, I see you've noticed a beautiful woman. Guess what? She's my daughter."

Alex turned to Lucia. "I know. We met." His eyebrows lifted. "I remember you mentioned you had a daughter getting married."

"Did I? I don't recall telling you that." A curtain of sadness draped across Lucia's eyes, but a moment later, she clapped, and a dazzling smile appeared. "Anyway, things can change." She cocked her head and stared at her daughter. "How did you meet Delphina?"

"On my way into the hotel." Alex grinned. "You might say we bumped into each other."

"Oh?" Lucia asked, eyes widening. "Good, and…?"

"Not much more, Lucia." His eyes wandered until they rested on Delphina as she placed handouts on each table. "We had little time for much of a conversation. She seemed determined to get to her destination."

Lucia called and waved to her daughter. Delphina lifted her head. Lucia curled her hand. "Come here."

Delphina's gaze bounced from Lucia to Alex. As if frozen, she stopped, and her mouth formed the letter "O."

Delphina

Delphina's lips wouldn't budge from the "O" position. Maybe thoughts of the Bellagio's Cirque de Soleil show, "O," oozed into her psyche. The sight of Alexander with her mother rendered her voiceless.

She shifted her feet, shook her head, and pointed to the pamphlets. By then, her lips moved but clamped tight.

No way will I go over there.

Delphina put her head down and stared at the elegant booklets that required placement.

But the corner of her eye detected movement, her mother dragging Alexander in her direction.

Need to keep going.

"Delphina," Lucia said, "I understand you met this special person."

At least she didn't say an old friend.

Delphina stopped and looked at her mother's beaming face.

"Yes, Mama, we met." Delphina forced her lips to tilt upward, and she turned her head to the aqua tie with an elephant on it. In slow motion, her eyes tiptoed up to a cleft chin, the same lopsided smile, and sparkling eyes.

She held her breath.

"Nice to see you again," Alex said.

Heat crawled up her cheeks. She adjusted her glasses, tapped her fingers along the handouts, and stepped away. "You too, but excuse me, I need to—"

Lucia grabbed the rest from her. "I'll finish this and leave you time to chat with Alex." Her eyes crinkled into a smile. "He loves dogs and elephants like you."

"No, Mama, let me." Delphina tried to wrestle them back, but Lucia pulled the pamphlets to her chest and backed away. "My darling daughter, I'm in charge here, and I call the shots." She pivoted, and as she ambled in the other direction, she tossed a few more words over her shoulder. "Besides, no hurry to start right on time."

To halt the jumping jacks within her, Delphina raised her chin and tucked her stomach muscles as much as they would allow before screaming *enough*.

Talk, Delphina. Say something.

"So, Alex, what a small world. How do you know my mother?"

"We met a few years ago." Alex said, with a twinkle in his eye.

Mama referred to him as special, so he wasn't one of her past clients.

"Hmmm. Interesting."

"If you say so." Alex's eyes probed hers. "Speaking of you, do you plan on partaking in tonight's event?"

Delphina bristled. "I'm just helping my mother keep things organized. I've no interest in being a part of this."

"Wow. You don't sound very positive."

"I'm not," Delphina said with a forced laugh. "No offense to you or anyone else who's here. Just not my thing." She folded her arms.

His mouth sprouted a lopsided smile, and she blinked, trying not to venture further into the ocean depths of his blue eyes.

"Yeah, I get it, but I trust Lucia. She convinced me to accept the invitation. Plus, I registered for a conference which I attended earlier this week."

Delphina glanced at the crowd and spotted her mother as she approached the podium.

"Well, Alexander, I mean Alex…"

"Did you just call me Alexander?"

"Sorry." Delphina knew her cheeks crested with pink, so she fiddled with her glasses again to distract.

"No, please don't apologize." His eyes danced. "I like the way you used my formal name."

"Well, Alexander," Delphina softened her voice, "it was nice chatting with you." She turned to the stage as her mother ambled toward the microphone. Without pivoting toward him, she said, "Looks like the show is about to begin, so I'll let you get to your seat."

Delphina spun around and stepped away.

"Um, excuse me, Delphina?"

She glanced over her shoulder, and Alex's gray trousers and black leather loafers appeared in her peripheral vision.

"Without sounding too forward, I hope to see you again. Maybe before we leave Las Vegas?"

The microphone boomed and echoed as Lucia uttered, "Testing, one, two, three," and shouted to a technician for help.

Delphina nodded without turning to him. As she moved away, a muffled "elephant" strayed behind her. But she refused to engage further and hurried toward the registration desk, where she would keep an eye out to ensure no problems arose. Lucia reminded her that no matter how many times you laid down rules, you couldn't predict if someone might break them.

After she jogged to the table, Delphina sat, folded her hands, and inspected the room.

Good. Excellent view of everyone.

With her index finger, she scrolled down the list and found Alexander's name. Table 15, close to the registration desk. Before she studied the roster further for any other Alexanders or Alexes, she looked up as he moved toward his table.

Delphina gaped at him. Handsome, but he knows it.

Alexander glanced at her and waved. A warm flush invaded Delphina's face again, and with a quick nod, she turned her head toward the stage, as her chair scraped the wooden floor.

"Welcome, Ladies and Gentlemen, to the First Annual Speed-Dating Event." Lucia said with open arms. "In case you forgot, my name is Lucia Tulasi, and I bill myself as the Old-fashioned Matchmaker."

As Delphina stared at her mother, a half-smile tugged at her lips.

My mother. Now a Matchmaker. Perfect transition for her.

Taking the mic off its stand, Lucia sauntered across the stage. "Tonight could be the night to find the one you love." Her voice lilted like a melodious soprano. "And if not, good practice. Agree, my friends?"

The audience cheered.

"As you know, I have matched you with ten people in 75 minutes, a random selection, like rolling the dice." Lucia waggled her eyebrows. "You never know."

The crowd laughed.

"You'll not meet everyone here, but that doesn't mean you can't approach them during intermission or chat with them at the after-party. Right?"

"Right," yelled many attendees.

"Now, you know the rules. I interviewed each of you, but in case I missed, or you forgot, tonight's event will be squeaky clean. Rated G. No foul language, no sexual innuendos. All of you know the purpose of tonight's event, to meet new people in search of a loving relationship, not a hookup. So, if you have other intentions, please leave now."

Delphina's gaze circled the crowd as silence stole the room.

Lucia clapped. "Good. Everyone appears to have found their seats. Let's begin with three minutes to ask one of the three questions you received with your package, and you'll switch. You don't have to ask the same question. Once three minutes pass, you'll have one minute to get to your next table. Not much time, but a spark of what might become a long, steady flame."

Her mother stopped, and another hush breezed into the room as the crowd waited for the signal. Lucia pulled out her phone. "Get ready." She pressed the timer. "Go."

With her hand on her chin, Delphina peeked at Alex and his first match.

Chapter Two

Alex

Alexander loosened his tie as the glass elevator took him to the tenth floor. He stayed close to the door, thankful it stopped at every level, and examined the crowd below.

She left early.

During the intermission, as he mingled with the crowd, she floated past him. At one point, he caught her staring at him, and scarlet tinged her face. He waved and raised his index finger, making his way to her. As she turned on her heel, the chandeliers blinked as they did every hour. He couldn't find her with flashes leaping between light fixtures and firework outbursts. *Oohs* and *ahhs* captured the room. Once the sixty-second display ended, Delphina appeared to have vanished.

Alex knitted his brows together. Wow, she sends interesting signals. What's her deal?

He shook his head. He'd like to ask Lucia, but he wouldn't go there with her.

"Hey handsome, I enjoyed our speedy conversation." Alex turned to the tall raven-haired woman, whose long fingers with even longer pointy white nails, skipped across his arm.

"Hi, there."

What was her name?

She wiggled her eyebrows. "Remember me?"

"Sure."

"Not my name though, right, Alex?"

He offered a lopsided smile. "Sorry, uncertain of anyone's, but let me try, Anna?"

"Close. Annalise."

"Ah, yes. Enjoying yourself?"

"I am, but I'd like to continue our conversation where we left off."

The lights began flashing, and Lucia's voice emerged from the stage, telling everyone to take their seats.

"Well, Annalise, nice seeing you again."

The woman took her hand of sparkling bracelets to toss her silky waist-length hair, behind her back. She leaned close to Alex's ear. "Let's try to catch up later." Pulling back, Annalise eyed him up and down. "The night is young." She winked, turned, and swayed her hips toward her table.

Alex shook his head, peered at the itinerary, and walked to his seat.

Annalise, a corporate lawyer, thought a lot of herself. The third woman to sit at his table for the first half of the event, flipped her hair, and insisted on going first. She took her questionnaire and, with delicacy, tore it into several pieces. After laying the tattered sections on the table, she folded her arms, lifted her chin, and said, "I know what I want and need, so Lucia's cute ice breakers aren't helpful to me. I have a two-part question I ask for those who interest me."

Alex arched an eyebrow. "Okay, so what would you like to ask me?"

"What do you do for work, and do you make over two hundred thousand?"

Alex's mouth dropped before he chuckled.

She gawked. "Yes, I know. Bold and beautiful."

He nodded and lifted his eyes. "Confident."

A husky laugh scraped from her throat. "Yes, so?"

"So?"

"So, what are your answers?"

"Um, I won't disclose my income, but you might figure it out when I tell you my profession."

She extended her hand, palm up, and nodded. "Fair enough."

"I'm the Chief Financial Officer for a biotech company."

Annalise bobbed her head. "You pass the test."

"All right. So, Annalise, I'm going to join you and go off script. How do you show humility when you're wrong?"

She raised her eyebrows, tilted her head back and forth for a moment, before putting her fingers under her chin. "I don't know because I'm never wrong."

Alex gave her a deadpan look to suppress a laugh. "What if you ever were? How do you think you'd handle it?"

"I don't know because, like I said…" Annalise leaned forward and folded her arms on the table. "I'm never wrong." She studied Alex. "For example, I know we could make, as they say, beautiful music and children together."

Ping. Ping.

Phew. Saved by Lucia's timer, the signal for the next person to sit down.

Thank you, God.

Taking her time, Annalise rose from her seat, flung her hair back, and purred, "Catch you later, gorgeous." And with the posture of a moving sculpture, she pivoted, swayed her hips, and headed toward her next date.

What a case! She and I would not make anything beautiful together.

Now Alex strolled toward his assigned seat. For this hour, he and the others who stayed at the same table would be the ones to move.

He sat down, listening to Lucia. Attendees hurried to reach their seats. Another woman from the last hour bent down. "Hi, remember me?" He slanted his head back and smiled. A bubbly woman, her red curls floating around her shoulders, shoved her card into his hand. "We forgot to exchange cards."

Alex pulled out one of his and handed it to her. She grabbed it.

"Let's text." Before she leaped to the next table, she said, "Later."

He put her card in his side pocket with the others given to him by the women he met. So far, a few seemed pleasant, but none intrigued him like Delphina.

The next seventy minutes brought some distraction for him. Each of the several women with whom he engaged for six-minute intervals was pleasant and attractive. But he widened and blinked his eyes, unable to erase the image of an oval face pushing through.

One of the last women, he met called him on it.

"Hey, did you fall in love already?"

"What?" Alex said, a blast of heat rising on his cheeks. "I apologize. Please understand. It has no bearing on you."

The woman, Nina, an attractive blonde, grinned. "No problem, Alex. I hope the woman who has your thoughts reciprocates. Just from watching you during the intermission, you seem like a nice guy. Lucky her."

Alex laughed. "We'll see. What about you?"

Nina blinked. "A couple of potentials, but the real prize looks like he's taken."

Alex shook his head, continuing to laugh.

They conversed about light topics for the rest of their session.

Ping.

Alex smiled as Nina stood up, stretched out her hand, and said, "In case it doesn't work out with your lady, I'd love to connect."

"Sure."

"Here's my card. So nice to meet you, Alex."

"You too, Nina." He bowed his head.

"Thank you for the lovely chat." She pivoted and sauntered to another table.

Nice woman.

If Delphina hadn't come along, maybe he would've called her, but that strange encounter changed everything.

Lucia clapped her hands. "Time for a slower pace. Ladies and gentlemen, whether you found love or not, I hope you enjoyed your time meeting new people. Now I invite you to go to the adjoining room to indulge in Bling's delicious food. There's plenty of liquor, but please not too much drink, thank you. Grab a plate. Then a time for dancing the night away."

She moved away from the stage and sprinted toward the disc jockey. She handed him a list of the requests she asked for during the intermission. The long-haired, young man nodded at her, scanning the list.

Alex's stomach rumbled, notifying him it was time to eat. He strolled into the other room, picked up a plate, ladled a few appetizers on it before his nose directed him toward the irresistible aromas of angel hair pesto and eggplant parmesan.

Lucia didn't skimp on anything. Sure, everyone paid a high price for this event, but he doubted she earned a huge profit. No, her financial windfall came from her Matchmaking services. Although she started her company a year ago, Lucia's reputation became renowned for helping so many people find love.

Makes sense based on her background.

After loading his dish, he wandered toward one table, where the other attendees sat. Carafes of water and wine were atop each table.

A natural extrovert, Alex enjoyed indulging in light banter, with questions about the usual, residence, work, or fun. Soon, a bombastic man joined the table and took control, with a booming voice of questions. Alex became quiet.

Good. Let him take over.

He ate a few bites, and his eyes skimmed the room.

No Delphina.

The music began, and people moved to the dance floor.

A tap on his shoulder prompted him to turn his head, and Annalise kissed him. "Come on gorgeous. Time for us to get to know each other better."

Alex shook his head and smiled. "You know, Annalise, I loved chatting with you and all the other beautiful women, but I'm going to call it a night."

Without looking at her, Alex put down his napkin and bounced up. "Good night, everyone. A pleasure. Enjoy."

He moved away from the table and strode to the elevator in the lobby.

He snapped out of his reverie as the elevator slowed to his floor. When the door opened, he stepped out and beheld a barefoot Delphina, high heels snug in her arms, galloping around the corner at the end of the hall. He started jogging and shouted her name. Right before he reached the bend, two doors slammed, one after another. He looked down at the lobby and slowed his steps, trying to figure out what room she had entered. He padded along the carpet, and when a door opened, he turned only to see a young, well-dressed couple emerge laughing and chatting as they strolled by him.

Except for a television droning from one room, silence unfurled. Quiet for Vegas at 9:00 PM.

Lights glittered along with the stars as Sin City yawned, rubbed its eyes, and awakened for the evening's mischief. Although an early riser, Alex would've stayed if Delphina hung around.

Yup, she seemed interesting, but interested?

Delphina

Delphina's eyes darted back and forth as she sunk into the door, palms securing her on the wooden surface. Footsteps meandered outside her suite and continued trudging back and forth until moving down the hall. Giggles became louder from a nearby room.

Like an Ice Queen, she refused to shift her position until the steps drifted away. A door opened and closed with a whisper.

Could Alex be on the same floor as her?

Okay, if you're on a diet from romance, what do you care?

Why did you peek at him so often? Huh?

Okay, admit it. Just because you're fasting from men and potential relationships, doesn't mean you're extinguishing them altogether.

His presence tweaked her.

When the event began, she focused on the booklet, forcing her eyes to scan each sheet with slow precision. Before she flipped the page, she picked up her cocktail glass, sipped on her virgin strawberry daiquiri, and peeked over the glass, observing Alex.

As a *ping* came from Lucia's phone, women flew to their chairs with their drinks, flopping down out of breath. Alex revealed impeccable chivalry as he stood for each arrival. Only one sultry, raven-haired woman, wearing a fringed sequin dress, sauntered over to his chair at a snail's pace. Admiring males and curious females watched her make her way to the standing Alex.

Before the woman reached Alex, he turned in Delphina's direction and caught her eye. She gulped her drink, the delicious strawberry concoction fizzling down her throat.

The raven-haired woman pivoted to see who drew Alex away from her. When she showed her face, Delphina blanched.

My God. Her chest heaved as if someone pulled the strings of a corset too tight.

The woman resembled Margo.

She needed to get out of there.

Delphina jumped up, took her bag, and forced her jelly legs to move. She headed toward the Ladies Room and as she opened the door, she almost collided with her mother.

Lucia's eyes widened.

"Delphina, you look like you've seen a ghost. Are you all right?"

"Mama, did you see that woman?"

"What woman?"

"You know, the one who seemed to draw everyone's attention."

"You mean Annalise?"

"Yes."

Lucia nodded. "Yes, she's attractive but arrogant, which I didn't realize until she arrived at the event, peppering me with questions."

"How could you have missed that in the interview, especially with your background?"

"Darling, many people disguise their true selves. You should know that."

"Is that a dig?"

Lucia grimaced. "Delphina, I know how much you hurt, but you can't assume every beautiful woman pulls the wool over every man."

"Well, I bet this Annalise will try with your friend, Alex."

Lucia lifted her full, arched eyebrows. "Oh, so my friend Alex piqued your interest."

"I don't know."

"That's a good sign, my beautiful daughter." Lucia's eyes softened and searched Delphina's. She then glanced at her watch. "Oh dear, I need to hurry back. A staff person took over for this one interval." Before she left, she touched Delphina's face. "No matter what happens, just hearing 'I don't know' made my evening." Lucia's eyes pooled.

"Oh Mama, I don't want you to worry about me." Delphina hugged her mother, wrapping herself in the cocoon of maternal love, and then stepped back.

Lucia's catlike eyes slanted into a smile, and she touched her daughter's face one more time before scurrying away.

Delphina inhaled every morsel of her mother's aroma lingering from the embrace and devoured the remnant before it trailed away. She closed her eyes for a moment.

Thank you, God, for gifting me with a mother like mine.

Entering the large women's bathroom suite, Delphina's eyes skimmed the interior. A mauve and light gray palette created a comfortable and inviting ambience for women to primp. She sat in front of the vanity again. The first part of the speed dating event would end in ten minutes.

She removed her glasses and studied her face.

Should I let my hair down in more ways than one?

Scrutinizing the golden streaks in her light-brown hair, not one strand slipped out.

Alex's lopsided smile loomed in front of her.

No!

Leave the hair.

Maybe at tomorrow's brunch, she'd allow a couple of curls to roam free.

Not tonight. Stick to the plan.

Delphina allowed herself to revisit the episode.

Margo. Her best friend's cousin. Dark, devastating, and devious. All three descriptions crammed into one dazzling package.

That woman, Annalise, reminded her of Margo, causing her tenuous scars to throb.

Those types of women duped many guys, wrapping their claws and roars in the most captivating silk.

Would Annalise mesmerize Alex?

She clenched her fist.

Delphina, what's the deal? What do you care?

If he fell for someone Lucia considered arrogant, what does that mean about him?

You know the answer.

That consequential night, when everything changed. She arrived home a day earlier from an advanced storytelling conference.

Because so many people requested storytelling during their therapy sessions, an idea began to unravel and transform her practice, knitting new perspectives about the role of stories. Instead of calling herself a therapist, she reincarnated herself as a therapeutic storyteller and incorporated her business, *Healing Through the Rewrite, LLC.*

Storytelling intrigued her since childhood and complemented her visualization techniques. Her clients loved her to start with a sentence or two, providing them with a foundation. They'd sit for a moment, then take their pen and write their narrative on top of the building blocks, coloring in the details.

She drove to their new home outside of Boston. A small house with gorgeous floor-to-ceiling windows. She couldn't resist roaming around the renovated kitchen where she'd slide her hands on the polished, green granite countertops. Next, she'd visit the great room and glide her fingers along the stone fireplace. Last, she'd head upstairs to the beautiful Master bedroom, and giggle. She couldn't wait to indulge in the sacred pleasure.

Over the last six months, they sacrificed going out to eat and vacation to save enough for the down payment. Jude earned a higher salary than her, so his allotment towards the house account tripled hers.

Anytime she complained about this, he'd grab her. "We're a team. Understood?"

She'd offer him a whisper of a smile.

Delphina's small Volvo SUV crept up the cobblestone driveway, and the top of Jude's car peeked through the garage windows, which surprised her. He must've completed his work early in New York.

She stepped outside of the car, and as she closed the door, Delphina whipped her head back to the garage. An Audi. Hmmm. Oh well. Maybe his vehicle went out of commission.

Didn't matter. They'd walk around holding hands and linger for a moment in every room, as lips caressed each other's face and neck. Coming attractions for indulging in greater intimacy. She disclosed to Jude an incident that occurred at the end of college, and he proclaimed his admiration for her traditional beliefs, a rarity in these current times.

The reason for a brief courtship and even shorter engagement.

Giggles and chitchat interrupted her visit to the past. Women flocked into the lounge, securing a spot in line for the restroom.

Delphina shook her head and dug into her clutch, within the Louis, searching for eyeliner and lipstick. She flipped through the items she stuffed into the smaller bag, not looking at anyone.

After refreshing her makeup, she lowered her gaze to her iPhone, scrolled through texts and emails, and avoided any contact with others by gluing her eyes to her device. Stilettos *click-clacked* past her, and layered dresses crinkled as some women settled in front of the mirrors.

No, not going out there until the session begins.

Soon the conversations dwindled. Women pattered out of the lounge, one-by-one or in groups screeching, then *shh*, laughing in hushed tones.

Delphina stretched her neck for any sounds, but now silence smothered the room.

She waited a few minutes before heading back to the event. As she reached the registration table, she looked up. Everyone sat across from their six-minute partners. Because a switch took place, those who didn't move in the first session, now rotated after each encounter.

She didn't know how her mother created such an outstanding and organized event, but she performed the feat.

Delphina's gaze circled the room and spotted Alex sitting across from a redhead, whose curls bounced with her head.

Enough. He's here for a reason. So, good luck.

But creeping beneath her rigid defenses lurked, an "I hope not."

She turned away, kicked off her shoes, and closed her eyes. Each time Lucia's phone *pinged*, she popped up. Now halfway through the second half, she texted Lucia, telling her to message if she needed her. Otherwise, she'd be going outside to watch the water display and then return to her room to read.

A text came back from Lucia.

> `You sure?`

Delphina shook her head, before taking her thumbs to type.

> `Yes.`

> `Okay, just let me know when you reach your room, so I know you're safe.`

Lucia couldn't help but worry about her. She understood her protective mother, who promised her she'd do the same once she gave birth to a child. Delphina's index finger pressed the two emojis, with a raised thumb and a heart.

Now traipsing across the hotel suite, she undressed and slipped on her red nightgown. Sitting in front of the vanity, she wiped off residual makeup and stared at her natural face, blinking back.

Would she ever trust again? Could she ever expose her true self to another man?

As she pulled out bobby pins, her fingers combed through her unlaced hair, and waves tumbled down. Tomorrow, she would indulge her head as she loosened the reins on her locks with a relaxed bun. Not as severe as the tight French braid, but like the rest of her, not carefree.

She jumped on the high mattress, plumped up four pillows, read her evening prayer, and started a romance novel. Soon her eyes fluttered, and sleep captured her for the next eight hours. While in deep slumber, a fuzzy outline formed of a familiar figure, which she couldn't discern, but she followed as the shape waved for her to join. Who? What? Where are they taking her? She hoped to find out.

Chapter Three

Alex

Alex traveled all over the world. Now, as he huffed, extending and contracting his arms up and down, he determined nothing compared to the Bling's fitness center. State-of-the-art equipment. The weights appeared brand new, as did the machines, with a few more advanced pieces for resistance training.

Maybe I'll suggest to management back home they consider investing in something similar.

Besides a daily conversation with God, nourishment for his mind and soul, his second commitment required exercising the body. Not surprising to him, research maintained that exercise boosted mental health.

He couldn't agree more. He pushed himself to a higher level of physical and mental endurance. No finishing lines. Without exercise and prayer, he wouldn't have survived.

Yup. Those who receive a great deal need to give back, so keep it healthy, pal.

Time for some interval training on the treadmill.

He jumped on the machine, pressed the manual button, and began a slow walk, increasing the level from flat to higher, upping the pace.

Push, pal, push.

Sweat dripped, showering his body, as his eyes swept over his sinewy arms. They rippled and glistened like polished apricot agate.

An attendant handed him an ice-cold face cloth dipped in eucalyptus. "Thanks."

Alex slowed the machine down to stop, putting the cloth over his entire face before stepping down.

He scanned the room and noticed a few familiar faces from last night. Sauntering over to the cooler, he filled his water bottle, tipped his head back, and gulped the refreshing liquid.

"Ah." He planted the water bottle on the floor and stooped down to tie the loosened shoestring of his sneaker. When he stood up, Alex did a double take.

In dark, loose workout clothes, a wide visor, and hair in a ponytail, Delphina collected her towel and bag. Almost incognito, but not to him.

Yup, that's her.

Should he try again?

Heck, what did he have to lose?

"Hi," he said, strolling over to her as she pulled her gym bag over her shoulder, getting ready to leave. "How are you? I almost didn't recognize you."

"Deliberate disguise. Since last night, several people approached me with questions. Even though I work out earlier than most, I didn't want to take any chances." She tugged on a large brim visor and gave him a half smile. "You know, exercise in peace."

Alex swallowed, wiping his face and arms with his towel. "I'm sorry if I interrupted."

"Of course you didn't." A rosy hue invaded her face. "I just finished."

She laughed and averted her gaze. "The redness just won't go away."

Trying to convince herself, me, or both of us that she's blushing?

"Sure." He nodded, preventing her further embarrassment. "Let's walk out together."

Delphina joined him with eyes straight ahead. Other than a thank you from her when Alex opened the doors heading toward the elevator, silence suspended any further conversation.

Although someone else might think it weird, Alex found a certain comfort in the stillness between them. When the elevator doors opened, he peeked at her. She bit her lip with her lower teeth.

"What floor?" he asked, feigning ignorance about last night.

"The tenth."

"Hey, we're on the same floor. How about that?" Alex's lopsided smile sprang forth.

She glanced at him for a moment before staring ahead and shrugging. "I think several of us are on the same floor, since my mother blocked out certain rooms."

The high-speed elevator reached the tenth floor, and when the doors opened, Alex brushed his hand out for her to walk in front of him.

"Are you attending the brunch later this morning?"

She stopped, and with a pinched expression, she said, "Do I have a choice? My mother would be apoplectic if I didn't appear even for a brief time."

Alex's eyes locked with hers for a split second before he grinned. "I never saw that side to Lucia."

Delphina cocked her head. "I never asked, but how do you know my mother?"

"Oh, a story for another time."

"Don't tell me you—"

"Not to interrupt, but I'm wondering if you'd be interested in attending a Cirque de Soleil show this evening. I know it's last minute, but I purchased two tickets in case I met someone, and..."

Delphina blinked, and pink blossoms formed on her cheeks again.

"And just so you know, I asked no one else."

She stood like a human statue for several seconds.

"If not, no problem, I'll go alone and leave the other ticket at the box office."

Delphina's eyes widened. "Oh, sorry, just thinking if my mother needed me." She stood with a timid smile. "I think I'd like that. I love Cirque de Soleil and have seen *O* and *Love* but wouldn't mind seeing one of those again or any other."

Alex beamed. "Fantastic. But it's neither of those."

"Oh. It's not the risqué one, is it?"

He shook his head and winced. "You don't know me, but I'd never take someone new or anyone who I thought might become uncomfortable."

She nodded.

"And to tell you the truth, I had the opposite in mind, a rated G-type."

"Which one?" she asked, wide eyes, amber flecks dancing with gold.

"*Mystere*, playing at Treasure Island," Alex said, as he took the towel hanging around his neck and wiped his face. "Have you heard of it?"

"I forgot about that one."

"Well, when I waited in line at the box office, I overheard people purchasing tickets for adults and children."

"Safe and sound." Delphina's lips attempted to curve upward.

"Yup."

A look between them lingered until someone barged into Alex.

"So sorry." The mother of a little boy said, as she grabbed his hand.

"No problem."

"Anthony, say 'Excuse me, sir.'"

"Skuse me."

Alex laughed and stooped down. "Hey, little man. Thank you." He put his palm up. "How about a high five?"

Anthony giggled and slapped Alex's hand. "High five." He then huddled behind his mother.

Alex stood up. The mother smiled, whispered a thank you, and hurried her son into the elevator.

More noise crept into the hallway.

Alex pivoted back to an expressionless Delphina.

"Little boys need to run and release that energy. They're the best." His eyebrows lifted. "Little girls, too. Hope to have a few of my own in the not-so-distant future. How about you?"

"How about me what?" Delphina bristled.

"Oh, I don't know. Just wondered your thoughts about kids."

"Well, maybe someday, but right now, they're not the first thing on my mind." Delphina grimaced and peeked at her watch. "I need to get ready and appear for this morning's brunch."

"Sure. Let me walk you to your room."

"Unnecessary." A polar vortex encircled her words.

"Well, where should we meet? The show begins at 7 so 6:15, 6:30."

"The lobby at 6:30."

"Sounds good, but will I see you at brunch?"

"Like I said, brief appearance. I have things to do."

Delphina rotated on her sneakers like a spinning top, dropping words as she jogged down the hallway. "See you."

Hey, pal, she's got walls. What's her deal? And how capable will she be of understanding yours?

Delphina

Bubbles brewed within her, gurgling from her throat into laughter. The first time in a long time.

Clowns bopped around in between the spectacular acrobatic show performed by Cirque du Soleil's gifted artists. *Mystere* offered a different display from the Bellagio's watery *O*, and the Beatles' *LOVE* at the Mirage.

For this themed show, more kids sat in the audience, parents whispering in their ears or gazing at them with eyes full of love. One little boy sitting on her left side kept peeking at her with his dimpled smile.

"You're pretty."

Delphina grinned. "Well, thank you …"

The mother murmured in his ear as the boy snuggled into her before turning back to Delphina.

The little boy said in a muffled tone, "Liam."

"Nice to meet you, Liam." Delphina winked at him. "What a lovely name for a handsome young man."

The little boy beamed.

"Liam has good taste."

Pleasure swirled through her heart as Delphina glanced at Alexander. "Thank you."

She turned her head back to the stage. The clown exited as the acrobats returned.

For a moment, Delphina imagined a little boy with golden hair and light blue eyes.

Prior to the breakup, she envisioned a little girl painted with olive skin, tawny hair, and brown eyes. A mixture of her and Jude, often alternating thoughts of a little girl for those of a little boy. She'd often shared these musings with Jude. He'd throw his head back, laugh, and wrap his arms around her.

"I can't wait to get started," he'd say with a lascivious grin, "and if you don't want to wait," his eyebrows raised, "no problem with me."

Delphina would extricate herself from his arms, fan herself, and move away from him. "Don't tempt me."

"Why not?" he'd asked. "We're getting married soon."

She'd shake her head. "No. Call me old-fashioned, because I am, and I want to keep my traditions even after what happened… Besides," she'd keep backing away from him, mirth frothing from her lips. "Good things come to those who wait."

Jude often crawled on his knees, panting. "I get it, but you're killing me, babe."

Alexander's brawny arm rubbed hers, bringing her back to the bookmarked chapter of now.

She peeked at the little boy again. His eyes remained glued to the acrobatic scene in front of them.

She followed his gaze to the flying figures above the crowd as they trapezed through the sky. Amazing gymnasts. Strength, balance, and agility. Pushing the limits with their sinewy bodies.

What a treat. Glad she accepted the invitation to attend.

"Fabulous, aren't they?" Alexander's peppermint-scented breath wafted around her.

Delphina bobbed her head.

For the rest of the show, she immersed herself in the artistry of the performers.

At the end, she and the audience clapped their hands. The little boy, Liam, said something to his mother, then to her. "That was so cool."

Delphina smiled at him. "Yes, Liam, I agree. Did you have fun?"

Liam bounced his head up and down, putting his fingers in his mouth, looking up at his mother before turning to her.

"How about a high five?" Delphina put her flat palm toward his.

Liam slapped his palm against hers before getting in front of his mother and exiting the theater.

Delphina followed them out with Alexander behind her.

"Boy, the little fellow liked you." His mouth glided across her ear again, awakening a delicious sensation. "Glad you took the idea of a high-five."

She nodded, and without turning around, she said, "Yes," letting it trickle behind her as she merged with the surrounding crowd.

Voices from all over the world reached her ears. At one point, she said, "Gracias," when a man allowed her to go in front of him. The man responded with, "De nada." Delphina turned her head to Alexander.

"Trying to use my Spanish more often."

"I think they speak Portuguese."

"De Nada?"

"Yes, in Spanish and Portuguese, but I heard him earlier, and he said to someone, 'obrigado.'"

"I see. You know the language?"

"Visited Rio years ago, and I never forgot."

"So, you enjoy traveling."

"I do, and you?"

"Yes, lots, but I have done little for the last couple of years."

"Well, maybe we can change that."

Delphina's eyes remained fixed ahead, but she couldn't suppress her lips from curling up.

"Did you eat?"

"I did."

"How about we go for some dessert, like ice cream."

Delphina turned and waded into his azure eyes. "Yes. I love ice cream but not too often." She tapped her stomach.

"Doesn't look like you need to worry." Alexander's eyes glanced down. "But that's why you stay the way you are."

She nodded and returned her gaze to those in front.

The crowd picked up the pace, carrying the chatter into the lobby. Delphina stepped ahead with Alexander striding alongside.

"I don't know if you noticed, but one of the coolest old-fashioned ice cream parlors sits right in the pavilion connected with the Bling."

"I didn't, but I'd love to explore and indulge."

Alexander offered his arm. "May I have the pleasure?"

Delphina hesitated for a moment before looping her arm into his.

"There. Now we won't lose each other."

Delphina permitted her eyes to ascend and reach his, allowing a brief but sweet surrender into his blue depths.

Uh-uh.

She shifted her gaze as he tucked her arm tighter.

His other arm reached up and pointed. "Look, right in front of us."

Delphina smiled as she followed his finger to the ice cream parlor. "Oh, my."

"Let's try to get ahead of the crowd." Alexander grabbed her hand, and they frolicked toward the shop. Organ music piped louder as they reached the door.

Gazing at the Tiffany-style lamps through the window, Delphina said, "I never heard that kind of organ music."

"I think they're emulating Welte's orchestrion, and look at that one lamp." Alexander pointed. "It contains a carbonated water dispenser."

"How do you know so much about an ice cream parlor?" Delphina's eyes searched deeper into the shop, taking in the backbar, stained glass, and mirrors.

"When I go anywhere, I look for interesting landmarks." Alexander grinned. "And because I love ice cream, I discovered the owner of this place referenced the one from his childhood home in Indiana, so I researched that. And…"

Delphina lifted her eyes, giving him a tilt of her lips.

"The place in Indiana, Zaharakos, maintains the largest collection of pre-1900 soda fountains on public display. How about that?"

An attractive woman in front of them spun around with a dazzling smile. "I didn't mean to eavesdrop, but thank you for the information." Her eyes lingered a bit as Alexander returned the smile, with an air tip of the hat. "Glad to oblige, ma'am." The woman's eyes moved to Delphina as they entered the shop.

A growl lodged in her throat before stuffing it back down.

Why do you even care? He's good-looking, and all the ladies and gents know it.

"You impressed her with your knowledge." Delphina bristled as they moved into the parlor.

"Nothing special. Like I said, just my thing, researching unusual places. Sometimes mysterious ones."

Delphina's inner spikes receded. Give the guy a break.

They reached the glass encasement of frozen confection vessels, and the symphony of ice cream flavors sang of whirling delights. A harried young man took their orders and scooped her favorite, chocolate-chip cookie dough, packed it into a small cup, and handed it to her.

"Thank you."

"Anything else, miss?"

Alexander said, "We're together."

"Sir?"

Alexander wiggled his eyebrows at Delphina's choice. "I'll have a large vanilla ice cream soda with lots of whip cream on top."

Delphina opened her purse, but Alexander put his hand on hers and closed it. "No. I invited you."

After Alexander paid, he placed his hand on her back, and they sauntered over to a round table with two wrought-iron chairs and velvet cushions. Alexander rushed in front of her, pulled out one, and swept his hand. "Madame."

Delphina's lips tilted up as she sat. "Ah, Merci, Monsieur."

He pulled out his chair and jotted a smile. "My few words in French. Et tu?"

As her cheeks warmed into Pink Lady apples, Delphina squinted one eye and touched her index finger and thumb together. "Petite."

Within seconds of sitting down, Alexander jammed a spoon into his soda, plopping a dollop into his mouth. "Couldn't resist." Whipped cream dressed his lips.

Delphina giggled, before taking a taste of hers, and the titanium shield around her chest loosened its grip.

Alexander took another scoop before slurping on his straw. His eyes twinkled, and he stopped for a moment, dazzling her with his lopsided smile.

Her cheeks toasted again. "You seem quite content."

"You betcha. How's your ice cream?"

"Delicious." Delphina leaned forward and, taking an extra napkin, dabbed at the whipped cream around his mouth.

"Thank you." His eyes invited hers to fly with him.

No.

Delphina inhaled. "So, Alexander. Besides learning about interesting sites, exercising, and ice cream, what else do you enjoy doing in your free time?"

"Wow." He dug his spoon into the soda and licked both sides. "I feel like I'm back to last night's speed dating questions."

Her cheeks burned like grilled cherries. "Sorry, I didn't mean to…"

"No, no, please. Good question, but for the last year, work, work, work, not much play."

"How come?"

"Oh, lots of reasons, but besides ice cream, ice hockey, travel, music, reading, dogs, elephants, and ties.

"Ties?"

"Yup. I collect them."

"But tonight, you're tieless." Delphina's eyes dipped toward his open shirt, catching gray curls lining the collar.

"Casual can be good."

His eyes skirted her light dress.

"What about you, Delphina?"

"Wait. Before me, you mentioned hockey. Do you play hockey or just watch it?"

"As far back as I can remember, glued myself to the TV screen with my dad and brother whenever the Grizzlies played. Sometimes, Mom joined us. I played in high school and college. Now I watch and play once or twice a week for an amateur league in Boston."

Delphina nodded. "My mother loves hockey."

"What about you?"

"Neutral. I like sports but I don't watch many games except during the playoffs. I know this will sound weird, but I love baseball."

"Why do you think that's weird? Lots of people follow the Sox, including me, but the game gets slow and boring."

"I view the slow and steady pace as a metaphor for life."

Alex placed his chin under his knuckles, with his eyes clamping onto hers. "Interesting perspective."

A heatwave rippled across her face, and she blinked.

"Think about it. Life can go along. Sometimes mundane, and then boom, a game changer." She paused, and her eyes descended.

"Yeah. Good point. It can become a fun, exhilarating ride."

Delphina pursed her lips, placed her palms flat on the table, and words scratched from her throat. "Not always. The change might become a major letdown."

Her eyes crept back up to his face.

Stay steady, girl. He's a good-looking guy, but so what?

"Enough about that. What else do you want to know?"

Alex raised his eyebrows. "Um, along with baseball, hobbies, interests, dogs, elephants?"

Without looking up, she laughed. "Besides dogs and elephants, I, too, love traveling, reading, dancing, but I've had little time for those activities. Been working a great deal these last couple of years."

"Yeah, you're a storyteller?"

"I am."

"Well, can you tell me more about it." He pitched forward. "How about a story?"

She shook her head. "No. I love my craft, but no work tonight."

Alexander leaned back. "Now, my turn for an apology."

"Please. No problem. Everyone asks."

"So, Delphina. I'll ask the same question. How come so much work in the last year?"

Jude's face loomed.

CHAPTER FOUR

Alex

Alex studied his reflection in the full-length mirror, unbuttoning and dropping his shirt.

"Yeah, God's been good, as they say, but pal, keep preserving the gifts he offered you."

Six-pack abs.

Yup.

Arms that stressed his sinewy physicality.

Yup again.

A chest of hair he refused to shave or laser, even with gray curls.

A third yup.

Although he dated several women after Daphne, no one complained about his premature coloring. Many of them swooned over him and offered a sensual delight on the first date. A few women traced their index finger along his lower lip and rolled it down his chin dimple. His passion ignited, but he'd remove their hand, kiss the top of it, and bid them good night.

Flings were never his thing, and after what happened, no way would he succumb to the hypnotic lure of a siren.

And, this woman, Delphina… She put him in his place.

"Oh, fast ride," Delphina said, when the elevator chimed for the tenth floor.

The doors opened, and he swept his arm as they stepped off the carriage. Delphina didn't respond and clasped her clutch, gripping it in front of her.

"Thank you for the lovely evening, but no need to walk me to my room." She thrust her chin toward the corridor. "The Bling ensures safety, so I'll leave you here."

"I look forward to seeing you again back in Boston, but Delphina, may I kiss you?"

She took her finger and pointed it to her cheek.

When his lips touched her smooth skin, allowing the peck to linger, she stiffened and stepped backwards. Her cheeks blossomed with high color. "Again, thank you for the evening. Have a safe flight home. I'll wait until I hear from you." She spun around and jogged toward her room. He watched her, and when she reached the bend, she didn't look his way. He waited until he heard the click of her door.

What the heck is her story?

She must have one. Her indifferent attitude stated something. What? Well, he'd find out. At least, he hoped he would. Besides beautiful, something intriguing about her. And being Lucia's daughter?

He peered closer into the mirror and rubbed his chin.

Still tender, and a reminder…

Chatter, laughter, and clinking of ice cubes. Inviting sounds to Alex as he entered the foyer. A hand-woven oriental rug commanded his attention first. Motifs with colors of cobalt blue and red waltzed together with a splash of gold singing in between. The carpet overlay a glossy hardwood floor with two sweeping staircases opposite one another like curving bookends. But those items slid into the background as his eyes caught the enormous portrait hanging from the balcony. The painting exhibited a red velvet background with beautiful people wearing white with red and gold accessories.

Wow. Logan seemed to have it all. Good genes.

Also, from everything Logan claimed, perfect health and financial wealth. Although he boasted to Alex and the rest of the team, he did it with humor.

"Gentlemen, I've done it, and so will you, not can, but…" He'd look at everyone. Full head of peppery hair, smoldering eyes, and pearly whites staring at each of them. "…Will. That's right. Will. Follow me, and you shall see."

Alex nodded his head as he studied the portrait.

"Hey, you. Glad you made it."

Alex turned as Logan trotted over to him. He hugged Alex and patted him on the back.

"Sorry, sir. Traffic."

"No apologies necessary. You've arrived in time for the sunset and the music." Logan glanced at his Rolex watch. "And please, no need to call me sir at this event. Logan will do. But come on and join the rest of the guests."

Alex followed the CEO, dressed in expensive jeans, a lightweight blazer, and an open-collared shirt.

Glad I did the same thing. Brought the tie just in case but looks like I don't need it.

Logan jogged down a hallway.

Alex moved at the same clip, but his eyes darted as they passed by artwork hanging from red walls with antique pieces scattered along the way. Large skylights illuminated everything.

"Impressive house."

Logan wheeled around and walked backwards with a grin. "I earned it Alex, and so will you."

He pivoted again, and they came to a set of French doors. About seventy-five people stood around a kidney-shaped pool.

Logan opened the doors to the outside patio and swung his

arm for Alex to step out first. "Salt-water. How about that, Alex?"

"Again, impressive, sir."

"Remember, for tonight, no sir, just Logan."

"Got it."

Alex looked around. A mixed crowd. Twenties to fifties. Everyone appeared toned. The women wore casual dresses, and the men donned attire like him and Logan. Everyone screamed *Wealth*… or at least getting there.

He waved to a couple of familiar faces. Servers passed around cocktails and hors d'oeuvres while the caterers organized food on long tables hiding in the background. Small, round tables with colorful cloths dressing them, and festive chairs for four held court around the patio section. Large vases of seasonal flowers positioned in between.

The aroma of food wafted by Alex. His stomach growled.

"Yay." An applause rose above other sounds as everyone watched God's unique uncovering of the night's sunset.

"Hey, O'Hara, come over here."

Two of his peers curled their hands as they sauntered over to an unoccupied table.

"Glorious, huh, Alex?" Logan approached him again with two women, both resembled the one in the portrait.

"Indeed, sir…" He halted.

Logan roared and turned to the two women. "Alexander, here, can't let go of his formalities even in this relaxed setting." He smirked at Alex and then turned to one woman. "I hope our sons…" Logan pointed toward two young sun gods who resembled the Winklevoss twins of Facebook fame, "…embrace the civility and manners that Alex developed."

"Logan, talk about manners? How do you expect our sons to follow such exemplary behavior when you aren't doing it yourself." The woman frowned at him and turned to Alex. "I'm *Sirena*. Pronounced *Si-Rena*, long *I*."

"Oh, oh, so sorry, my love." Logan furrowed his brow as crimson

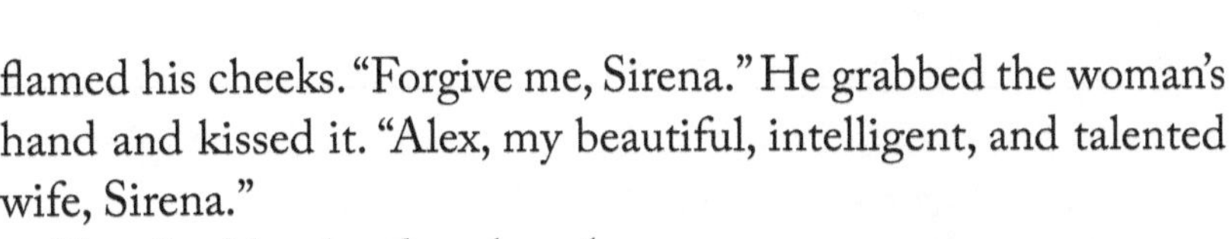

flamed his cheeks. "Forgive me, Sirena." He grabbed the woman's hand and kissed it. "Alex, my beautiful, intelligent, and talented wife, Sirena."

She tilted her head to the other woman.

"Oh, of course, and her stunning twin sister, Isolde."

Alex gazed at each of them. "Pleased to meet you." He recalled his father talking about an older French actor, Catherine Deneuve. Yes, they looked like her. Blonde, brown-eyed, and gorgeous.

Need to share that tidbit with Dad.

"You too, Alex." Sirena purred and pecked his cheek. "We've heard much about you in our house." She glanced at Logan. "Logan talks about his protégé. Alex this, and Alex that."

Sirena stepped back. Her eyes roamed up and down his body.

Whoa. Logan's wife doesn't hold back.

Alex shifted his eyes to her sister, Isolde. She smirked. "Can't wait to get to know you, Alex." And she stepped back to link arms with her twin. Both stared at him with slow, steady blinks.

A tense pause clawed its way into the space.

Logan cleared his throat and winked at his wife before turning back to Alex. "Well, Alex, please mingle. You know a few people here, and now you know more. Excuse me for a few minutes." He kissed his wife and trudged toward some other guests.

"Alex, would you like to sit with us for a bite to eat?" Sirena asked.

He pivoted toward voices. "O'Hara? We saved you a seat."

"Mrs...." About to say McCormick.

"No, no Alex. First names only. No work and all play." Sirena offered a throaty laugh and glanced at her sister.

"Yes." Isolde clung to her sister's arm and turned to Sirena.

Alex's stomach roller-coasted, and his cheeks heated.

Hey, pal, don't let them unnerve you.

"Ah, Mrs., I mean, Sire..."

A powerful voice boomed toward them like a baseball roaring into the outfield. "Sirena, come over here. The boys are leaving."

Alex's head followed Sirena's as Logan waved to his wife.

Sirena moved closer to Alex. "Well, saved by the call. Please get a bite to eat. I know Logan invited a couple of other employees." She grinned like a satiated cat. "We'll talk later."

As she turned, Isolde leaned forward. "Yes, like my sister said, later."

They strolled away with arms still linked.

What is it with twins? Do they ever separate after leaving the womb?

He moved toward the table where two of his peers sat.

Quinn Stotsky and Bart Palermo stood up.

"Hey, you two, I didn't know you'd be here. Logan swore me to secrecy."

"Did the same for us." Quinn, a golden-haired Brad Pitt-type, smirked and glanced at Bart, a younger, darker Colin Farrell look-alike.

"Yup. Didn't know what to expect."

"Interesting." Alex cocked his head at the two of them as they sat. "The three of us. The chosen ones. What do ya think?"

Quinn took a sip of his martini and leaned forward. "Let's face it. The three of us are…" He gulped another sip. "No less than tens in looks and intelligence."

"Don't want to seem cocky, but I couldn't agree more." Bart scanned the crowd and turned to them and snorted. "Most of these people fall in the average lane."

"How about some humility?" Alex said with a sarcastic tinge to his voice.

"Why? You've got it. Flaunt it." Bart chugged on his beer. "So, no coincidence that Logan invited the best-looking guys in the firm."

"Hmm. I'm not sure about that." Alex tilted his head and laughed.

"You're too modest, O'Hara. I see the gals studying you." Bart wiggled his eyebrows.

Alex jutted his chin. "You too, Palermo."

A server approached them. "Gentlemen, please join the others for some delicious food." He bowed and scurried away.

"Shall we?" Quinn lifted his eyebrows.

Alex plodded behind his peers and smiled at women who waved hello as they passed him.

Their ages varied, with the youngest being about his age. The men appeared older, thirties, forties, fifties.

"Look at all this." Quinn passed plates to Bart and Alex.

Alex took a deep breath again.

Blackened salmon, grilled shrimp, fillet, strip steaks. Man. Typical Logan. Goes all out.

The men loaded their plates, returned to their seats, and chomped on their food.

A guitarist strummed classical music in the background.

"Do we know the agenda for tonight?" Alex asked.

Both men shrugged.

"He said something about conversation and dancing outside until dark, then… You know, Logan, he grinned and hinted how pleased we'd be with what he had in store." Quinn chuckled.

"Yup, sounds like a night of pleasure if you know what I mean." Bart said, before biting into another piece of food.

Alex knitted his brows together. "Yeah, he told me something similar, but I didn't question the meaning."

"Dude, what do you think he meant?" Bart stared at Alex. "Besides, he clarified that anything happening tonight needed to stay behind closed doors. Didn't he say the same thing to you?"

"Yeah, and I hesitated about attending, but he implied he expected my presence with no if, and, or but about it."

"Three handsome guys, and look around, a beautiful crowd." Quinn's eyes conveyed mischief. "We fit right in."

Bart took another gulp of his beverage. "What did the Baby Boomers say? Sex, drugs, rock 'n' roll?"

"Well, alcohol in moderation. But drugs and hook-ups aren't my thing." Alex sipped on his wine.

"Dude, we know Logan's position on drugs. Not okay with it but alcohol and sex… look at the people in front of us." Bart swung his head toward people chatting, hugging, and drinking. "Come on, O'Hara. You're not seeing anyone special. Right?"

Alex nodded.

"Have some fun. Will ya?"

"If I meet an interesting woman, I might ask her for a date…"

"Date? Who said anything about a date? You old-fashioned or something?" Quinn snickered. "Huh?"

"Yeah, I am. Tried not being, but that way of life didn't work for me." Alex sat up straight, eyes steady on Quinn for a moment. "And you know what, man? I'm good with my position on love, sex, and the rest of it."

"Gotcha." Quinn shifted his eyes.

"O'Hara, if some beautiful woman approaches, you gonna ignore her?" Bart scoffed, still chugging on his beer.

"Like I said, I'm going to do things the way I prefer."

"To each his own." Bart sniffed. "But for me, if some luscious treat wants to engage in extracurricular activities, I'm not going to say no." He snapped his fingers at the server to bring over another drink.

"Whatever." Alex's gaze skimmed the room. "And I'll see how it goes, but if things get weird, I'm out of here."

"People may hook-up, but I think they'll go elsewhere. At least I will." Bart's eyes became unfocused. "As much as I might enjoy a one-timer with someone, I believe in privacy."

As Alex nodded, Sirena sauntered back to their table.

"Hello again, you three." Her eyes stayed focused on Alex. "May I borrow you for a few minutes?"

The music became louder. An electric guitarist and drummer had joined the acoustic player. The speakers, placed outside of the house, streamed the music inside and out. A song oozed about the delights of the evening.

Alex shook his head from the pages of the past and touched his jaw. The claws from yesterday dug into his psyche.

Why am I going there? The past belongs in the past.

If things developed with Delphina, he'd share it with her. And maybe it could be healing.

Early flight tomorrow. Go to sleep, pal.

He fell into bed, with his eyes insisting that he pull the lids down.

As he drifted, a voice whispered, "What if she doesn't believe you?"

CHAPTER FIVE

Delphina

"Your captain, here again. It looks like a beautiful day in Boston. Clear skies. Temperatures registered in the low eighties with little humidity. We should land in less than two hours."

"Smooth voice, and so far, smooth flying." Lucia leaned into Delphina.

Delphina nodded as she lifted her window shade and stared at the white clouds, sitting like cotton balls on a blue canvas.

"You've been quiet."

"Nothing to say, Mama. Plus, I'm engrossed in this book you recommended. Look how much I've read." Delphina turned the book to her mother and flipped the few pages left.

"I thought you'd like her. Family drama, romance, history. Penny Vincenzi, God rest her soul, knew how to write a story." Lucia winked at her daughter. "The romance tingles, wouldn't you say?"

Not going there with her.

Delphina laughed and brought her hand to her mouth to cover a yawn. "Wow. I guess the time change still affects me."

"Well, I'm glad you came."

Delphina nodded, with her eyes straight ahead.

"And you went out with Alexander."

Delphina continued to nod without turning to her mother.

"Are you going out again?"

"Mother?" Delphina tilted her head and narrowed her eyes to Lucia.

"I know. I know, but you know how much I want for you."

Delphina kissed her mother on the cheek. "I'm okay."

"But you haven't mentioned going out with anyone since... what happened."

Delphina slapped her thighs and sighed. "So, I will tell you. Yes, I have seen no one else until we arrived here, and because Alexander, I mean, Alex invited me to Cirque de Soleil, I couldn't resist."

Lucinda tightened her shoulders, gave her a mischievous smile, and squealed.

"What's that supposed to mean?"

"Nothing, nothing."

"Besides, you never shared with me how you met Alex."

"Ask him."

"Please don't tell me he saw you in your previous profession."

"I'll leave it up to him to share our introduction." Lucia drained the rest of her Diet Coke and crunched on some ice cubes. "And, since you evaded my question, I'm going to assume you're seeing him again."

Delphina shrugged. "Maybe. We'll see."

The loudspeaker clicked on. "Ladies and Gentlemen. It looks like we're headed into some turbulence, so please fasten your seatbelts again."

Delphina buckled up and slouched back in her seat. "I'm going to close my eyes for a few minutes."

As her eyelids shut, Lucia touched her cheek. "Good idea. I think I'll do the same."

Last night popped forward. Sizzles streaked through her each time Alexander leaned into her, and as his lips touched her cheek, the tingling ignited into flames.

She moved away from him and stood erect, trying to prevent any visible response of what he evoked in her.

Do I want this now in my life? Do I need it?

The memory shifted to an earlier time, two months before the devastation. Jude's forehead touched hers as his hands cupped her face.

"Babe, I love you so much. Can't wait to show it more." He kissed her, and his tongue grabbed hers as his fingers twisted around her hair. He halted in the middle of it. "Almost there, but I want you so bad."

"I know, but no, babe. I can't. Besides, the wait makes it even more special."

He nodded, and his charcoal eyes came closer with his nose touching hers...

A few weeks after that exchange, she stretched her body in the three-way, full-length mirror.

"Turn around." Her mother flashed a couple of photos from her iPhone. "Gorgeous, my daughter. You need to let your aunt see you."

"Okay, Mama." Delphina preened at her reflection, twirling around to see every angle. "Yes, this dress couldn't be more perfect."

"You will be Queen Delphina." Lucia's voice broke.

"Oh, Mama." Delphina lifted the layered dress and hugged her mother. "I'm so excited."

"That Jude doesn't know how lucky he is."

"I think he does." Delphina laughed.

"Where has he been?" Lucia frowned. "He should come around more often."

"Mama, he has much to do before the wedding and honeymoon."

The image shifted again. A month before the wedding...

Her heart lurched like a runaway elevator.

Every time I open things up again, I'm reminded how palpable my scars are. Why am I doing this to myself? When am I going to sit down and do what I tell my clients?

Delphina shifted in her seat and opened her eyes. Sleep lost out to the insistent memory scratching its way into the present.

Let me write instead.

She bent down beneath her seat and pulled out her journal.

Pink with sparkles. Brushing her hand along the leather covering, Delphina glided her fingers over the raised language embossed on the cover, *"Be Still & Know That I Am God. Psalm 46:10."*

Delphina closed her eyes and brought the journal to her chest. God's salve for me.

"Yes, my darling daughter. We know where to find comfort when something troubles us. Don't we?"

Delphina opened her eyes and smiled at her mother, who touched her cheek and turned away.

I know Mama doesn't want me to see her tears.

Delphina touched her mother's hand. "Mama, I'll be okay." She pulled out a pen, flipped her journal to an unwritten page, and wrote;

August 21st. A new chapter.

My visit to Las Vegas brought an interesting scenario. I don't know what will come of things, but I met someone who seemed interesting and polite. My mother invited someone whom she knew already but wouldn't share how they became acquainted. Alex, or as I referred to him, Alexander, which he didn't seem to mind, will have to earn his trust with me. Betrayals tainted my view on relationships, and my trust has turned to ashes. He will need to prove himself before I let him into my inner world.

I need to relax. How do I know he'll even contact me? But if he doesn't, at least I had an enjoyable experience with a gentleman...

The plane began to shake and vibrate. Things rolled around, and as Delphina's pen tumbled away from her, she tucked her journal into the carry-on bag. Her mother grabbed her hand.

"Hold on everyone. Just a rough patch." A smooth voice interrupted the clamoring within the cabin.

The winged machine rattled as it wrestled for control over a larger-than-life opponent.

Delphina clasped her mother's hand and scrunched her face as the vibration shuddered through her body like a booming drum. A reminder... Six years ago...

Boom, boom, boom…

Flocks of students shrieked as they pushed their way into the fraternity house, and the drummer, positioned outside the door, didn't hold back. Delphina flattened her hands over her ears and pushed through the crowds.

Way too loud for me.

She scanned the room in search of her sorority sisters. No familiar faces. She wiggled through the groups of students holding drinks, laughing, and chatting together.

Where did they go?

A man wearing snug khaki pants and a white polo shirt that showed sinewy arms bent down and cupped his hands into one of her covered ears. "Hey, gorgeous, you look lost."

Delphina released her hands, being further from the live band and glanced at the blond man, a Thor incarnate, big, bronzed, and beautiful. "Just looking for my friends."

He grinned. "Haven't seen the likes of you around here."

"Nope. Not my style. I'm a dual major and spend most of my time in my books."

"Aww, that's no fun. All studying and no play."

Delphina shrugged and giggled. "Well, I'm here now." She peeked at her watch and stood on her toes in search of her familiar pals. "I think I may have come to the wrong house."

"Nah, we planned to make our party the solo event for the weekend. I'm sure your friends have found their way, or will. By the way," he put out his hand, "I'm Chad, the House President, and you are?"

"Delphina." She placed her hand into his enormous paw.

"Nice to meet you, Delphina. Follow me." He kept her hand in his and led her through the crowd.

They passed through student groups dressed in jeans, holding drinks. He strutted and offered light fist-bumps and "Hey, man," along the way until they reached a bar area. Chad patted the stool and helped Delphina plop onto it.

A large young man with a baseball hat sitting backwards on his shaggy head tapped beer from an enormous keg. Delphina blinked, mesmerized by the foamy liquid swirling into the cups. Another young man pointed his index finger on the bar slap insisting on the show of an ID before giving anyone a drink.

"We have an over-twenty-one-rule for guests because we don't need any problems with the authorities." Chad winked. "Tim, here, makes sure that no one gets alcohol without showing proof of age."

Delphina lifted her eyebrows. "Well, I would hope so."

Chad chuckled. "Ah, a rule follower?"

Delphina's lips curled up. "I try, but it doesn't matter because I don't like beer."

"How about another adult beverage?"

"Maybe. Since I'm twenty-one and eleven months, I'm willing to try something."

"Like what?"

"How about a cosmo?"

Chad threw his head back and roared. "Wow. Fancy, beautiful Delphina. Not sure we can accommodate right here, but let's see what I can do for you…" He slipped off his stool and stood. "Follow me." Chad grabbed her hand and led her through the throngs again. They came to a locked portal, and he pressed a few buttons into a safety code to open it. Turning the knob, Chad opened the rickety door, and a steep set of concrete stairs loomed in front of them. Still clutching Delphina's hand, Chad climbed to the second step. Delphina hesitated, and her feet remained planted on the ground.

He turned, and without releasing her hand, he gazed down at her. "Just taking you upstairs so you can drink what you want."

No harm, Delphina. He's president of the Fraternity House.

"Okay. Just let me text a couple of my friends." Delphina wiggled her hand from Chad's, unzipped her tiny crossbody bag, and tugged out her smartphone. She stooped down, and with both thumbs, she pressed onto the keys to send a group message, telling them her whereabouts.

With his muscular arms folded, Chad shifted back and forth on one step and arched an eyebrow.

"Ready, beautiful?"

"Yes."

Chad reached for her fingers, and she followed him. He opened another door. "Welcome to our palatial home." He swept his arm, and Delphina found herself in a large living room, with a long, cracked leather couch and a variety of shaped chairs. A stone fireplace stared back. Her eyes roved to a gigantic TV screen, which took up most of the wall.

"We love our sports and binge-watching. As you can see, it's the most important fixture to the brothers." With hands on his hips, his gaze circled the room. "Been my home away from home for almost four years." He gestured toward the couch. "Please sit while I get Madame her drink."

"Thank you." Delphina smiled, feeling her cheeks blossom.

He's gorgeous and seems so nice.

"I'm going to the kitchen, where I have some ingredients for your cosmo and a shaker. I think I'll make myself a dirty martini."

Chad sauntered towards the kitchen and spoke behind the half wall. "Hey, Delphina. I assume you're a senior, as well."

"Yes. I plan on becoming a Mental Health Counselor and will attend graduate school next year."

"Fantastic." He unlatched the cabinet doors. "Can't believe it." His head turned toward Delphina. "You're in luck because we have Triple Sec." His smile lingered for a moment.

The heat in Delphina's cheeks spread like red bee balm.

"How about you, Chad?"

He turned back as he mixed the ingredients together. "I got accepted to medical school and hope to become a dermatologist."

"Good for you. If you got into medical school, you shouldn't have a problem choosing the specialty you want. Am I wrong?"

Chad dropped some ice into the cocktail tumbler and shook. *Click-clack.* "You are correct if I ace everything. And I'm determined to not let anything interfere with that." He poured the drink. "One down, and one to go."

He whistled as he prepared the second martini. "Yup. We've got olives and lots of juice for the dirty one." He glanced up at her and waggled his eyebrows.

Delphina extended her arms out and slouched on the leather couch. "Wow, I could fall asleep on this." She rubbed her hands along the rough leather grain.

"Aww. Don't do that gorgeous. You'll deprive me of your glorious company."

Chad strolled into the living room with the two martinis on a tray. "Don't mind the plastic cups." He laughed and offered Delphina her drink. "Here you go, but don't sip yet."

"Okay." Delphina placed the drink down on the long, large-plank wooden table in front of her. "I want to check my phone." She pulled it from her bag. No texts. "Hmmm."

Chad settled himself next to her and raised his glass. Delphina did the same. "To a memorable evening and maybe more." He clinked glasses with her, and she sipped on her drink as he did the same.

"Delicious, Chad." She positioned her glass on the table.

Chad's eyes became hooded, and he reached over and brushed her lips.

Delphina's insides combusted, and she accepted more from him. His kisses became deeper.

Delphina pulled back and fanned herself. "Ooh." She grabbed her glass and sipped.

Chad's eyes bored into hers as he pulled one of her locks, closed his eyes, and swept it across his lips. He opened his eyes and took her glass and placed it back on the table.

A wooziness blanketed Delphina. "Umm. Wow. What did you put into that drink?" She gagged on a laugh.

Chad pitched forward. "Hey, just a little extra to relax you." He grabbed her face and gave her a hard kiss.

Slurred, stretched words propelled from her throat. "Ooh. Slow-ow-ow down, puleeze."

"Why?" Chad's voice became muffled between kisses. "Let's enjoy each other while we have the time. I can't keep the door locked forever."

"Whaaat?"

"Yeah. Secret code for downstairs, which only a few of the brothers have, but an extra lock up here."

Chad kissed her all over, and Delphina couldn't move.

"Gosh. Everything seems so heavy." She tried pushing him away, but she couldn't move her arms from his embrace.

Tingling spread through her as if someone gave her a shot of Novocain.

Chad became blurry and fuzzy as he blended into the background.

Static replaced it like the beginning of an HBO episode followed by blackness.

Thrum, thrum.

A voice beat into her ears, unremitting and growing louder as if someone pressed the button higher and higher.

Her head pounded, and finger pressed into her shoulder, shaking her.

"Come on, gorgeous. Time to wake up."

Words remained stuck in her throat until two scurried out. "Wha-a-t happened?" She rubbed her eyes as he leered at her. "You're a lucky girl, Delphina. You got Mr. It-Guy on campus to help your entrée into womanhood. That will be a story to share over the years."

Delphina eyes filled as reality hit. She lifted her hips and pulled up her jeans.

"Oh, honey, it won't hurt for long. Before you know it, you'll want more."

She trembled and struggled to raise herself up. The surroundings remained wavy and watery. "I-I-I want to go back to my house."

"Sure thing. I'll help you." Chad grinned and yanked her up. "See, chivalry never dies."

Delphina wobbled, and he took her arm. "Hey, gorgeous. I'm not up to carrying you, so let me get you an Uber."

She fell back and could see Chad pull out his phone and click an App. "Okay. I'm going to bring you out front." He put his hands under her armpits and jerked her up again.

Delphina limped as Chad pushed her along. "Come on. I need to get back to the party."

She stumbled down the wooden steps and screeching voices and laughter surrounded her.

"Hey Chad. Another night of fun?" A male voice yelled.

"Just helping the little lady here. The alcohol went to her head. Going back to the party."

"They can't resist you, can they?"

Chad chuckled, and Delphina swayed.

"Woah." He dragged her toward a fire hydrant. "Here. Hold on to this until the Uber gets here. You'll be Okay. I paid the driver and gave him a good tip, so you don't have to worry your little head."

Chad stooped down and kissed her on the lips. "See you around, and if not, at graduation for sure. Two more weeks, baby." He jogged away and shouted to a couple of people in the distance.

Delphina held on tight to the yellow object in front of her. The night surrounding her, blacker than ever. No stars in sight like her current state. A chill shuddered through her as if she tumbled in icy waters, and she leaned on the hydrant to wrap her sweater tighter. Thumping music from the house reached her ears. Other than that, nothing until a rattling car with bright lights approached her. The driver, an older man, got out and helped her into her seat. He turned around.

"Ya live close by and wouldn't need me, but I see you can't walk in your condition. Gonna say something ya might not want to hear. But I pick up a lot of girls leaving this Frat, and from the stories told to me, they're a bunch of Bad Boys. Ya know what I mean?"

Delphina grunted. "Um."

"And how do I know a Bad Boy?"

Delphina met his eyes in the rear-view mirror and shrugged.

He raised his finger. "Cuz I was kind-of one until I met the wife." He chuckled, "And boy, did she yank my chain. Forty-five years ago. The best thing that happened to me. Let me just say, though, I didn't act like these characters nowadays."

Delphina gulped.

"Okay, I know. I talk too much. I'll shut up."

He moved his old Toyota Corolla at a snail's pace. It wailed as if protesting when he shifted gears, then halted in front of Delphina's sorority house. "This the place?"

Delphina uttered a hoarse, "Yes."

"Let me escort you up the steps."

With gentle hands, he led her to the door. "Young woman? In the future…" His eyes studied her for a moment, swooshed his hands down like paws, and pivoted. As he *click-clacked* down the steps, words trickled behind him. "Ahh, never mind. What's the point. Take care of yourself, miss."

"Thank you," Delphina muttered, and she wobbled inside.

Silence razed the entire house.

Good. Don't want questions.

To describe her body right now? A gummy doll. She turned and lowered her butt. One step at a time, her derriere led her up the carpeted stairs. At the landing, she crawled until she reached her room. With as much strength as she could, Delphina turned the knob, and her head propelled her forward. She fell flat on her face but kicked the door shut.

A streak of determination bolted through her foggy brain before she grasped the frill on her comforter and dragged herself on top of the bed.

No one, but no one, will know about this. Who would believe me except my mother and maybe a couple of friends? And my mother? She'd go out of her mind. Not worth it.

I wanted to save myself. Old-fashioned? Yes.
Now what? Wait, a minute…

Delphina fluttered her eyelashes as the plane settled down, flying like a bird in the eye of a hurricane.

Peering at her mother, Lucia caressed her cheek again. "My darling, all seems well now."

She nodded and shut her eyes. Yes, she made the right decision long ago. Her mother's fury, more like a saltwater crocodile than a Cape Buffalo, would have chomped Chad alive.

And the debacle with Jude reinforced that.

Chapter Six

Alex

Alex leaned back in his high-back, ergonomic chair and laced his hands behind his head, staring at the computer screen. After returning from the fitness club, he'd showered, dressed in jeans and an open-collared shirt, and sat with a strong cup of French Roast. He was working from home this morning as he did two to three times a week, depending on the needs of the day.

Leaning forward, Alex took a sip of coffee and rubbed his eyes. Although his return flight got in late, he refused to deviate from his regular schedule of listening to a biblical reflection as he walked to his fitness facility, within a few blocks from his condo, and pushing his body to the limits afforded him.

His fingers glided over his sinewy arms.

Sound mind. Muscular body.

Yeah, yeah.

Not vanity alone. I want to keep everything going as long as possible. When I need to slow down, I will, but right now, push, pal, push.

He glanced outside and scanned the city of Boston. Windows stretched across the front, the reason he chose this unit in the Seaport district which gifted him an unobstructed view of the harbor. The boats at the pier shifted with the water's movement, a perfect nautical snapshot, while each waited for a Poseidon-like captain to release them onto the ocean.

The city, one of the most desirable in the country, continued to drive prices up, making it quite unaffordable for many. Alex purchased his condo during the first phase of construction, a deal he couldn't refuse even though some would've blanched if they heard the price. Delays ensued for a couple of months, but he didn't mind the wait, continuing to save money for extra amenities.

His eyes skimmed the surroundings. Man Cave, sort of. Lots of light, but you couldn't disguise the masculine air swirling around the place. A lion's domain, matching its mane with tawny, brown, and streaks of ebony.

He kept his computer in the living area, which included a few comfortable, wing-back chairs of neutral colors and a chocolate leather sectional that seated ten people. His mother insisted he accept her gift of a dark-brown oriental rug woven with motifs of gold, red, and black.

She winked when he invited her and his father for a tour of the furnished condo.

"See, Alex. An excellent color for camouflaging in case you and your friends get riled up over the games and spill beer or anything else." His mother shook her head, and her ash-blonde hair, now in a bob, bounced along. "I don't want to know."

His father, whose image mirrored his, chuckled. "Son, she knows her boys. Remember when you and Nick watched the games with me?"

Alex nodded, and a smile jotted across his face as he considered those days watching football or hockey, his favorite, with Nick and his dad.

His eyes found the 75-inch TV. A prize. This weekend, taco party and a Red Sox night game.

At least ten people were usually expected even in the late summer, and before you know it, the Pats and his beloved, Boston Grizzlies.

Man, what a treat to live in Boston. A real sports town. Everyone could choose. Baseball, basketball, football, and hockey.

Does Delphina like sports? She said little about it except that her mother shared his love for hockey, but she claimed she preferred baseball.

Okay. Slow for his tastes, but he enjoyed a Red Sox game if they played a strong competitor like the Yankees.

Take note, Pal. Think about bartering some precious hockey tickets for those Fenway box seats from one of your buds. If watching sports didn't appeal to her, not an issue, but accepting his love for it is another thing, with hockey being number one.

Okay, time to get a sense of Delphina. Not a lover of social media, but why not learn more about her?

Alex gulped his coffee, the dark roasted drink swishing around his mouth before warming his throat.

Delicious.

No matter what season, a hot and strong brew for him.

Alex pressed the button to power up the computer. A picture of one of his Grizzlies, holding a hockey stick as he glided the puck along the ice to the netted goal.

Peter LaFlamme, one of the greatest stars from long ago, and good friends with his parents.

Alex's hand glided the mouse, and he clicked on Google search. His fingers tapped the keys, typing in Delphina Tulasi.

A list appeared.

Healing Through Story landed at the top. He moved the cursive and pressed the link.

The summary explained Delphina's shift from traditional psychotherapy to therapeutic storytelling. Within the synopsis, she emphasized the history of the narrative, and how every human being develops a unique story through their lifecycle. She further stated that some people view their lives as boring, but she helps them pluck the strings of glory within their tale.

She suggested people follow her on social media, but if you wanted to choose one, select Instagram, where she posts every few days about storytelling.

Okay, Storyteller. You've convinced me.

Alex avoided social media except Instagram. He used to enjoy Snapchat, but not anymore. His last serious romantic relationship ended that relationship.

His Instagram account revealed specific topics, sports, and gatherings around the various games. His postings occurred once every couple of weeks.

Click.

Alex's Instagram account popped up, and he scrolled through a few notifications.

Dogs of different breeds, elephants, and his friends appeared. Okay. Done.

He moved the cursive toward search and typed in Delphina's name.

Private.

Hmmm. I guess she keeps personal and professional separate, and it makes sense if clients want to know more about her than she'd prefer.

He rubbed the scars and even though they appeared invisible to the eye, every so often, his heart would crack, with a drop of blood trickling out.

All right, pal. You know, sometimes this happens, like right now.

Dropping his hand, he typed in *Healing Through Story*, and in feminine font, the company name appeared with delphinium flowers surrounding it. Her professional headshot showed her gazing to the side, with a pearly background. Wearing an open-collared cobalt-color shirt, she smiled wide, and her golden curls shrouded her, coiling down like…

Alex snapped his fingers twice. What was her name? The lady whose hair grew and tumbled out the window?

Thumbelina?

Nah. Too little.

Tangled?

Nope. Too recent, and no tangles within Delphina's glorious mane. His fingers froze in midair.

Rapunzel.

Yeah, that's right. *Rapunzel.*

Alex moved the mouse to the first video and tapped on it. With a background of the signature flower coupled with a gentle piece of classical music, Delphina spoke.

"Let me tell you my first story about the origin of my name." She paused, tilted her head, and smiled. "Delphiniums. What a glorious species." She shifted her head for a moment, swept her arm up, and returned to gaze into the camera. "Don't you agree?"

Lacing her hands together, Delphina said, "The delphinium gets its name from the Greek word *delphis*, meaning dolphin. Delphiniums, celebrated in Greek mythology and named after the Delphi temple, became a favorite of the sun-god Apollo."

A smile bloomed across her face. "My mother graced me with a derivative of the name."

She opened her palms and directed them to the screen. "What about you? What's the story around your name? Check it out and write it down." She crossed her arms on top of each other. "Until next time."

The video halted, and Alex's eyes skimmed her face.

"Hey, gorgeous, could play this forever, but I won't. Nothing beats meeting in the flesh, but let's see what else you have."

A beautiful arrangement of colorful quotes and videos.

He glided the mouse to the quote, scripted in a fancy, feminine lettering.

Alex grinned. I'll name it the Delphina font—elegant, curvy, and curly like her.

Click.

The quote squiggled across the screen, which he enlarged, inviting him into her estrogen world.

Flowers surrounded it: *Fortune sides with him who dares. ~ Virgil.*

Are you a risk-taker, Storyteller? I guess so, since you're the sole proprietor. I wonder where else you might take risks? You gonna let me know?

Let's see what else you might offer.

Hmm, a bible verse. I guess you're not afraid to share that you're a woman of faith.

Click.

Same flowery background. *Weeping may stay for the night but rejoicing comes in the morning. ~ Psalm 30:5*

Wow, Storyteller. Pretty courageous during these hyper-secular times. But the quote has merit with offering hope. Speaking of hope, I hope to find out more about you.

Alex glanced at his watch. One more, because I could drown in your videos, Storyteller, but I need to get to work.

He moved the computer cursor and pressed on the video next to the Bible verse.

Delphina leaned forward in a white blouse, her hair bunched into a loose bun, with tendrils flowing down alongside her face and shoulders like hanging ivy.

"Good day, everyone." She cocked her head. "Are you surprised that I inserted a few Bible verses in my Instagram posts?" She paused and clasped her hands. A ring flashed on her left finger with little sparkles flashing.

Alex halted the video and pitched forward. Must be an engagement ring. I assume someone called off the wedding. Wait, a minute... How do I know?

Mom's older friend got jilted at the altar. Josh's girlfriend broke off the engagement the weekend before. How about Tallie? She left Mike two months after their big bash of a wedding.

Alex lifted his eyebrows. What's your story, Storyteller? Don't know Lucia that well to ask, and besides, she could get offended if I bypass her daughter. And Delphina?

He grinned as his head bobbed.

Don't need to nudge a porcupine's spikes.

Click.

"As you can assume, I'm a woman of faith, but let me be clear." Her index finger rose again. "I don't impose my beliefs on anyone, and I've seen all kinds of people from religious to non." Delphina relaxed her hand and smiled. "Why, then, do I scatter a few Bible verses here and there?" Another cocooned, silent moment.

Not sure, Storyteller. Hope?

"If you answered, inspiration, you're correct."

Okay. Can see that.

"Did you know that without the Bible, so many stories and books and movies wouldn't exist? From Shakespeare to *Star Wars*, what do you think of that?"

Delphina gulped, allowing the viewer a moment of reflection.

"If you doubt me, think about all the quotes you hear, such as, *he's a wolf in sheep's clothing,* or *the truth shall set you free.* And did you know a famous novelist, Betty Smith, from long ago, wrote a book, *Joy in the Morning,* and the title comes from? Yes, you've got it…" She nodded her head. "The verse I shared here."

She clapped. "Okay. No matter where your belief system lays, inspiration comes from many sources." She bowed her head. "Have a lovely day. Until next time."

The video froze.

Okay, one more.

One post with bold letters, *Challenge,* beckoned him.

What'cha got here?

In the same luxurious typeset, she penned: *Can you create micro-stories for 365 days? Consider yourself a modern-day Scheherazade, female or male.*

Alex scrunched his eyebrows.

Who the heck is Scheherazade?

Chapter Seven

Delphina

Delphina swung her hip, slammed the door of her white Volvo, and pulled the horizontal-shaped yoga bag over her shoulder. She pressed the car key.

Beep.

A couple of people ambling in front of her looked back before resuming their chatting.

Everyone headed in the same direction.

Yoga. Sunrise Power Session.

Delphina's eyes ascended.

Dawn attired herself in a unique splash of rose, silver, and purple, teasing everyone as they waited for the Sun to reveal her splendor.

The familiar faces of the usual crew in their yoga pants, flip-flops or Birkenstocks, showed up every week, often yawning, and like her, remaining committed to several early morning sessions. More women, but a few men, became regulars.

Delphina's teal-colored yoga mat swung from the outside of her long bag, and she unzipped it to look inside.

Good. Blocks, blanket, and strap.

She made sure she carried her own. One time, she forgot, and although she sprayed down the blocks before and after, germs floated their way and captured her with a flu-like virus.

Never again. She checked no less than three times, becoming

obsessed about not forgetting her equipment. No guarantees about warding off illness, but why not try.

One of her favorite refuges, home away from home. Delphina drank in the enchanting pink stucco building with long windows. Planter boxes projected forward, full of marigolds, zinnias, impatiens, and petunias. Large pots near the entrance housed similar flowers, and a wide white arched wooden door beckoned, *come on in.* The owner, Marquesa, hailed from California, and wanted to create a French-country-California-Dreaming scene.

Everyone loved it.

Delphina stepped closer to the window boxes and gazed at the velvety lavender petunias, peeking through the other annuals, luring her to touch.

Uh-uh. Don't want to disrupt your bloom.

A slight breeze prompted the marigolds to wave, inviting her to approach them for an intoxicating extravaganza.

She closed her eyes, inhaling their musky aroma.

A silver-streaked head with a lopsided smile protruded into her mind.

Hmm. You carry a certain scent, Alexander.

Musky? I think. I'll find out.

Her eyes popped open, and two Monarch butterflies, her favorites, fluttered around the marigolds, feasting on their nectar before continuing their long journey to Mexico.

What a treat! Sluggish caterpillars metamorphosing into this glorious species. A sign for me to transform again?

Scratchy voices interrupted the spell as yogis shuffled inside the building. She smiled as she followed.

The interior of the studio displayed similar themes with mirrors between murals of enormous waves, pearly sand, and blue skies. White-washed hardwood lined the floors like an added layer of beachfront. A sprinkling of a variety of delicious aromas lured each person to breathe deep as if they could hold on to the scent-of-the-day forever.

Although the aesthetics created an atmosphere misted with peace, calmness, and restoration, the major attraction of this sanctum differentiated itself from most.

Blessed yoga.

It took the principles of yoga and entwined it with the teachings of Christianity.

The owner, Marquesa, described her story on her website.

Ten years ago, at 29, I became a Christian.

Raised in a household of nonbelievers, God didn't come up, which I never questioned. I attended college, and like my peers, I partied and drank to escape any sense of discomfort around partaking in hook-ups and the "culture of now." After a turbulent four years of this, something roiled within me, like a sporadic storm of restlessness, but I didn't understand for many years. After my graduation, I became disillusioned with modern-day casual relationships and no longer believed in love. I focused on building a business around yoga techniques, traveled to India, and studied with experts.

In my late twenties, I fell in love with a man of faith, who never pressured me about God, but I became intrigued about his commitment to a faraway, invisible being. After he proposed, I agreed to get married in church but not convert.

Three months before the wedding, he died in a motorcycle accident.

My anger towards this God of his had no bounds, but something happened.

I tripped on my gown at a formal event, fell down the stairs, and died. While they tried resuscitating me, I floated above, went through a dark tunnel, and found myself in the splendor of an eternal home, Heaven. The visuals, smells, touch, and sounds…Beyond the imagination. I cannot express the glory of it in human language.

I saw my fiancé, glowing, and wanted to stay, but a mellifluous voice whispered, 'Not your time.'

Returning to my body, I converted and devoted my last ten years to sharing my Christian faith, not celebrating Gaia. I direct my praying hands to God with blessings rather than Namaste.

Welcome again to Blessed yoga. May God guide you in mind, body, and soul to the best version of you.

With much love, Marquesa

Delphina discovered Blessed yoga two years ago, and after the tumult of last year, her dedication to routine saved her from sinking into the bowels of darkness. She attended classes no less than five times a week and sometimes twice on weekends.

Now walking in, she turned toward her usual spot. Josie, her only best friend now, waved from a mat with raspberries speckled across it and tapped the place right next to her.

Delphina slipped off her clogs and glanced at her peach parfait nail polish painted across each toe before peering again at her coral-colored spandex outfit.

She padded over toward Josie, reached down, and hugged her.

"Hey, Delph. I see you checking those pretty toes of yours. Only you could have beautiful feet. Another inheritance from Lucia?"

Delphina grinned at Josie. "I don't know about beautiful, but I make sure I don't appear like an adolescent girl with chipped toenail polish—but speaking of beautiful, look at you."

Garbed in a one-piece, red yoga outfit, Josie, slender and tall, straight golden hair, caramel-colored skin, big dark eyes fringed with curly lashes, and an upturned nose, widened her smile. "Oh, come on. No more or less than you."

Josie stretched her scarlet scrunchie, bent her neck, and tightened it around her long tresses before popping her head back up.

"Okay, girl. Spit it out. I want to hear all about Sin City and..." Josie lifted her thick brown, Brooke Shields-like eyebrows.

"And what?" Delphina unwound her mat, pulled out her purple blocks, turquoise strap, and wool, teal and white yoga blanket.

"Come on, now. Didn't you hint about some cutie-pie?"

Delphina kept her head down as she stooped, rolled up, and placed the blanket at the top of her mat before her eyes brushed over Josie's. "I did, and I'll feed it all to you at breakfast." She laid down and shut her eyes.

"Ha, ha, ha." Josie's voice crinkled. "Not even a crumb?"

Delphina extended her arm outward, and Josie grabbed her hand. "Okay, sis, in another life. I'm starving for the story."

As she inhaled the warmth of her friend and the cocoon of the heated ambience, a set of familiar footsteps cushioned across the floor.

Delphina placed her hands behind her, raised her torso, and extended her legs.

The under five-foot Marquesa, wearing a black, two-piece yoga outfit and a long braid, flashed a toothy smile. "Blessings to all of you."

The chorus of participants synchronized their responses. "Blessings, Marquesa."

"Let us begin for a moment in a seated position, bow your heads, and offer a prayer of your own, expressing gratitude for our gathering today."

Delphina sat cross-legged and gave thanks.

"Good," said Marquesa. "Now please stand and let us begin with a sun salutation. Take a deep inhale, sweep your arms overhead, and bring your palms together."

For the next hour, Delphina flowed into a variety of stances that fortified her body. From downward facing dog, to warrior one and two.

As much as she loved the strength and flexibility poses, her love for the positions of balance stirred appreciation into her soul. As her right foot climbed up the side of her left calf and situated itself on her lower thigh, Delphina's heart rose with delight. She brought her hands into a prayer position before lifting her arms toward the heavens.

For several seconds, she stood stationary, until Marquesa directed them into the tree pose on the other side.

With ease, she performed the same way on the left.

I've worked at this. Less wobbly than a few years ago.

Since giving up her higher heels, Delphina concentrated on posture and balance.

Balance.

As her leg slid down, and she proceeded to another position, Alex's eyes loomed in front of her.

Okay, Alexander, I need balance beyond the physical.

But right now… She scrunched her eyelids, to swat his image away.

For the rest of the class, she concentrated on breath and Marquesa's gentle guidance.

At the end of the class, a soaked Delphina glanced at Josie, who dripped sweat.

"Time for a quick shower."

"You got it, girl. Can't wait to peel this off and let the suds pour over me."

After showering and changing into a loose-fitting cobalt-colored shirt and a pair of purple-turquoise colored harem pants, Delphina capped her head with a baseball hat, embroidered with delphiniums and her logo, *Healing through Story*. Her long curls cascaded down her back, unfurling the folds of a silky, golden blanket.

She sprinted out to her car, and Josie, always ahead of her and attired in a tunic dress, folded her arms, and giggled.

"Beat you, Goldilocks. And look at those springy coils of yours."

"Josie, your golden locks have less curl but do more to frame your stunning features. Okay?"

"You got it, girl." Josie's enormous eyes flickered. "Besides, we've got lots to talk about beyond a ping-pong game about looks. And a cutie pie comes to mind." Josie walked backwards, glancing over her shoulder. "So put your gear in your car and meet me at Ernie's." She rubbed her stomach. "I'm starving." Turning around, she jogged toward their favorite breakfast place.

After dropping her equipment into the SUV, Delphina stepped toward the old-fashioned diner. Gleaming chrome in the shape of a railroad dining car, the bright red sign embossed with a sparkling Ernie's Diner, had developed a reputation for a cozy, inviting atmosphere, delicious food, and fast service. Although a few from the highfalutin' crowd at yoga turned their noses up if someone mentioned eating at Ernie's, Delphina and Josie, joined by others, laughed. Josie often spoke up. "You don't know what you're missing."

As Delphina approached the door, chatter, laughter, and clanging swallowed the space. She pushed it open, and small bells jingled. The variety of aromas—of sizzling bacon, cooked eggs, and toasted English muffins—streamed around her nostrils, awakening her now-alert stomach to growl.

"Hey, Delph," said one of the male servers as he cruised by her along the long, narrow corridor of a black-and-white checkered floor separating the counter and swivel stools from the booths.

Did she arrive?

"Hi Tom. I…"

Words trailed behind him. "Yup. In the usual spot."

Josie peeked out from around a large person in front of her and waved.

"Almost didn't see you."

"I had my head down, checking out the choices to see if anything new might tempt me, but no. I'm starving."

Delphina slid into the turquoise booth, scanned the menu, and placed it down. "I'm ready. Let's face it Jos. We stay creatures of habit."

Tom came over with a pot of coffee, poured the steaming brew into each cup, and placed hands on his hips. "Ladies, the same?"

Both nodded.

"See. Even Tom recognizes we never deviate from our routine."

Josie smirked. "Thanks, Tom. We are boring gals."

Tom chuckled. "Not quite how I would describe either of you."

As he trotted away, Josie gulped on her drink and stared at Delphina.

Looking at her friend, Delphina couldn't resist examining Josie's features inherited from a Caucasian mother and half-Black, half-Spanish father. The DNA blender had mixed elements from the pool of genetics, creating a spectacle of perfect symmetry.

Josie placed her cup in the saucer, brought her knuckles together, and said, "While we wait, will you get to the point about cutie-pie?"

Delphina sipped on her coffee. "Okay. Let me give you a quick synopsis before the food arrives."

Delphina shared with Josie everything that happened while in Las Vegas.

As she finished her summary, Tom delivered their egg-white omelet meals.

"All set ladies?"

Both nodded and thanked him.

"This guy, Alex, sounds nice, Delph."

Delphina cut a piece of her egg and chewed it before responding. "Delicious. Love the avocado and tomato mix."

Josie munched on hers and tilted her head. "I haven't heard you be enthusiastic about anyone since Jude."

"I wouldn't go that far."

"At least, you're willing to go out again. Tomorrow, right."

"Yes, but we'll see."

Josie shook her head as she cut another piece. "Delphina…" She stopped and chomped on a piece of her English muffin.

"I know. I know. Time to give romance another chance, but Jos, after what happened, I'm not sure I'll ever trust again."

Josie scoffed and pitched forward with her fork in her hand. "What do you say to your clients? No problem. Never trust again."

Delphina knitted her eyebrows together and didn't respond.

"How about that corrective experience that they drummed into us in graduate school? It doesn't just refer to a therapeutic relationship."

Delphina nodded.

"This guy could have stuff of his own. He said he knew your mother but wouldn't tell you how. You sure he never became a client of hers."

"I'm certain from what they both showed."

"Did you mention Jude or Chad?"

"What? Are you kidding? No. We didn't go there, and it will take a while with anyone before I do."

Josie continued to hold her fork in midair.

Delphina's mouth curved into a smile. "And will you please put down that utensil before someone thinks you're going to poke me with it?"

Josie laughed, cut another piece of food, and before placing it into her mouth, she said, "Girl, you need to live and rewrite the story like you tell everyone else to do."

A set of ocean-colored eyes floated in front of her.

Chapter Eight

Alex

Walden Pond in Concord, Massachusetts, received much notoriety after American transcendentalist, David Thoreau, authored his book, *Life in the Woods*, in the mid-nineteenth century. He built a cabin in the wooded area owned by his mentor, friend, and fellow transcendentalist Ralph Waldo Emerson.

For the next two years, he described simple living in natural surroundings. Themes of independence, social experimentation, spiritual discovery, and, to a degree, self-reliance became the focus. Satire also peppered the text.

Alex's father shared a great deal about his 1970s Catholic education, which included an English Literature course describing the Transcendentalist movement.

Now flocks of people visit the famous pond. The regular jaunts had nothing to do with Thoreau's footprint in history. Instead, walkers, joggers, hikers, and birdwatchers gorged on its natural delights traveling along a popular 1.9-mile loop. Whether they realized it, their enchantment with the area simulated Mr. Thoreau's.

With tanned, brawny arms folded, Alex stood, gazing at people. A few sat near the edge of the body of tranquility, immersed in a book, writing on a notepad or journal, or closing their eyes and breathing in the wooded and earthy fragrances that drifted in the air surrounding the pond.

Perfect day.

The sun caressed the landscape with her warm rays, a gentle reminder to New Englanders she'd remain bright but less balmy as fall approached.

Glad I chose this. Delphina agreed. She mentioned something about *Little Women* being based in Civil War Concord.

No idea, but a point of conversation.

Too bad she wouldn't allow me to pick her up.

Whatever.

With so many deceptive people out there, I guess she requires extra caution.

Alex arrived at 2:30, ten minutes earlier than their designated meeting time. He knew little about her, including her relationship with time. Would she be prompt or late? He glanced at his watch, then took a few steps back and forth.

Beep.

Alex looked up.

A small white SUV, like a baby harp seal, slid into a vacant parking space. Dressed in Nikes, gray casual shorts, and a white polo shirt, he sprinted over to the vehicle.

The door swung open, and a pair of thick sneakers stomped onto the pavement. The rest of Delphina jumped out, dressed in beige cargo shorts, a yellow three-quarter length top, and her long golden hair woven into a long braid.

Wow. She let her hair down. Kind of. A sign?

Gracing her with a wide smile, Alex said, "Hello, Delphina. Great to see you here at home."

Delphina stood, and her golden orbs sparkled and danced. "Yes. Nice to see you as well in more familiar surroundings." Her eyes skimmed the area. When she returned her gaze to him, she swallowed, and a smile flitted across her face.

He reached for her hand and bent down to kiss her cheek. Although she bristled, she stayed put for a moment before releasing his grasp and stepping back.

"So…before we get started…" She pivoted to the back of her

car and opened the hatch. Her arms shot out, like a martial arts master, gripping two bottles of water. "Since you're into fitness like me, I wanted to make sure we'd be hydrated."

Alex lifted his eyebrows, and his fingers touched hers as she handed him the drink. "Thank you. I didn't think of it because I thought we'd go slow, but it makes sense."

Delphina turned back to her car and lifted a delphinium embroidered, lightweight, gray knapsack. "I brought this to carry them in."

Thoughtful. Good. Not used to it.

"You don't have to do that."

"I want to."

Her cool silky hand touched his again and stayed for a moment. A tingle boomeranged through his body.

Pal, simmer down. Stay in control. Too soon to let her overwhelm you.

As if sensing his response, she retracted her hand, grabbed the bottle, and threw it into the backpack which she hooked over both shoulders. Standing straight like a soldier, lips penciled into a straight line, her eyes hopped from his to the pond. "Let's go."

She can't hide her nervousness.

"Sure." Alex swept his arm out.

Taking a long step, Delphina strode in front of him, swinging her arms.

Alex rubbed his chin.

Really, so you want to do it this way? Okay, I'll play that game.

He knelt to tighten his laces.

Crunch, crunch, crunch.

She halted and glanced over her shoulder. "Coming?"

"Yup." He leaped ahead and sidled alongside her. "Didn't know you wanted to work out."

"I don't, but why not use our muscles as we take in everything this place offers."

"Great."

He tilted his head, and her profile displayed eyes straight ahead, with pursed lips.

For several seconds, he followed her tempo, and from the swishing of her arms, he wondered how long she'd keep this pace before slowing down.

As silence echoed between them, nature's voice came alive, with blue jays squawking at robins, sparrows flying from branch to branch, and chipmunks and squirrels scampering around them.

Not so bad walking without words, I guess. If that's what she wants, for now, fine with me.

After what seemed like several minutes, she halted and removed the bag. His fingers touched her shoulder and wound around the straps. "Let me help you."

Words scratched from her throat. "All set." She dropped the bag by a tree, plopped down, leaned against the trunk, and reached for the bottles.

Alex stooped in front of her.

"Here." She handed him a bottle, unscrewed the cap of hers, tipped back her head, and chugged on it.

He lifted his eyebrows and offered a sliver of a smile.

After drinking most of the water, she tapped her chest. "That helped."

"You were moving at quite a clip."

"Aren't you thirsty?"

Alex removed the cap and took a few sips. "That's all I need right now." She held out the bag, and he planted his bottle of water inside over a thin blanket.

Afraid of touch, Storyteller?

She bounced up, strapped on the backpack over her shoulders. "Ready?"

Alex rose, and his eyes clamped onto hers before she shifted her gaze.

"How about we go at a slower pace, you know, so we can chat and get to know each other?"

Her eyes darted back and forth. "Hmmm." She lifted one knee up and down and repeated it on the other side before turning her head and tiptoeing her eyes until they reached his. "I guess. Okay."

Alex's eyes became hooded, and for a moment, her golden gems accepted the invitation to waltz in his ocean waters. A redness crept up her neck and rose buds sprouted on her cheeks.

She spun her body toward the trail, cleared her throat, and said, "Let's go."

They sauntered side by side, with another hush surrounding them for several more seconds.

"Um..."

"So..."

Their words collided, and they turned toward each other.

Delphina covered her mouth, trying to stuff the giggles fizzing in her throat.

He tipped his head back and chuckled. "Look at that. The adage, great minds think alike, bears merit here."

She dropped her hand, and laughter catapulted, slicing through the left-over quiet.

With her infectious light-heartedness igniting sparks within him, he swallowed, trying to dampen the intensity.

She mesmerizes me, and I haven't even heard her story or anything about her storytelling yet.

He followed her eyes as they moved and expanded. Hopping and pointing toward the pond, she squeezed his arm. "Look over there."

Alex turned his head.

Because the late afternoon sun mellowed, softening her rays, a subtle movement around the perimeter of the pool became more visible.

A small bird, garbed in magnificent, wooded plumage, pecked its way around the water's edge.

Delphina leaned closer to him, providing him with a moment to inhale and savor the subtle fruity aroma she emitted.

"What kind of bird do you think it is?"

As he pitched his face closer, he put a finger to his brain and coated his voice with exaggerated intellect. "Ms. Tulasi, let me wear my ornithologist hat. Hmm. I'd say it's some kind of heron?"

Giggles floated up again, and swathing her words with a similar quality, she said, "Mr. O'Hara, in my estimation, I'd say you're correct."

Alex glanced at her, and she gifted him with a wide smile.

"Ms. Tulasi, it looks like we share a sense of humor."

Pink blossomed on her face. "Mr. O'Hara, let us carry on."

A relaxed warmth spread throughout him, and he bowed. "Please, Delphina. Ladies before Gents. You go first."

A smile jotted across her face. "Well, sir, I appreciate the chivalry, but why don't you share more about you?" She turned and walked backwards.

He followed her and smirked. "Are you playing therapist with me?"

She laughed again. "Moi?" But then she halted and narrowed her eyes. "Wait, a minute. I don't recall sharing my past professional role as a therapist."

He nodded and raised his palms. "Guilty." Advancing closer to her, she traipsed back. "I explored your website."

Delphina cocked her head and squinted one eye. "Are you sure my mother didn't tell you that?"

Alex threw his head back and roared. "No o o. My exchange with Lucia involved nothing about you."

She pivoted and ambled forward. "Okay. Please tell me how you know my mother."

As he strolled beside her, Alex dipped his head. "Ah. All in good time, but for now, we'll stick to lighter subjects, so here's a bit more about me. Born and raised outside of Boston, by both parents. An older brother. Close family. Testosterone fueled the house, but the last word came from Estrogen."

Delphina stopped again, and her eyes dazzled as she flashed her pearly-white smile. "I never heard male-female relationships put that way. I love it."

"Mom used the expression sometimes when we resisted certain chores. She didn't let us get away with too much."

Alex locked eyes with her for another moment before she directed her gaze forward, walking again.

"She loves her boys as she calls us, and I get the sense Lucia's maternal instinct equals Mom's." He shot her a sideway look, but even with the mention of her mother, no return gaze as she continued to nod.

"I told you about my love for hockey, but the whole family fell in love with it. Some people thought I had the talent to go pro, but I knew deep in my heart. No. After college, I joined a league where I still play once a week when not traveling."

His eyes skirted in her direction, but her gaze didn't waver, fixed on the horizon as she nodded.

"Your turn."

She gulped and pressed her lips. "What would you like to know?"

Careful, Pal. Tread with caution.

"How about telling me about Scheherazade?"

Delphina flashed him a half-smile. "What makes you ask?"

Alex's eyes coaxed hers, which she allowed for a longer delicious moment. "Ah, again, your website."

She nodded before peering ahead. "You never heard of her?"

"A bit from google. Sounds like she needed to regale her husband with stories. Otherwise, the end for her. Am I right?"

"Yes, I know little more, except her storytelling took much ingenuity, of which all of us are capable even if we don't realize it. I brought her to light because she tapped into her creative juices to entertain and stay alive."

"Did they fall in love?"

Delphina cocked her head, and her eyes captured his. "I believe they did," she said, a sliver of a smile caressing her face. "Lived happily ever after. The legend became so popular that a Russian composer created an orchestral piece based on the Arabian Night tale."

"Wow." Intoxication flooded Alex.

A magnetic pull dragged his feet closer to her, causing Delphina to jump, and with a jagged pivot, stumble forward. As he followed, her words straggled behind, cracked with bitterness. "Too bad it doesn't happen as often in real life."

What the heck?

Alex trotted beside her, and his eyes skimmed her profile. Lips stuck together like cement.

"Delphina. Can I ask you something?"

She tilted her head back and forth without glancing at him. "Go ahead."

He swallowed. "Have you ever been married?"

Delphina skidded to a stop and stared ahead.

Caw, caw. A bird's announcement interrupted.

And nature started conversing. Trees rustled, and animals scurried and splashed along the pond.

In slow motion, Delphina pirouetted around, stood erect, with hands grasping the shoulder straps. As she blinked, her mouth gaped open.

Nature's voice thundered.

Chapter Nine

Delphina

The square-shaped Waterford vase, filled with delphiniums and coral roses, demanded eyes on it. No matter how glorious the bouquet, the sparkling crystal refused to let the blooms capture all the attention, and the blue-purple flowers, sharing their home with long-stem roommates, vied for center stage.

Dressed in jeans, a long-sleeved, button-front, rib-knitted top, and leopard clogs, Delphina's lips flipped up as she immersed herself in the commanding centerpiece which now sat on the coffee table.

She nodded, and with hands on her hips, Delphina bent down, shut her eyes, and inhaled the spicy fragrance bellowing from the roses.

Umm. Clover, cinnamon, and nutmeg breezed around her.

Opening her eyes, Delphina touched one of the delphinium's dolphin-shaped flowers.

Don't you worry, namesake. Nothing mars your beauty. You and your pal, here, make a splendid team.

The resplendent display hypnotized her as its message whispered, "You can't resist, so don't try."

Could that have been Alex's intention?

I guess I'll find out, but for now, don't focus on it even if the flowers beckon you to do so.

Delphina plodded over to her small but elegant kitchen of maple wood cabinets and beige granite swirling with gold and green. Her hand slid across the cool countertops that allowed small, stylish, thin, high-back chocolate suede chairs to sit. The coffee pot awakened, gurgling as it announced brewed Italian Roast, and two mugs sat ready for the pour.

She traipsed back to the living room and flopped against her periwinkle, modern Victorian Chesterfield sofa. Her fingers glided over the soft, velvet covering, and her gaze shifted to the wrought-iron, glass coffee table. Surrounding the centerpiece lay colorful ceramic coasters, flowered mats, and small plates as she waited for her guest.

Placing an embroidered throw-pillow behind her, Delphina leaned back, and knitted her hands on top of her head.

Wait until I tell…

Buzz, buzz.

Delphina jumped up.

Right on time as she skipped to the microphone and pressed the receiver.

"Hell-o-o-o, Delphina. Ready for scrumpchar-o-o-o?"

"I'm starving. Hurry."

"I'm starving too, honey, but more for the story than the food."

Delphina clicked off the button and opened her door.

Like a gazelle leaping across a field, Josie swished up the stairs with the scent of fresh bagels wafting around her.

Delphina plucked the bag from her hands and hugged her with one arm, as Josie's embrace cocooned her. "Okay, you, since you're now my only sis in another life, let's eat."

Rounding her hands into fists, Josie swung them up and down and stomped her feet. "I can't wait!" She frolicked toward the living area. "Oh, my God. Look at those gorgeous flowers." In a sing-song melody, Josie asked, "Should I assume they come from Alexander?"

Warmth streamed through Delphina's body to the tips of her fingers and toes, and her lips refused to suppress a ballooning smile. "Yes, they are. And read the note."

Josie hurried toward the bouquet, and her long nails clicked as she flipped open the card.

Dear Delphina,
Thank you for the honor and pleasure of your company yester-
day. I look forward to learning more about you as we embark on
a new adventure.
Yours truly,
Alexander

Josie put her palm on her chest. "Oh, my God." She pivoted to Delphina. "I want to hear about this guy, so hurry."

"Coming. Sit and get comfy. Everything's ready except toasting the bagels. I assume you got our favorites?"

"Yes. *Everything* for me, and *Garlic Galore* for you."

Delphina smiled as she sauntered into the kitchen, pulled out the cut bagels, and put a half of each in the toaster.

Placing the cream cheese container on a tray, she paused as Josie's words bounced toward her. "So, you messaged me an hour ago, telling me about his question, and you leave me hanging with *later?* Come on Delph. I'm dying, so get to it. Tell me what happened."

With her back to Josie, Delphina peered outside the window. Her book of thoughts arranged themselves in the conversation's sequence flow.

Pop, pop.

She fluttered her eyelashes and spun around as the toasted bagels announced their readiness, reinforced by the pungent smell of garlic. Pouring the coffee, she placed food and drink on the tray and plodded over to Josie.

"Get ready for your *Everything*." She winked. "And I'm not talking about bagels alone."

As she positioned the tray on the table, Josie bent forward and spread the cream cheese across her bagel. "I'm all ears."

Delphina sat upright on the sofa, and with her hands clasped around the steaming brew, she took a sip and nodded as she skimmed back to the page of yesterday.

Her mouth dropped open, and words scattered along her throat, unable to string together a sentence.

Alex's eyebrows knitted together, and he pitched forward, grasping her wrist.

"Oh, no. I didn't mean to offend."

Her body froze, and she allowed his fingers to warm her.

"I, um." Tears cascaded down her cheeks.

Alex shook his head, as turmoil carved into his face. "You don't have to answer, Delphina. It's just…"

A downpour of sorrow flooded every cell, and she swallowed, ready to slump over. "Wh-a-a-t made you ask me?"

With features softening, Alex's eyes caressed hers, and he took a deep breath and emitted a broken laugh. "I confess. Not only did I study your website, but…" He tipped his head, and scarlet bloomed up his face. "I visited your Instagram page."

She gulped and shook her head. "I post nothing personal on there, so what does that have to do with the question you're asking?"

He released her wrist, looked down, and shuffled the dirt in front of him.

A stillness amplified the scraping and joined with nature's cacophony of peeps and chirps.

Several seconds passed as if the hourglass dispensed an over-abundance of sand into the lower chamber.

Delphina noticed his furrowed brow, and the torrential downpour softened to a sprinkle of sadness. "You look like you're thinking about what to say."

Alex nodded, as his eyes remained focused on the creation, the tip of his sneaker carved into the ground. "I am." His head popped up, and again his eyes found hers. Touching his jaw, he said, "In one of your videos, you wore a diamond band."

I guess I didn't think of removing any of the reels showing my ring. Didn't even consider it. I wonder how many.

Her gaze became unfocused, and tree branches rustled as robins and blue jays landed there, bickering again. She sighed, and her eyes wandered to his. Panting joggers clomped by, and routine walkers strolled past them deep in conversation.

"I'm not ready to talk about this episode in my life right now. I'll say only one thing." Tears leaked into her eyes again, and she blinked, trying to prevent them from streaming down her cheeks. Words trembled as they propelled from her vocal cords. "Everything in my life fell apart about a year ago, and even though other not-so-good things happened to me, by far, this surpassed all of it."

Alex's head bobbed up and down, and with a tight jaw, a tick flitted across his cheek. "You know, Delphina…" His eyes descended again, and he stroked his jaw.

What's up with him and that jaw area?

His head bobbed up and down, and he bit his cheek, appearing to wrestle with his response. "Things have happened to me also, which I'm not ready to discuss, so…"

Pausing, Alex's eyes widened, and his gaze meandered past her. "I guess we'll need to become more acquainted with one another, before either of us dabble into those events."

He continued to nod before he stared at her again, with his lopsided smile visiting in full glory. "And…" His eyebrows lifted. "I hope we get that opportunity in the future. What do you think?"

A shower of relief spread through every vein and artery of her body, and the corners of her mouth tugged upwards. "I think I'd like that."

Alex shifted his head and peered toward the trail. "Looks like we have a little left on this loop." He cocked his head at her. "Shall we?"

"Yes." Her smile reached her eyes and inverted deep inside of her. "That sounds like a plan."

"So, that's what happened." Delphina bit into her bagel. "Hmm. Delish, Jos. So, what do you think?"

Josie finished chewing, put down her bagel, and wiped her hands with the napkin in her lap. Swallowing, she lifted her index finger and took a deep gulp of coffee. Placing it onto the coaster, she dropped her palms together in her lap. "Okay. So you want me to diagnose the situation first or ask questions?"

Delphina laughed, almost choking on her coffee. "Do we never not use therapy language, Jos? But okay…" She swayed her body, used air quotes, and in a snobbish voice, she said, "Madame Therapist Turned Dream Inspirer, please give me your Evaluation and Assessment." She sat back and chomped on another hunk of her bagel.

Josie tilted her head. "First, Miss Oversensitive Friend, I'm glad you didn't bristle at him when he asked."

Dabbing her mouth with her napkin, Delphina picked up her mug and raised it in the air. "I might have if I hadn't cried first."

"Glad you didn't, because this guy said nothing wrong. If he sees a sparkler on your hand, of course, he might wonder."

"Yeah, but since he's acquainted with my mother, you'd think he'd know."

"Ms. Delphina, what makes you think they're that close? Huh?"

Delphina lifted her eyebrows. "Good point."

"We don't know the nature of their connection, since both refuse to share at this point. From what it sounds, he met her in the professional realm, but we don't know how. Maybe she tried to match him with someone?"

"Maybe."

"But let's put that aside." Josie grabbed Delphina's hand. "Girlfriend, he sounds like a gem."

Delphina moved her head around. "Not sure yet."

"Fair, but at least he's courteous, and from what it sounds, sensitive to your…"

"Go ahead."

"Well, you know, you're like a pin cushion waiting for the pricks to invade you."

Delphina nodded. "I know. My oversensitivity."

"I love you, Delph, and what happened, beyond unfair, but not everyone will become a Judas, so tell me the rest of the story, puleeze."

Delphina sipped on her coffee and held the mug in her lap, turning to yesterday's page in her mind.

A comfortable stillness billowed between them, and the area-at-large seemed to hitch a ride on their tranquility.

Delphina's steps slowed down, and Alex's movements followed her rhythm.

A balmy breeze circled around them, and Delphina inhaled, allowing her insides to dip into a warm, frothy bubble bath.

"Hmm."

"Yeah, perfect day, wouldn't you say?"

Without glancing at Alex, Delphina nodded. "Yes."

"You know what I think, Delphina?"

She shifted her gaze, waded into his ocean eyes with an upward pull to her lips.

"I think the day became better because we tightened some of the loose bolts people encounter getting accustomed to each other."

Delphina lifted her eyes. "I agree, Mr. O'Hara, and an interesting metaphor. You sure you're not a storyteller?"

Alex chuckled and focused ahead. "Oh, I have a few stories or two to tell, as I hinted to you. But I think every human being has stories to share, which I'd venture to say, you agree?" He peeked at her.

The shackles around her heart slackened from earlier today, and a foamy laugh lilted her voice. "Yes, as a therapist turned storyteller, my focus remains on the story, rewriting the old with new."

"You let me know you preferred not to discuss your work, but I find it fascinating, so hopefully in time, without identifying the people, you'll share more with me."

"When did I say that?"

"Ah, I think in Vegas."

"Well, that was early on."

Another slight breeze invited nature to dance again. Trees swayed, shedding some of their aging green attire. Golden Rod waltzed in concert with New England Aster, and a couple of squirrels scampered by with acorns in their mouths, preparing for the changing season.

Huff. Puff.

Indistinct words ping-ponged between shuffling runners as they whizzed by them.

Alex stopped for a moment and jutted his chin. "Look, we've come to the end. What do you think about sitting for a few minutes?"

Delphina glanced at her watch and jerked her head. "Wow. I didn't realize the time."

Alex's lopsided smile dazzled her as he bent his arm, offering his elbow. "Would the old saying, time flies when you're having fun, apply here?"

She looped her arm into his, tilted her head, swimming deeper into his azure-sea eyes. "What do you think?"

Throwing his head back and chortled, Alex said, "Ah, playing therapist with me again?"

Delphina shook her head and rounded her lips into a perfect O. "N-o-o-o..." She lowered her eyes, closing her index finger and thumb. "Maybe a little." Her eyes skimmed his face and grinned. "It's in the genes."

"Yup. Like mother, like daughter."

"Uh-huh. You can take us out of the profession, but you can't take the profession out of us." Slowing down, they reached an unoccupied bench and plopped down. Delphina squinted and tilted her head to him. "Does that make sense?"

His eyes twinkled. "Sure does."

Placing her palms on the bench, Delphina slumped down and dug her heels into the ground.

Another cozy silence wandered around them, and other than a few chirps, nature joined them.

Delphina sipped on her coffee, stared past Josie, and her lips curled into a smile.

A hand waved in front of her. "Hey girl, don't leave me hanging."

With the smile embedded on her face, Delphina reached for her bagel. "Let me finish this half, and I'll tell you."

Josie rounded her hands into balls. "I'm dying. Before you take a bite, give me a hint."

"Movies and the Melkites."

Chapter Ten

Alex

Aloud roar rose, and people jumped up as the baseball made its way over the Green Monster. Alex and Delphina stood and clapped. One of Boston's favorite Red Sox players chugged around the bases, pointed to the sky, and tipped his hat after delivering a three-run homer for his fans.

Alex chuckled. Everyone from the area understood the reference to the great green wall in the left field of Fenway Park. A challenge to the most talented players. Not today. A huge treat as the Red Sox scored past their greatest rival, the New York Yankees, in the top of the seventh inning.

As they watched from their box seats behind third base, Alex breathed in the early fall air. What a glorious ride over. New England unveiled some of its splendid attire before it prepared for the long winter sleep. Fire red, burnt orange, and gold. Perfect day for a game.

Fenway Park. Man. 1912. Amazing. So glad they didn't tear it down. You can modernize without eliminating.

He peeked at Delphina, and she winked back at him, twirling one of her coils around her index finger.

Wow, what a difference since that first date in Las Vegas.

They sat, and turning to Delphina, he asked, "Are you having fun?"

"Are you kidding?" Delphina's eyes grasped his and sparkled with dancing gold flecks. "I'm having a ball. No pun intended."

She laughed and pulled on his arm. "Look who's up next? Maybe another homer?" She started banging on her chair.

Alex's eyes lingered on her for a moment.

What a beauty. A tumble of golden curls met him on their second date in Boston. He almost didn't recognize her. Not only did she allow her hair to roam free, but she seemed more relaxed after their first on Walden Pond.

The corners of his lips flitted upwards. Take that, Mr. Thoreau.

What could have been the collapse of a fragile beginning, steadied itself. Her porcupine spikes retreated when he did his best to allay her fears.

Phew.

Sitting for another hour. A soothing balm of safe topics.

Movies. One of her favorites? *The Age of Adeline.*

Why? To her, eternal youth, a curse. Growing old with a loved one, a blessing.

One of his? *No Country for Old Men.*

Why? One reason. Interesting.

She gaped at him, shook her head, and birthed a slow smile. "Every guy I come across says the same thing. I saw it once with someone and thought it was depressing." A faraway look invaded her face.

Hmm. Wonder if it was her ex? Right now, ask nothing, pal. Look what happened. Repeat. Let her tell you.

"I can understand that, but the characters reveal the evil nature of human beings, so it makes you think. Like your favorite makes you do."

She cocked her head, and her eyes danced with his. "Are you kidding? Comparing a sociopath to a tortured woman?"

"Hear me out. Human behavior on display. Good vs. evil."

With mirth trickling from her, Delphina grabbed his wrist and said, "I'll give that one some thought, sir."

"You do that, ma'am. Because interesting can mean something other than warm and fuzzy."

Delphina jotted another smile as her eyes skidded over her apple watch. "Oh, my goodness, I have to leave in fifteen minutes."

"Aww. Another date?"

"Yes."

Alex's stomach descended like a free-falling elevator, but he plastered a half smile on his face.

"With the Melkite Maidens."

"W-h-a-a-a-t?"

Delphina's head tipped back, and a laugh squeaked from her. "A group of ladies from my church get together once a month for dinner and a game, which we've been doing for the last five years."

Alex's lurch to the abyss halted, and his smile shifted into a relaxed curve.

"Too bad for me, but it sounds like fun for you."

Delphina fluttered her eyelashes and shifted her gaze for a moment. "I'm having fun right now, but…" She returned her eyes to his. "I don't want to cancel at the last minute."

A foamy sensation surfed through his body, and he bobbed his head up and down. Keeping his words tight, Alex said, "Of course, you need to keep your commitment."

Delphina's eyes caressed his. "Thank you for understanding."

"We'll have more time soon," Alex said, wiggling his eyebrows. "Wouldn't you say?" He held out his palm.

Delphina's eyes tiptoed down to his hand and she moved hers into his.

Swallowing, Alex squeezed it, and a warm wave of stillness encircled them.

As if following in their steps, nature remained mum, and Alex drank in the soothing, momentary calmness.

Delphina sighed, continuing to allow his hand to cup hers.

"Delphina, before you go, could you share more about Melkite Maidens? I don't even know what Melkite means."

Another laugh sang from her throat. "Sure. But do you know anything about the Eastern Catholics?"

"Nope."

"If I hadn't grown up in the church, neither would I, but the Syrian/Lebanese Catholics, different from Orthodox, follow the same rites of the Catholic Church but vary in how they display them. I won't get into all of it, and it doesn't mean we don't attend Roman Catholic church. I often do, but what I love about my…" she used air quotes, "…Mother Church is the community feeling. Lots of Lebanese people, food, celebrations, including a festival called a Mahrajan."

"Wow, never heard of it. I come from parents with mixed religious orientations. Dad, Roman Catholic and Mom, Evangelical. Spent time in both churches. Not great at practicing anything until the last year, a story for another time, but I knew nothing about Catholicism other than Roman. I had a Syrian Orthodox friend from college. I attended his wedding and got to see him and his wife wear the crowns. Long ceremony but cool."

"Yes! Oh, my goodness, you know about the crowns. Aren't they magnificent? Someday when I get married…" A door slammed shut on the rest of Delphina's sentence. Her eyes widened, and she turned away as a tear splashed across her cheek. Brushing it with her free hand, she sniffled.

Alex gulped.

What do I say?

Delphina swung Alex's hand in a playful pattern, and her face found his again. "Don't mind me… Anyway, my maiden friends, some of whom I've known since our days in Youth Group, reconnected. We thought about forming a book club, but had different reading tastes—romance, thrillers, suspense, romantasy—so we decided on games. Ten women in the group, and no less than eight show every month."

"And what made you decide on the name Maidens?"

Delphina's eyes brushed his again. "At the time we reconnected, all of us were single, so someone said, 'How about Melkite Maidens?' And everyone agreed. About half are matrons now, but we'll keep the name even when the rest of us marry."

So, she never married. The ring must have been an engagement one. Lucia mentioned her daughter was to marry.

What happened?

Delphina shuffled her feet, released his hand, and bounced up. "I need to go now."

"Let me walk you to the car." He picked up her backpack, slung it over his shoulder, and extended his hand.

Entwining her fingers into his, an infinity symbol blotted onto his mind's landscape.

They strolled toward her car, and she unlocked it before reaching the driver's door.

Beep.

Alex rushed forward, opened the passenger side, and situated the bag on the seat. He stood back in front of her, and his knuckles nestled on her cheek.

Delphina tilted her chin, and another smile calligraphed across her face.

"Delphina, may I kiss you?"

A languid expression coated her eyes. "Yes."

Alex bent down, and his lips nuzzled hers.

Man, I don't want to stop.

For a moment, he pressed harder, savoring the delicious moment, then softened the electric current into a peck. Pulling back, his index finger zig-zagged along her braid before tugging on it. He took her hand, and she slid into the car and looked up as Alex's fingers curled around the top edge of the door. "Have fun with your friends, Delphina. Until next time." Without taking his eyes off her, he closed the door with slow precision.

A poignant expression sculpted her face, as she waggled her fingers, pushed the ignition button, and drove away.

With one hand on his hip, Alex waved. As the pearly white car whisked her away, he stayed until it shrank, becoming invisible, until another day.

Now their fourth date.

Crack. The player watched his ball fly as he slung his bat.

"Ooh. Another homer?" Delphina bounced in her seat and grabbed his wrist.

The crowd moaned as the outfielder jumped, lengthened his arm, and stretched a gloved hand to capture the ball, robbing the player of a home run.

Elongated rumbles of *Aww* groaned from the spectators.

Alex's eyes locked onto Delphina's. "Well, we can't complain."

"Maybe a little." Delphina laughed.

He peered at her outfit. Jeans, a cream-colored wool sweater, and New Balance sneakers.

"Okay. But a beautiful day."

Her cheeks blossomed with a peachy-rose hue, reminded him of awakening peonies, and she smiled. "Yes." She shielded her eyes. "Let's get ready for the wave."

Delphina and Alex stood and sat as part of the ceremonial seventh-inning ritual at Fenway. She slurped on her soda and offered Alex a sip.

He waved his hand. "No, thank you."

Delphina stretched her legs and sighed.

Alex stroked his chin, and Delphina tilted her head. "You seem to rub that same area."

Slapping his hand against his leg, Alex said with a sheepish grin, "I know. Bad habit."

"You can't see the scars until you bring attention to them."

Alex shifted his head side-to-side. "Need to work on not going there. Maybe the storyteller can help me write a new story."

Delphina's eyes lit up. "Sure, but you'd have to share the old story first."

Alex inhaled. "Got it. Not sure I'm ready to return to that episode." His head lowered and touched her forehead. "Besides, I don't want to burden you. I've done therapy on it."

"It wouldn't be a burden." She gave him a nondescript look. "Both of us can share more when we, ah, you know…" she blinked, "…are more comfortable with each other." Delphina's eyes shined. "And glad to hear you sought help for it."

Alex's gaze lingered for a moment on Delphina, interrupted by the voice booming from the intercom.

"Here we go." Delphina grabbed his wrist, releasing it to pitch forward, and stomped her feet with the rest of the crowd.

As Alex turned his head to the infield, he noticed a hand of red, pointed nails waving her fingers. He did a double-take and pressed his chin as if a sharp weapon sliced into his scars again.

Logan's pool. The evening unfurled, and a haughty moon took center stage with a wink. "Let the games begin."

Sirena clasped Alex's wrist. About to lead him away from his two gaping friends, an older gentleman tapped her on the shoulder and whispered in her ear. She grimaced with lips curled up and leaned into Alex. "I'll be right back. You stay put."

"O'Hara." Quinn wiggled his eyebrows. "What kind of fun does Logan's wife have in store for you? Did she and Logan plan this party around the full moon? You know, ancient ceremonies focusing on celestial bodies celebrated with orgies and sacrifices."

Bart howled.

"Come on, you two. His wife might be a flirt, but guess what, she's married. And, may I remind you, to our boss. I doubt she's up to anything beyond some light and playful banter. Don't act like an older woman has never come on to you."

"I don't know, O'Hara. Ever hear of open marriages, swingers, polyamory?" Bart devoured his drink, snapped his finger at the server nearby, and snatched another glass.

Alex gritted his teeth. "First, Palermo, I'd suggest you be more polite to the servers. Second, I don't think that's Logan's thing. And if I'm wrong, to each their own, but not for me."

"Alex O'Hara—Boy Scout. I don't need lectures from you or anyone else about manners. And…" Bart stood, hooked his thumbs into his belt, and looked around. "Do whatever you want, but I'm off to check out the scenery." He nudged his chin at Quinn. "You want to come?"

As Quinn rose out of his seat, Logan shouted and curled his hand. "Okay, everyone. Time to move the activities inside." The musicians closed their instruments and followed.

Alex peered at his watch. He'd pop inside, chat for about twenty minutes, and unless anyone interesting came his way, he would say his goodbyes. As he stepped forward, fingers curled around his wrist, and a sultry aroma wafted close to him.

"You're all mine, gorgeous. I'm capturing you before anyone else tries."

Alex looked to see Sirena. She changed her more subdued dress for a scanty one, slit up her leg, and a gold choker with a long keychain dangling from it.

He noticed a rush going through him. "Um, Mrs.…"

Without releasing him, she pressed her index finger to his lips. "Shh. Remember, Sirena only." She dragged a long pointy red nail down to his chin and allowed it to linger on the Y-shaped dimple in the middle of his chin. "Ooh. I love cleft chins." She tugged and led him in the opposite direction of the crowd.

"Sirena, I think…"

"Don't think. Just follow. We'll see the others soon enough. Maybe." Sirena giggled.

Alex turned his head and noticed some couples embracing and laughing as they stumbled through the French doors. He could see musicians now wearing blindfolds, and a server handing masks to each guest.

Sirena brought him to a glass door with drapes covering it. Her lips curled up, and she pivoted and unlocked the door.

"For you and me only."

Alex shook his head. "I don't think so, Sirena."

"Oh, come on. If you're worried about Logan, he knows all about this. We agree on having an openness to our marriage, and I whispered to him you would be my afternoon delight." She snickered. "More like evening."

Alex planted his feet and folded his arms. "Sirena, I don't have an issue with how people conduct their private lives…"

She placed her finger against his lips. "Shh," and she gripped his wrist, almost dragging him forward.

Another whiff of her exotic aroma entered his nostrils and intoxicated him.

Oh, man, instead of the Sirens' song luring the sailors, this Siren tempted with her scent.

They entered a room of different shades of bright red.

"I designed it myself, Alex." Sirena's tongue rolled over her lips. "As you can see, I love red. Imperial, Scarlet, Ruby, Poppy, Chile. Bold, passionate, lush, spicy."

Alex nodded. Dread, like an inferno, began erupting in his chest.

Sirena began kissing him. Her mouth roamed over his face, and she began nipping his neck.

His body started responding. Sirena released the top button of her dress, tipped her head back, and a guttural laugh erupted from her throat. "Come on, lover boy."

Alex grabbed her chin, and for a moment, his eyes mauled her body.

"You want me, so have me." Sirena curled her tongue against her teeth.

Crack.

Alex blinked, returning his attention to the present.

The player threw the bat as he ran to first base.

"A line drive deep into center field," the announcer boomed.

The crowd stood and roared. Delphina jumped up and clenched Alex's arm.

He touched the side of her face, and their eyes locked before she turned her head back to the game.

I think I'm falling in love with her. No, I know I am. But will I be able to trust her with this? In these current times, with nasty men being exposed, will she believe the truth about me?

Alex stooped down to tie a loose shoelace, and as he stood up, his eyes caught those of a man of similar in age glowering at him. He turned his head side-to-side to see if he misjudged the man's glare. Perhaps it was intended for someone else. When he glanced again, the man appeared to have vanished. Guess he mistook me for someone else.

Chapter Eleven

Delphina

Delphina breathed in the crisp fall air. Chilly, but she loved the colorful season. The end of October. And starting a relationship during the fall.

What a treat and not a trick.

The trees undressed and threw off their obsolete attire of leaves, blanketing the ground. Bright pumpkins, some carved into Jack-o'-lanterns, witches' hats, goblins. Preparation for Halloween and Trick or Treat. This year, a special one if the momentum with Alex continued, even if he went away on business.

Bump, bump.

A late afternoon hayride. Still light out and a great way to see the apple orchards. Delphina wore fingerless gloves, and her hands wrapped around a thermos of hot cider. She snuggled closer to Alex, and his lips caressed her hair.

Shutting her eyes and sipping the warm liquid from her thermos, Delphina allowed the cider to linger in her mouth. She savored the tastes of the apples, cinnamon, and nutmeg and puckered her lips before allowing it to roll down her throat.

"Yummy," Delphina hummed.

"Who? Me?"

With a languid voice, Delphina said, "You and the cider."

He chuckled. "I'll take yummy. You, my beauty, I'll describe as sumptuous. How about that?"

Joy spun around Delphina's heart. "I love it because I adore the word *sumptuous*. I use it myself because of its meaning. Valuable, precious, splendid. A prettier synonym." She laughed. "Of course, I don't refer to myself that way."

"And why not?"

"I don't know, except I don't want to sound conceited, but I like you applying it to me."

"Liking it for you but liking you even more."

"Good."

She nestled closer as daylight yawned, readying itself for sleep. A comfortable quilt of silence enveloped them.

"I could stay here forever," murmured Delphina.

Alexander nodded, and his fingers glided over her face, touching, exploring.

"You know, Alexander, I'm more than liking you." Delphina shifted her head as his finger went under her chin. Warmth seeped into her cheeks.

"And?"

She poked her finger into his chest. "Scary for me to admit."

Alex grabbed her hand and brushed his lips across each fingertip. His peppery hair fell over his azure eyes. "Glad you said it, because Delphina, I'm more than liking you. I'm falling in love with you." He cupped her face with his hands. "And I don't just think it. I know it."

Alex bent his head and locked his mouth on hers as his hands combed through her hair. Sparks ran through Delphina like an electric current, drawing her closer, and wanting more.

She clasped his neck, awakening the waves that lay dormant.

After several seconds, she pulled away, and her eyes latched onto his. Strands of silver threaded through his magnificent pupils, seducing her to wade into their depths.

"I-I believe I'm ready to share with you the start of my issues around trust. You know. Need to change my story as I encourage clients to do. Time to write a new chapter."

Alex lifted his eyebrows. "The beginning." Gravelly laughter scraped out of his mouth. "A great place to start."

Clasping her hand, Alex brought it to his lips again and kissed it. His gaze lingered on her. "Yes. New chapters for both of us."

"I wish you didn't have to go tonight."

"Me too." His forehead joined hers. "See. I can't help myself from copying you."

"Alex, I really want you to hear this before you go."

"Wherever you want to begin, I'm ready to listen."

Delphina exhaled and blew a raspberry.

"Are you sure? Because I don't want you to feel pressured, after all," he said, concern sprinkling his tone, "we have all the time in the world." His muscular arms wrapped around her like protective tree branches.

Delphina's heart swelled from the magic potion implied in his words.

Yup. Love. Two-way street. Don't deny it.

She turned her head and looked up at him. "I need to get this out because while you're gone, I'll start a new story in my journal."

"In a journal?"

"Yes. I have one which I jot down daily musings, but now, I'm going to write *The Next Chapter*. The journal stares back at me, and without sounding ridiculous, I swear it's inviting me to do this." Delphina laughed.

"Not silly at all." Alexander shook his head. "Sometimes we miss clues laying right in front of us."

"My journal has a pink cover with sparkles."

"Perfect for her scintillating owner."

Delphina shut her eyes, leaned into Alex's chest, and his chin moved to rest on her head. "Okay, Alexander the Great, here goes."

As she pulled on one of her curls, Delphina unlocked her secure vault. Broken words about the assault catapulted forth, bringing unleashed relief.

With each sentence she uttered, her voice shook, and tears

tumbled down her cheeks. Alex squeezed her tighter. "You can stop anytime."

Delphina sniffled and accepted the handkerchief he offered. "No." She dabbed her eyes. "I'm more okay than I sound. I trusted two other people with this. Big mistake, which I'll get to another time."

Alex kissed the top of her head and nodded.

She let out a forceful breath, and in her zeal to release the dark tale, all restraints lifted. Alex's embrace spun a cocoon of safety which fortified her.

"I never thought something like that would happen to me, and for a long time, I blamed myself."

"Hey." Alex changed his position and cupped her face again. "Never, ever allow yourself to think that way. No means no, and that guy… well, calling him a creep minimizes the description he deserves after the harm he inflicted on you. If you ask me, he's a criminal."

In a wispy voice splashed with relief, Delphina said, "Thank you."

"Did he end up becoming a doctor?"

She nodded. "Yeah. In the alumni news, under our class, it stated that he graduated from medical school and began his residency in dermatology. In the writeup, he claimed his goal was to help people maintain a healthy appearance."

"Yeah, right. So he didn't mention his true intentions of making tons of money by administering Botox, Restylane, and other fillers?"

"That's right. Also, no sign he wanted to treat people who suffer from chronic acne or other skin afflictions."

"Not surprised, but you know what, Taibhseach?"

Delphina cocked her head and laughed. "What?"

"Taibhseach. It means gorgeous in Irish or Irish Gaelic."

"Yes, how could I forget. O'Hara—Irish."

"One hundred percent on both sides, and while my paternal grandfather learned English when he came over, he never forgot the old language and taught us a few words."

"Say it again."

"Let me drawl it out. Taibhseach." Alex's eyes shined on hers. "Now you try it. Taibhseach."

"Taibhseach. I like that, even if I'm a Middle Eastern one." Delphina settled back against his chest, and he hugged her again. She kissed his wrist.

"That's right. I forgot your grandparents came from Syria. What a splendid mix, Syrian and Irish." He squeezed her tighter. "But more about that later. Yes, Taibhseach, I like the name because it describes you to a T."

"I can say the same thing about you." She giggled. "Taibhseach."

Oh my God, I can't believe it, but I'm falling in love with this man.

Alex chuckled. "Maybe starting pet names for one another? At least to start?"

Delphina's heart ballooned again, and she murmured. "Uh-huh."

A cozy pause cloaked them as dusk opened the door for the evening. The wagon slowed down. Crunching leaves and its pungent scent signified their arrival at the orchard station.

The driver turned to them. Although night veiled his expression, Delphina detected a lilt in his voice. "Looks like you two enjoyed yourselves."

Delphina locked eyes with Alex, and they said in unison, "We did."

The driver chuckled. "You two sound like you're in sync."

Alex placed his finger under Delphina's chin. "We think so."

"Ah. Young people in love."

Alex stood and grabbed Delphina's hands to lift her up. He pulled out his wallet and gave the driver a fifty-dollar bill. "Thank you for such a great experience."

The driver tipped his hat. "My pleasure. Thank you, sir, and miss."

Jumping out, Alex hoisted Delphina from the wagon.

She glanced at him. "I won't see you until after Thanksgiving?"

Alex laced her hand as they walked toward his car. "I know." He sighed and brought her hand up to his lips. "I'm already missing you."

They stopped, and he bent down with his eyes caressing her face.

Delphina stood on her toes and clasped her hands around his neck. "Me too."

He kissed her eyes, nose, and then her lips, deep and long.

"I'll be in meetings day and night, but I'll do my best to text."

"Let's pray the weeks go by fast." She touched his cheek. "It will be like you never left."

"I hope so."

Alex

Alex gawked at the massive jewel standing in front of him.

He jerked his neck as far back as it could go to gaze upward. It rocketed toward the clouds with no end in sight. The Burj Al Arab Hotel, a replica of a boat sailing in the ocean, fit its description. Luxurious, unique, and expensive. He stayed in many spectacular hotels, but nothing compared to this.

Wow. The executives of this company don't scrimp. They invited us to discuss a partnership and pulled out all the bells and whistles.

"Sir, may I take your bags?"

"Thank you. I think I'll just stand here for a moment and take in the scenery."

The young man bowed. "We will bring them to your room."

Alex pulled out some cash. "Much obliged."

The man bowed again and slipped away.

The tipping policy seemed murky, so Alex did it anyway. Even for business, he preferred to give.

Dressed in trousers and a light-weight cotton shirt, Alex remained hypnotized by the stunning view of the Arabian sea. The morning ushered in three-foot waves, whispering with a kiss as they lapped. Alex folded his arms and closed his eyes. A golden-haired mermaid with ringlets appeared. Luscious lips framed white pearls, and a laugh erupted from her throat.

Ah. Delphina. Gorgeous. Not just on the outside. Inside too.

Could she be the one? He hadn't felt that way about anyone for a long time. Daphne came the closest, but something held him back from proposing. After two and a half years, she clarified she wouldn't wait any longer. She watched her older sisters and cousins. They expressed misery being without a potential partner or dating a non-committed guy.

In the beginning, Daphne—tall, willowy, and blonde—painted her face with a permanent smile. In her mellifluous voice, she would have said, "Whatever works for you, Darling. I'm easy." But in the last year of their relationship, a less saccharine disposition chomped on her sweetness, bit by bit.

Daphne erased her smile and replaced it with a permanent scowl directed toward him. By the end of their couplehood, every plan and decision went her way. One morning, he stared at himself in the mirror.

Alex, I don't even know you.

He became robotic and agreed to everything she asked, except for her greatest desire.

"Alex, I've arranged for us to get together with Kate and her boyfriend on Friday at 6:30."

"Sure."

"We need to attend my parents' brunches every other week. They insist."

"Okay."

"Alex, jeans and a sports jacket won't cut it. Suit and tie, please."

"Got it."

"We can't meet with your friend, Drew. I refuse to sit with his new girlfriend. She bores me."

"No problem. I'll meet Drew on my own."

"Alex, where are we going with our relationship? I told you I'm ready for the next step, so I'll start looking at venues. Hint, hint."

"What?"

"Yes, Alex. What?"

He shrugged and remained mute.

"What's that supposed to mean? Huh? So, how about when?" Daphne's dark eyes raged like an impending storm, and she jabbed her ring finger at him. "I don't want to wait any longer for the diamond. I thought Christmas, Valentine's Day, any day, and no ring. So either promise me you'll talk to my dad and get on you knee soon, or—or it's over."

"Okay."

Daphne screeched. "Okay, what?"

"Okay. I guess it's over because I'm not ready to commit to marriage."

Daphne put her hands on her hips, stomped her feet, and screamed.

"Whaaaat?! I've had it. Do you understand?"

She ranted for several minutes. As a finishing touch to her tirade, she swung her arms up and slapped them against her hips. "I'm not wasting any more time. I'm not waiting. You've seen what's happening to my sisters and cousins as they search for Mr. Right. Desperation and misery. Well, guess what? Not me, so get ooooout!"

"Okay."

And he did.

A day or two after she broke it off, a dam opened, flooding him with relief.

Pal, talk about being out of touch with your emotions. Good thing she called it off. Yeah, you would have ended it, but why wait? What if you became complacent and entered a marriage with the wrong person? You know you, unless one of the three A's happened—abuse, addiction, or adultery—you would have stayed and made the best of it. Yup. She did you a favor.

Some people assumed he wanted out because of commitment phobia. But they didn't know the nuances of the situation. Daphne put on a good front. But in a marriage, he wanted a partnership, not a boss.

And Delphina? How did she differ from Daphne?

You couldn't compare the two. Right from the beginning, her

authenticity sparkled. And he could be himself with her. At first, she maintained a brick wall, but after what happened at the end of college, you couldn't blame her. Yesterday, she released the mortar that bound her blocks. He hoped more would loosen to allow her to divulge the other major issue, about an ex, which she referenced. And what about him? Could he trust her to disclose his situation?

Hey, pal. Maybe her courage will catapult you to spill. Yeah, trickier, but if she believes you, a breakthrough.

He stroked his chin, gulped, and to ground himself, he breathed along with the gentle rising and falling of the waves.

Pal, you did nothing wrong. Keep reminding yourself.

He shut his eyes and re-examined the details of that consequential night.

His breath became harsh, and his eyes returned to hers. A voice screamed in his head; *Married. Boss' wife. Married.*

Never been your thing, so don't start now.

"Hey, um." Alex grabbed her wrists and pushed them down. "Sirena, you're a beautiful, sexy woman. And like I said, if people want to involve themselves in these kinds of escapades, to each their own." He shook his head hard. "But not my thing. Believe it or not, I'm kind of old-fashioned."

Sirena pouted.

"Hey?" Alex placed a finger under her chin. "Please don't personalize this."

Sirena's eyes widened, and her voice brought forth a growl. "Are you rejecting a glorious goddess who could have anyone she desired but chose you for tonight?"

He sighed. "Look, this has nothing to do with you, but…"

"But? But what?" Sirena's face became contorted. She grabbed his cheeks, dug her fingernails into the left side of his chin, and in a downward motion, clawed the area.

"What the heck?"

Alex slapped her hand away, and he pulled back as far as possible. He brought his hand to the lower part of his face. Blood spouted out like a spigot being turned on. He extracted a handkerchief from his pocket and pressed it on the wound.

"You can leave now."

"Don't worry." He trudged away from her as he kept the drenched cloth on his face and opened the door leading outside.

"And I will tell Logan how you treated me."

"What?" He turned as she hung back in the shadows.

"You got it. Rejection equals maltreatment. And there are cameras in this room to prove it."

As Alex stepped outside, the door slammed, and high heels clicked toward the party.

Plodding to his car, he winced as his face burned, and he looked at the handkerchief. Even in the dark, the blood-soaked cloth blared its scarlet color. He sat in his car, switched on the dome light, and studied the red tide overflowing from his face.

Oh, man. How do I explain this. Do I go to Urgent Care? No way. I'll just keep applying pressure until the bleeding subsides.

Ripped skin as if placed in a shredding machine.

He clicked open the glove compartment, retrieved the extra napkins he stored, and pressed them against his chin.

Knock, knock.

Alex recognized Bart's knuckles wrapping on his door. He lowered his window a few inches.

"Where ya going, Boy Scout? Last time I saw you, the Mrs. led you like a puppy on a leash." Bart smirked. "Did she forget the dog collar?" He pivoted to the woman standing in the dark. "This is…" He crouched down to Alex and, in a low tone, slurred, "I can't remember her name. All that alcohol."

A singing voice echoed. "Chloe. Chloe."

Bart squinted. "Hey, what happened to your face."

Alex shook his head and turned on the ignition. "Just scraped it on some branches that I missed on the way out."

Bart garbled something, but Alex said, "Gotta go. Enjoy your time with Chloe... and try to remember her name."

Thud. Thud.

Alex opened his eyes to a bellman banging a piece of luggage. All in good time.

Breakfast hour in Dubai. Alex left Boston yesterday at 6 PM and slept off and on. The time change would be a challenge, but he'd adjust.

Time to go inside. His boss insisted they meet for a breakfast pow wow and prepare for the marathon ahead. He texted Delphina as soon as he disembarked, and she responded right away. She delivered a lengthy message about how much she enjoyed him and capitalized *very much in more than like*. She topped it off with rose and lip emojis.

Not one for long texts, Alex kept his correspondences short and sent, *Me Too. Will be in touch*, with claps and hearts. He glanced at his phone as the bellman opened the door to the iconic hotel. A big GIF heart spread over the entire message screen. A warmth rippled throughout his body.

She got me from the first time I laid eyes on her. Rather, when I barged into her.

As he entered the lobby, Alex whistled under his breath. Towering. Bold colors of red, blue, and gold taunted its visitors with opulence, but hey, over-the-top here and there, not so bad. His eyes scanned as much of the scenery he could absorb. Mosaics, marble floor, fountains, and torches. The Middle East bragging with its finest.

Delphina.

Alex nodded. The perfect place to share with her.

Unusual, exotic, and mysterious.

Like Delphina, with her unique style and flair. From their dates, hair up or hair down. Curls cascading or silky straight.

They talked about roughing it during the day.

Yup, he envisioned it now.

Off-road driving in a sturdy 4X4 Jeep through the Arabian Desert. He grips the steering wheel and wiggles his eyebrows at Delphina. "Hold tight my partner-in-adventure as we embark on a thrill-ride."

They bounce over the undulating dunes in the Arabian Desert. "Delphina, do you know what creates sand?"

"No, Taibhseach, I do not."

"Crushed shells and coral."

"You never cease to amaze me."

"We'll learn from each other forever, Taibhseach."

They slow for a minute. "Let me grab some." He sweeps a handful of the gritty material through his fingers and drops a few grains into her hand.

"What do you think?"

Delphina shuts her eyes and shakes her head. "God blesses our world with so much, including me finding you."

"I can't top that one." He navigates the steep slopes and sharp turns with deft precision. Her hand touches his knee, and their laughter connects their souls.

And glamorizing at night?

They'd splash themselves in formal but chic attire.

For him, a dark blue linen suit, a cream-colored, French-cuffed shirt, and Scully and Scully gold rope cufflinks, a gift from her. And bringing it together with an embroidered cream tie of navy-blue elephants.

For her, a gold, sequined, high neck, low-back dress to stress her golden locks and eyes. Curls dangling beneath her shoulders. Diamonds peek from her ears. The only other pieces of jewelry adorn her left hand. A sparkling pear-shaped diamond and a thin eternity band. In the years to follow, more rings for significant anniversaries and the birth of their children.

Yup, Delphina, my wife.

Not scary, so say it again.

Delphina, my Taibhseach,

And while at dinner, I'll ask my Scheherazade to regale me with a story, and another, and another, bringing forth her inner and ancient Middle Eastern heritage with a Christian touch.

Alex took a deep breath and chuckled. He pulled out his phone again and videoed the lobby.

I'll add some voice later and send this to her.

He raised his eyebrows and then plodded toward guest services.

Okay, pal. Time to prepare for a heavy-hitting three weeks, so stop dreaming.

Wait. Not dreaming. I want to make this a reality if—if what?

If she trusted him once he shared the truth.

Chapter Twelve

Delphina

Delphina stared at her twenty-three-year-old client, Glori. The young woman, wearing a black dress, stockings with pumpkins on them, and flats, arrived early for her weekly appointment. Now halfway through her session, she wrote with long, methodical strokes as she penned her story. Every few minutes, Glori paused, tapped her journal with the pen, before returning to her task.

"Ten minutes completed. Five more."

"Okay."

Storytelling sessions with Delphina required no less than six visits. In their first meeting, each person shared the story they wanted to rewrite. Many clients remained with her after she closed her therapy practice, determined they wanted to hone their storytelling tools for a new chapter. Some saw the therapeutic value of rewriting the earlier story and how it might have unfolded under healthier circumstances. But the majority agreed with Delphina. Crafting a new chapter provided a better path toward healing.

Delphina's eyes skimmed her office surroundings. Shabby Chic. A mix of soft pastels and flowers. Distressed furniture with curves and muted linens. The Tufted Chaise she purchased from an estate sale created loud *oohs* and *ahhs*.

The room yelled feminine, but her male clients didn't seem to mind. Everyone commented on the elegance and comfort of the room. But the biggest attraction? Her books. Wall to wall. When clients stepped into her cozy, bookish office, they stared at the bookcases. Personal development, the classics, and lots of fiction. Also, she kept several extra notepads and pens. Most brought their own personalized journals, but some sauntered into her office clutching a laptop bag or holding a large smart device. When that happened, Delphina shook her head and reminded them of the agreement they signed during their initial contact.

"Remember, pen and paper. The old-fashioned way."

They would hit their foreheads or grimace. "Darn. Sorry."

Most of her clients, older Gen Zs, and younger Millennials, asked the reason for pen and paper. "Ms. Tulasi, no problem, but curious, why?" or "I work faster with my computer," or "My hands haven't held an instrument like that in a long time."

"Many believe pen and paper deepens and increases learning and creativity."

All of them would either cock their heads, rub their chins, or nod.

"And it helps with thinking and memory. And…the most important issue? It focuses on you, your uniqueness, and your individual touch. How about that?"

Grins or laughter often emerged with, "You've convinced me, Ms. T."

A few of her clients crowned her with the single initial of her name, so she offered it as a choice when people expressed discomfort calling her Delphina.

She scanned her office, and her eyes landed on the poster she created with Canva. She inscribed it with one of her favorite quotes by Cicero: "A room without books is like a body without a soul."

Now, every time she read the quote, a lopsided smile from a nodding silver-streaked head popped into her mind, causing her heart to *zing*.

Next, with Alex's influence creating a semi-permanent smile, her gaze moved to the childhood books she inherited from her mother—Nancy Drew, Trixie Belden, Donna Parker. Good, clean stories devoted to fun, friendship, and exploration. She zeroed in on one Nancy Drew novel and spanned her life pages back to adolescence.

Thirteen-year-old Delphina stomped her feet when her mother suggested she read one from the series. "Too old-fashioned. Plus, if I tell my friends, they'll think I'm weird."

Lucia's eyes twinkled. "I dare you to read two or three books. If they don't transport you, we'll find something more current. And who says you must share with your friends? Besides, if you like the book, who cares about what they say, my love. Remember, what I told you about confidence?"

"Okay. So, what do you suggest first?"

After a year of reading Trixie and Donna, she asked her mother, "What's next?"

Her mother placed a load of Nancy Drew books in her arms. "Let's see what you can do with these."

One rainy day, Lucia knocked on her bedroom door, telling Delphina she could use the family computer, a permanent fixture in the kitchen, and a nonnegotiable rule for its place in the home.

"Okay, Mama."

Lucia peeked her head inside Delphina's room.

Delphina, lying in her bed with three pillows propped behind her, glanced at her mother, and returned her eyes to the riveting print in front of her. "Mama, *The Quest of the Missing Map*, so like chill, ya know?"

The tale offered an exhilarating journey. With each passing page, she flew as if riding a magic carpet to join Nancy. They put their heads together, stroked their chins, and studied the torn map. What could be the connection between a small ship cottage and a faraway island, carrying a buried treasure?

"We must figure out who has the other half of the map." Delphina said out loud.

During these mystical journeys with her books, Delphina paid little attention to time or voices.

When clients studied the titles, some cocked their heads. "Yeah, I think my grandmother read some of these books. Nancy Drew sounds familiar, but why do you keep them here?"

"Ah, good question. I'll answer it, but first, please tell me what you think."

They would share their perspective, and two or three got it right.

"Yes, nostalgia, and a yearning for the surprise that lies within a good book. Instead of reading on a computer or kindle, I invite people to hold a hardback as they prepare themselves for an adventure to another world?"

Delphina would grab one of her books and bring it to her nose. "If a scent travels into your olfactory lobes, it could percolate creative energies."

Next, she'd tiptoe her fingers along the binding and the cover, floating her thumb to the body, and flipping the pages. "Skim the words and, as the black print flies by, consider its ability to enchant you with the unforgettable."

Each client who asked nodded.

"And I invite you to read a few pages when you need inspiration. If you're intrigued and want more, borrow the book with the promise of returning it in the same condition."

"Not much of a reader these days, Ms. T.," more than one client said.

So glad Alex joins me in love for reading, rare for our generation.

"I know. Our generation grew up with devices, so as we scroll down on our phones and pads, we miss out on the entertainment a delightful novel provides." Delphina smiles. "And not only could it help with your story, but who knows what else—like relationships."

They'd often tilt their heads, then stand. "Wow. You've convinced me. Can I look for one now?"

"Sure."

Several of them would walk toward her wall of books, glance at a title, and put their hands on one. "Going to try this."

"I think you'll enjoy it."

As she looked at Glori, Delphina sighed.

Glori suffered from orthorexia, obsessed with healthy food. For Glori, it didn't interfere with her physical well-being, but her emotional state? Another story.

The young woman exercised at a fitness club seven days a week and maintained a strict diet of healthy food. She refused to deviate even for an occasional dinner with others. Friends stopped inviting her out. Each of them either avoided her, insisted they had little time, or yelled, "I'm sick of you lecturing me about healthy eating. Don't call me until you get help for your food obsession."

Glori met with a few traditional therapists, but she found them too silent for her tastes. Recommended by a friend, she sought Delphina's storytelling services. In their first visit together, she said a few words before dropping her face into her hands and sobbing. As her long golden hair fell forward, her body shook. A minute following this release, she looked up and shared her tale. "I hope storytelling can help me."

On her fourth visit, Glori shared good news with Delphina. "I went out with friends, ordered an ice cream, and didn't say a word about food."

Delphina grinned. "Great. Now time for you to write the next scene or chapter."

As she waited for the timer to stop, Delphina smiled and considered her own next chapter.

What made her feel so safe with Alex?

Could climbing a mountain have clinched her trust?

A few weeks ago, it dawned on Delphina how calm she felt around Alex. She didn't realize to what extent until the hike in New Hampshire.

Her heavy shackles loosened. Any time Delphina and Alex got together, he'd ask her about her week, even though they texted in between dates. His eyes would capture hers, and when he sensed her fatigue, he'd explore other topics or make her laugh. Delphina often examined his face. "I bet your eyes hypnotized the girls from a young age."

"Yeah, some referred to me as a pretty boy, but I did not know. I felt shy, goofy, geeky, and hunched over. He would glance at her, shrug, and sprout his signature lopsided smile. "At 14, my mother threatened to send me to male charm school if I didn't start standing straight. She'd march around, pull her shoulders back, and say, 'Watch me,' and force me to walk back and forth like her."

"I didn't know a male charm school existed."

"It didn't, but how did I know? It sounded horrifying, so I endured my mother's scrutinizing until I perfected my posture."

Delphina laughed. "Mothers can be annoying but are often more correct than not."

"Yeah, and over the years, when I caught her studying me, I'd cock an eyebrow and swagger toward her. 'How's that, my beautiful mother?' She'd giggle and swat at me. 'Don't push it.'"

These light-hearted conversations fertilized an unexpected change. One she could no longer resist because of Alex's authenticity and kindness plumping her heart.

Yes, something shifted. During the Fenway date? The next date? Maybe their time on the mountain?

Alex suggested a hike on Mt. Monadnock in southern New Hampshire. While trekking along the White Dot trail on a cool day on the last day of September, Delphina's heart bloomed like a budding flower as she shared her love for storytelling with Alex. He stopped, took a sip of water, and touched her cheek. "You amaze me, and I'm so glad I found a bibliophile like me."

Delphina laughed and glanced down at his shorts, wool socks, and heavy-duty hiking boots. "Me too."

"Are you amused by my getup?" Alex folded his arms, with a smile peeking through.

"Don't think so, because look at me." Delphina pulled down her baseball cap, brushed her hand down her baggy sweatshirt and shorts, and pointed to her hiking boots.

Alex's eyes caressed hers, and a sweet silence connected them like a silk rope. Seconds passed before a loud cawing interrupted and broke the spell.

Alex blinked. "Curious though. Getting back to your profession. Couldn't you have done this as a therapist?"

"Yes, but I wanted to offer something different. Many coaches claim they practice strength-based help compared to therapists who emphasize pathology. False. But rather than push against the tide, I thought about using all my skills, so I focus on creativity and writing the next chapter."

"Got it. So, what people do you see?"

"Good question. Because I've done this for only a couple of years, I seem to attract people our age. You know, older Gen Zs and young millennials."

"Hmm. Why do you think they choose a storyteller versus a therapist or a coach?"

"Another brilliant question. From everything I heard from my mother, things move at lightning speed compared to her generation. Ours want quick results. Even though I love being a therapist, I'm not so different from the rest of our age group. I became restless and wanted to try something more niche. What better way than introducing storytelling? And the sessions are therapeutic, but the clients become more active participants through writing."

Alex smiled. "Can't wait to hear more. Let's go further and take a break, say…" Alex glanced at his watch. "In twenty minutes." He looped his arms into his knapsack. "Does that sound like a plan?"

Delphina saluted him. "You lead, and I'll follow."

She stepped behind Alex as he maneuvered his hands on the White Dot Trail. Delphina watched his movements, grabbed the same stone, and placed her foot on the same ridge. She loved the feel of the cool, worn rocks and allowed her fingers to glide over them.

When they stopped three quarters up the mountain, they looked out at the trees dotting the New England landscape. Their branches continued to wear green garb longer, but in October, they would stun an eager audience as they changed into their spectacular garments. But even with a duller green, a glorious view.

Alex studied the ground's surface. Finding a flat area, he laid out a blanket, patted a spot next to him for Delphina to sit down, and snuggled close to her. He handed her a peanut butter and jelly sandwich, napkins, and sparkling water.

Delphina munched on a potato chip and glanced at Alex. "You said you had a few more questions about my work."

"Yup. Mine's boring. Not much to share about numbers, so Madame," he waved his hand. "Please tell me more about your services."

Delphina told him about some of the newer phenomena originating in the twenty-first century. Disclosing no identifying information, she detailed the rise of another eating disorder, orthorexia, and snapshot dysmorphia.

"Yeah. I've heard about orthorexia, without knowing it had a label. Our generation seems consumed by perfection." Alex gulped. "Like you, I believe in exercise and healthy eating, but man, not deprivation."

"Agree."

"And what the heck—snapchat dysmorphia? Never heard of that one."

Delphina explained how social media fueled young people's desires to pursue cosmetic surgery to perfect their selfies.

"Some of the thirty-somethings who come into my office, talk about going to the dermatologist."

"Should I assume it's not for acne?"

"You got it. Younger and younger. I read some research that people under the age of nineteen have sought treatment for another new trend—*prejuvenation*."

"Whaaaat?"

"I know. I guess they think they can ward off wrinkles by doing it at an early age, but there's no evidence of its effectiveness."

"God. What's that about?"

Delphina shook her head. "Focusing on the outside and not on their inner beauty. Thank God, the young people who come to see me about this issue want to avoid succumbing to peer pressure. So I encourage them to write a story about their uniqueness."

"Good." Alex nodded, with eyes darkening like a gray sea.

"And I'm glad I see adults because, according to The American Society of Plastic Surgeons, a small minority of under eighteen have undergone Botox treatments."

Alex scowled. "Man, when we have…" His cheeks became like candied apples, and he lowered his eyelashes. "When *I* have children, no way will I let them do that."

Delphina saturated herself in the magic swirling around them, and she cocked her head. "Nor I." A toasty warmth baked her face, and she twirled one of her curls.

And that was that. The rest of the chains surrounding her heart? Yanked off, tossed over as if she flung them off the mountain and yelled good riddance.

Alex. Could he be the one?

She missed him, and even though they texted when possible, she couldn't wait for him to come home from Dubai.

He revealed that a surprise would reach her as he flew back to the United States. Also, he promised to tell her the extenuating circumstances that led him to meet her mother.

Beep, beep, beep.

Before she attended to Glori, who reached into her pocketbook to place her signatory pen, Delphina said to herself, "Could he have been one of my mother's friends after all?"

Alex

Alex scanned the luxurious bedroom and took in his surroundings for the first time since he arrived.

Man, the businesspeople in this part of the world didn't deprive their American counterparts or themselves of anything.

Every time he encountered his personal butler, the man bowed and reminded him not to hesitate to ring for any requests he had. And like the first time, Alex put his hands together and bowed back.

"Will do."

The butler smiled and slipped away.

"They treat us like royalty. I can't wait until I share this with Delphina."

His eyes roamed over the various shades of purple and blue that colored the opulent interior. A long, white rug bordered by purple and blue trim overlaid the cobalt blue carpet. A bar with a similar theme sat across a king-sized bed swathed in white with decorative pillows displaying Middle Eastern themes.

Alex whistled as he changed into his sweats. The company kept him busy, so he had little time to check out the room. For the last five days, he'd fallen into bed late and risen before the breakfast meeting to work out. He had little time to devote to his special project for Delphina.

He rubbed his hands together.

Not tonight.

They let him and his colleagues loose.

Good. He'd work on the video he created for Delphina. He played the clip.

First, a scene revealed pinks and peaches blushing the sunset sky. The sparkling blue sea, hypnotized by the ephemeral painting, danced a splendid finale for daylight's curtain call as it awaited the stars to shine upon it.

Next, in slow motion, zeroed in on the bold and majestic lobby. Colors symbolic of the Middle East unrolled.

Another segment revealed the glittering chandelier in the renovated exit lobby.

A few days ago, he tipped his head back and shifted the camera to get every angle possible.

Daily workouts gave him much flexibility and agility, and he turned his neck like an ostrich. But he couldn't capture the detail he wanted.

After several attempts, he glanced at his watch and plodded over to the manager of the back desk.

"Hello, I don't know if someone could help me, but I'd like to get a closer look at the chandelier."

"What would you like, sir?"

"Could I get a ladder to…"

"No sir. We don't allow our guests such, how do you say it, dangerous endeavors on our grounds."

"Got it."

"But sir, there's a way we can send you a 360-degree closeup view of the lighting."

"Yeah?"

"Yes. We provide any service within our means. Give me about one hour, and I can send it to you via Google drive."

"Sure thing. Do you want my Gmail…?"

The manager nodded. "I believe we have everything we need to provide you a spectacular vision of the chandelier."

"I can't thank you enough."

The manager bowed. "We do everything we can to make your stay at the Burj-Al-Arab Hotel an unforgettable experience. In the meantime, I suggest you visit the concierge who can provide you information about the sparkling object that graces a guest's departure."

"Thank you. I hope to bring my bride here when the time comes."

"Please do. We shower our newlyweds with many delights."

On break from the meeting, he jogged over to the concierge, who discussed the story about the unique chandelier. A Czech company, Sans Souci, adapted it from its signature Symphony collection. 210 crystal tubes, each coated in gold and engraved with a unique leaf motif taken from the hotel's wallpaper.

Now he examined the scenes he compiled so far.

A few days ago, Alex attended a business dinner cruise around the hotel. Grilled octopus. He closed his eyes, still tasting the delicacy. After dinner, his iPhone captured the evening view of the hotel.

He stared at the video of the magnificent spectacle. In a few minutes, he'd guide his camera over the suite and glittery ocean view.

What a creation.

Anyone who doesn't believe in God, think again. You can't overstate the inspiration and creativity He gifts us. So glad Delphina shared such a strong faith with me.

Right before he dropped her off, she told him another piece of her story.

"I wouldn't have bounced back from the date rape or the other betrayal which, um, I'm ready to share with you."

"A man?"

Delphina nodded.

"He cheated on you."

Her lips quivered. "When you come back."

Her departing words as his fingers lingered in hers while he turned to leave.

Delphina.

He knew. Yup. She's it.

As if reading his mind, his FaceTime rang, and her name appeared.

Alex shifted his gaze to his iPad and grinned as he pushed the button to accept.

Delphina's face appeared.

"Hello, Taibhseach."

Delphina's golden eyes sparkled. "Oh, I'm so glad I caught you." Roses flowered on her cheeks. "Taibhseach, yourself."

Alex placed his hands on top of one another in front of his mouth. His eyes clasped onto hers. Golden-brown hair flowing from her loose bun, oversized glasses, and a blazer over a plain white blouse screeched "gorgeous" to him.

He placed his hands on the desk. "Yeah." He nodded, not removing his eyes from her. "Glad this worked."

She bobbed her head, and pink turned to red, budding like perennials over her entire face.

"I miss you, Ms. Tulasi."

Her eyes widened, and she pursed her lips. "Mr. O'Hara, I miss you." She sighed and leaned forward. "But I can't think too much about you, or you'll distract me from my clients."

"You distract me all the time."

Delphina tipped her head back and emitted a throaty laugh.

"You find that funny?"

Her eyes fastened on him again. "No. I'm flattered and," she inhaled, "I can't believe I found someone I can trust." Her smile faded.

"You can. I promise." Alex furrowed his brow. "I'm as flawed as anyone else, but I'm loyal to the core."

Delphina closed her eyes and took another deep breath. "I hope so." She opened her eyes.

Alex pitched his face forward. "I don't know what happened to you, but Delphina, no way would I ever betray you. You'll see, and I feel like I can trust you with my, ah…" He scratched his head. "You might call it a past crisis. Different from yours, but, well…" His head moved from side to side. "Devastating. A breach that affected my ability to have faith in anyone."

Delphina swallowed. "I'm so glad you feel the same way. And…" She gave him a half smile.

"What?"

Delphina bit her lip.

Alex raised his eyebrows.

"Does your situation have anything to do with my mother?"

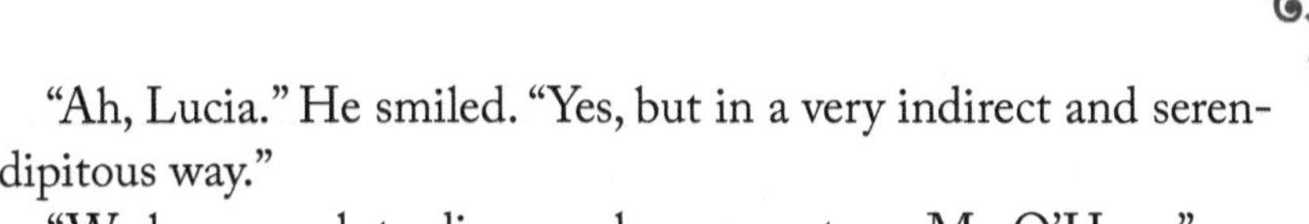

"Ah, Lucia." He smiled. "Yes, but in a very indirect and seren-dipitous way."

"We have much to discuss when you return, Mr. O'Hara."

"We do, and we might as well get to it, since we know we have so much in common already. Books, dogs, more books, elephants, books, owls, more books, travel, and a desire for," he cocked his head and said, enunciating each syllable, "marriage, children."

Delphina lowered her eyelashes, and more coils slipped over her poppy red face. She lowered her voice to a whisper. "Some couples are never themselves with each other. I don't see that for us."

"Me neither." Alex's eyes grabbed hers again.

Another enchanting moment. The connection? Two magnets drawn together.

Man.

Delphina lowered her eyes.

Alex put his hands behind his head. "Hey, guess what I'm doing?"

"What?"

"Creating a surprise, which I'll give to you when I return."

Her eyes changed from amber to gold and sparkled. As she leaned back in her seat and clapped her hands, more coils fell from her bun, and she roared in laughter. "I can't wait."

Alex studied her and blinked. A gorgeous lion in all its splendor, a female one with a mane.

Yeah, pal, only males have manes, but so what, you can pretend.

"What are you thinking about Alexander O'Hara?"

"Lions."

She squinted and giggled. "Lions?"

"Yup."

"You know what? You make me laugh."

Alex wiggled his eyebrows. "My intention."

"Good." Her eyes remained locked on his.

"More to come, so prepare yourself for my return. I plan on regaling you with lots of stories about this jewel in the middle of the desert. So, Ms. Scheherazade, you aren't the only storyteller. I hope you don't mind me calling you that. But after you explained her ability to entertain by spinning a thousand tales, the name seems perfect for you.

Her eyes sparkled. "I love it as long as you promise not to…" Delphina slid her hand across her neck with a *crrr*.

"Are you kidding?" He raised his eyebrows. "I would never give up my own Scheherazade, Taibhseach. Instead, I would guard her with my life. I mean you."

Delphina shut her eyes, rubbed her hands together, and she blinked. "I…"

Ring. Ring. Ring.

Clearing her throat, she shook her head and glanced at her watch. "She's early, but I should get going."

"Oh, all right." Alex pouted. He leaned toward the screen again. "My schedule will be tight for the next few days and nights but try me anyway."

Delphina threw a kiss and hugged herself.

Alex leaned forward and kissed the screen.

"How about that?"

"Oh, Alexander. I can't wait to feel your arms wrapped around me again."

"Umm, and nothing will prevent that from happening. Will it?"

"Not anything or anyone." Delphina puckered her lips again, waved, and disconnected.

Alex sat back for a few seconds, and a slow smile crept onto his face.

Ah. Scheherazade. Yup. That's the theme for the video, and yes, Delphina, you're the one. I'll echo you. Nothing and no one can interfere with our future together.

Chapter Thirteen

Delphina

Delphina's focus on her last client wavered. Three days since she and Alex met on FaceTime.

Excruciating, but he'd arrive home soon.

He's the one. Less than three months, but she knew. At least she did until doubts cut through her like a razor slicing into skin.

Last night, she visited her mother in her small but lovely condominium. As she sprawled out on Lucia's turquoise, suede chaise lounge, her mother handed her a glass of San Pellegrino and settled into a complementary, oversized chair.

She and Lucia maintained a very close relationship, but she refused to share many details with her mother about Alexander.

"Anything else you want?"

"Mama, you don't have to wait on me. I'll get anything I need. The pizza should arrive any minute."

As Delphina and her mother readied themselves for the third episode of the series, *The English*, Lucia asked how things were going. Delphina nodded and said, "You know he's in Dubai, and things are looking good. But don't ask me more about it."

Delphina smiled at her mother, clad in loose jeans and a wool sweater. Still beautiful for her mid-fifties. Olive skin, large green eyes framed by thick black brows. Silky white hair falling below her shoulders.

Lucia had a glint in her eye. "What are you looking at, my love?"

"You." Delphina rose and kissed her mother. "Still beautiful, Mama."

Lucia sighed. "Not as beautiful as my greatest creation who deserves the best."

"I know, Mama, but you don't have to worry about me. I can take care of myself. You taught me well. And Auntie helped." Delphina spawned a smile. "As much as she could."

"Yes, your aunt never let her traumas interfere with her life. Less fiery than me. Even though she's in her fifties, I hope she finds a lovely man, but…" Lucia's gaze became faraway. "I leave it in God's hands. Right now, her work sustains her."

"Mama, you found that work fulfilled you as well. I know you don't like to talk about Papa, but besides me…"

"I'm not talking about me." Lucia's voice flattened Delphina's sentence like a rolling pin.

"Okay, Mama."

Lucia lowered her eyes, as she did every time Delphina raised the subject of her mysterious father. "Although you're an adult, you're my child, and my purpose remains to ensure your happiness and safety for the rest of my time on this earth."

Delphina shook her head and rolled a curl around her finger. "Mama, the twenty-first century offers people of your age with…" She puckered her lips and threw a kiss. "Dating, romance, and love. I bet you have some older clients seeking your services. Riiiight?"

"Yes. But I'm not interested in finding someone for me, and love comes in other forms besides romantic." Lucia gazed at her daughter, and a glow surfaced on her cheeks like soft light from a dimming lamp. "Besides, my family and the matchmaking role provide me with total fulfillment." She tapped her daughter's knee.

"Okay Mama, but I'm immersed in my work as well."

"My dear, you were readying yourself for marriage until…" Lucia's eyes welled up.

"Oh, Mama. Please." Delphina hugged Lucia.

"What a traitor. Jude couldn't have been a better name for him."

Delphina's lips curved into a smile. "Mama, I know, but I'll tell you this, my time with Alexander, well…"

Lucia sprang up like a morning bloom, wiped her face, and widened her eyes. "Well, what, daughter?"

Delphina inhaled. "He makes me laugh."

Lucia leaned forward, grasped Delphina, and held her eyes. "Just as I thought. And I knew."

"Knew what, Mama?" Delphina placed her hands on her hips. "My goodness, if he wasn't one of your special ones…" She made air quotes with her hands. "Why can't you tell me?"

Lucia shook her head. "I can't." She folded her arms. "You need to let him tell you his story, and…" Her eyes captured Delphina's. "You must believe him."

Delphina frowned. "Why wouldn't I?"

Her mother blinked. "You need to discuss it with him. I'm not at liberty to talk about it."

Buzz.

Lucia stood up, and as she glanced at her ring video, she strolled to the door with words dropping behind her. "It's complicated, and I'll say no more." Lucia opened the door to a young man, dressed in jeans, a sweatshirt, and a backwards baseball cap, holding a large, boxed pizza.

"I paid online."

"Yes, Ma'am."

"But for you." Lucia handed him a ten-dollar bill.

The young man grinned. "Whew. Thank you, Ma'am."

Lucia shut the door. "They make very little money."

"Mama, you're so generous."

Lucia's eyes twinkled as she sauntered into her elegant rustic kitchen, placed the pizza in the heated oven, and brought a Ceasar salad and bread sticks to the coffee table. Delphina poured more San Pellegrino into their glasses as Lucia tossed the salad with her wooden tongs, spooning a robust portion into each of their bowls.

"Yummy, Mama." Delphina's nose followed the aroma emitting from the kitchen.

"As always, my darling."

"Mama?" Delphina gulped.

"Yes?" Lucia munched on a breadstick and peered at her with a wrinkled brow.

"I guess I don't understand why you can't…"

Lucia wagged her index finger. "Because he shared the entire situation in confidence. Not as a so-called friend, but…" Lucia stopped with her eyes on her food. "Well…" She glanced back at Delphina and fluttered her fingers. "Enough before I say something I'll regret." She took a sip of the sparkling water. "Umm. I'm so pleased I gave up wine. Now eat."

Delphina nibbled on her salad and savored the comfort from the unconditional love surrounding her like a cocoon of maternal protection.

Her mother swallowed a bite of her food and stared at her daughter. "Besides, I haven't seen you light up like this since the end of your engagement."

Delphina couldn't resist spawning a smile. "You know what, Mama? You're right."

Jude. Margo. How could he? That night. Oh, what a night.

"Good. I hope this relationship provides you with healing and much more."

"We shall see."

"A much better match for you."

Delphina laughed. "So says the Matchmaker. And speaking of…" Delphina dipped her head toward her mother. "Did you have me in mind when you invited him to the event?"

With sparkling eyes, Lucia's lips curled upward. "Maybe my unconscious…"

"Oh, come on Mama."

"All right, perhaps…" Lucia brought her index finger and thumb close together. "This amount from the conscious part of my mind."

Delphina laughed. "Okay. Let me serve the pizza." As she padded to the kitchen, Lucia sputtered, "I promised not to mention Jude, but I hope any thought of him has evaporated."

Delphina stopped, turned her head, and her eyes softened. "Mama, I understand. He occupies my mind less and less."

"Whew on two counts." Lucia clapped. "You didn't bite my head off, and better, you've extinguished him from your mind."

Delphina slipped on an oven mitt, opened the oven, and as heat hit her face, she retrieved the pizza and gulped. She didn't want her mother to worry, but memories of Jude popped up. How could they not?

She tilted her head over to her mother and painted a smile on her face. "Of course, Mama. Let's eat and watch the next episode."

As her mother clicked on the TV, Jude emerged from her locked vault. Black eyes, olive skin, and ebony hair. Cocky, but with her, the quintessential gentleman.

How could she have missed? For heaven's sake, she became a therapist because of her ability to assess others.

"Everyone misses," said her therapist friends. "Love conquers all, including our doubts. Got it. Jude exuded the ultimate alpha dog. Magnetic and confident. He'd snow anyone."

She agreed, which made her cautious about prospects.

Until Alex.

But…

How did she know he might not be like Jude. Yes, he presented himself as a unique specimen, but she could be wrong. Less of an alpha dog, but charming and at ease with himself.

Delphina shook her curls as she tried to disentangle the snarls infesting her thoughts.

Alex, please come home soon. Reassure me.

Now, as she sat with her last client, Jude came alive. His musky scent, his enormous eyes, his hairy arms, and massive hands.

Stop, Delphina. Pay attention.

Chiara, her sweet twenty-two-year-old client, sobbed while reading her story. She plucked several tissues from the Kleenex box and dabbed her red, swollen lids. Tears streamed down her cheeks onto her notebook, blurring the ink on the pages.

The young woman heaved in between but waved her hand when Delphina asked if she needed to stop.

"No," she whispered, "I must get this out." Chiara often wore various shades of amethyst to match her eyes and today was no different. Dressed in a long-sleeved sheath dress, solid stockings, and platform shoes, the petite woman resembled a garden of periwinkle vinca flowers—a pastel monochromatic extravaganza.

Even her cologne splashed purple onto her, with various scents of lilac trickling into the room.

She bent her head, pushing her wavy chestnut hair away from her face, and read more of the next chapter. Her enormous eyes pooled and lips quivered.

"I know I lost my boyfriend because of my beliefs, but I'm sticking to them." Her clenched fist smacked her thigh. "There."

"Chiara, you sound very determined." Delphina jutted her chin out. "Good for you."

"I-I did some things in college." Chiara swallowed. "And even though I remember little, I recall bits and pieces that make me cringe. Not the real me. Followed the crowd. Never again. I wanted to start afresh. I thought Todd understood, but…" She shook her head. "What did he do? He lied to me about having a fling with coworkers. And when he confessed," she whispered, "not one but two."

Delphina's heart ripped like paper shredding into thin strips, and she coiled a curl around her finger.

Jude's face emerged, and she almost stumbled back in her seat. Stop.

She rubbed her eyes, trying to swat the image away.

Chiara sniffed and peered at Delphina.

"You okay, Delphina?"

"Oh—oh, yes." Delphina's head sprung up. "Just digesting every-thing you've said." She moved her head up and down. "The new chapter you've begun emphasizes your convictions."

"Yessss." Chiara enunciated.

Whew. Glad I recovered from that mishap. Not fair to Chiara.

"And…" Chiara looked down at the wrinkled pages with smudged ink. "I think I'm going to look for someone on a Christian dating site. Just writing this makes me feel even stronger about my faith."

Delphina nodded.

"Hold on. I just thought of something." Chiara pressed her fingers on the pen, and as she scribbled a few words, she said, "just reminding myself, 'no situationship.'" She stopped and looked up. "A lot of guys my age aren't interested in a relationship, just a situationship."

"Yes." Delphina furrowed her brow. "I heard about this new phenomenon a few days ago."

"You are kind of in a relationship, but you don't label it as that. And you go out with other people, so no commitment, I guess, except you might be the most important person. Not for me."

Delphina frowned. "Doesn't sound very special or safe to me."

"Me neither. But lots of people say they don't care about that."

"Don't let anyone kid you. They do but won't admit it."

"I know. They pretend. Lots of people my age claim it's no big deal. Part of the culture. But not me, so I hope the men on the Christian sites aren't into that."

"I bet most aren't, and you can let the man know when you come across a potential match."

"I will." Chiara sighed, and her gaze became unfocused. "So many of my friends don't believe in God. One time, I tried to talk about God with three of my besties. And you know what they did?" Chiara tossed her hair behind her and stared at Delphina.

Delphina inclined her head. "What?"

"Samantha kind of made a weird face and said, 'Chi, I'm not

religious, so I don't want to talk about God.' Her twin, Olivia, shook her head. 'Ya, Chi, Sam and I stopped going to church as soon as we hit college.' My other friend, Eden, who reminds us of her feminist status anytime she can, raised her head. 'You know me. I'm super spiritual and believe in the goddess, Gaia. So, I don't want to talk about any male deity.' I let it go, and I guess I don't care, but for a relationship, I want someone who shares my belief system."

"I know. The world seems to have forgotten about God, so we must learn how to navigate our way around it. But in pursuit of a life partner, you should be selective, woman of the light."

Chiara bubbled over with laughter. "I love you remember the symbolism of my name."

"I do. It suits you."

Chiara beamed. "Hey, you're a person of faith. Right?"

"I am."

"How's it been for you to find someone?"

Delphina blinked. "What do you imagine?"

Chiara's violet-blue eyes dazzled. "Ha ha, Delphina, turning it back to me like a therapist." She knitted her eyebrows together. "Wait a minute, I thought you no longer practiced as one."

Delphina gazed at her client, and a smile jotted her face. "Not in the same way, but it will remain part of my identity forever."

"Got it." Chiara tapped her index finger against her chin, and in slow motion, she repeated Delphina's question. "So, what do I think about your ability to find someone?" She cocked her head. "I don't know. Are you in a relationship with someone of faith?"

Delphina swallowed.

What do I say?

"Chiara, I…"

"I don't mean to pry," Chiara said, waving her palms back and forth. "Please… but you're so kind and beautiful inside and out."

Delphina laughed. "I appreciate your sentiment, but I think we should focus on you. At least for now. How's that sound?"

Chiara's dimples appeared, and she bobbed her head with a flashing smile. "Okay. But I hope… well, you know."

"I know." Delphina bowed her head. "And again, thank you." Her eyes moved to the clock. "We have only a few minutes left, so let's return to your story."

Chiara read the rest of her chapter. When she closed the journal, she lifted her head and peered at Delphina.

"My new chapter, Delphina. I'm going to find Mr. Right and not settle for anyone less."

"Wonderful. A woman of the light deserves more brightness, and on that note…" Delphina's eyes found her clock. "Time to say goodbye for now."

Chiara stood up and padded across the quilted rug that lay beneath her feet. She hugged Delphina. "Thank you." She smirked and pointed her index finger at her. "And you deserve the best, too."

Delphina tipped her head back and laughed. "Thank you again."

Chiara pulled the knob, stepped out, and shut the door with a soft touch.

Rustling movements and footsteps came from the waiting room. Some of her colleagues worked Friday afternoons. Not her. 12 noon. Done.

She glanced at her office again.

Even some of her young men admitted the ambience made them consider romance and courtship, and some included bits as they wrote their next chapter.

With a sheepish look, one said, "Ms. T, I never considered myself old-fashioned. Just not cool, you know. But I think I might be." Another said, "Ms. Tulasi, your office prompts me to wonder why chivalry gets a bad name? I'm a big guy, and I enjoy opening doors for women or letting them go first."

Delphina would smile. "Don't let anyone make you feel bad about that, and I think more women yearn for those polite overtures even if they don't verbalize it."

She brushed her hand along the armchair with soft, floral fabric, locked her file cabinet, and gathered her belongings.

Could things be changing in the world of dating. A return to courtship? She hoped so.

As she pivoted to ensure she forgot nothing, a familiar voice uttered something from behind the door.

No. It can't be.

Delphina's legs became like jelly, and she forced them forward. Her hand hesitated and trembled as she twisted the doorknob.

She stuck her head out and gasped, bringing her hand to her mouth, as she opened the door wider.

The familiar face gazed at her, and a signatory smile sprouted on his face.

"I know. What a surprise? Right?"

PART TWO
A Year Earlier

Chapter Fourteen

Alex

Round. Curvy. Feminine.

Muted pastels, ruffles, arched doors, high ceilings, and windows galore.

Swathed in a soft blanket of comfort.

Every time he came for a session, he saw only female therapists.

The decorations made sense as they reflected a woman's touch.

Never studied the waiting room this much, but a pleasant distraction as he waited.

Alex glanced at his watch. Fifteen minutes passed, and no sign of his her.

In their four meetings together, at the exact hour, the door opened, and there stood his elegant, older therapist. Long hair, stilettos, and tall, very tall. A six-footer, he guessed, by the way she met him. Eye to eye, not needing to tip her head upward, as most women did while conversing with him.

Wonder what happened to her?

He pulled out his phone for the umpteenth time. No call. Text? Uh-huh. No email. Nada. No Bridget.

Yup, yup, yup.

He leaned forward and dropped his laced hands between his knees. Since he arrived, three other people, two women and one man, had risen from their seats to enter their therapists' office.

Good. Or more like relief. Not the only guy choosing to see a shrink. Alex sighed. He'd wait for another ten minutes. With no time to change out of his suit, he flicked off a speck glaring at him from his otherwise immaculate black trousers. Alex peeked at his jacket. Nothing there. He leaned back, and his eyes moved to his silk tie. He pulled on it and examined the details. Red with embroidered gray elephants. A Christmas gift. Everyone knew his penchant for animals, with the majestic giants sharing top prize with dogs.

With no one in the waiting room, he played with his tie to occupy himself.

Five more minutes.

A door creaked open. One therapist he saw another time came out. Older, slender, and well-dressed like Bridget, but not as tall.

She smiled. "May I help you?"

Alex cleared his throat. "I'm waiting for Bridget."

"Oh, dear." The woman grimaced. "You didn't receive a message from her."

"No."

"She must have missed you because she alerted her clients that she would be unavailable today."

"Ah, nooo…"

Wow. That makes me feel wanted.

"Well, I'm so sorry, but please understand, these things happen, and believe me, they have nothing to do with the client."

A nervous laugh crawled out of his throat. "If you say so." He stood. "Not an emergency, but I could have used the session. Oh well, thanks."

The therapist blinked hard, cocked her head, and studied Alex for a moment. "How about this? I've finished my work for today. Why don't you come into my office and tell me a bit about what's going on for you. We can chat for some time."

"Are you sure?"

"Yes, I am."

"I'd be happy to pay for the session."

The therapist flicked her wrist. "Don't worry about that right now." She swept her hand toward her office.

"Thank you."

Alex's eyes roved around the office. Not so different from the waiting area except for more beige and whiter, with a stunning Pressley lamp with glass in jewel and pastel tones sitting on an end table.

"Beautiful lamp." He crouched down and examined the glass and base. "Art nouveau."

"Yes. You have a good eye."

"My mother studied art history and taught me a thing or two." He stood up.

Already seated in a high office chair, the therapist said, "Please sit wherever you want." She sipped from a mug with a name plastered on it. "By the way, what's your name?"

"Oh, uh, sorry. Alex. Alex O'Hara."

"Nice to meet you, Alex." She placed the mug down. "And in case you missed my name on the door…" She pointed to the name in large calligraphy on her cup.

"Got it."

"Good. So, please tell me what weighs heavy on your heart."

Alex placed his ankle on the opposite leg and bobbed his head. "Yeah. Yeah. That's what's going on with me. A heavy heart."

He peeked at the therapist. She seemed warm and caring, like Bridget.

Alex loosened his tie and removed his jacket. "Okay. I told Bridget about some of it, so I'll provide you with the homogenized version before…"

"Stop, Alex." The therapist put up her palms. "I'm not in a hurry. In fact, I'm closing my practice in a few weeks, so please give me as much of the story as needed."

"I appreciate that."

His hair flopped in front of his eyes, and as his fingers combed it back, he noticed soft eyes like velvet.

Pal, she gets you. Turn on the firehose.

Words sprayed from his throat.

Alex began with the events of that consequential evening. He fidgeted a great deal, but the therapist didn't seem to notice. She nodded, and her eyes locked with his.

He went from crossing one ankle over the other, switching legs, stretching them, and leaning back in his seat. He didn't pause as he shared the encounter with Bart as he got ready to drive away.

"That was just the beginning." Alex lifted his eyebrows. "Things went from bad to worse." He shook his head and stared at the lamp behind the therapist.

Quiet breached the room.

Alex slumped and studied the elephant on the tie.

"Well, Alex, it sounds like something most unfortunate and unfair happened to you."

Alex nodded, and he glanced at the therapist. "Yeah." He gulped.

"The next morning, I examined my injury. In retrospect, I should have seen a doctor, but I was too embarrassed. Even though I did nothing wrong, what do you say? Uh, my boss' wife came on to me, and she clawed my face."

The therapist nodded with eyebrows knitted together.

What's her name? You forgot already? Nerves. But who cares. She won't even notice. You hope.

"You know what I mean?"

"I do, but again," she said. "Not your fault."

Alex swallowed. "Ah. I know that, but I didn't feel comfortable. Besides, I thought it would heal."

"I understand."

"So, Monday arrived, and I woke up with a pit in my stomach."

The therapist pitched forward, with a tense look.

"I can see it now as if it were yesterday."

He stopped and stroked the area of his scar.

"I walked into the building, and Charlie, the security guard, the first person I saw each day, stopped me. Big guy about my age. A gentle giant. Curious about self-improvement. Every day, he'd pepper me with questions around exercise and healthy living but not this morning. With his hand up, he said, 'Hold on, Mr. O'Hara,' and made a call. I knew…my chest tightened like…Ya know, a snake, more like a python, twisting around it. I waited and calmed myself, focused on the ultramodern foyer, stainless steel and sharp angles. Cold and sterile."

Alex strung his fingers through his hair, and a few locks flopped over his eyes. He gave the therapist a half smile.

She bobbed her head, and compassion beamed from her eyes.

"So, Charlie narrowed his eyes at me and didn't return my smile. He gestured for me to go into the elevator. 'The boss said for you to sit in the conference room.' Charlie joined me. A chill followed us into the elevator and man…" Alex folded his arms. "By the time we reached the top floor, and the glass slider opened, an arctic vortex."

He shivered. "*Brrrr.* I can still feel it." He tightened his arms.

"With Charlie glued to me, I chugged through the hallway, and no one had their doors opened."

The therapist said, "Eerie."

"Yeah." Alex stared at her. "Eerie?" He nodded. "A perfect word. Because it felt like everyone ghosted me."

"*The Twilight Zone.*"

"What?"

The therapist chuckled. "A sci-fi and horror television show that played long before you arrived on this earth."

Alex smirked. "Oh yeah. I remember my father mentioning that show, but I caught none of the reruns."

"I watched one or two and decided, no thanks. Too dark for me… Anyway, Alex, how are you doing with all of this?"

"Better as I unload things."

"Please continue."

Alex rubbed the scar again. "So, Charlie dropped me off, and I entered the conference room. I sat for a few minutes. The glass partition prevented me from hiding. Familiar people passed by. When they noticed me, they averted their gaze. Only Bart halted and frowned when he caught me sitting there by my little old self. He stretched his neck around the hallway and then stuck his head into the suite. 'Hey, O'Hara. What's up?' I said, 'Not sure.' Bart waved his iPhone, tapped his fingers against the screen, and mouthed 'text me.' Right then, someone yelled his name, and he bolted."

Alex leaned forward again and clasped his hands between his legs.

He peeked at the therapist.

"I couldn't stand seeing more people walk by, so I took a seat with my back to the door. Less nerve-wracking. In between, looking at the view of the city and scrolling through my phone, I eyed the room in a way I never did before." Alex shook his head. "Like the rest of the building, very contemporary, minimalist, and expensive. Modern art hung on white walls and abstract sculptures sat on glass tables. I remember scrutinizing everything and thinking about what human characteristics might apply to the room. And I concluded, cold and stoic, with little personality."

The therapist snuggled her sweater around her shoulders. "As I listen to you, I can almost feel a chill from the frigid atmosphere."

Alex chortled. "You got it. After what happened next, you might say I suffered from frostbite.

Alex waited.

Power and control. Nothing I can do. Logan's company. King Logan rules.

He glanced at his watch. Forty-five minutes passed.

Alex turned around. Charlie paced back and forth. He returned his gaze to the windows overlooking the city. Several minutes passed until footsteps approached, and the door opened.

Dressed in a monochromatic gray suit, shirt, and tie, Logan entered with a leather binder. Alex shifted his head toward his immediate boss.

"Alex." Logan jutted his chin.

"Sir." He nodded.

Logan's lips retreated into a straight line. Without taking his eyes off Alex, he sat down and laced his fingers over his mouth.

A tap at the door.

Logan curled his hand, and a server entered the room with a tray, holding a pot of coffee, two mugs, and milk and sugar.

The server poured a cup for Logan, and to distract himself, Alex watched the steam rise, float, and drift away.

Logan waved off any milk or sugar and took a sip with no thanks to the server.

Hard. Alex never saw this side of his boss. A shiny veneer of kindness and compassion cracked open and shattered.

People used to rib Alex about his favorable status with Logan.

Some referred to him as Logan's golden boy. Others said, "Heir apparent."

Um. Not anymore, as Logan's eyes bore into his.

"Sir?" The server, an older woman, smiled at him.

"Please, and I, too, prefer it black." Alex forced the corners of his lips to rise for her. "Thank you."

The woman nodded and scurried away.

Logan continued studying Alex in between sips.

All right Logan. I'll do it your way.

Alex took a gulp and glanced outside.

Thumbing began on the table, and Alex's eyes found Logan's again.

"Sir, I…"

Logan put his hand up and took another sip of coffee.

"Mr. O'Hara, we have some things to discuss."

"Sir?"

Logan nodded at him. "The bandage on your chin area says all we need to know."

"Mrs.—"

"Stop." Logan licked his lips, pulled out a manila envelope from the binder, and slid it toward Alex.

He took the package, glanced at Logan, and lifted his eyebrows.

"Open it."

Alex squinted and bent the two-pronged metal clasp. He slipped his fingers inside and plucked out large black and white photographs of him and Sirena from the party. The first photo revealed him smiling in the red room with her. A second caught them kissing. The third displayed Sirena clawing Alex. And the fourth and final one? The most damaging. Sirena's tear-streaked face, hair mussed in different directions, black and blue marks on her wrists and arms, and a dress torn down the middle.

Alex's heart drummed against his chest. He shook his head, gaped at Logan, and yelled, "Sir, this doesn't depict the true events of what happened."

"What?" Logan's eyes widened and blazed into Alex. He stood and leaned forward with his hands pulled back and forth like a bull pawing its forefeet about to attack.

Alex jumped out of his seat and pounded the table. "Sir, these photos don't reveal the context."

"Are you accusing my wife of lying?"

As Alex's face burned with rage, he tried to measure his words. "The pictures display a moment in time."

Logan's mouth twisted. "Sirena likes to flirt and bring things close to the edge, but she's blamed no one when her antics go over the top."

Alex remained standing, and he placed his arms on the table.

Stay steady, pal. You know the truth.

"I will repeat what I emphasized to Mrs. McCormick. I don't care what people choose to do behind closed doors, but when I say, 'not my thing,' I mean it. Your wife selected not to hear me, but more importantly, when I left, she didn't appear in that condition." Alex picked up the last photo and ruffled it.

Logan took another sip of coffee and pivoted away from Alex.

A stillness iced the room.

Alex began rubbing his palms together.

You can't stay working here. Time to resign.

Logan's hands went into his pockets, and he rotated his stance to face Alex again.

He had a remote look in his eyes and nodded. "So, we have a problem, but an easy one to remedy."

Alex cocked his head and squinted. "Sir?"

Logan clasped his hands. "O'Hara, I thought you would've been the perfect guest with your two colleagues. Fun. Discreet. Everyone gets a bit carried away with alcohol. But you…" Logan jabbed his finger toward Alex. "Went too far."

Alex scoffed. "Hey, Mr. McCormick…"

"Don't 'hey' me."

Alex halted.

"Now, Charlie will walk you out, and he'll have your belongings shipped to your home, and I never want to see the likes of you again. Do you understand?"

"Fine with me, but I will not admit to something I didn't do."

Logan glowered, took a breath, and tilted his head back and forth. "Well, Mr. O'Hara, you can't dispute what the camera caught. What's that old saying? 'A picture speaks a thousand words?'"

Alex growled. "The picture misses the rest of the story, Sir."

"We have the video as well. Would you like to see that?"

"No, because I'm sure it's an inaccurate portrayal."

Logan scowled. "Before I say, 'get out,' I want to remind you I have copies of these photos and the video. My wife and I decided not to press assault charges against you, but remember, before the statute of limitations, Sirena can and will if you caused her more harm."

"What are you trying to say?"

"Do not, and I repeat, 'do not,' mention a word about our party and events that followed. Also, don't expect a reference from me." Logan's eyes simmered like hot coals.

Alex bobbed his head up and down.

Logan nudged his head at the door. Charlie's heavy footsteps plodded into the conference room.

"Please ensure that Mr. O'Hara hands you his keys before he leaves this building."

Alex glanced at Charlie, whose eyes softened from earlier. He shifted his bulky body from one foot to another.

"What are you waiting for, Charlie?"

"Sorry, sir."

Charlie gave Alex a sheepish look. With heavy breathing, he grabbed the lever on the glass door and swept a beefy hand for Alex to walk in front of him.

Alex headed to the elevator. Although he kept his eyes straight ahead, his peripheral vision revealed a few people standing. Chatter trailed behind him. As Charlie opened the door for him to leave the main office area, Alex twirled around. Bart grimaced and nodded at him. The other staff scurried in different directions. Alex saluted Bart and left.

Now Alex peered at the therapist and did a raspberry.

"That's some of it."

He focused his eyes back on the therapist.

What's her name? How could I forget?

She shook her head and scoffed. "Horrible."

"Yup." Alex puckered his mouth. "Yup."

"You know, Alex. You're so right about a snapshot. I don't know if you ever heard about this." The therapist's eyes danced. "But long ago, someone snapped a photo of George Schultz, President George H.W. Bush's Secretary of State. I'll never forget it. The picture showed his face dropped in his hands, appearing upset or distressed. When you saw more of the unfolding, he had been rubbing his face. No evidence of turmoil or tears, just exhaustion, perhaps."

Alex nodded. "I didn't know that story, but thank you. It validates what happened to me."

"Yes, the perfect example of freezing a moment in time, and the danger of deciphering a piece of something taken out of context."

"That's what the photos did, and the one of her with bruises, I swear…" Alex slapped his thighs and locked eyes with the therapist.

"Never in my life would I do that to a woman, even if they wanted it. I had a buddy who dated someone that asked him to hit her for pleasure." Alex shook his head. "He told me, 'No way,' and walked away."

"Yes, Alex. Not all men are brutes, and not all women are innocent and fair, but you know that now, don't you."

Alex bobbed his head up and down and glanced at his watch.

The therapist waved her hand again. "Don't worry about the time. Please continue if you wish."

Alex gulped. "Yeah. I do. I need to question my ability to trust again because what happened and what happened next led me to do so."

The therapist spun her chair and poured a cup of ice water from a crystal pitcher sitting on a nearby tray. She handed him the cool beverage.

"Thanks." Alex's parched throat cried for hydration, and he guzzled the liquid, an ice cube clinking as he emptied the cup.

"Ah. Needed that." Alex bent forward again, tapped his knees. "This next part, well." Slumping back in his seat and allowing his arms to dangle, Alex let out a long exhale and rolled his head back and forth. "You don't realize how tense you feel until you stop for a moment."

The therapist scrunched her eyebrows together.

Wow. What's it like to listen to everyone's problems? This woman doesn't miss a beat.

"You look a bit out of sorts."

"No. Just wondering how you and Bridget and any therapist, I guess, listen to so much pain?"

"What do you think?" she asked with mischief speckling her tone.

Alex grinned. "Oh, I don't know, but I bet it isn't dull."

The therapist blinked and smiled. "You're correct, because I have the privilege of listening to people like you, even if it's only for one time."

He whipped off his tie and unfastened the top button. "There. That's better." He fixed his collar and returned his gaze to the therapist. "I appreciate your kind words and giving me the time." He tapped his knees again. "Now that I'm more comfortable, I'm ready to share Act Three.

"So, Bart must have been chomping at the bit because when I got home, five texts and three missed calls showed up on my phone."

The therapist reached for the pitcher again. "More."

"No, thanks."

As she poured some into her glass mug, a few ice cubes splattered. *Clink, clink, clink.*

He stared at the ice cubes, and the therapist glanced at her beverage, then back to him. "You sure?" She picked up her drink, and the cubes shifted around.

Alex chuckled and waved his hand. "No, I'm sure. It just reminds me where to start next." Alex leaned forward. "A few days later. In a bar."

Pop, fizzle, and crackle.

The sounds punctuated the chatter as he stepped through the alley door and made his way into *Pluto,* an underground bar in the Back Bay.

Leave it to Bart to scout out unique places. This one didn't disappoint.

Alex's eyes adjusted to the dark surroundings. Onyx walls, black interiors with gold, and a dark-gray marble bar.

Not much light or much seating.

"Hey, O'Hara." Bart waved from a small cocktail table.

"Got here early. Only thirty seats. Cool, huh?"

Alex's eyes skimmed the room. "Yeah, if you like subterranean, which right now I do."

Bart chuckled and took a gulp from his drink.

He swept his hand. "Have a seat."

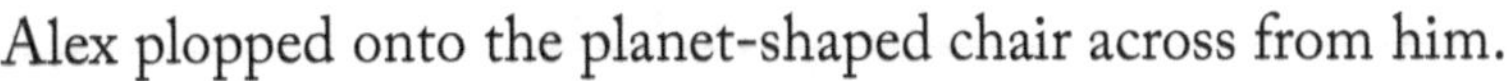

Alex plopped onto the planet-shaped chair across from him. "Let me get you a drink."

"Unnecessary."

"Come on. By the way you look, you could use one."

Alex knew he appeared haggard after being persuaded to go out for the first time since Monday's meeting.

For the last three days, Alex dragged himself out of bed and worked out from home.

First weights.

He went from light to heavy, depending on what muscle he used.

Pump, pump, pump.

Huff, huff, huff.

He pushed the limits to avoid the intrusions squatting in his brain.

Don't think about that, pal. Just keep grinding but know your limit. You're not Hercules.

He ignored the salt from sweat trickling into his mouth and the familiar odor wafting toward his nostrils.

Keep going. You'll shower soon enough.

He put down his hand weights, took a cloth out of an icy bucket, and wiped his face.

Cardio next.

He didn't want to see anyone, so he avoided his running routine. Instead, he grabbed his jump rope.

Forward jump. Twenty-five seconds. Side-to-side jump. Twenty seconds. Backward jump. Fifteen seconds. Single jump on each leg. Ten seconds.

I need to work on those single leg jumps.

The exercise focus became his sanctuary from the inner jabs.

Other than returning a few texts to Bart and engaging in brief conversations with his parents from his landline, Alex shut down his iPhone for most hours that week.

As he sat across from Bart, he watched the server pour the dirty martini from the cocktail shaker and fill it to the brim without spilling a drop.

"Good job." Alex said and opened his jacket to pull out his wallet. "Hey, I'm running a tab, and the drinks and dinner are on me."

Alex squinted. "Bart, you don't have to…"

"Listen, Alex, with what you've endured, let me do this."

Alex nodded at his friend and sipped his drink.

"I'm glad you agreed to meet."

Alex raised his eyebrows.

"Before we get into it, look around." Bart said with hooded eyes. "The ladies are purring." He grinned. "Meow."

"Are you kidding? That's the last thing I need right now."

"I know. I know. But like I said before, we're handsome dudes."

"Yeah, and like I told you before, a little humility."

"Okay, Boy Scout." Bart tipped his head back and drained his glass. He snapped his finger at a nearby server. "When you have a chance," he gave Alex a sheepish look and said, "please."

Alex snorted. "Talk about a tepid please."

"Hey dude, I'm trying." Bart snickered. "But on a serious note, I watched Sirena's reel on social media. Even though she mentioned no names, she created quite the embellished sob-story."

Alex's insides tumbled over like clothes in a dryer and caused him to teeter.

Bart's face paled. "Alex, you, okay?"

Alex nodded and sat back. "Yeah. Give me a moment."

"You know. We don't have to talk about this."

"I need to find out how much is out there for damage control."

"Look, Alex, you're a Boy Scout. Everyone knows how well you treat the ladies, and you're…" Bart shook his head and raised his hands. "I guess, the word, old-fashioned?"

"Instagram, TikTok, what the heck?"

"Yeah, but again, coy Mrs. Logan withheld your name. She claimed that someone got out of hand, and she clawed his chin."

"Man, I'm glad you chose a dark setting."

"Sure, but I have to say, the skin-colored tape blends in and does a good job covering your chin."

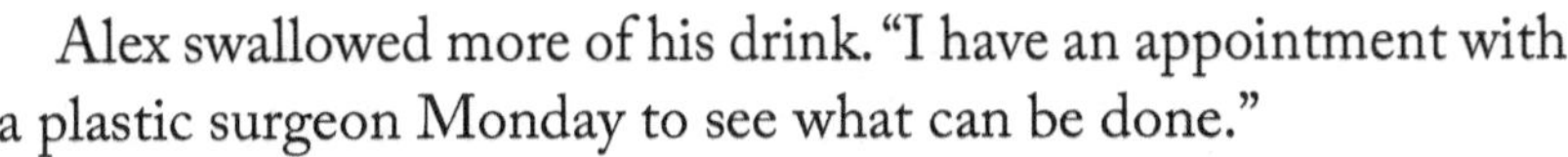

Alex swallowed more of his drink. "I have an appointment with a plastic surgeon Monday to see what can be done."

"You going to wait to look for a job?"

Alex knitted his eyebrows together and bobbed his head.

"If you need a reference…"

"Will take you up on it because I think Logan will try to black-ball me."

"You'll be okay. You have an excellent reputation, and I've heard rumblings that Logan's parties and open marriage aren't so discreet."

"Although I should be, I'm less worried about the job prospects and more concerned about the emotional toll these lies have taken on me."

"This might not be your thing, but would you consider talking to someone?"

"You mean a therapist?"

"Yes."

Alex leaned into his seat. "I've thought about it, but you're the last person I'd expect to make that suggestion."

Bart bit his upper lip. "What would you say, if I told you I see one?"

Alex widened his eyes. "Surprised, but good for you. What made you decide to go?"

"Ever since Sarah and I split, I became lost. Too many drinks, too many women." He rolled his tongue in his cheek. "I think, uh, time to man up."

Alex shrugged. "Good for you. Whatever works best, but I'm going to hold off for now. I'm a God man, so I'll do some praying to figure out what to do."

"Religion?" Bart jutted his chin.

"Yup."

"Didn't know you were a religious kind of guy. Not my thing, but…" Bart gave a sliver of a smile. "Maybe it should be."

"Up to you, but since Daphne and I ended it, I gave a lot of thought about what it's all about and what do I want in life. I started reading and playing podcasts, and because I go between

Catholicism and Evangelical Christian, I've listened to people like Greg Laurie. And you know what? I feel good after hearing his sermons."

"Who's Greg Laurie?"

"A popular evangelical minister. You should check out his podcasts and catch the movie *Jesus Revolution*."

Bart tilted his head back and forth.

Alex leaned on the table, dropped his chin into his hand, and his gaze became unfocused. "I need all the help I can get because after what happened…" He paused, noticing the background chatter as if someone had increased the volume. Bart stretched his neck back, his eyes roaming over the scenery. Alex bobbed his head up and down, took another sip of his drink, and glanced at Bart.

"Trusting another woman? I don't know."

Now, as Alex sat across from the therapist, he stroked his chin.

"Following that get-together, I couldn't get over the feeling…" Alex shook his head, laced his fingers, and dropped his hands between his legs. "You know." For a moment, his eyes brushed the therapist's face before they shifted to her high heels and the oriental rug beneath them. "A heavy gray shrouded my spirit. The workouts? A pleasant distraction but temporary. Who could I tell? My parents? My friends? I shared a bit but not much. At least not right away. Too embarrassed."

Alex fell back in his seat. He peeked at the therapist again before he stared into space. "How do you tell your parents that you found yourself in a compromising position with an older woman…" He grunted. "And married to your boss, and oh, they're swingers, but I didn't know?" He folded his arms. "But I shared some of it."

He smiled at the therapist, whose soft eyes remained welded on his. "I'll have that refill."

"Of, course." The therapist extended her arm with bracelets jiggling as she took the mug from Alex.

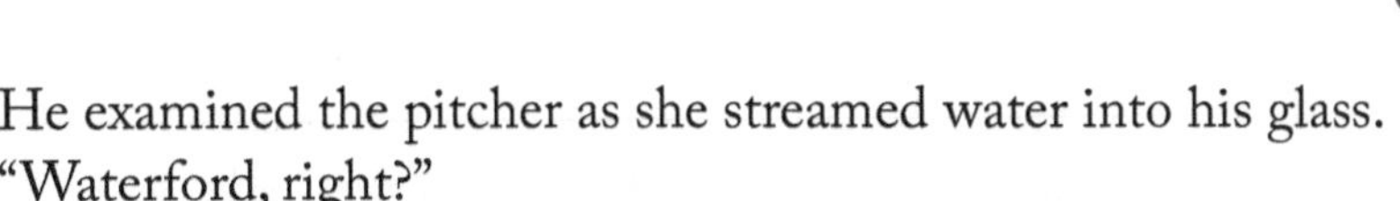

He examined the pitcher as she streamed water into his glass. "Waterford, right?"

"Yes, you have a good eye."

"My mother again, plus she and my father have wine glasses, goblets, bowls, plates, I don't know, Christmas ornaments. Even a clock. The house glitters with Waterford." Alex laughed. A moment of lightness. "When she says 'we,' Dad winks at me because everyone knows the collection has her name all over it. He goes along for the ride."

"It sounds like you have a close relationship with your parents."

"Yup, me and my brother were fortunate. My dad started his own manufacturing business. We grew up privileged but not spoiled." He chuckled again. "They made sure of that."

"Well, from everything I'm hearing, they raised a lovely son."

Alex nodded. "I appreciate that."

The therapist cocked her head.

"All right. Back to my somber," Alex blinked. "That's the word, somber, story, which I told my parents after I showed up for dinner two weeks later. They took one look at me, and my mother put her hands together and cried. Dad's mouth opened, and he stepped forward. 'What in the world…' So, I told them, and they couldn't have been more supportive. They offered money, and Dad clenched his fist. 'I'll call around.' I waved him off. 'Dad, I'm, ah, an adult. I'll handle it.'"

The therapist smirked. "A parent never stops being a parent, no matter the age of their children."

I wonder if she has children.

Does it matter?

I came to spill, not to have a tête-à-tête with her.

"I guess." He sighed. "I share little about my private life, but this one… A necessity. Next, I told two close buddies of mine."

"How did it feel?

"To share?"

The therapist nodded.

"I suppose a relief. All of them got a bare-bone version, but their responses let me know they believed me." Alex drummed his fingers on his thighs without looking at the therapist. "I felt better, but it didn't last. Nope. Things got darker."

Alex fidgeted, took a gulp of water, and stared into the mug.

He tilted his gaze to the therapist. "Yup. Very dark. I started questioning everything. Other than close friends and family, who could I trust? Beyond what I imagined. So dark that every morning I woke up with this," he took his fist and hit his chest, "unbearable feeling. Hard to put into words. I tried to escape it, but every time I came close, this hulking monster appeared, latched onto my soul, and tried to gobble it whole. I prayed and listened to podcasts, but it wouldn't retreat."

Alex took a deep breath.

The therapist's eyes watered.

"Ma'am, are you okay?"

"Yes, Alex. Please don't worry about me. I've been doing this work for eons, and my experiences with clients evoke intense emotions. Empathy on steroids." Her eyes glimmered. "I'm fine, but from what it sounds like, you haven't been, so please continue."

He nodded. "One morning, I called the priest, and he saw me within the hour. He must have mental health training because he asked a bunch of questions. I reassured him I wasn't suicidal but agreed I suffered from a major depressive episode. He scrolled through his phone and texted me Bridget's name. He claimed I'd like her."

Alex looked up. "The rest is history except for what led me to need tonight."

"And?"

"I met a woman through one of my buddies. He worked with her, and thought we'd be a good match, but I-I…" His eyes found the lamp again. "Last night, we got together for a drink. She seemed nice enough, but I don't know…" Alex laced his fingers. "She—Cheryl, I think—started twirling her hair, put her hand on my knee, and I freaked. That never happened to me before. Not to sound arrogant, but I never had that problem." He gulped. "I felt that weird sensation in my chest and grabbed my phone, pretending I got a text message. I stood up, threw a hundred-dollar bill at her, and bolted." Alex looked at the therapist. "Now, as I'm talking about this, I realize I need to go deeper. Not quite ready to date."

"How are you doing?"

Alex nodded, and his eyes clamped onto the therapist's. "Wow, a lot better. Thank you."

The therapist nodded. "You are most welcome, Alex. It sounds like you know what you need to do, but not tonight and…" Her eyes softened like a silky sheath, "… not with me."

Alex pulled on his tie again.

"Bridget will return, and you'll do your work with her." Her eyes danced, and her lips tilted upward. "My daughter is getting married soon. If she weren't, I'd introduce you to her." She sighed. "Oh well. But when you're ready to date again, please let me know." She handed him a business card.

Lucia Tulasi, Matchmaker.
"Embellish: Old-Fashioned Love Story."
Romance, Courtship, and Marriage

Chapter Fifteen

Delphina

Delphina jumped out of the car, took a few steps, and her gaze floated to the heavens. A smiling moon and stars appeared to flicker and dance across the midnight sky like glitter shimmering on velvet.

God, you never cease to amaze me with the many gifts You offer us. Your artistry has no bounds, as displayed by tonight's performance.

She wrapped her arms around herself.

I can't wait to see Jude, but first…

She skipped to the end of the brick walkway, and with her hands on her hips, she studied the special dream house she and Jude stumbled upon.

The previous owners built this Tudor with four floor-to-ceiling windows on the ground level. Although it conveyed some modernity, it didn't remove the charm of a more traditional, medieval-type home.

So many features created a fairy-tale abode.

The sloped slated roof, lots of brick, and arched entryway.

Magic. Like her and Jude.

What are you waiting for, Delphina?

She pranced to the domed wooden door and pulled out the tarnished skeleton key. Jude had suggested a locksmith create a custom-made item to match the antique-quality of their home.

Her index finger grazed over the ornate bow before she inserted it into the keyhole and unlocked the door.

Delphina ambled into the foyer. "Hey, Eros, where are you?"

She waited.

Hmm, I know he's here.

In a sing-song voice, she said, "Where are you?"

Footsteps thumbed above, and Jude called out, "Hold on."

Delphina stepped toward the staircase when a barefooted Jude peeked from around the bend and jogged down the stairs. He wore a robe, and his hair dripped. He grabbed her shoulders, and his mouth dropped open.

"What are you doing here?"

Delphina jerked backwards. She didn't expect this and bristled.

"What do you mean, what am I doing here?" she snapped. "What are *you* doing here?"

Jude hugged her and kissed her hair. "Babe, just didn't expect to see you."

He grabbed her elbow and pushed her into the great room. Most of their furniture hadn't arrived, but like an only child, a small, two-seater, velvet-curved sofa sat in front of their stone fireplace.

Jude nudged her into the seat, and he put his arm around her. "There. Here we are." He chiseled a smile, but when she glanced at him, his eyes didn't share the sentiment.

Delphina's eyes narrowed, and she cocked her head. "What's going on with you?"

He pinched his nose, and his eyes darted. "What? Oh, I don't know. Long day."

"You never answered me."

"About... Oh, I thought it would be fun to sleep here, and..." He wiggled his eyebrows. "Imagine you with me."

She giggled. "Soon."

"Yeah." He took his arm off her shoulders, yawned, and rubbed his eyes with his palms.

Delphina's heart pricked.

Stop silly. He's tired. And pay attention. He told you he came here to experience you.

She stuck her lower lip out. "I thought you'd be more enthusiastic seeing me." She peeked at his muscular, hairy calves.

"Um, whatcha looking at?"

Delphina's cheeks blazed, with the flames spreading to every part of her body. She said in a purring voice reserved only for Jude. "You know."

His eyes became hooded. "Hmmm, I do. Just say the word, except not for tonight. Too tired. I wouldn't want our first intimate moment to fail, if you know what I mean."

"I wasn't even considering it for tonight. You can preserve your magical tricks for our wedding night because I'm staying true to my commitment."

Jude laughed. "And babe? Believe me, Eros' wand will immortalize his Psyche."

Delphina shook her head and stretched out her mouth. "Jude, it's a good thing I love you because your humility is scarce."

"What can I say? Confidence, Babe, confidence."

Jude gulped as he tried to suppress another yawn.

Delphina tilted her head and grabbed his chiseled, unshaven chin. "Be careful, my Eros. Confidence? Fine. Arrogance? Uh-uh."

"Yeah, yeah, yeah." Jude stood up, stretched his arms out, and yawned again.

A Greek God. Black thick hair, dark eyes with flickers of caramel, crowned by long black eyelashes, and bronze-olive skin, kissed by the sun. Tall, broad, and sinewy.

They loved Greek mythology. He crowned her with the name Psyche, and Delphina embraced it.

When she told him it meant soul and referred to him as Eros, his face softened, a rarity for Jude. "Perfect. Together forever."

Right now, her heart surged. Soon, marriage, the sacred connection, binding them into perpetuity. Mind, body, and soul illuminating and lifting to the heavens.

His powerful fingers entwined her wrists and tugged. "Come on, my temptress. We…" He circled her mouth with his index finger and caressed her lips. "…need our beauty sleep." He kissed her hard. "Okay, come on."

Jude dragged her behind him as he padded toward the door. He opened it for her and gave her a quick peck on the cheek. "Tomorrow. Bright and early, but not too early."

Something seemed off.

Jude did his best to maintain his usual Jude, but she knew.

As Delphina pivoted to leave, a crash came from upstairs. Jude flinched, his lips pressed together, and his cheek twitched.

An uncomfortable silence thundered between them.

Footsteps came from above.

Delphina's eyes skimmed the room and tucked below the table in the corner sat Jude's Samsonite Freeform, a gift from her, and a small carry-on. Pink, expensive, and not hers.

Delphina's heart teetered, tumbled, and broke into fragments. She swayed.

"It's nothing. I-I…" Jude uttered.

Delphina put her palm up. "Don't." She pushed past him, and he grabbed her arm.

"I can explain."

A wispy voice. "Jude? Is she gone?"

Familiar.

Words lodged in Delphina's throat.

At the top of the stairs, a long-haired head and shoulders peeked from around the wall.

Delphina squeezed her eyes tight. "No." Tears overflowed. The cracks in her heart spread to the rest of her body. Her breath became shallow, and she shook like a tree being whipped around in a torrential storm.

Jude gripped her arms, but she stepped back.

The woman said something inaudible.

"Not now."

She slipped away, and only the creaking sounds above revealed her presence.

Jude combed his fingers through his hair. "Psyche…"

"Don't you dare."

"Okay. Delphina, this means nothing."

Delphina jutted her chin in the luggage's direction.

"It's not what it seems. You gotta believe me."

"Of all people."

"Hey, she came on to me. I never wanted you to find out."

"What?!" A raucous chortle battled through Delphina's throat. "So you think it would be okay to cheat on me?" Her laughter became out of control. "And as long as I didn't find out, all would be well?"

"Listen to me." Jude gritted his teeth. "I'm a young, virile guy, so you're lucky it didn't happen sooner."

"Oh, I see." Delphina rested her chin on her hand and tapped her cheek with an index finger. "My, my, so I deprived you even though, from the get-go, I minced no words about my beliefs and what happened to me. You claimed you respected me and could restrain your…"

Delphina made air quotes. "Vir-il-ity and male urges, so we became engaged after three months and set our wedding date for three months later. And you forget that women also experience sensual feelings."

"Look. I'm sorry for my weakness, okay? And I messed up. I will force her to leave right now." He snatched her wrist. "C'mere. We can get past this."

Delphina recoiled and yanked her arm from him. For the first time since she met him, Jude's eyes widened and pooled.

Delphina plucked her keys from her hobo bag, brushed away some tears with the back of her palm, and grabbed the doorknob. "You think so, huh?" She swallowed, and her voice quivered. "You betrayed me on so many levels. How could I ever trust you again? So, Jude…what a fitting name for you…" Her head bobbed up and down. "I don't think so."

She stumbled out the door without turning back.

Click, click, click.

Delphina pressed the television control and channel surfed. She lay on the couch in her mother's condo, where she lived for the last two days. She refused to do anything else, unless Lucia pressured her to rise from bed by seven and shower.

"Seven o'clock. Time to wake up." Her mother pulled back the bulky comforter and sheets.

Delphina rolled over. The smell of citrus and roasted coffee waded into the room.

"Up," Lucia barked. "You'll recover from this, my love, but you must not succumb to sleeping all day."

"Mama, leave me be."

"No. If you were learning to walk again, the physical therapist would have you moving right away. How's it any different with depression, huh?"

Delphina placed her feet on the hardwood floor and noticed the peeling polish on her toenails.

Who cares?

She looked at her fingernails. Same thing.

Lucia's gaze tracked hers. "Maybe I'll arrange a Mani Pedi for us."

Without looking at her mother, Delphina shook her head.

"Not today, but later this week."

Lucia, wearing jeans, a T-shirt, and clogs, appeared fresh, like a cool glass of sparkling water.

Delphina couldn't move.

"Take a bite of this." Lucia offered her a dish of peeled sliced oranges with a cherry tucked in the middle. The bright sunflower tempted her to pluck a piece with her fingers.

She blinked at it, turned her head, and waved her mother off.

"Just one. I insist."

Delphina took the slice from the plate and chewed on it. The citrus streamed into her tongue and throat.

Lucia linked her arm under hers, and like a Raggedy Ann doll, Delphina let her mother move her into the bathroom.

Steam surrounded them. "Everything is ready for you, as I always do when you stay over." Lucia swept her hand toward the thick folded towel and washcloth made of Turkish cotton, and the shampoo, conditioner, and French almond scrubbing soap.

Lucia laid out Delphina's favorite sweats.

She mumbled, "Mama, you don't have to take care of me."

"Oh, my love, I do, and I will do extra under the present circumstances."

Delphina nodded.

"Get going, and when you come out, coffee awaits you."

Delphina plodded into the shower, and the hot water seared her body. She rubbed soap onto the washcloth and scoured every inch of her, exfoliating skin and thoughts of Jude.

When she came out, she trudged into the living room. The aroma of French roasted java beckoned her. She plopped on the couch, removed the towel from her head, and an avalanche of damp curls spilled around her shoulders.

A tangled mess. But who cares?

Lucia entered the room with a cup of coffee. "A grilled English muffin for you. Just the way you like it."

"Stop fussing over me, Mama. Don't you have new prospects to see?"

"No, I canceled them for the week. I told them something came up and invited them to reschedule their appointment on *Calendly*."

Without looking at her mother, Delphina snapped. "That wasn't necessary. My God, I'm not suicidal."

"Listen to me Delphina. I'm going to take care of the arrangements, but…" Lucia took a deep breath and shook her head. "If you will not see a therapist again, you need to talk to me. As far as Jude is concerned, words can't express my disgust for that narcissist."

"Yes, Mama, you've mentioned the word narcissist umpteen times since I arrived here."

In a broken voice, Lucia said, "I can't help it. My beautiful daughter duped by that, that—creepola."

The corners of Delphina's lips couldn't resist slanting upwards.

"See. I got you to smile." Lucia beamed.

"Not for long."

"Oh, my darling, instead, not for now."

Delphina's nose twitched and the buttery smell coming from the cracked muffin beckoned her. She reached over and took a small bite.

"Good. I allowed you to skip food yesterday, but today? A new day."

Delphina nibbled on the crispy slice and sipped on some coffee. "Mama? When you asked me if I recognized the woman, I told you no because I didn't want to get into it."

"What do you mean?"

Delphina held the coffee cup, and her gaze became unfocused. "Margo."

"Who? Margo, Margo…" Lucia's eyes darted around before she leaned into Delphina and gasped. "Tanya's cousin?"

Delphina's head moved up and down, and she muffled, "Yes."

Lucia stood up and started pacing. "Oh, my God. What in the world… Tanya and you have been best friends for years. How could her cousin do that to you?" Lucia's eyes narrowed. "Over the years, during events at Tanya's parents' home, when I've chatted with Margo, I sensed something sneaky about her. Unlike Tanya, she seemed spoiled and self-absorbed. I try not to judge, but now I will."

"I know." Delphina hugged herself. "It gets worse."

"What do you mean?" Lucia's voice cracked.

"My friendship with Tanya. Please get my iPhone, and I'll read you the text exchanges from yesterday morning. I think I left it in the bedroom."

Lucia marched into the other room, hurried back, and handed Delphina the device.

She read the back-and-forth messages to her mother with the last being:

Delph, I've loved you like a sister, and this breaks my heart to say it, but our sisterhood is not enough for me to stand by you. Margo, for better or worse, will remain connected to me through flesh and blood. I don't sanction what she did, but I must remain loyal to her. I thought nothing would break apart our sistership, but who knew this situation would arise. Under any other circumstance, I'd be with you, but in this case, I cannot. I hope you understand and find the support you need to get through this. Stay well! Love, Tanya.

Delphina threw the phone onto the cushion next to her.

She peeked at her mother.

Lucia stood still, and her mouth twisted into a frozen snarl.

"I know Mama. I know. Your Mama Bear instincts ring loud and clear. All you need are fangs and claws."

Lucia's expression softened, and she flopped onto one of the plush chairs and shook her head.

Before she said more, Delphina surveyed her mother's living room for the first time in the last couple of days.

Oh, Mama, I feel like I'm cloaked in beauty, safety, and affection. A Middle Eastern jewel.

Long, flowing sheers highlighted floor-to-ceiling windows. Deep-blue velvet, low-slung armchairs with carved wooden legs and intricate patterns complemented the vibrant red velvet couch with rolled armrests and gold-embroidered pillows.

So like Mama to bring in her Syrian roots. Warm, jewel-like, and elegant like her.

Oriental rugs with vibrant red-browns, beiges, and golds over-laid a custom parquet floor centered by a Moroccan, brass coffee table resting on a mahogany, star-shaped base. Tapestries, original paintings, scaled the walls, and Arabic urns sat on top of smaller tables with geometric shapes.

"What are your thoughts?"

For the first time since she knocked on her mother's door two evenings ago, Delphina's smile bubbled into a laugh. "So much for you leaving the therapy world."

"First, I get you to smile. Now I get you to laugh." Lucia's eyes caressed Delphina.

Delphina put her hand out to her mother, and Lucia clasped it with both of hers. "My dear, please, tell me what is going on in the storyteller's head?"

She released her hand, grabbed a pillow, and pressed it to her chest. "I'm looking around because I forgot how comfortable I feel here. When you sold the house, I worried if you could transport the safety to your new condo, but you did. And with an even more elegant touch."

"Not my home, ours, and you need to stay as long as it takes to heal. One week, one month, one year."

"Nooo, Mama. I'll be all right at some point. Everything comes in threes." Her mouth twitched. "With two in one."

"Did you say threes?"

Delphina's head moved up and down as if in slow motion.

"What do you mean, three? Jude, Tanya, and her cousin—I won't even say her name?"

Delphina laced her hands together, and without looking at her mother, she rocked back and forth.

Should I tell her what happened in college?

"Yes, Mama, three betrayals, and no, I'm not talking about Margo." Her eyes tiptoed up to her mother's. "Remember how quiet and moody I became after college, and you suggested I get myself into therapy?"

"Yes?" Lucia tilted her head, and her green eyes darkened to a night forest.

"And remember until I met Jude, how I bristled at anything or anyone who suggested I date more often?"

Lucia squinted and bobbed her head.

Delphina squeezed the pillow tighter. "Well, here's the truth. I didn't want to worry you about," she hesitated.

"About what?"

"Something I never mentioned, but this guy, Chad…we met at a party…"

"What? You never mentioned a Chad to me." Lucia's voice became volcanic.

Her mother's tone never erupted unless it related to someone hurting her daughter.

"Because you sacrificed so much for me as a young widow, I tried never to burden you. But I-I—"

A ringtone of Andre Bocelli's song, *Time to Say Goodbye*, shrilled. Her aunt.

Lucia glanced at the phone, face down on the coffee table.

"Mama, it must be important for Auntie to call instead of text."

"Yes." Lucia's eyes locked with hers. "But hold that thought."

Lying beside her, Lucia picked up her phone, stood, and started pacing as she spoke to Delphina's Aunt Lydia.

"Lydia, everything okay?"

Lucia nodded and stared at Delphina.

"Ya? Let me go through some of my material later and get back to you." She continued walking back and forth.

Delphina inhaled, held her breath, and expelled it a little at a time. What should I tell her?

A few minutes later, Lucia pressed the end button on the phone and padded back to Delphina.

"Everything okay with Auntie?"

"Yes, yes. She wanted to verify something about the family history, her pet project."

"She's become so immersed in this when I spoke to her last week. How's it going?"

"Fine, fine." Lucia twisted her hand. "You know your aunt. Once she gets going on a project…" She slapped her thighs. "But now, my darling daughter, I'm eager to hear more about this young man, Chad? Is that his name? He broke your heart, didn't he?" Lucia bobbed her head up and down. "You could have come to me."

Delphina blinked.

"So, what happened, Delphina?"

Silence coiled around the room.

"Delphina?" Lucia sat down, with eyes searching hers.

"Oh, some guy that swept me off my feet. You know a bad boy?"

Lucia's lovely features contorted into a Medusa-like Gorgon, ready to turn anyone harming her daughter into stone.

Oh my God. No way will I share the truth. She'd scare Chad enough where he might turn into stone.

"I'm tired Mama. No more talk."

Delphina shut her eyes. As her mother's footsteps sank away, gifting her a present of uninterrupted space.

She sighed.

Close call.

Tightness released like a gentle massage sweeping her body.

PART THREE
Mesmerize

Chapter Sixteen

Alex

The FaceTime call rang as expected, and Alex pushed his finger on the accept button.

Bart's face appeared on the screen. His arresting eyes and pearly smile etched his chiseled features.

"Dude." Bart lifted a wine glass with a sparkling liquid and a slice of lime on the rim.

"Hey, glad you suggested this call."

"Yeah. We haven't connected in a few months. When was the last time? June, July?"

"Could be."

"Lots to tell you, O'Hara."

Alex bobbed. "Yeah, I've got some things to tell you as well."

"All good, I hope?" Bart cocked his head.

He broke into a chuckle. "Yup, so far."

Bart stretched his mouth out and lifted his thick eyebrows. "A lady?"

Alex inhaled and widened his eyes. "A beauty, inside and out."

A howl erupted from Bart's throat as he tilted his head back.

"Palmero, still doing that wolf call, huh?"

"Yeah, but…" Bart leaned into the screen. "Without booze, weed, or any other substances." He then sat back and stretched his arms out. "How about that?"

Alex jutted his chin toward the glass. "What's that you're drinking?"

Bart nodded and raised the glass again. "I took a page from you. San Pellegrino."

"Wow. What happened?"

"Before we get into, a couple of things… First, show me the palace you're staying in."

Alex took his iPhone and moved it around the room. The purple and blue silks and velvets waved like a midnight sky and ocean in concert.

Bart whistled this time. "Boy, your company's clients know how to provide the best, huh?"

Alex positioned the phone back in its holder. "Yeah, they do it right." He laced his fingers together and pitched forward. "Okay, Palermo. What's the second item on your list?"

Bart smirked. "Guess who's getting a divorce?"

Alex's eyes widened. "Logan?"

"You got it. Even though I left a few months after you, I keep in touch with some of the executive assistants who feed me bits and pieces about the happenings both onsite and off, if you know what I mean."

"Tell me more."

"From what I heard, Logan tired of the swapping thing, so he gave Sirena an ultimatum. From what I've been told, she agreed. No more extracurricular activities, but also, no more Logan and said bye-bye."

"How did he take it?"

"I don't know, but within a few weeks, he strutted around with new arm candy."

"And her?" Alex asked as the aching scar memory punched his heart.

"I heard she closed all of her social media accounts, accepted Logan's settlement for millions, and moved to Miami with a new boyfriend."

Alex gulped, leaned back in his seat, and looked past Bart. "I try not to revisit that situation."

Bart snorted. "O'Hara, you didn't deserve what happened, but like I said many times, everyone has ADD. By the end of the week, the chitchat switched to some other juicy tidbit. And I'm convinced that Logan knew the truth but felt compelled to stand by his Sirena."

"Yeah, I try to close the photo album any time the picture emerges." Alex bit his lip. "So, let's move back to you."

Bart's teeth retreated as his lips pressed together, and the sparkle in his eyes faded. "I didn't tell you in our last call because I didn't want to jinx anything."

"Do tell."

"Well, Boy Scout, you had more of an influence on me than you realized."

Alex lifted his hands. "How so?"

"I know you saw a shrink like me, but it wasn't enough. So, our conversations rolled around in my head, and…" He gave Alex a sheepish look. "I explored the faith thing and come to find out… my therapist told me she was a person of faith."

"Wow." Alex's head popped up, and he stroked his chin.

"Yup, O'Hara. I found God. Big time."

Alex nodded. "And?"

Bart glanced inside his drink before taking another sip. "You saw the amount of alcohol I consumed."

Alex kept nodding.

"Well, I started using some other drugs for fun. First weed, then meth, then coke, and one day I said to myself, 'What are you doing?' I took a shower, trying to wash away the debris infecting my life."

"Good way to put it, Palmero."

"I appreciate that, O'Hara."

"Full transparency. I had my share of alcohol, weed, and hook-ups in college. Brief but impactful. Because I viewed myself as an athlete, I stopped imbibing and indulging, and by my junior year, like you're doing now, I drained the desire for those, um, how do I say it? Seductive extracurricular activities."

"So, that's how you became a Boy Scout, O'Hara?" Bart grinned. "Looks like I'm following you even if I'm late for the clean-up party."

"Never too late."

"Yup. AA conveyed that message."

"What happened next?"

"AA kept mentioning a higher spirit, and as a lapsed Catholic, I got thinking about God, so one day, while driving around the burbs, I landed in Lexington and came across Grace Chapel. Have you heard of it?"

"Yeah. A few of my friends attend."

"You seem to go with Catholicism, which works for you, but this place…" Bart shook his head. "I don't know. Something resonated for me, so to get to the point. I dropped out of AA and attended Grace. And the best part? Guess. I'm engaged. Met her there, and after four months of dating, I knew. Last week, I proposed, and we're set to get married late next year."

Alex gasped and sat up straight. "You're killing me, man."

Brad gave a half-smile. "Yup, and I want you in the wedding."

"Sure."

"Now that I've dominated this conversation."

Alex shook his head. "No problem. A lot has happened to you. All good."

"Yup. But Karla—that's my gal's name—she's a teacher and has taught me to focus better, so…"

"Well, like I said, Delphina, my girlfriend, has turned me upside down and all around."

Bart cocked his head. "These ladies. You find the right one, and *ping*, we become like panting puppies."

Alex chuckled. "I didn't look at it that way, but yeah, she's amazing. A therapist turned storyteller, and can you keep a secret?"

Bart saluted him with three fingers. "Do I need to say scout's honor?"

Alex bent his head, and a piece of hair flopped down to cover one eye. "Nah, I believe you." He lifted his head. "When I get home, I'm going to propose. We've been together for three months, but she's the one. I know it, and from everything she's said, she does, too."

Bart fist-bumped through the screen, and Alex returned it.

"And Palmero. I don't know what's going to happen regarding a wedding party, so I can't promise I'll reciprocate. It depends on what Delphina wants."

"Hey, I get it. The ladies have their way for that special day. Lisa wants a big, bold bash. I couldn't care less, but she told me to consider no less than four ushers. So, no problem if you don't do the same."

"Yeah. From everything Delphina's told me, I get the sense she wants elegant but small."

"Hey, O'Hara. Like I said, up to the ladies, but tell me more about your gal." Bart waggled his eyebrows. "A therapist turned storyteller, huh?"

Alex inhaled and smiled. "Yeah, and she's good at it."

"Does she know what happened to you?"

"Not yet. But I plan on letting down my guard when I get back. I can be myself with her, and not just because she has a therapy background."

"Speaking of therapy, O'Hara, do you still go?"

"I took a break. We agreed I'd call her as needed, and the cool thing was that she hinted she believed in God. Bridget. Yeah, I liked her a lot."

"Good to know. I stopped seeing mine because she closed her practice. Bummer, but what are you going to do? So, if I need another, which right now I don't, can I get Bridget's information from you. Or would that be weird?"

"Sure. I've no problem with that, but what happened to your therapist? Did she retire?"

"Nope. She went onto develop a Matchmaking service."

Alex flicked both eyebrows up. "What was her name?"

"Lucia Tulasi. The best."

Alex's mouth dropped. "Palmero, are you kidding?

Delphina

Delphina's feet cemented into the ground as the rest of her tried to rebound from the shock reverberating through her body.

Her waiting room, with its white fireplace, wicker furniture, and confection of sugary pinks, whites, and purples, a refuge for her, now felt like enemy territory.

The towering man with medium-length, shaggy black hair, and olive skin now sported a mustache and beard. The dark eyes remained fixed on her. Rich chocolate with a tinge of honey, reminding her of expensive chocolate bars embossed with an edible gold leaf.

They coaxed her, inviting her to come forward.

He stood, stepped toward her, and brought his subtle but intoxicating scents of vanilla, musk, and cinnamon.

Her knees buckled, and her heart bounced. But Delphina couldn't figure out if the reaction meant desire or dread.

Both, silly. You can have two feelings.

She thrust her arm out, turned her palm up, and spread her fingers. "Hold on." Her voice shook, an alarm buzzing through her heart. "What are you doing here?"

"Okay. Fair enough."

"You didn't answer my question?" Delphina's voice trembled.

"What do you think, Delphina." Jude gritted his teeth. "I tried calling, writing, begging, and you ignored me, so…" He folded his hairy arms. "What's a guy supposed to do after blowing it and losing the woman he loved?" He cocked one of his striking eyebrows, as he often did. "And I see you still have that feisty streak in your personality, which I always found attractive, but…" A frown forged across his face. "Challenging, like right now."

Delphina gasped and shook her head.

"What?" He coated his tone in smugness and lifted his eyebrows.

"What do you mean what? Did you expect me to welcome you with smiles, hugs, and kisses?"

Jude's demeanor softened, and he swallowed. "No. I didn't, and I'm sorry I'm showing that brash side of myself." He lowered his eyes.

Oh, no. Watch out for him. Smooth voice. Enchanting eyes fringed by those lustrous black lashes that so many women coveted.

Delphina plodded toward the closest chair, a lilac tufted wing-back, and sat. Garbed in a simple monochromatic outfit of a black, long-sleeved, high-necked, Vince dress with Wolford stockings, and Donald Pliner pumps, she peeked at Jude. His gaze roamed over her body. She placed her leather bag and briefcase on the floor and hugged herself.

Mauling me with his eyes, as usual. Glad I wore this.

Jude sat across from her in the higher wingback and placed an ankle over his knee, cajoling her with his eyes.

He leaned closer. "Delphina, I want to try…"

"I'm seeing someone, Jude."

He slumped back and raised his eyebrows again. "I'm aware."

Her head snapped up, and she snorted. "How do you know?"

"I saw you at Fenway Park a few weeks ago."

"You did?"

"Yes, Ma'am." He nodded. His eyelids teased like a slow waltz.

Tension slithered through Delphina's body. "How come you didn't say hello?"

Jude's eyes widened, and he pitched forward with his hands on his thighs. "Yeah, Delphina. Right. So, I'm going to approach you and your new prince and say, 'Hey, Delphina, how are you?' And turn to loverboy and say, 'I'm Jude, Delph's ex. Nice to meet you.'" With an open mouth, he shook his head. "Huh, Delphina?"

"I get it, but you could have texted me and let me know."

"No, no couldn't do that because Ms. Tulasi made it clear through her actions. You blocked my calls and returned my written correspondences."

Jude tilted his head back and forth. "Well, I know who you're seeing, Delphina. Alex O'Hara, and I'm surprised based on what happened to you."

A chill rippled through the room, and Delphina tightened her arms around her torso to prevent an icicle from piercing her heart. "Alex, what—what are you talking about?"

Jude laced his fingers again, and his gaze became unfocused. "Well, Delphina, I hate to inform you of this, but I heard through the grapevine, that Alex O'Hara has another side to him." His eyes found hers. "A dark side, and well…" He bobbed and stared at her without a trace of a smile.

"I hope you know no matter what happened and…" His eyes nudged hers. "I, uh, I want what's best for you."

Frigidity now permeated the room and slinked throughout Delphina's entire body. From head to toe, numbness. Her lips froze.

"Delphina?" Jude waved his hand. "Are you there?"

She swallowed. "Yes." She stared past him. "I'm trying to digest everything you just told me." She stopped for a moment. "So far."

"I-I didn't do this to upset you…"

A blaze ignited within her, thawing a momentary freeze frame, and fiery words erupted from her vocal cords. "And tell me, Jude, how did you expect me to respond? Hmmm? Like, oh, thank you for sharing?" She folded her arms and turned her head away from him.

"I, uh…"

Delphina glared at him. "Besides, how do I know what you're saying is true?"

Jude stuck his tongue into his cheek, nodded, and raised his eyebrows. "Delphina?" His eyes grabbed hers. "Do you want me to show you the evidence? Because I have it. A reel on a very public Instagram account."

Delphina folded her arms, grimaced, and blinked hard. "Show me."

He tugged his iPhone out of his leather jacket sitting beside him and began typing on the device.

His eyes found hers again. "Before I show you this, did he…"

"Alex."

Jude nodded. "Ya. Right. Alex. So did, A-l-e-x, tell you anything about his firing by his CEO, Logan McCormick?"

"He mentioned something happened connected to the job before this. Why? Did he embezzle or commit some kind of malfeasance?"

Jude's lips rounded into the letter O. "Oh, no. Worse. At least. Your boy-wonder became a bad boy."

Delphina scowled. "Don't call him that. You sound so holier-than-thou when you do that."

He tipped forward, handed her his smartphone, and jutted his chin. "A friend sent this to me. You know what to do."

She studied the image. The blonde-haired woman, fiftyish and stunning, with lashed, soft brown eyes and a set smile, cocked her head.

Delphina scrunched her face. "Who is this?"

"Sirena McCormick, Logan's wife, and you should hear what she has to say."

Her index finger wobbled over the visual.

Get it over with.

She pressed the screen, and her wrist snapped back like an elastic band.

Sirena started talking. "Hi. You know me. But in case you're new, Sirena, here." She tilted her head back and forth. "Ladies, I want to alert you I've become one victim of an almost sexual assault, which I escaped." Her hand glided along her muscular arm and brushed across large and smaller bruises. "Ouch." She squeezed her eyes and swallowed. "Okay, the other arm. Her fingers breezed along her shoulder, past chiseled biceps, to her wrist. Oooh. As you can see, he pressed harder into this arm."

As she watched the reel, Delphina's chest became constricted, and the experience of suffocation took over her like a serpent tightening its coil around her.

Oh my God! She can't be talking about Alex.

Sirena shook her head. "I'm lucky because I escaped his clutches.

How, might you ask?" She lifted one of her hands, fingers decorated with a perfect French manicure. "I dug my nails into the left side of his jaw and carved into that area of his face." She nodded and lowered her hand. "Ladies, we must remember our tools. If not fingernails, I would've used my teeth. That's right. Whatever it takes, but for this nasty creature, the nail treatment worked." Sirena cocked her head again. "And if you don't have long nails, jab his eyes with your fingers or take your shoe and, well, you know what to do." She paused for a moment.

This could be anyone. There's no sign of Alex being involved.

Sirena's eyes pooled and widened, and her mouth quivered and sprouted into a grim twist. "You must wonder why I didn't press charges? Let me tell you it's difficult if it becomes a he said/she said scenario. Plus, I'll be Okay." Sirena clenched her fist as tears from her velvety eyes rolled down her cheeks. "Also, I won't say his name, but ladies, watch out for a handsome man with an unusual hair color, and…" She smirked and turned her fist into a claw. "The mark of Sirena sliced in the chin of his pretty face." She blew a kiss and waved goodbye.

Delphina's hand trembled, and she dropped the phone in her lap. She slumped back in her seat and refused to look at Jude. Her eyes remained downcast, and tears streamed down her face.

A vapor of silence curled into the room. No feeling to it. Numbness. Nothingness.

Thump, thump.

Jude assembled one of the stackable chairs and padded toward her. Legs came closer with an accompanying aroma. Jude's enormous paw covered her hand and brought some life back to it.

I can't believe this is happening to me.

A sigh from Jude.

She blinked and blinked again, and the limp hand remained under Jude's. If someone pushed her, she'd fall like a rag doll.

"Delphina?"

Her eyes made her way to his, and she shook her head.

Jude's eyebrows knitted together. "I know you don't believe me, but I never stopped loving you."

Her mouth dropped open, but nothing emerged from her parched throat except for a brief snigger.

"Look." He squeezed her hand. "I take full responsibility. I messed up, and I admit I could've had more restraint and not acted like a caveman. But you know me. I'd never push myself on you and never have. No is no, so when I learned about this guy…"

"How did you learn about Alex?"

"A friend of a friend. Pictures snapped of his aggressive overtures, and his boss walked him out the Monday after the party. I guess the office gossiped about this for about a week. The boss viewed Alex as his boy wonder until this happened."

"I see." A hysterical laugh protruded out of her mouth. "Another man who hides behind the shroud of deceit."

"Ouch."

Delphina gritted her teeth, pulled her hand from his, and tipped her head forward. "What did you expect, Jude? Huh? That I'd welcome you back like a panting puppy?"

Jude dipped his head and lowered his eyes. "You're right again, and knowing the feisty you, no, I didn't expect that response. The truth? I thought you might have thrown me out of your suite."

Delphina glared at him. "I still could."

"But you haven't."

She pursed her lips. "So, tell me Jude. Where did pretty little Margo go?"

Jude snarled. "Babe, she doesn't…"

"Don't even…"

Jude raised his palms up. "Nope. Sorry… Delphina, you're right, but she doesn't come close to you. I got home early from my trip, and she must have followed me and just showed up. And after you left…" Jude grabbed her hand. "Look at me."

Delphina brought her gaze back to him, and the hard edges around her soul began softening.

His eyes bore into hers. "I told her. 'Get out and never contact me again.'" His thumb whirled around her palm and moved across her lifeline, evoking something familiar, something delicious, like a swirl of chocolate syrup.

"And other than dating a couple of women once or twice about six months ago, no one since. Nada."

Now the edges melted.

"Delphina…"

Without removing his eyes from her, Jude brought her hand to his lips.

So good… Wait a minute!

As if coming out of a trance, her hand recoiled, and she flinched.

Jude's eyes became hooded, and his lips turned up.

"Still so cocky, Jude." Her head bobbed, and she glowered. "Don't get ahead of yourself."

He pulled back, lowered his head, and steepled his hands in front of his mouth.

A harsh stillness streamed into the room, and Jude's chair squeaked his discomfort.

Delphina gripped her laced fingers, pulled back her shoulders, and held her head high.

Jude's arms dropped to his lap, and he exhaled. "Again, you're right. These things take time."

She shifted her head and squinted. "And what makes you so certain I'm going to see you again?"

Jude shook his head, bent his elbows, and opened his palms before collapsing them. "I-I just thought you might be willing, but…" His eyes captured hers again. "Even if you're not, I gave you the information about Alex because I still love you and have your best interests at heart." He stood up. "And by the way, within the rumor mill, there were photos taken of the incident."

A wildfire invaded her, and flames reached her face.

"Hey, don't take it out on me. I'm an open book now." He gave her a nondescript look.

What do I say?

Jude trudged to the door, and as he turned the knob, he pivoted and glanced at her.

Chapter Seventeen

Alex

Alex arrived thirty minutes ahead of time. He strode into the main room and scanned the panoramic scene.

Bold, ruby curtains towered over the stage, demanding attention, teasing, and readying the audience for delights to come. Art déco features, gold motifs embellished like sparkling gemstones, creating a wistful charm to a theater long in the tooth.

Every two to three years, the owners enhanced the video quality and fine-tuned the sound system. They also refurbished the interior, with springy seats, shiny hardwood floors, and plush carpeting. Tradition and modernity joined as they meandered through time. How much better could that be?

Alex's lips sprouted his signatory-lopsided grin as he took in the magnificence laid before him. The aroma of buttery popcorn wafted in his mind, and he envisioned inhaling it and crunching on every morsel.

His imagination summoned Delphina. Golden curls cascaded around her. She unsealed her rosy lips, inviting the tasty kernel like a flower, opening its petals for the morning sun.

Delphina kissed his fingertips as he dropped one popcorn on her tongue. She shut her eyes and chewed.

Crackle, crackle, crackle.

"You like it?"

She nodded and curled her hand.

"So, you want more? What about me?"

Delphina plucked a popcorn from the bag. "Close your eyes."

"Yes, Taibhseach."

Alex opened his mouth. Her fingertips placed the kernel on his tongue, and his mouth played with them.

She laughed and removed her fingers.

"Umm."

"Sir?"

Alex blinked and bounced out of his reverie. The usher stared at him.

"I know we have another twenty minutes, but I wanted to know if you have any other special requests?"

"No. I don't think so. Just the movie and popcorn when my guest arrives." Alex glanced at his watch. "I think I'll go make myself comfortable in the private room."

With the usher ahead of him, Alex proceeded to his destination.

"Thanks, man."

The usher nodded and left him alone in the small space that seated less than thirty people.

Perfect. Based on what Lucia shared with me, I can't wait to see Delphina's expression.

He stroked his chin area where the undetected scars remained.

Yup. Full transparency tonight. Lucia believed it should come from me and that Delphina, a therapist by training, would understand.

Lucia. We'll be relatives soon if all goes well.

His memory flipped through the pages of his life book, to the calligraphy written two nights earlier, and a smile etched his face.

Clap, clap, clap.

Lucia's hands came together, and her eyes lit up.

"Alex, I'm so pleased you contacted me." She flicked her slender wrist and pointed toward the open door. Her stack of bangles jangled like wind chimes. "Please come in. You'll see similarities to my office down the hall, but I've added some features that represent even more of me."

Alex rose from the curvy couch, swathed in magenta, like the one from the therapy suite, but newer and more Lucia. And Delphina.

Lucia's radiant smile triggered an injection of solace, dissolving the pulsating anxiety coursing through his body. Clad in a turquoise suit and stilettos, with silvery tresses flowing to her shoulders, Lucia embraced and wrapped him in a quilt of warmth and familiarity.

Alex stepped into the office where the warm blanket of estrogen thickened. A round bleached desk, a plush camel-back couch with rose-colored hearts, and velvet chairs with gold high backs—all in shades of white and red—floated around the pickled hardwood floor. A ruby-red oriental rug with bold patterns extended beyond the furniture and gestured 'look at my offerings.'

Lucia's fruity-floral scent curled around the space and wafted toward his nostrils. Alex inhaled. Peach and gardenia.

Different from Delphina's.

"Wow, Lucia. I bet Delphina loves this." His words trailed behind him as he padded over to the chairs and glided his hand along the gold frame. "Beautiful. And these?" Bending down, Alex studied the design. "Swans?"

"Yes, when I typed in my keywords in a search, these Infinity Gold Swan chairs popped up. I couldn't resist, Alex. They breathed beauty and love like the goddess Aphrodite promising, 'Sit here. And you'll find your soulmate.'"

Alex chuckled and bobbed his head up and down. "They represent you, Lucia. Offering hope with a touch of elegance."

Lucia's eyes crinkled. "Yes, I'm glad that's how you perceive it."

His eyes skimmed the entire space again. "When you contacted me over the summer, I should've dropped by to experience your new digs. A little more feminine than your therapy office. But hey, you're a lady, right?"

She laughed again. "I am. XX chromosome from head to toe, inside and out."

"Like that gorgeous daughter of yours who gives me the privilege of keeping her company."

"Ah, yes." Her eyes twinkled. "So, I assume you came because of my splendid daughter?"

"I did." Alex's head went up and down once, as he sat back, crossed his legs, and bent his body close to hers. "I understand Delphina's father visited Iran and died under mysterious circumstances."

Lucia's smile faded like a snowy owl, blending into the pale, wintry sky, and a chill punctured the air between them.

Alex flinched. "Oh, Lucia, I hope I didn't cause you discomfort. I just, well…"

"No, no, no, Alex. You said nothing wrong." Lucia pivoted in her chair and poured some water from the Waterford crystal container. "Familiar?"

Alex nodded.

She sipped from her glass and turned back to Alex with soft eyes. "Dear Alex, I don't discuss Delphina's father very much these days, even with my daughter or my sister." She gulped.

Pal, you hit a sore spot. Get to the point.

"I only brought it up because I wanted to make sure I'm doing everything right."

A dazzling smile glittered Lucia's face again. "Alex, if you are the one making my Delphina happy, I'm beyond joyful." She shut her eyes, took a deep breath, and crossed her arms in front of her.

A glow radiated through his core, emboldening his optimism about what would happen next.

A broken laugh emerged from Alex, and an internal warmth flamed his face. He stroked his chin and swallowed. "Okay. Here goes."

Lucia's hands pressed on her seat, and she gritted her teeth. "I'm ready."

"Lucia Tulasi, I'm requesting your permission to ask your daughter, Delphina Tulasi, to become my wife."

Lucia stomped her feet and shook her fists up and down.

"Ooooooh." Her palms came together, and her gaze moved to the sky. "Thank you, Lord. You answered my prayers." Lucia stood up and inched over to Alex. "Yes, yes, yes. With the utmost pleasure, I welcome you to the family." Alex came out of his seat, and being a foot taller than mother and daughter, shut his eyes, and rested his chin on the top of her head.

She released him, dipped her head back, and nodded. "You and my daughter mingling together. Ahh, you'll give me exquisite grandchildren." She returned to her seat. "And I don't mean on the outside, which…" She gestured with her palm. "I don't even need to say, but on the inside because you and Delphina are people of faith with old-fashioned values—rare jewels in this day and age."

Alex flashed a smile. "I'm so glad you're sanctioning our marriage. And by the looks of that speed dating event, more people are seeking a traditional approach to relationships."

"Yes, I agree. Too many people have followed the motto of 'if it feels good, do it.' And they discover that quick and casual results in nothing but emptiness and self-loathing. From the calls I've received since providing this service, people yearn for something more. The fireworks may elicit fun, but they dissipate. The long, steady flame may flicker, but it endures if one keeps it alive."

"Funny you should say that because a buddy of mine made an about-face in his behavior." He shook his head and chuckled. "He refers to me as Boy Scout. I guess he wanted the title for himself. Now he has it. I know you can't respond because you were his therapist."

"You're right, Alexander, but…" She lifted her eyes with mischief dancing within them. "I can listen."

Alex tipped his head back with a chuckle. "I'm sure he'd want you to know that you had a role in his conversion. Bart Palmero."

A smile jotted Lucia's face, and her eyes sparkled with tenderness. "Good. See. And maybe more, as others watch the two of you, but…" She shook her head. "We can't control that, and what matters to me is that you found each other." Her eyes pooled. "I

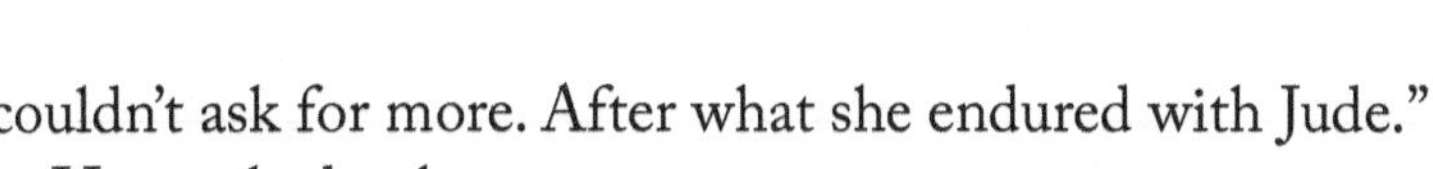

couldn't ask for more. After what she endured with Jude."

He gawked at her.

"You know about Jude, don't you?"

Not really.

Alex lowered his eyes. "Not much. She planned on telling me more when we reunite. And I'll tell you after what she went through in college, she didn't need more."

"You mean Chad the cad?" Lucia scoff.

Alex raised his eyebrows. "I think I'd call him something stronger."

"Why?" Lucia peered closer. "I know he broke her heart, which…" Lucia shook her head and pursed her lips. "I learned about him last year, but—" She stopped, narrowed her eyes, and inclined her head toward him. "Is there something more?"

She doesn't know about the date rape, pal. So, keep your mouth shut.

"No, Lucia. No worries. I'm being protective of Delphina, and I promise to do so all the days of our lives."

"You, you…" Lucia puckered her lips and blew him a kiss. "Sweetheart, you."

Whew. Got out of that one.

"I love your daughter, Lucia."

She beamed, and her green eyes appeared like jade gemstones. "Well, I'll let her tell you about Jude, and as you told me in confidence, you can share with her."

"Sir?"

Alex shook his head, and for a moment he wondered where he was.

"Sorry, I must have nodded off. It's been quite a… It doesn't matter." He wagged his head back and forth.

Wow. I didn't realize how anxious I'd be.

"No problem, Mr. O'Hara, but we have the movie ready, and…"

Alex widened his eyes and blinked. "What time is it?"

"5:15."

Alex knitted his eyebrows together and fished for his phone. He placed his hands in his pockets. "That's weird…" And bent over, doing the same with his back pockets.

Alex jumped up. "Not like me to misplace…" He glanced at the floor, and his device vibrated from the ground, like a friend waving *over here.*

He smiled at the usher. "It must have fallen. Let me see what's happening here. Could you give me five minutes?"

"Yes. No hurry. You rented out the room for a four-hour block, so I'll check back with you."

Alex nodded and gave a sliver of a smile. "Thank you."

The usher slipped away without a sound.

He took a deep breath.

An iMessage blared from the screen next to Delphina's avatar, and Alex sighed and stared at the device.

His fingers crawled to their familiar position, and he stroked his chin area.

What are you waiting for, pal?

As he rubbed his chin harder, his right thumb clicked on the phone, and a long text appeared. Scrolling through the sentences, the sharp edges from words like "I can't" and "I'm so sorry" sliced through Alex's heart. His breathing became shallow, and to calm himself, he paced back and forth, hitting his chest with his fist.

"Mr. O'Hara, I'm just checking back."

Alex turned and blinked at the usher. "Ah, Tom, is that your name?"

The young man nodded, and Alex tugged at his pocket, pulled out a couple of twenties, and handed the money to him.

"Thanks, Tom, for your time." He sculpted a smile on his face and widened it to disguise his trembling. "If there are any other charges, tell the theater to email me."

Wobbling like an injured person learning to walk again, Alex stumbled toward the exit.

CHAPTER EIGHTEEN

Delphina

The humming sound scratched at her concentration, an uncommon phenomenon for her.

She couldn't remember a time when the blow-dryer's white noise didn't provide an invitation to sink into another world of confectionary daydreams or melodious somnolence, but not today. No, today it annoyed her, but now, everything did, with her mother receiving first prize.

Waiting for the foils to perform their magic, Delphina studied the scene in the mirror. Two hairstylists chatted as they wove their fingers through their customers' locks, fluffing, and drying. Another one layered her customer with the same treatment given to Delphina. Others were washing or cutting.

Delphina shut her eyes for a moment and inhaled the vanilla extract, streaming through the sprays, shampoos, and conditioners, with the aroma curling its way into her olfactory glands.

Now that's not annoying.

Her hairstylist, Cindy, plopped into an unoccupied seat next to her. "So, Delph, I forgot to mention that Lucia came yesterday for her keratin treatment."

Delphina erased any remote sign of a smile and penciled her lips into a narrow line. "Yes, I know."

Cindy, a forty-two-year-old woman with scribbles on her face from years of smoking, stared at her in the mirror.

"Wow, hon, you and your mom are simpatico." Cindy grinned. "When I told her you'd be here today, she kind of grunted the same words as you."

Delphina shook her head. "And did she mention, Jude?"

Cindy's head shifted back and forth, with a half-smile emerging. "Well, she said something about Jude snaking his way back into your life again." Cindy put her palms up. "Not my words, hers."

"And did she exaggerate her fingers like this?" Delphina stretched out her mouth, brought her hands closer to her face, and shifted them from right to left with fingers wiggling.

Cindy cackled, bowed her head, and smacked a hand over her mouth, trying to suppress the giggles from overflowing. "Sorry." I couldn't have imitated her better, and you weren't even here."

"I know my mother well. Sometimes, she forgets where she ends and I begin."

"Yeah. You're tight."

"I love my mother, but sometimes she takes our closeness too far and crosses the line."

"But Delphina, she's pretty good about respecting your boundaries, and compared to my mother, I'd take yours any day."

"I know, and she's learning. I've pointed out that we can be like this." Delphina pressed her index and middle fingers together. "But it's not healthy like this." She crossed the fingers on top of each other. And based on what you know and saw the other day, she can forget."

"Cindy?" The receptionist curled her hand.

"I'll be right back." Cindy strolled toward the young woman, new in her role, who interrupted Cindy three times since Delphina sat in her chair.

She shut her eyes and opened the latch to her memory vault, and her mother's two-day-old grinding words tumbled out.

"Whaaaaat?" Lucia's voice exploded like a burst of gunfire, which didn't surprise her daughter.

Delphina removed the phone from her ear, stood up, and plodded around barefoot in the living room of her tiny condo. She stared down at her pedicured toes, colored in shiny Peachy-Rose, and rubbed her feet into the soft, plush oriental rug, a gift from her mother. She halted for a moment and zig-zagged her big toe into one of the ruby-red patterns woven into the teal-colored carpet.

"Are you listening to me?"

"Yes, and I'm studying my toes that replicate yours."

"Well, I wish you'd replicate me about Jude. I can't believe you're dating him again."

"I didn't say we were back together. We went out on one date. I have another later in the week, and one over the weekend."

"Why? And what about Alex? I thought you were falling for him."

"I told him I needed to take a pause."

"So, you're giving up a loving man to give your cheating ex another chance?"

"That's not the only reason."

Silence creeped into the conversation.

Delphina waited for a moment. "Mama, did you hear me?"

"I did." Lucia's tone shifted to neutral.

"Don't you want to know what I'm referring to?"

No utterances from the other end.

"Mama?" Delphina plopped down on her sofa, pressed the speaker app, and glided her fingers across a rose-gold pillow before placing it behind her.

"I'm here."

"Well?"

"Well, what?"

"Okay, Mama, Alex presents a good front, gentlemanly and all, but I learned that he's not who he seems—"

"Stop right there, Delphina!"

Delphina bristled at her mother's demand. As she often imagined, the Goddess of War, a helmeted Athena, with a shield in one hand and a palm raised with the other.

"Let me preface this before I tell you what I know. Alex was never my client, but one day, he sat in the waiting room, not receiving the emergency cancellation from Bridget. Because I was closing my practice and he appeared quite upset, I offered to meet with him."

"And?"

"He shared with me the false accusations hurled at him after being lured by his boss's wife at one of the swinger parties, partner-swapping events or whatever they call it these days. I say stupid, even if it's judgmental because it's a lose-lose for everyone, but I digress."

"I saw the Instagram reel made by Sirena McCormick, Mama."

"What? How?"

"Does it matter?"

Her mother hissed. "Jude showed you. Didn't he?"

Delphina bolted from the couch and started pacing. "Mama, he did it because he heard the stories and wanted to warn me."

"Oh, I bet he did." Lucia's tone remained rough but now more tinged with sarcasm.

"Mama, how hypocritical. You used to tell your clients that everyone could change. Listen to yourself."

Lucia sighed. "All right, Delphina. If you say so, but now tell me how you left it with Alex?"

"I told him that someone shared the reel with me, and because of betrayals I experienced in the past, I didn't know how I could trust him. I asked him to give me some time."

"Delphina, Alex didn't assault that woman. In my role as therapist, I've heard stories about the sex parties that have taken place at the McCormicks."

"Well, if it was so awful for him, then why didn't he leave?"

"It sounds like the summer evening event, converted into a late-night, drunken affair, which took him by surprise. Anyway, what did he say?"

"Nothing. I considered meeting with him, but at the last minute, I decided against it. He never responded. I guess he didn't feel a need to defend himself."

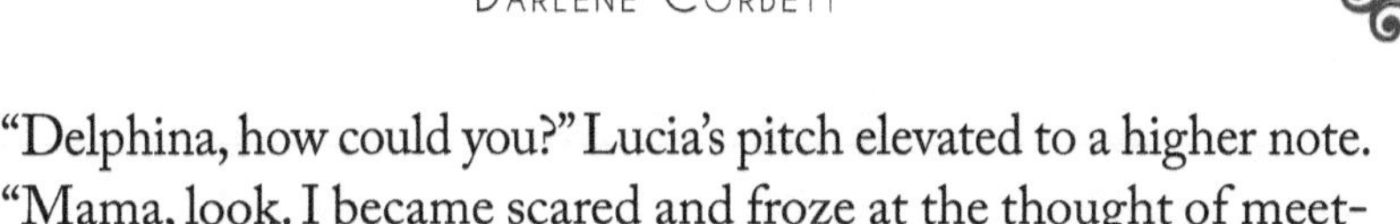

"Delphina, how could you?" Lucia's pitch elevated to a higher note.

"Mama, look. I became scared and froze at the thought of meeting him. Maybe later, but right now I'm trying to sort this out. I don't know who or what I can trust, but…" Delphina braced herself as the next sentence propelled from her throat. "You will not like this, but I need to give Jude a chance. No, I don't trust him, but he's beyond contrite, and so far, he's doing everything possible to win me back."

"I love you, Delphina, and I want what's best for you. You are my daughter, and I'll accept whatever you choose to do. Just be careful, my darling, please. You don't need a rerun of what happened to you."

A voice catapulted her back. "Hey, Delphina, did you go somewhere?"

The whirling of blow dryers became louder, and again Delphina focused on her reflection. She gazed at the foiled head blinking back, with a rhythmic background of endless tresses being fluffed or curled.

She turned to Cindy, who leaned forward in another stylist's chair with her hands on her thighs.

"I'm here. Just thinking about the exchange with my mother."

Cindy raised her eyebrows. "Based on Lucia's reaction here, I can imagine. But she just sounded concerned."

Delphina nodded.

"Delphina, tell me if it's none of my business, but can I ask about Jude? Because the breakup devastated you."

"Not sure what's going to happen, but he seems quite remorseful. Still, I'm taking it slow."

"What about the other guy—Alex?"

Delphina swallowed and shook her head. "I learned some things about him that might be true or not, but I can't see him right now."

"Wow. Okay."

"That's all I have to say about that."

"Got it. On another note…" Cindy glanced at her watch.

"We've a few more minutes for the treatment. So, I've got to ask you a favor."

"Sure."

"Well, I've been smoke free for over a week."

Delphina clapped. "Good for you because that's tough to do."

"You're telling me, but your mother suggested I ask you to give me a visual or something like that to help."

"Sure. I have a perfect scene for you to imagine. I have my nicotine-addicted clients practice this."

Cindy rubbed her hands together. "Goody. I'm ready."

"Okay. Close your eyes and take a few slow and deep breaths. Imagine a life-size, lit cigarette with disgusting smoke seeping from her. Yuck. Now glare at her. We'll call it her because she was once your best friend."

With her eyes closed tight, Cindy nodded and smiled.

"Now, you tell this gal she betrayed you."

Cindy took another deep breath.

"Yes, you had good times together, but she went behind your back, not telling you the truth. She lured you, teased you, and made you feel you couldn't live without her, but she betrayed you. She carried a poison, and when you heard about it from others, she pooh-poohed it."

Delphina's heart inflated like a pufferfish, as it always did when she used her craft. She knew her calling of being a therapist, now a storyteller, but still a therapist in disguise was God's gift to her.

Delphina growled. "Goodbye traitor. We had some good times, but not only did you take advantage of me, but you bullied me into staying. No more. I'm finished." Delphina slapped her palms across each other. "You can't get me back, no matter how hard you try. Stay away from me. Go away."

Lustrous black locks bore through her concentration.

Stop. He changed, and this isn't about you or him.

Lucia's face popped in with a cocked eyebrow, shaking her finger. No, Mama. Wrong.

She pushed out the pesky doubts.

Focus.

Cindy's mouth fell open as her head bobbed up and down.

"Take another deep breath, and when you're ready, open your eyes."

Cindy mumbled, "I feel so relaxed that I don't want to."

"All good things must end." Delphina laughed. "Now stomp."

Her hairstylist raised her feet and came down.

Clunk. Clunk.

Her eyes blinked open.

"Wow, Delph. Amazing."

Delphina grinned. "It came from you."

"Yeah, I know but…" Cindy stood. "Let's go rinse you off and make beautiful you even more so."

"You're too kind."

Delphina trotted over to the sink, and she sat back.

"I wanted to tell you that in the visual, the cigarette came at me and said, 'You want me.' So, you know what I did?"

With her head leaning back on the rim of the sink, Delphina raised her brows. "Tell me before you turn on the hose."

"Look."

Delphina lifted her head.

With her fists, Cindy struck blows into the air and bounced side-to-side like a UFC fighter preparing for her latest. She halted and bowed.

Delphina chuckled. "Okay, Rhonda Rousey. I love it."

"Yup. Every time the urge tries to lure me, I'm going to close my eyes, pretend I'm Rhonda, pound that sucker, with quick jabs until she's knocked out. I'll use my knuckles, Delph." Cindy tightened her fist. "Because I heard it's all in the knuckles."

Laughter stirred in Delphina's belly, erupting into a roar. She popped up from her seat, and a few stylists and customers looked their way and smiled. "Cindy, you're making me laugh so hard my stomach hurts."

Cindy smirked. "That a girl. Glad to see you can do that again. Now lay your head back down."

Delphina nodded and rested her neck against the rim of the sink.

"Know what else, Delph? I pray. I questioned God and the whole Jesus thing for years, but I listened to you and your mother about how faith helped you get through tough spots. So I'm copying you. How about that?"

"Oh, my goodness, Cindy. I'm so pleased for you, and remember, it came from your great imagination. A gift our creator endowed every one of us with, but it's up to us how we use it."

"Aww. Delph, you're the best, and," Cindy pointed both index fingers toward the sky, "so is He."

"No, Cindy, you're the best. And your experience not only makes my heart sing, but reinforces my choice of going beyond the traditional therapy role and marketing myself as a Therapeutic Storyteller with the focus on healing through story."

"Yup. It looks like you're in the perfect place, and I hope I'm not overstepping again, but Jude should take more of an interest in your work. And tell him you've become a Rhonda Rousey, so he'll never mess with you again."

"He admitted he didn't do enough and promised that would change. We'll see, but I'll visualize Rhonda or some kind of Warrior Queen."

Cindy waved the hose. Warm water massaged Delphina's skull as Cindy's nails scrubbed every inch with vanilla shampoo. A rinse and repeat, and a slathering of conditioner in between.

"Didn't this recent beau have more of an interest in your profession?"

"Yes, but I can't think about him now."

Cindy shut the water, wrung out Delphina's hair, and toweled it down. "Honey, you can go back to the chair. I'll be right with you."

Delphina trudged over and stared in the mirror again. The image of Jude loomed in front of her.

She cringed for a moment.

Could the story I suggested to Cindy be about me again?

She gripped her arms. Stop. He's a new man.

Her eyelashes fluttered, and the picture changed. A silver-threaded head appeared. Azure eyes, long, black eyelashes, and a lopsided smile shone like the mythical Apollo.

She shut her eyes to erase the image.

Instead, it enlarged. Alex pitched forward and touched her face.

Delphina shook her head.

Go away, Alex.

The image wouldn't budge.

The tall, lavender-colored candles flickered as Delphina whisked around the rustic, pedestal, dining-room table, a perfect piece for her open kitchen, complementing the maple cabinets.

Her insides lobbed back and forth like a tennis ball.

With her fingers gliding over the Maison D'Hermine Tropiques Placemats, she ensured they sat straight, their design of humming-birds feeding off foliage and ushering in a wildflower garden into her home. Matching napkins, shaped into a fan, graced each plate, enhancing the MacKenzie-Childs' Rosy-Check dinnerware and glassware, a gift from her Aunt Lydia for the wedding that never happened. Auntie insisted Delphina keep them, suggesting she treasure the unique stoneware as Delphina's Delights.

She fidgeted with placemats to distract herself.

Ten minutes late.

Typical Jude. Not a great sign.

Her eyes roved over the silverware, which didn't require an umpteenth repositioning.

Now her heart bounced up and down like a basketball.

Although always tardy, it became worse towards the end of the relationship.

Anxiety nipped at any remnants of calmness.

Here we go again.

Stop! He's coming.

Plodding into her bathroom, she twisted back and forth at her reflection in the full-length mirror. Her eyes scrutinized the woman returning her gaze. Dressed in a high-neck, simple black jumpsuit and inky-colored mules, she focused on her loose bun of spiral locks, with tendrils trailing down her neck like a philodendron plant. Cocking her head and lifting her thick eyebrows, she blinked at her curly eyelashes, crowning her eyelids brushed with taupe eyeshadow.

Ooh, I forgot my earrings.

Delphina went over to the vanity. The David Yurman eighteen-carat gold earrings given to her by Jude stared back at her, shouted, "Why did you keep us locked away for so long?"

You deserved it because he deserved it. Now a second chance… Maybe.

Lifting one earring up, she allowed it to dangle for a moment before looping it through the piercing in her earlobe and doing the same with the other.

Could this dangling before looping symbolize my feelings about this second time around?

Hmm. We shall see.

She picked up her phone. No texts.

What's going on?

Stay steady, Delph. You're in charge of you. Not Jude.

Delphina pirouetted back to the long, antique looking glass and nodded.

Not bad.

She coiled her tendrils, puckered her lips, and splayed her fingers.

Staring at her index finger, the broken nail reminded her of this morning.

As she gulped from her water bottle, walking out of yoga with Josie, Marquesa approached them. Wiping her face with a cool

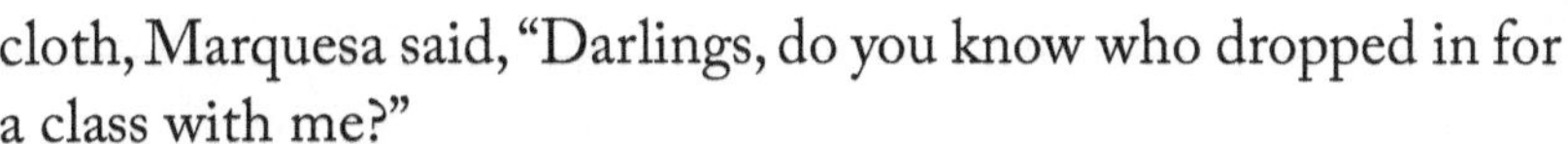

cloth, Marquesa said, "Darlings, do you know who dropped in for a class with me?"

Delphina and Josie shook their heads.

"Lisa Ming, the founder of *Heavenly Souls*."

Lifting her eyebrows, Delphina said, "Really? My mother and I fell in love with her program a few years ago."

"Yes. I remember you told me, and…" Marquesa wiggled her eyebrows, "I let her know she might meet some fans next time she attends a class."

Delphina nodded.

"Wow, Marquesa, you're attracting all kinds of people." Josie grinned. "And well deserved."

"I couldn't agree more," Delphina said. "Do you think it is the faith-based foundation."

Marquesa's toothy smile sprang across her face. "Yes. She approached me and said that she heard about me through others. And being an avid Yogi and a person of faith, she wanted something that married both."

Delphina beamed. "I bet she'll take some classes as she prepares for this year's program, and being a faithful attendee of her annual production, I hope I get to meet her one of these days."

Marquesa nodded. "At the end of the sunrise class, she told me she came home one day for her mother's birthday and needed to get an early flight the next morning. But she promised she'd be back soon for the Boston holiday extravaganza."

Delphina's lips tugged up. "I can't wait. The annual mother-daughter date, thanks to Auntie."

Josie smirked. "Lucky you. I'm always away for the holidays, but one of these days, I'm going to catch her show even if it's in another city."

Throwing her hand cloth aside, Marquesa leaned forward and grabbed Delphina's wrists. "Darling, I heard you found love again."

Delphina plastered a smile on her face, and out of the corner of her eye, she caught Josie grimacing.

Marquesa's smile slinked away as her gaze went from Delphina to Josie. "Am I wrong?"

"Well, Marquesa, you're right and wrong. It's complicated." Josie snorted.

"What am I missing?" Marquesa's mouth quivered in an attempted half smile, with dimples shadowing her cheeks.

Delphina inhaled and dipped her head for a moment.

"Delphina found the most amazing man, but someone from the past revisited and erased his presence," Josie said.

The petite yoga teacher, with her braid askew and little ringlets framing her face, touched Delphina's arm. "Oh my. Do you mean Judas?"

Delphina bristled, and her words grated from her throat. "Jude, not Judas. Like Jude Law."

Marquesa's cheeks seared with redness, like residual marks from a slap across the face. "I'm so sorry, Delphina. I didn't mean to insult you."

Ignoring the sweat soaking her body, Delphina reached out and hugged Marquesa. "I apologize for being defensive. It's just that…" She released Marquesa. "I know you and Jos here and," in a sing-song voice she said, "my mother, all want good for me, but I must give him another chance. We had been building a life together, and—he seems quite remorseful."

Marquesa nodded. "I see." Her gaze moved to Josie.

"Like you, Marquesa, we saw what happened, but…" Josie's eyes shifted to hers. "We love her and have to believe she knows what's best for her future."

A full, toothy smile expanded across Marquesa's face. "Yes, and I love both of you and want good for you, as I had long ago."

"Maybe again?" Delphina asked.

"Bah." Marquesa curled her hands down. "It would take a miracle."

Delphina wiggled her eyebrows. "Miracles happen."

Marquesa smiled. "Yes, they do, but let me get back to you, and may I ask what happened to…"

"Alex." Josie squeaked out.

"Ah."

"Al-ex-an-der." Delphina said

"Well, do you feel comfortable telling me what happened to him."

"She sent him a Dear John text." Josie's words skittered out of her mouth.

"Josie!" Delphina turned to her friend as a slow internal combustion flamed within her.

"Sorry, Delph, but didn't you?"

Delphina blinked. "I called it a pause."

"Whatever."

Marquesa's gaze shifted back and forth between her and Josie. "Delphina, I hope all goes well, and again, I meant no offense."

"I know Marquesa. Just protecting one of your flock."

Marquesa's dimples blossomed like chrysanthemum petals kissed by the sun. She hugged both. "Until next time…" Her eyes scanned the empty studio, and she said in a wispy voice, "My two pets."

Delphina and Josie laughed as they sauntered out of their yoga habitat.

Quiet squeezed between them until they reached their cars. Placing her yoga bag on top of her Mini Cooper, Josie's dark eyes rippled with solemness. "Delph, I'll support you no matter what, but…" Josie embraced her for a moment. Letting go, she said, "Just be careful. Okay?" She opened her car door and nudged her chin toward Delphina's index finger. "You broke a nail, girl, but don't let anyone break you again."

Now Delphina stared at the cracked nail.

Can we mend this relationship?

We shall see.

She glanced at her watch. Almost fifteen minutes late.

The nipping of her nerves had become a crunching chomp.

Buzz.

Whew. He's here.

She exhaled the invasive anxiety, and a vanilla salve spread throughout her being.

Delphina took another look in the mirror before ambling toward the door.

Knock. Knock.

That's weird. Did someone let him in?

She pursed her lips, walked over to the peephole, and squinted. Dressed in a white, open-collared shirt and dress jeans, Jude stood smirking and holding a bouquet of red roses, with a bottle of wine under his arm.

She turned the locks.

"Hi, Delphina. So sorry for the delay. Got here as fast as I could, and lucky for me, I swept through the door as a female neighbor of yours walked out. I guess I looked safe to her."

Jude, the charmer.

As Delphina swung the door open, Jude's eyes sparkled, his pearly whites glowing across his face. Her mouth wrestled with a smile, evaporating any words of chastisement crawling from her throat.

Instead, fireworks exploded inside her chest, causing her to hold her breath for a moment.

God, he still electrifies me.

Jude stared at her, and an unusual softness brushed over his face. "Hello, beautiful Delphina."

Her lips tugged upwards. "Hi, Jude. Let me take these gorgeous flowers from you."

Her fingers grazed his knuckles, and again the sparklers streamed through her veins.

She grabbed the flowers and spun around, with words trailing. "Please come in."

As she traipsed toward the kitchen, she laid the roses on the counter, stopped, and opened the cabinet holding her crystal. The

Waterford vase towered in front of the rest. Delphina blinked at it, and coral roses and delphiniums emerged.

She fluttered her eyelashes as the swaggering Waterford signaled that the time came for a refill and something fresh.

Jude's scent curled towards her, causing her nerves to sharpen. Placing the bottle of wine next to her, he said. "Really nice place, Delphina."

His manliness secreted his presence, and without shifting her focus, Delphina poured water into the vase. "Thank you, Jude, and thank you again for these beauties."

"Ah, they don't live up to their gorgeous owner."

Calm down Delph. His magnetism is on steroids right now.

"Let me give them a temporary arrangement, and I'll cut and rearrange later."

"Sure. Do you have a corkscrew to open the wine?"

Without glancing at him, she pointed to the top drawer. "In there."

Whoosh.

"Here it is."

Jude unscrewed the wine.

Pop.

"Wine glasses?"

"Cabinet above the microwave."

"Ah, here they are. Elegant, just like you."

A faint *glug-glug-glug* as Jude poured the wine.

Pulling some leaves from the stems, she placed them into their new home, stepped back, and cocked her head.

"What do you think?"

"Like I said, the flowers pale compared to you." Her gaze drifted toward him, and his powerful fingers wrapped around her arm, drawing her nearer. Gliding his hand under her chin, he coaxed it to rise, and her eyes found his, dancing with the waves in their ebony depths, like waltzing on a rhythmic, dark sea.

He bent down, and his mouth covered hers. Lips entwined with his.

His breath sped up. "I've missed you, so much." And his tongue grazed her cheek and moved down to her neck.

Intoxicating. Her breathing joined his as she surrendered to his lure.

I can't give in…

Her palms pushed against his chest, and Delphina staggered away from him.

"What's up, babe?"

"Whaaat?"

"Sorry. No *babe* right now, I get it. But…"

Jude crossed his arms, shook his head, and his gaze became unfocused.

He thinks I don't know, but he's pouting. Too bad.

Delphina positioned the floral arrangement in the center of the table and flopped her arms down. "There. What do you think?"

With his arms still folded, Jude nodded. "Yup. Good taste, wouldn't you say?"

She flicked her wrist, and with a fake grimace, shook her head.

"What? Nothing wrong for a guy to have confidence about what his fian…I'm mean his *lady* desires." His eyes shifted to the wine. "Let's make a toast." Handing her a glass, his fingers brushed over hers.

Another tingling sensation from even the slightest touch.

Uh-huh.

Pulling her hand away, Delphina lifted her goblet. "I'll give you the honors."

Without removing his eyes from her, Jude's mouth curved into a glistening smile. "To us, may we journey together forever." He raised his goblet, reached over, and tapped hers.

Clink, clink.

Delphina took a sip and averted looking back at him. Planting the glass on the counter, she handed him a tray with hummus, pita bread, and napkins.

Holding his wineglass in one hand, Jude balanced the platter in his other. "Wow, my favorite dip."

"I know."

He wandered over to the sofa, with the appetizer. "Where's your remote?"

As she placed the tabouli on the table, Delphina turned and jutted her chin. "Right there."

She scurried around the kitchen, and no words offering to help her trickled from Jude's lips. Instead, he increased the volume of the program.

Whatever. Some things won't change. The thought wouldn't cross his mind unless prompted. Let it go. Think of the good.

With her mitts, she removed the Syrian rice dish, hushwee, from the stove, ladled some into a large bowl, and placed it on the table.

Taking another sip of wine, she leaned against the counter.

Jude, preoccupied by the television program and munching on the hummus and bread, didn't look up.

"Ready to eat?"

He didn't respond as he leaned forward, munching on the dip and pita bread.

"Hey, Jude?"

His head jerked up. "Already?"

"Yes, come on over."

Jude stood, but his gaze remained fixed on the TV.

Walking backwards with the napkin in his hand, he wiped his mouth, took a seat, but kept glancing back. "Hey, b... I mean, Delphina, how about we sit in there. You know." He waggled his eyebrows. "We could dim the lights, get cozy, and I could restart the movie."

Scratchy words propelled from Delphina's throat. "What movie?"

"Oh, come on. Don't get pouty. It's not anything like *No Country for Old Men*, I promise."

Delphina crossed her arms. "How about this, Jude? You scoop the food onto the plates, help me bring them over to the table, and we'll pick a show together?"

"Deal, except I think you'll like the one I chose."

"And if I don't?"

Jude nodded, plastering an exaggerated smile on his face. "All right, Delphina, then we'll choose something else."

Strolling over to the table, his eyes scanned the place settings. "New dinnerware?"

As Delphina handed him a serving utensil, she turned to the pink checkered dishes and lasered in on the pastel design. "Aunt Lydia surprised me with these. She wanted me to have them—regardless of my marital status."

Jude's powerful fingers entered her periphery as he picked up a plate. "A wedding gift, correct?"

Delphina's fingers curled around one chair, and the word scraped out of her mouth. "Yes." She turned away, gathering the placemats, silverware, and napkins as Jude spooned the steaming hushwee, next to the tabouli on the dinner plate. "Let's make this easy with everything on one dish."

"Fine with me."

Stepping toward the coffee table, Delphina laid them down, and Jude positioned the plates for her.

"Oh, I forgot my wine." She rose.

Jude pressed down on her shoulders. "Sit. I'll get it." Delphina plopped on the couch, took the remote, and muted the program. Jude returned with her glass and the bottle of wine, and as he sat next to her, his powerful leg touched hers, with one of his arms placed along the edge of the couch behind her. When he offered her the goblet, his fingertips brushed her hand.

Sparks ignited as his masculinity gobbled every inch of her being.

Delphina, stop. You're in control of you. Practice what you tell your clients.

"How about another toast before we indulge?"

She refused to give Jude eye contact, and cocking her head, she embellished a display of nonchalance.

"I don't care. Sure."

"You give the toast this time."

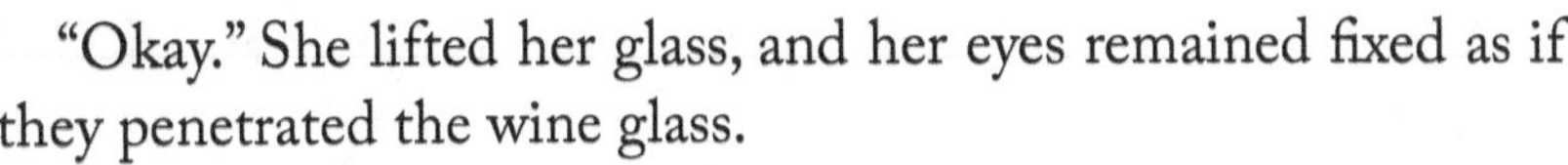

"Okay." She lifted her glass, and her eyes remained fixed as if they penetrated the wine glass.

"Ah, Delphina, how about looking at me."

Attempting to camouflage the nervous energy invading her, she forced a sliver of a smile. Her eyes tiptoed up to his, cavernous and forbidden, luring her to enter his realm.

Hold your own Delphina.

She pulled her shoulders back, raised her chin, and widened her eyes to shield them from his enticement. "To new explorations as we journey together again."

Their goblets met with a light clink, and they sipped. Jude's eyes tried piercing hers, but she turned her head, placed her glass on the coaster, and picked up her plate. "Let's eat before the hushwee gets cold."

Jude took his dish and forked some Hushwee into his mouth. "Hmm. Delish. So many things I missed about you, Delphina."

With her eyes steadfast on her food, Delphina scraped some tabouli on her fork. "Good. Glad you like it. Try the tabouli as well." Her eyes skimmed his face, as he munched on some of the Syrian salad.

Other than some clanking and scraping as they ate their meal; a strange silence burrowed into the room.

This seems weird. Neither one of us has much to say.

Munching and the pouring of more wine interrupted the still-ness. After several minutes, Jude tapped her knee. "How about we watch the movie? I'll rewind it."

She shrugged her shoulders. "Fine."

"Hey, if you don't want to…"

"No, let's try it."

Jude clicked on the remote and rewound the film.

"We saw this. Didn't we?"

"Yeah, but it was so riveting that I think we should watch it again."

"I need to clear these dishes and put the food into the refrigerator."

As she stood, he yanked on a piece of her jumpsuit, and she fell back into her seat.

"Sit down. I'll clear the dishes." Jude rose, lowered his head, and gaped at her. "Man, you're ravishing."

Her mouth twitched into a half-smile. "You're too kind."

With his black eyes boring into hers, Jude shook his head. "Oh, no. I'm not." He picked up the plates and silverware, and his head shifted to her. "Don't go anywhere. I'll be right back."

Shuffling toward the counter, Jude twisted the faucet, rinsed off the dishes and silverware, and placed them in the dishwasher. Walking over to the table, he took the bowls of food and brought them to the counter. Glancing at her, he asked, "The foil or the stretch-it?"

Delphina nudged her chin. "The compartment next to the refrigerator." He opened the drawer, pulled out the covering, and masked the food. Grasping the refrigerator handle, he settled the food on the shelf and slammed the door shut.

He's trying to impress me, but something doesn't seem right.

Jude strolled over to the couch, flopped next to her, his leg hugging hers, and he smirked. "See. I've changed."

"We'll see."

His brows lifted, and a flare blazed across his eyes. "We'll, see? Really, Delphina?"

She cocked her head. "What are you expecting from me, Jude."

He turned his head and steepled his fingers together. "You're right. I—uh—I'm just trying to go out of my way."

Her gaze went outward, and a salt and pepper head came forward. Azure eyes, lopsided smile, and cleft chin insisted on staying. She fluttered her eyes.

Jude's fingers dabbled over her hand. "Listen, you're right. I need to lower my expectations from you."

Delphina blinked, and as the silver-streaked head receded, his neck twisted back and forth, with azure eyes storming and a smile shriveling into a straight line.

"Delphina?"

She cocked her head and stared at him. "Sorry. I thought of something I forgot to do."

"Hear me out. Let's watch the movie. No funny business from me. I'll go home when it's over, and tomorrow, I'll take you to that surprise I promised."

"Sounds like a plan, Jude."

Alex's image popped back, wagging his finger as if to say, "Watch out."

Alex

The cigar lounge outside of Boston offered some of the finest smoke products in the Northeast. Bart insisted Alex meet him there after hearing about the break-up with Delphina.

Alex never smoked much, but every so often, he indulged in a good cigar, so he agreed to join him a few days later.

He hadn't slept or eaten much. Nor did he shave, which was unusual for him. Sauntering into the lounge, attired in jeans, a sports jacket, and open-collared shirt, he scratched the spread of stubble spreading across his face, except for the scar tissue from Sirena's claws.

Man Cave.

Dark and smoky.

Rich chocolate swirled around with splashes of gold and black. Many women visited, but beware, the owners made it clear, no feminine touches, with the lounge displaying its XY attire without hesitation. The King of the Jungle roared, shaking his magnificent mane and baring his teeth to anyone who questioned his domain. No woman ever complained.

Bart, clad in similar clothing, sat on a brown leather couch, puffing a cigar. Alex smiled, and pointed his chin at him, breathing in the coffee and licorice flavor of Bart's favorite, the Romeo y Julieta Aniversario.

"Hey, Boy Scout." Bart stood up and reached his hand out. "Let's go get you a Man-o-War, isn't that what you like?"

Alex flapped his hand. "Nah. Not yet. Sit."

Bart plunked back on the soft seat and glanced at his cigar. "Me, here, is smoking the Romeo y Julieta and drinking sparkling water."

Alex dropped into a seat kitty-cornered to him and slumped back. "Good to see you, Palmero."

"You too, O'Hara. Looks and sound like you've had a tough go of it."

Alex placed his arm on the top of the chair, crossed his ankle over his knee, and scanned the room. A woman walked by and winked at him.

Bart laughed and inhaled his cigar. "Jeeze, O'Hara. You still attract them."

Alex cocked an eyebrow and grunted.

"Without sounding pompous, I do too, but I'm taken now and won't ever look back."

Alex smirked. "Good. A wildcat now tamed, huh?"

"Yes sireee. You'll meet her soon, but right now, I want to know what's happening with you."

"Like I said, she sent me a Dear John text." Alex's gaze became unfocused. "Kind of."

"What d'ya mean?"

Alex pulled out his phone from his jacket, scrolled through the texts, and handed the device to Bart. "Read it yourself."

A server approached. "Sir, would you like something to drink?"

Alex flashed a smile at the young female. He jutted his chin at Bart. "Same as him."

With his cigar between his teeth as he held the device, Bart nodded. "O'Hara, nice to see you reveal those pearly whites. Atta boy."

"Just being here makes me realize I don't need a weak-kneed woman."

Bart held the device, took another puff on his cigar, and placed it in the ashtray. "Good, man. But let me read this."

Alex tapped the back of his chair as Bart perused the text and knitted his eyebrows together.

A drink appeared in front of him, and without glancing at the server, Bart said, "Put it on my tab."

Alex's lopsided smile widened. "Thank you again, Miss."

Bart glanced up. "Yeah, Miss?"

"Jaime."

Bart expanded his canines and charm to her. "Thank you so much."

She batted her eyelashes and slithered into the background.

"Palmero, you've, ah, come down to earth. Influence of your lady?"

"Yup." Bart grinned and inhaled again before reading more of the lengthy message.

As Alex waited for his friend to scroll through the rest of the text, time dragged like a slow exhale from one of the smoky cigars in the cozy lounge.

Bart rubbed his forehead, bobbing his head up and down.

Alex scanned the room. A few women sat together, but the atmosphere growled men, men, and more men.

"All right, O'Hara." Bart handed the phone back to him, took another drag from his cigar, and blew out a smoke ring. "Before I give you my honest take on all of this, let's visit the humidor for your favorite."

"Not yet. I want your thoughts."

Bart leaned forward and laced his fingers. "This chick, I mean gal. Trying man."

"Yeah. Okay. Get to it."

"She sounds confused. She says she loves you, but the Instagram reel caused her to question who you are."

"Nice of her to give me a chance to explain. Huh?"

"Right, but it sounds like she communicated with her ex-fiancé, Jude…"

"Which I knew little about. She planned on telling me about another betrayal, but…" As if he choked on rancid oil, Alex gritted his teeth and coughed up words of disgust. "She… I don't even know how to respond." He leaned back in his seat and grimaced.

"Jude, Jude. That rings a bell." Bart's gaze became unfocused.

"I dunno any Judes." Alex scratched his head. "But if he betrayed her, the name fits, right?" He snickered.

Bart took another puff. "Jude?" He bounced up and snapped his fingers. "Wait, a minute. I know him. We met him at some business event when we worked for Logan, remember?"

Alex extended his arms over his head and laced his fingers. "If I recall, we imbibed a bit more than usual, so my memory stays hazy. Give me more details."

"Handsome guy, like us, but dark looks like yours truly." Bart wiggled his eyebrows.

"Not coming to me." Alex sighed.

With measured words, Bart said, "Well, let me illuminate you. Remember that event when Quinn pointed to this slick dude, his sister's best friend's cousin." Bart's head bobbed up and down. "Yeah, A+ in the looks department, but a you-know-what. Trying to watch my vernacular." He smirked. "Anyway, this dude boasted about being engaged to a beautiful, intelligent woman, and we commented on how his engagement didn't stop his flirting."

"Now that you say it…" Alex tilted his head back and forth. "But we never got his name."

"You didn't, but I did. And found out later, his lady broke up because he had a fling with her bestie's cousin. Of course…" Bart stared at his cigar, gaped at Alex, and snarled. "He justified it."

Alex folded his arms and blinked. "Now that you say it. I remember, and you know what. I saw him at Fenway, staring at me and Delphina."

"There ya go, buddy. He must've shown her the reel."

A hammer of despair pounded his heart like brass knuckles slamming into his chest.

His facial expression must have exposed his raw insides.

"Hey, O'Hara. Don't let this keep bringing you down. Look what you've got to offer. Not only in the looks department, but you're a a genuinely good guy." Bart gave him a half smile. "Not like me. It took lots of therapy, faith, and a beautiful girl to show me the way. And you know what else? Watching you—even though it seems to come easy for you—I thought, 'try it, man. Maybe you'll become a Boy Scout too.'"

Alex nodded with a slow exhale and tightened his jaw.

Wow, Bart's changed. Who knew? His words soothed like a salve coated over his wounded heart.

"Thanks, man. It sounds like you wanted to make the change. Otherwise, it wouldn't have happened." Alex's gaze became unfocused. "And regarding Delphina, as they say, her loss."

"Before we go further," Bart leaned forward. "You ready for that cigar that beckons you?"

"Finish your thoughts, then I'll sit back and enjoy."

"Sounds to me like she's mixed up."

"Ya, think?" Alex's question punctuated with sarcasm as he lifted his eyebrows.

"She says she needs to meet with her ex-boyfriend twice and put you two on pause. But then," Bart cocked his head, "she wants to have a conversation with you in the not-so-distant future."

A fire simmered in Alex. "Yeah? Well, she can't have it both ways."

"Agree, but, well, I don't want to tell you what to do, Boy Scout…"

"Go ahead. Tell me."

"Have you thought about talking with her mother about this."

Alex scoffed. "No. I'm not involving Lucia, and as much as I think she's great, I'm not looking for an intervention."

"Well, as a former client, I know she might have some interesting insights."

"It's her daughter, dude. No matter what she thinks, their relationship remains sacrosanct."

"I hear ya." Bart pitched forward. "What about her father? Lucia told me she became a young widow and devoted her life to raising her only daughter. But that's all I learned about her

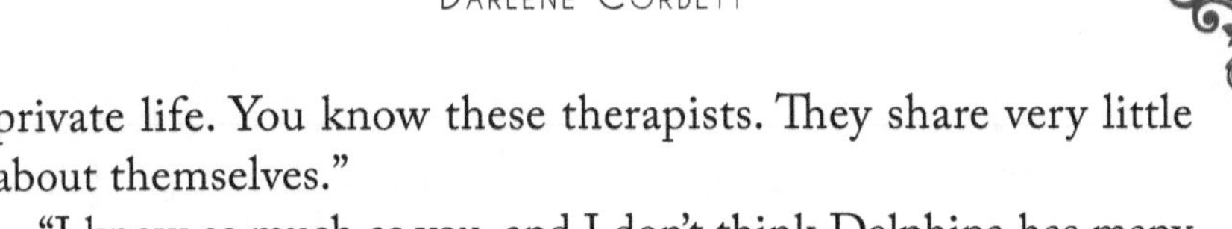

private life. You know these therapists. They share very little about themselves."

"I know as much as you, and I don't think Delphina has many details about her father. He returned to Iran to visit his family of origin and died under mysterious circumstances."

Bart jutted his chin. "Ya think she's got daddy issues?"

"Nah. Lucia raised her well from what I saw, but who knows. Everyone has issues."

"True, and we sound like a couple of therapists commiserating about," Bart made air quotes and smirked, "issues."

Alex chuckled and stroked the scar area of his chin. "Any other comments?"

"Here's my advice, Boy Scout."

"Listening."

"Live your life. Start dating when you're more fortified and see what happens. This may not be the end of you and her."

Alex nodded and widened his eyes. "Well, right now it's the end, and I'm going to start anew." He stood. "Let's go get me that cigar and you a second. The rest of the night is on me."

Bart bolted out of his seat and patted his friend on the back. "If she were here, I'd say, 'Hey, Delphina, you do not know what you're giving up.'"

Alex tipped his head back and laughed.

As they strolled toward the humidor, his eyes skimmed the room and immersed himself in the scenery. A dark and rich treasure chest with shiny brass and gold buckles— the perfect place for gentlemen to indulge in its smoky delights.

A woman waved at him. Pushing his hair from his forehead, his gaze captured hers, and he dazzled her with a smile before looking away.

Not yet, pretty lady.

Delphina

Delphina stared at the key chain. An elegant, textured gold stiletto inlaid with tiny sapphire butterflies and ruby elephants. She glided her fingers over the gift that her mother and aunt presented to her on her twenty-fifth birthday. Although insured and kept out of sight most of the time, every so often she pulled it out in front of friends and clients. "Oohs and aahs" echoed whenever it happened.

She knocked on her mother's hand-engraved, wooden door. Like everything else in her mother's exquisite home, it whispered Middle Eastern with a contemporary touch.

As she inserted the key into the door, she rapped her knuckle against it. "Mama, it's me."

Turning the knob and almost slipping as the door swung open, Lucia pulled on her wrists and hugged her. "What a wonderful surprise." She let her go and kissed her cheek. "I'm glad you're here, but why didn't you tell me you were coming?"

Delphina pursed her lips. "I thought you were mad at me."

"My darling, I was." Lucia's eyes danced with hers. "But like I said, you're my daughter, my greatest creation and gift from God. Even if we fight, I never stay mad. You know that. We're entwined forever, as you'll be with your children. But now, tell me…" Lucia studied her. "How is it going with…" She tightened her lips. "Jude?"

"Well, Mama. You were right."

Her mother's body swung back like an archer preparing its bow before it snapped forward again. "Do you mean what I think?"

"Yes, and I realized it at the Guinea Pig Refuge."

Lucia cocked her head. "What? Guinea Pigs and you?"

"No. I mean, I love all animals, but Jude thought it would be his display of generosity by taking me there. And his true colors came out about dogs and everything else."

Delphina inhaled and nodded. "Earlier today, Jude took me to the refuge located north of here, and this happened."

Sunrays from the ceiling basked the Guinea pigs in a fluffy bright light, and pungent smell from fresh grass and basil teased the human nose as the rodents chomped on their food. Cool fresh air and sunlight from an open window cut into its overwhelming aroma. Jude's long fingers entwined hers as they gazed at the number of Guinea pigs the refuge sheltered. Furry animals with coats of cinnamon, cream, brown, and white scurried around as Delphina peered into their cages. "Wow, they don't look deprived." She laughed at their abodes full of food, chew toys, water, and treats.

"Would you like to hold one?" a volunteer asked.

"I'd love to."

The young volunteer took out one pig and handed it to Delphina. "Here's Dame. We gave her that name because she looks like a Dalmatian."

"Ooh. So, cute. Who knew? A Dalmatian guinea pig." Delphina stroked the black and white mammal with a couple of fingers. Her eyes locked with Jude's, and he grinned at her with arms folded.

"Do you want to hold him?"

"No." Jude trod back. "The rodent seems content with you, Babe."

Delphina's eyes narrowed. "Babe? Not yet."

Jude's palms went up. "Sorry." He moved further away and glanced at his watch. "I'm going to go outside. You know animals aren't my thing, but I'm trying to show you how open I've become. Like I told you, this is just the beginning." He turned his back, and as he strutted away, his trailing words pierced his silky tone like knives cutting through chiffon. "We'll buy that dog you want, but when the baby arrives, outside it goes."

"What?"

His back had turned as he trudged away and tossed back more. "Look. Dogs don't belong in the house." The sharp edges from Jude's words caused Delphina's heart to crack. And a shudder went through her. "This conversation isn't over, Jude."

Jude didn't turn back as he made his way to exit the building.

He promised he had changed. I'm not so sure.

The warm creature in her arms wiggled as it must have sensed the anxiety emanating from her. She brought her lips to it, cooing and petting it.

After a few minutes, she called out to the volunteer.

"Here you go," Delphina said, depositing the guinea pig into the young woman's arms.

Her eyes searched the room and landed on a small window positioned at the top of the door. The old but authentic Jude revealed himself as he conversed with an attractive woman. He leaned into her, and his gaze roamed up and down, mauling the stranger with his eyes.

Delphina stood erect and placed a hand over her heart, directing it to become a shield against further disappointments from Jude.

Oh, no you don't, Jude. I needed to see this as a reminder, reinforcing what lurked deep within me. A marriage to you would be a repeat of the Humpty Dumpty show.

She pivoted, tip-toed toward the volunteer, and whispered, "If you don't mind, could you direct me to another exit?"

The volunteer looked past her toward the window before finding her eyes again. Without a word, the young woman padded in front of her and pointed. "Here you go, Miss."

"Thank you." Delphina pressed on the crash bar of the stainless-steel door, and with trembling fingers, she gripped the edges so she could close it without detection.

She stepped outside, drew her phone from her purse, and pressed the Uber app. The virtual map showed a vehicle could collect her in two minutes. She tapped on it for her choice and followed the visual icon on her screen, forking its way to her location.

Delphina stretched her neck and waved with both arms to a white Honda Civic rolling in her direction. As it slowed, Delphina yanked on the handle and jumped into the back seat. The driver, an older, bearded man, turned, tipped his Veteran's Cap, and smiled. "Miss, I'm the old-fashioned type and would have opened the door for you in my new Toyota. Glacier white, you like?"

"Yes, yes. Lovely and thank you. But I'm in a hurry."

"Okey-dokey. Where to?"

Delphina gave him the address as her eyes darted around.

"You okay, Miss?"

"Yes, please just go."

After buckling the latch of the seatbelt, she looked up and noticed him glancing in his rear-view mirror. "Looks like someone's yelling."

Delphina hunched her body and peered over her shoulder. Her periphery brought Jude into her visual landscape as he ran toward the vehicle.

"Please go. I don't want to speak to that man."

"You got it." The driver slammed on the gas.

Vroom. Vroom.

And his glacier-white car burst onto the street like an Arctic wolf.

As they sped away, she pivoted her body to look back. Jude flapped his arms and shook his head, shrinking into the distance until he was no more.

How appropriate, Jude. You disappeared, and I banish you to the past.

Delphina exhaled, and relief flooded her. She suspected Jude hadn't changed after that first date, but now…

And what about now?

Alex?

"Miss?"

"Yes?" A smile insisted on gracing her face.

"I know nothing about you, but I hope you'll do what's necessary if that man made you feel unsafe."

"Thank you, sir. No, I don't fear bodily harm, but emotional safety? Another story."

The driver glanced at her in the mirror. "Gotcha."

"Thank you." She knew he meant well but doubted he understood. How could he?

Slumping into the leather comfort of her seat, her hands slid across the smooth grain, and she inhaled. The aroma of lemon and orange from the upholstery flirted with her nostrils. A sign that the driver cleaned his vehicle.

Delphina shut her eyes, and a scene of her wiping away every speck of Jude blasted forth.

She lifted the corners of her mouth. Yes.

Within five minutes, Delphina's eyes became heavy, and with tension evaporating, she visualized a Monarch Butterfly fluttering to its next Sunflower. Magnifying the picture, she imagined her finger touching the intricate wings as the majestic creature fed from the nectar of the towering blossom.

What glorious flower could be next for her?

Did she dare say, Alex, after what she wrote to him?

Her eyes glistened with tears.

What did she do? Could this spreading Silver-King Artemisia push out the weeds of bad boys forever?

A chiseled face crowned with silver and black hair and eyes of a crystal-blue liquid sprinkled with green came in front of her. Perfect canines sat behind his lopsided smile, with lips inviting hers.

Umm. A smile sprouted within her.

Oh, my goodness.

Wait, a minute… How do I get him back? What must I do?

Delphina stared at her mother. "I made a big mistake."

Lucia blinked, inhaled, and held Delphina's arms. "My darling daughter, you did. I need to share something with you…" Her mother's arms dropped, and she laced her fingers.

"What, mother?" Delphina snapped.

Lucia swallowed and sighed. "The night before you were supposed to meet, Alex visited with me."

Delphina's eye bulged, and her hands rounded into fists. "What? What did he say, and…" She gaped at her mother. "Why didn't you tell me?"

"Because…" A fire ignited Lucia's tone. "I promised him I wouldn't ruin his surprise."

"Will you tell me now?"

Lucia pursed her lips and blinked.

"Mama?"

Her mother folded her arms. "He loves you very much."

"You mean loved?"

"I suspect he still does."

"Why? Did he call you after I sent him the text."

"No." Lucia shook her head. "He did not, and even if he tried contacting me, I would've redirected him to you."

Delphina plopped onto her mother's couch, removed her overcoat, and stared into the distance. "I need to get him back."

Her mother sat next to her and leaned close.

With a voice cracking like a broken eggshell, she asked, "Do you think I can, Mama?"

"Maybe." Lucia touched her daughter's cheek. "He seems like a reasonable man, but as you understand, Delphina, he's no pushover."

"Where do I begin?"

"Where do you think?"

"Oh, Mama." A groan erupted from Delphina's throat. "We're both therapists, so please don't therapize me."

Lucia lifted her eyes. "I'm not, but you already have the answer."

Delphina's eyes caressed her mother's, and a sliver of a smile budded. "The truth."

Lucia's face radiated, and her head bobbed up and down. "See. It came from you."

Delphina jumped out of her seat and whooped. "Alex, Alex, here I come. Get ready for the untold story."

She beamed and glanced at her mother. "I'm going to call him right now, and if he answers I'll move to the bedroom."

Her mother's eyes sparkled. "I'm going to prepare a meal for us, and…." She looked to the sky, put her palms together in prayer, and plodded to the kitchen.

Delphina clicked on Alex's number, put the device to her ear, and walked in circles to calm the somersaults in her stomach.

A ringing tone persisted. About to press "end," a voice picked up. "Hello."

"Um, Alex?"

"No. You must have the wrong number."

"Sorry." Delphina cocked her head. "That's weird." She looked at her screen and redialed with Alex's name lighting up the screen.

"Hello, again." The unfamiliar voice chirped. Older, with a slight accent. "Check your friend's number because I just moved to the area, got a new cell phone, and this number came with it."

"Oh. Okay. Sorry to bother you." Delphina ended the call, dropped onto the couch, and studied her contacts. "Hmmm."

"You talking to me." Lucia called from the kitchen area as she clanged pans. The sizzling garlic aroma wafted into Delphina's nose, cozy and delicious. Tomato, garlic, and ricotta over pasta. Her favorite.

"I don't know. Alex changed his phone number."

Her mother turned the knob on the gas stove, and it ticked. "All set. A delicious meal soon." Her mother trudged over to her, wiping her hands on her apron.

"What about emailing him?"

Delphina nodded. "Good idea. Although not as instantaneous as his texts, he flags his emails often enough."

She plunked down on the couch again, and with her thumbs, Delphina pressed onto the keyboard. She typed two lines about talking soon and explaining what happened. Studying the sentences, she paused for a moment, and her index finger lingered above the space before clicking send.

Okay, Delphina. Did you just lose your nerve. Just press it.

She pushed the key, and her finger sprung back like a mattress coil. Within a moment, an autoresponder answered:

Thank you for your email. I'm unavailable and will have limited access to any correspondence. I will return after the new year. In the meantime, if you have an urgent need to reach me, please reach out to Bart Palmero at bart@bartpalmero.com, where you'll find further contact information for him. Thank you very much. Merry Christmas and Happy New Year. Regards, Alexander O'Hara.

Doubt swirled in, and words of "Gone, Your Fault, and Too Late" popped up. Delphina swatted them away.

No.

"What's the matter? He couldn't have responded so fast." Lucia joined her on the couch.

Delphina handed her mother the device. Lucia glanced at it, and her head shifted back.

"What?"

"Nothing." Lucia gave her daughter a nondescript look. "So, he's out of town. Not unusual since he travels for his job."

An acidic laugh spewed from her. "For two months, Mama? Around the holidays?" Delphina shook her head. "I don't think so. Let's face it. I blew it." She folded her arms, sat back hard against the couch as droplets fell on her cheeks.

"Settle down, Delphina. You don't know the circumstances. It could've been work." Lucia turned to her. "Oh, my dear." Her mother touched her face. "You've already given up."

Sniffing and reaching across the couch to pull a tissue, Delphina nodded.

"Delphina, why don't you contact the man whom he cited in this email."

"You mean, Bart?"

Lucia lifted her eyebrows, got up, and turned her back to Delphina as she strode to the kitchen.

"I guess I could." She nodded with a titter. "I never met him. Alex referred to him as a wildcat but thought he'd tame his excesses once he met someone like me."

"Maybe he did." Lucia tossed out as she whipped open the silverware drawer, inviting a loud clinking. "But either way, that has nothing to do with you."

Delphina extended her legs and put her feet on the coffee table. "I guess you're right. Maybe tomorrow."

"Why not, now?"

Delphina's gaze became unfocused. "I guess it wouldn't hurt to email him and ask if he could give me an address to reach Alex. But…" She glanced at her mother, who continued cooking over the stove. "But what if he doesn't respond?"

With the water boiling now, Lucia moved to the refrigerator, and without pivoting to her daughter, she retrieved a bottle of minced garlic and ladled some into a skillet. "He won't if you don't try."

Sizzle.

The aroma curled its way into Delphina's nose.

"I don't know. Oh, Mama, it smells delicious."

Lucia clanked a spoon against the pan. "It will be, but while you wait, do what you tell clients. Take advantage of what might be a fleeting opportunity. Email him right now and see what happens."

Delphina smirked. "You're right, Mama. Some people even have auto responses that carry their cell numbers."

What do I say, but more importantly, how will I get Alex to believe me? What if he wants nothing more to do with me?

Delphina grabbed her phone again and wrote a short but friendly email to Brad, asking if he could either text her or email Alex's contact information.

Please, God. I messed up. I need a miracle. Please give me a sign about how I could win him back?

Wait, a minute… An idea scribbled across her mind's terrain. Then another in bold letters with vivid pictures towering behind them.

Of course.

She looked up to the ceiling and threw a kiss.

Thank you, God. As usual, you provide the answer if we're paying attention.

She pulled out her stiletto keychain. Holding the point of her keys, the gold links secured the elegant ornament as it dangled and circled, and her fingers dabbed at the elephant.

Her head bobbed up and down.
Yes, you will be a part of it.

235

Chapter Twenty

Alex

"Dude. How's Dubai?"

Alex grinned and nodded at his friend on the screen. "Good. Glad the boss called me, even at the last minute. Couldn't have been a better time." Alex jutted his chin at his friend. "Hey, Palermo, you didn't greet me with Boy Scout."

Bart smirked and leaned forward. "Ya noticed. Well, guess what Karla, my lady, started calling me? Boy Scout." Bart nudged his chin. "And before I tell you why, tell me what ya eating there, O'Hara."

Alex munched on a piece of pita bread before he answered. "Baba Ghanoush." He blotted his mouth with a napkin.

Bart shut his eyes and took a deep breath. "Umm. I can smell from thousands of miles away. Love that stuff."

Tearing off another small piece of the bread, Alex inhaled the nutty flavors of roasted eggplant, tahini, and garlic, coated the pita with the dip, and dangled it in front of the screen. "Here's one for you, Boy Scout." He popped it into his mouth, chewed, and brushed his hands off with the napkin.

"Thanks, O'Hara. You've tempted me. Need to take my lady to a Middle Eastern restaurant."

Alex bobbed his head. "Sounds good." He pitched back in his seat. "Now before we get into things, what made your girlfriend call you a Boy Scout?"

"My Lady, a pet name from the man here, appreciated my honesty and willingness to mend my ways, so she decided there's room for more than one Boy Scout. I took it as a compliment."

"It sounds like you earned it, Boy Scout." Alex chuckled and folded his arms. "And your lady sounds like a wise lady."

"Yup, and…" Bart cocked an eyebrow. "So isn't yours."

In the smaller picture on the computer screen, Alex observed his own smile converting into a penciled line. "Not sure about that." Keeping one arm around his chest, he extended his other hand with a beckoning palm. "Okay. Tell me what she said."

"Well, she got my cell number from my auto responder and left ah…" Bart shook his head. "Man, a message that… well, it even got to me. But you're my bud, Boy Scout, so I was gonna wait a day. But I played it for Karla, and she said, 'No. The woman sounds like she's suffering. Call her back.' My lady, who's been waving her magic wand, tapping into my male sensitivity gene, convinced me. So, I did."

With narrow eyes, Alex tightened his arms over his chest again to protect his heart from another tear.

"Are you ready?"

"Listening."

"I called her back. And at first, she sounded stiff, you know, stand-offish but polite and asked if I'd give her your contact information. When I told her I'd have to check with you, she burst into tears, and O'Hara, I was, like, flabbergasted. She kept blowing her nose and must've used half the Kleenex box. I didn't know how to respond. She said, 'Mr. Palermo, Bart, are you there?' And I cleared my throat, and she started crying again about how she made a big mistake and just wanted to communicate with you."

With another slit in his heart, Alex laced his hands and brought them to his lips.

"So, O'Hara, she got to me, and I promised I'd check with you as soon as possible. But she wanted to go further and insisted on sending a video to forward to you. I agreed, and I swear…" Bart raised his right hand, palm facing outward, and pointed his three middle fingers to the sky. "Since we're both Boy Scouts now, scout's honor. I didn't peek at it." He grinned. "Even the old me wouldn't have done that."

Alex nodded, let his arms dangle, and stretched his neck from side to side, skimming the luxurious suite.

Different from last time but no less opulent. Towering pillars with carvings of the desert. A color scheme of peach-rose and gold created a glittering spectacle. Alex laid against a couch of amethyst purple with lemon-colored fringed throw pillows. His legs stretched out on a long rose coverlet, overlaying a leopard ottoman.

She would've loved this.

"Not waiting, Boy Scout. I just forwarded the video to your alternate email. You decide if you want to view it, but if I were you…" Bart lifted his eyebrows. "I would. She sounds decent and remorseful about the mistake she made."

"Thanks, Boy Scout." Alex allowed a hint of a smile.

"Hey, O'Hara. I support whatever you want to do. Up to you. Looks like they put you up in royal digs again."

Alex put his fist to his mouth as he yawned. "Yeah. Next time we communicate, I'll use my iPhone and give you the virtual tour."

Bart gave a quick dip of his head with a salute. "Until next time, O'Hara, and good luck with this."

Alex saluted him back and clicked the red symbol, ending the conversation. He pressed the icon to his email account, sat back with his hands behind his head, and stared at Bart's subject line, Delphina.

What to do? Tonight, or tomorrow?

Alex stood up, moved to the floor-to-ceiling window, and immersed himself in the murmurs of the lapping Arabian Sea. Night's hand glided a comforting blanket over the water, inviting tranquility and sleep.

Okay, pal. You know you want to hear what she has to say.

He padded back to the couch and extended his legs again onto the ottoman. Placing the computer back on his lap, Alex rubbed his chin and clicked on the video attachment to the download. As he waited, his heart became a flame of determination, ensuring she wouldn't wound him again.

Alex nodded as Delphina came to life. Curls floated around her shoulders, eyes glistened, and a tentative smile dominated her face.

"Hello Alex." Her voice quivered. "I'm not even sure this will reach you, but if it does, please listen to me before you shut it down."

With hands laced together, she lowered her head for a moment before popping it back up.

"I didn't write any of this down because I wanted the words to come from my shattered soul along with my heart."

Alex nodded. The flame within him blazed into a roaring fire.

So, this is about you, Delphina? And why should I keep listening to this?

"You're saying, and so, your heart? What do you think you did to me?" Her head bounced hard. "I shouldn't be so narcissistic to imagine I damaged you, but I know we expressed our love for one another, so I assume it did."

Her head dipped down again before rising in slow motion. She stared back at the camera, and other than blinking, she remained still and voiceless.

Alex flipped his palms up. "And?"

"I made a grave mistake." Her head bobbed up and down. "Coerced by false promises." She paused again without removing her eyes from the screen. "I never discussed Jude with you, but he cheated on me a month before our wedding date. I caught him in our future home with another woman."

Delphina shook her head and grunted. "The other woman was my best friend's closest cousin, so I lost both my fiancé and best friend within twenty-four hours."

Her gaze became unfocused, and a laugh trickled from her, bordering on hysteria. "You are saying. So what? And you know what? You're right."

She tapped her hands, and her eyes widened, rays of gold beaming into his. "After I ignored him for months, Jude came into my office and cajoled me into thinking he had changed."

Delphina closed her eyes and took a deep breath. "Not only did I believe him about that but also, about you. And whose fault was that?" She opened her eyes, gritted her teeth, and pointed to herself. "Mine."

Her voice grew louder. "Mine." She screeched. "One more time." Delphina jabbed her index finger into her chest. "Mine."

She clasped her hands, then let them drop. Anguish seeped into her words. "You wonder what this has to do with us?"

Droplets showered on her cheeks. "It doesn't. That's the folly of my choice."

Her head shook. "I should've trusted our relationship, but no…I swallowed sugary words that promised an elixir but delivered more toxins."

Another momentary silence as Delphina's gaze returned to the screen. "The storyteller and therapist being fooled by a well-rehearsed, fabricated tale. Again, not your problem, but I wanted you to know that Jude doesn't come anywhere near your platinum status. I realized it when he took me to a Guinea Pig Refuge. That's right."

She laughed. "But I'll reserve that story for you when we meet in the flesh." She coughed. "If we do."

Delphina clasped her hands together. "So, dear Alexander, I can't say enough how sorry I am, for my thoughtless behavior. No excuse. My cowardliness. But if you're willing to hear me out, I'll show you how much I want us to try again."

She turned, plucked a couple of tissues, wiped her cheeks and her nose. As her swollen eyes returned to the screen, she sniffled. "Sorry. I get emotional. As you know."

Continuing to dab at her cheeks, Delphina's mouth delivered a sliver of a smile. "So, that's it for now. I don't expect to hear from you right away."

She pulled out another tissue and took a deep breath. "Or maybe never, but this isn't the last you'll hear from me, Alexander, unless you tell me it's useless."

She waved. "Until next time."

The clip ended with Delphina frozen into virtual perpetuity.

Alex stood up and looked out at the sky. God sprinkled outstanding glitter across night's canvas, another wonder that so many took for granted.

Not Delphina.

Amazement about God's gifts entwined many of their conversations.

You should be here, Delphina. If only…

He rubbed his chest. Less painful as her message provided a scant amount of healing superglue to his tattered heart, but it would take more salve to heal those deep cuts. As he sighed, Alex pivoted back and sat across the screen, holding Delphina's eternal pause. Golden from head to toe. The woman he thought would be his wife.

Nope. Not enough.

He slammed the laptop door shut, and his jaw clenched and hardened.

You're right, Delphina. A beginning, but you've got to do far better than this. Show me what you've got, Storyteller, and don't make it anything less than the best. Otherwise…

Delphina

It had been a few days after Bart let her know he forwarded the introductory video, and until further notice, she'd continue using him as the messenger.

Phew. At least Alex accepted her correspondence.

Don't get ahead of yourself, Delphina. Curiosity tantalizes even the resistant.

She prepared for another video, which she'd record in the next half hour. Gazing into a mirror, she cocked her head.

Get ready, Alex, for the first faith-based story.

Two more would follow, one about hair and a chapel, and the other about an angel and a sword.

She clapped and laughed. No matter what happened, at least she'd entertain him.

Alexander, you wanted Scheherazade. Guess what? You'll get a Scheherazade. A modern-day one, tinted with Christianity.

Delphina stuck her hand in the bag.

Crinkle. Crinkle.

Shoveling through the items, she dug until she touched the prosthetic.

Ah. There you are.

As she held the fake mustache, her fingers brushed along the crafted fibers.

Before applying the hair above her lip, she glanced into her lighted mirror, poured dark liquid foundation in her palm and fingers, and stroked the fluids over her entire face. A browner version of her stared back.

Next?

Bronzer.

Her fingers flitted through her makeup bag to find the right accessory. A fluffy brush promenaded in front of the others. 'Please let me be the one.' She twirled it, dabbed bronzer onto it, and slid it along her cheeks, chin, and forehead.

Next, she picked up an eyebrow pencil and began drawing upward motions along her brows to gain an oriental look and followed the same direction with her mascara.

One more application before the mustache.

Delphina brushed her hair into a tight ponytail, and with a coated elastic band, she pulled it tight away from her face.

Ready for the final adornment. Delphina grabbed the mustache, pressed it against her upper lip, and gazed at her reflection.

Her fingers became claws.

Grrrr.

Sudden laughter bubbled from her throat. Delphina couldn't stop the mirth, and slumped back in her chair, clutching her stomach. After a few seconds, she plucked a tissue to wipe her tears, inhaling, and stretching her arms and legs out.

Get it together, honey. Otherwise, it will be difficult to pull this off without laughing your way through it.

Glancing back in the mirror, Delphina cocked her head and tugged on one end of the mustache.

Not bad for a female version of the male warrior.

Before she began recording, Delphina went to her settings to ensure she uploaded the photo.

Pressing a button on the computer, she clapped as the scene came to life.

Pearly giants radiated from a backdrop of palatial columns, encircled by ribbons of gold, silver, and bronze.

Yes. Perfect. What a beautiful surprise for the finale.

Delphina switched it back to a colorful etching. Created by a student artist she had hired, a fifth-century, eastern-Asian man sat on a horse wearing layers of greased leather clothing, a steel-lined helmet, and a chain mail around his neck. He carried an iron sword in one hand with a bow strapped to his back and the quiver of arrows secured beneath his chest.

Alex, if nothing else, you'll learn something.

Time to start the story.

Delphina rubbed her hands together, adjusted her webcam, and switched on her microphone. She grasped the mouse and dragged it along the pad. For a moment, her index finger hovered over the right side of the cursor.

She stared at her reflection on Zoom.

You've got this girl. Let's roll.

She clicked on the record button and leaned forward with her right hand resting in the crease of her left elbow.

Delphina spoke with her lowest pitch, traced with a slight accent. "Hello, Alex, or should I say, Alexander. You must wonder who I am."

She steepled her fingers together. "My name? Infamous in history. Yes. Some referred to me as a barbarian."

Shaking her head back and forth, she gripped her fist and banged on the edge of her desk. "No. Such a label, doesn't do me justice."

Delphina chuckled and wagged her finger at the screen. "With so many attributes, I, Attila the Hun, prefer the title of Great Warrior."

She pulled out a miniature stuffed horse, laid it onto her palm, and using her other hand, she created air gallops. "A skilled horseman."

Placing it down, she ducked underneath her desk and retrieved a toy wooden bow and arrow. With as much grace as possible, she closed one eye, pulled the bowstring back, and with the flick of her wrist, released the arrow, which fell in front of her. "Although I'm rusty, an expert archer too, and…"

Delphina laid down the bow, and with both hands, she raised up a large rubber sword.

Swish. Swish.

"And a superb swordsman, even with the heavy metal of iron."

She dropped the toy and laid her palms down. "Examples, but you get the point, and you know what, Alexander?"

She paused. "Jealousy evokes all kinds of names for me, trying to diminish my character."

Waving her hands, she said, "Okay. Okay. Me and my soldiers hacked people to death. What can I say?"

Delphina threw her hands in the air. "And, yes, yes, I assassinated my brother. You would've done the same. I had no choice. Me or him."

She sighed and lowered her hands. "Such were the times. The early-to-mid-fifth century. You needed to walk in my foot coverings to understand, which I believe you call—*shoes*."

A slow, sinister laugh erupted, and she tipped her head back.

"Ah, Alexander. I presided over a vast empire and needed to stand tall against my enemies." Stretching out her arms, Delphina flipped her palms up. "Can you imagine, Alexander? Oh, the glory. Which I deserved."

Pausing for a moment before letting her head drop back, she released her arms and pitched forward. "Speaking of Alexander, why did Alexander the Great receive more praise than me? Huh, Alexander, huh?"

With tight fists, Delphina grunted. "Again, I say a false narrative. They, the history writers, documented that Alexander inspired his troops and carried the gift of tactical genius."

Her thumbs pointed backwards. "I, they claim, used brutality and intimidation."

She sniffed. "Maybe I did, but so what? Unusual times called for unique styles."

Delphina moved closer to the screen. "And you know what else, Alexander? Historians discovered that Alexander the Great wasn't so great the way he treated others, so there." She leaned back in her chair. "So much for historical accuracy."

Clapping her hands together, Delphina stared into the screen, allowing a slow smile to blossom. "Now, getting back to you, Alexander, and not the Great, I heard you have some greatness yourself, and again, you ask, why am I sharing all of this with you?"

Without shifting her gaze, Delphina clicked on her virtual setting which displayed Attila the Hun and a Pope. "Because miracles can change the course of history."

Delphina returned her gaze to the camera. "Here I am with Pope Leo."

She nodded and returned her gaze to the camera. "Correct. I, the so-called barbarian…" She raised her chin. "Met with this ordinary man."

Delphina cocked her head. "Okay. I'll give him a bit of credit. It took courage for him to meet with me." She smirked. "If I were him, I wouldn't have met with me, but…"

Delphina lowered her eyes and pursed her lips for a moment. Good. Keep him in suspense.

"I'm not as arrogant as the historians purported, but another story for another time. For this tale, Pope Leo faced me with humility—kneeling and acknowledging my strength."

She raised her index finger. The virtual setting changed without Delphina shifting her focus on the screen. "As you can see behind me, while Leo expressed his truth, these winged figures, I think you refer to them as *angels*, flanked him and wielded flaming swords over his head."

She nodded. "Yes, this man, who pledged his allegiance to a carpenter from Nazareth, spoke from the heart. And with those powerful beings next to him, I thought, 'Nah. They can have their city.'"

Delphina's eyes widened. "So, as history recorded, I departed and left Rome alone. Something about him touched me in a way that I never admitted to anyone, and," she leaned close to the screen and whispered, "between you and me, those angels frightened me."

Her head popped up and shifted from side-to-side. "No one can know."

Silence bathed the moment as Delphina removed the mustache, pulled out the elastic band, shook her hair out, and used her fingers to fluff out her curls. "There. I'm back to me."

She fluttered her eyelashes and allowed a smile to flow across her face.

"Alexander. I'm no Attila the Hun, but when I heard this legend, I thought I would use my Scheherazade techniques to entertain you."

She inhaled, plucked a tissue from the nearby Kleenex box, and dabbed at the shower, sprinkling her face.

"Even when one thinks it's too late, sometimes love, humility, and the truth changes the course of an almost dead-end. With the right ingredients, one could conquer the insurmountable. Miracles happen."

She shook her head again. "What do you think about this tale, Alexander? Do you believe in miracles? How about the truth?"

Delphina paused again, as the sprinkling became a streaming

flow of tears. She took the scrunched tissue and blotted her cheeks. "I-I do, Alexander."

As Delphina swallowed, her eyes widened, creating a dam to hold back the deluge of waterworks.

"This Pope's authenticity and faith conquered the unthinkable. And although I faltered, I'm hoping you will believe my remorse about throwing away the best thing that ever happened to me."

She pointed at the screen. "You. That's right, you, the best. And…" The corners of her mouth curled upwards and she clapped. "I promise you, I, a Christian Scheherazade, will regale you with more stories of faith, miracles, and love."

She took a deep breath and waved. "Goodbye, Alexander."

Moving the cursor to the red icon, she pressed the button to end so the Zoom recording could convert into the MP4 file. As she waited, Delphina pulled out some cotton balls and wiped the rest of her makeup the tears didn't erase. With the conversion completed, she switched off the microphone and camera and stared at her screensaver of a mother elephant with her calves.

"Don't you worry, Mama. As I promised, you're one of God's magnificent creatures, and I'll include you in one story."

Before shutting down her computer, Delphina grabbed her favorite cosmetic and slid it across her lips to the corners. Perfect.

Satisfied with the application, she puckered and blew a kiss. "For you, my love, Alexander."

Shutting her eyes, a subtle curve shaped her mouth. Yes, a rose-colored kiss, breezing along the waves, until it reached Alexander, with its trace brushing along his handsome cheek.

Delphina placed her hands in prayer. "Please keep inspiring me, dear God, and if it's in your plans, help me find my way back to Alexander."

Bringing her hand to her mouth, she whooshed another kiss. And with her palms pushing it upward, she willed her gift toward the celestial world, hoping her gratitude would reverberate like an exquisite musical note.

Chapter Twenty-One

Distraction pricked him.

Curiosity poked him.

Discipline shielded him. He wouldn't allow Delphina to claw at his attention. As meeting after meeting unfolded into the night, his mind meandered. If it centered on Delphina, he'd grasp his wrist and squeeze as inconspicuously as possible. The pressure halted his wanderings, and he focused on the speaker within moments.

Sometimes, his eyes skimmed the room. Those from other western countries dressed in similar attire. Black, Blue, Gray suits made with Vicuna wool. Tailored shirts of the finest Egyptian or Swiss cotton, and ties woven from luxurious silk. He couldn't see their shoes, but he knew. The most common? Cap Toes, Oxfords, and Venetian loafers.

Dotted in between his western counterparts sat their Arab colleagues. Most of the men wore loose-fitting white robes and headscarves held in place by the agal, a black cord. The few women in attendance donned a loose-fitting head covering, the hijab, and a dark-colored abayas adorned with exquisite embroidery, embellishments, or jewels. Wealth echoed throughout the emirate.

A contrasting world to the West. At least they allowed different religions to worship here.

Whenever he prepared to speak, a surge of anxiety entered

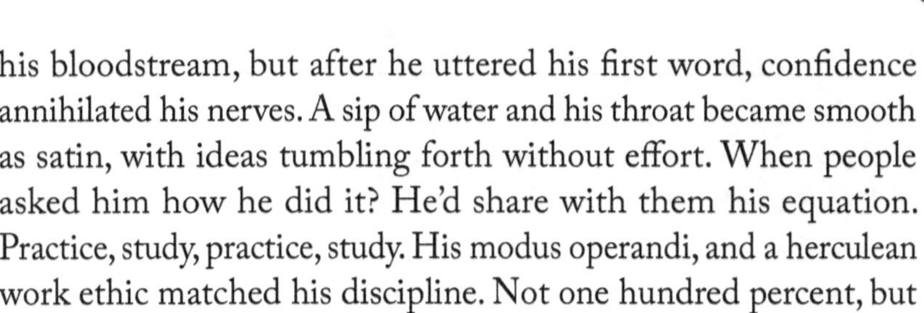

his bloodstream, but after he uttered his first word, confidence annihilated his nerves. A sip of water and his throat became smooth as satin, with ideas tumbling forth without effort. When people asked him how he did it? He'd share with them his equation. Practice, study, practice, study. His modus operandi, and a herculean work ethic matched his discipline. Not one hundred percent, but one hundred and fifty.

Now the weekend.

After pumping iron and joining colleagues for breakfast, Alexander sat in front of his laptop, sitting on a granite counter in his suite. He sipped his third cup of Arabic coffee spiced with cardamom, in between bites of middle eastern butter cookies, Ghraybeh, that melted on his tongue. After each nibble, he shut his eyes. "Um-Um, good."

He waited five days before he viewed the first video from Delphina. Every time he scrolled through his inbox, her email waved at him like a mellifluous voice whispering *open me and see the delights*. The subject line, *A Story Created for YOU*, tantalized him.

No way, Delphina. I'll open you on my timeline.

Last night, he succumbed. The first video tweaked his tight resistance to a smile, and soon, the corners of his lips crept until giddy laughter percolated from his belly. Attila the Hun and the Pope? Good one. And he surprised himself, as he viewed her performance. Not feeling so bad. Her storytelling provided a few more sutures to his wounded heart.

Now, brushing his hands off with a napkin, he glanced at his watch. Another hour before meeting the guys for a camel ride in the desert.

Okay, Delphina. Two more videos, huh? Let's see what else you have for me.

He glanced at the subject line of the second. *A Tale Like No Other For YOU*. Clicking on the email, he read her instructions and opened the attachment. Alex's index finger roved around the right click of the cursor before pressing down. The back of her head appeared in front of him. Ringlets cascaded down, fastened with burlap bows, and locks twisted on top.

Alex bolted up, and his eyebrows knitted together.

What the heck?

Another smile whisked across his lips.

In slow motion, Delphina dipped her head, rotated her neck with her chin leading the way, and the rest of her body following.

With hands laced, Delphina lifted her head. "Hello, Alexander. You never heard of me, but I'm referred to as Theodora of Vasta." She leaned forward. "And I hail from a very long time ago, centuries past."

Whipping her hair around, Delphina said, "You can see the power that lies within my tresses. Close to a female Samson but less ferocious and the strength of my locks revealed later, in another way." She slowed down the circular motion. "That's right, as a mighty tree. Roots coiled into the ground, a thick-crusted trunk, and branches extending out, but let me get to the story."

Delphina halted, pulled her shoulders back, and stretched her neck out. "By now, I've piqued your curiosity. I hope."

A smile budded on her face, and she fluttered her eyelashes. "I have quite the tale, one speckled with suffering, but…"

Her eyes widened. "Back then, fight or die. I did both."

Bending down, Delphina brought forth a spear in one hand and beat the top of her chest with another. "Like the courageous men in my village, I joined them in thwarting the bandits who raided us. How did I do that, Alexander?"

She paused for a moment.

Alex stroked his chin, before letting it drop into his palm, as warmth flowed through his limbs.

Trying to mesmerize me, Storyteller? Not so easy, second time around.

He folded his arms tight, guarding himself from the temptation to cave, but surrendered his mouth to his signature lopsided smile.

"I disguised myself as a soldier. And the other women?"

She stomped her spear and pulled on one of her coils. "I challenged them. 'Come with me and rise against these invaders. We can assist the men in defeating them, and if we succeed, word will spread about the bravery of Vasta's female warriors.'"

Shaking her head, Delphina screeched. "And what did they say? 'No.' Not only did they refuse me, but they pointed at me and called me derogatory names, which I won't repeat."

She steepled her fingers, and with narrowed eyes, she came closer to the screen. "Cowards, I yelled, and they huddled together, cackling, and turning their backs on me."

Grabbing a handful of ringlets, Delphina tugged on them. "My hair. My strength. I'm repeating myself but a softer Samson."

Delphina cocked her eyebrow. "But I needed to cover my…" Her hand stroked the top of her head.

"So what did I do?" She dunked beneath the desk and rustling floated through the computer speakers.

A moment later, Delphina popped back up, and a few unfastened bows veered to other parts of her hair. "Lost some burlap here." She shifted back and forth, peering over her shoulders. "Oh well."

Grinning and lacing her hands together again. "I can't find it, but I wore a helmet. And…" In words brushed with pastel tones, Delphina said, "No one knew."

She clapped, and a frothy laugh gurgled from her. "Alexander, just visualize me, Theodora, a magnificent warrior queen."

Delphina cocked her head. "Okay. Delphina fed me that one, which she uses in her storytelling, but I digress."

Trying not to laugh, Alexander paused the screen with Delphina's head tilted.

Storyteller, you're quite an entertainer.

Sipping a long gulp of java, he placed his cup on the counter and studied the expression freeze-framed on his screen. He noticed his heart pinged less. The only thing that hurt came from the relentless laughter crackling in his belly.

Scheherazade, Theodora, whoever, Delphina, I'm ready for more.

Alex pressed the start icon.

Delphina raised her chin. "I, Theodora, sword in hand, and spear tied to my back, marched with my comrades and fought."

She pounded the table with her fist. "And fought again."

With eyes wide. "Picture it. My shield in one hand and weapon in another. And wearing valor under my vest, I battled against the enemy's strength."

She swiveled to the side and extended her arms with an imaginary sword. "*Swoosh, swoosh. Clang, clang, and clank.*"

Turning back to the screen, her voice elevated. "Steel against steel. You should have seen me. There I rose, twisting and turning like a huppu, what you now refer to as an acrobat. And then…"

Delphina tightened her fists, crossed her arms against her chest, as words scraped from her throat. "Something sliced through my upper leg, and a red fountain spurt forth."

Her chair squeaked as she placed her hands under her thigh and lifted a knee. "I believe you refer to it as the femoral artery?"

Releasing her leg, she pitched forward. "So, Alexander, my fate? Death, but…"

Her index finger rose. "Not before I pressed the villagers with: 'Let my body become a church, my blood a river, and my hair a forest.'"

Delphina shut her eyes, lifted her face to the ceiling, and extended her arms out. "As I departed from this earthly existence, I saw and heard my fellow warriors converse and promise me they would build a church in my name."

Dropping her arms, Delphina dipped toward the screen. "Guess what happened, Alexander?"

She halted as she waited for him to respond.

After another swig of coffee, Alexander chortled and almost choked as he swallowed. Grabbing a napkin to ensure he didn't spill any on his clothes, he wiped the dribble on his chin, shook his head and smirked.

He spoke aloud. "Delphina, now that your performance made

me laugh so hard, I almost spit out my coffee. Do share because I can't imagine."

As if on cue, Delphina's mouth curved into a smile. "They built a chapel and named it after me."

She shut her eyes for a moment and took a deep breath. Puckering her lips, she exhaled long and steadily, and her eyes fluttered open. "My chapel, Agia Theodora, built long ago, survived through the centuries. And not only that, Alexander."

Delphina's fingers combed through her locks, knocking down a few more bows, and spreading a few strands outward. "Trees representing my mighty mane sprouted. Not…"

One hand went up.

"Or…" The other hand sprung up, with ten fingers splayed.

Delphina's head shifted back and forth, and her lips scrolled up. "Uh-uh. Alexander, I bet you can't guess."

She dipped her head and played with a curl, teasing him, and releasing a purr.

Alex leaned back in his high-top seat and folded his arms. "You're right, Storyteller. I've got no idea, so please do tell."

Delphina couldn't have timed her response better. "Seventeen."

Her head bobbed up and down. "Our great Creator fulfilled my wishes, and you know what else, Alexander?"

Delphina slung her arms out, and her eyes gleamed. "My body, the stone chapel, remained intact even as tree limbs pushed through it. The trunk spiraled and grew in a way that strengthened the structure. Like the strongest metal, I believe you call it titanium. The building endured the heaviness of the trees, now weighing about five and a half metric tons."

Alex bobbed his head up and down and dabbed the laparoscopic scars on his chin.

Riveting, Storyteller. I knew nothing about this.

Tilting her head, Delphina's face displayed a landscape of expressions, from subtle to extravagant. "You continue to wonder, don't you, Alexander? How could this be true? Yes. An enigma. A miracle, and in 1996, scientists determined the roots grew along the church stones without damaging them."

She blew kisses toward the ceiling before her eyes returned to the screen. "And now, Alexander, you must visit me in Greece, with, what's her name…"

Delphina raised her eyes, hummed the Jeopardy tune, and tapped the side of her head. "Oh. Of course."

A calligraphic smile swept across her facial canvas, and her eyes shone. She positioned her hands under her chin. "Who is Delphina?"

Alex chuckled and nodded. "Good one, Delphina, merging the present with the past."

As if reading his mind, Delphina peered at him with a sheepish grin. "Okay. I time-traveled and brought past and future together." Her palms turned up. "Who cares?"

She blinked a few times, clasped her hands, and a feathery tone caressed her throat. "I want this for us, Alexander. Miracles happen, and maybe…"

Delphina dropped her head for a moment, and tresses tumbled forward. Stillness gathered for seconds until she lifted her chin. With glistening eyes, her mouth quivered, and fragmented words dangled together. "Maybe it—it will happen for us."

Delphina puckered her lips, threw a kiss, and waved goodbye.

Hands found their way to his pockets, and Alex stared at the frozen image. As his jaw tightened, he shook his head and glanced at his watch.

Storyteller, you've given me much to think about, but for now, I have a date with a camel.

Spanning almost eighty-seven square miles, the Dubai Desert Conservation Reserve became the first national park in the UAE. Founded in 2002, HH Sheikh Ahmed Bin Saeed Al Maktoum created the DDCR to preserve the original landscape, protect the flora and fauna, and stimulate processes to re-wild the environment.

As Alex shaded his eyes against the relentless sun, he scanned his surroundings. The desert, like other terrains, revealed a unique beauty. Sand dunes swept across the landscape like mounds of golden sugar.

Dressed in a long-sleeved cotton shirt, light linen trousers, a scarf, and sunglasses, Alex nodded at the enthusiastic tour guide, Omar, a replica of Sheikh Ilderim, the owner of the Arabian horses, from the movie, *Ben Hur*.

Before they began the trek, Omar gestured and curved his lips at his small caravan of camels, instructing the guests on the how and what to do as they rode the humped-back animals.

Sitting on the back of Emma, Alex inhaled the dry air. Tangy and inviting, until Emma relieved herself. The slow flow dripping down her legs created a pungent and unpleasant scent. With a slight accent peppering his English, the guide, Omar, warned them this would happen, so Alex's hand cupped his nose for several seconds.

A strange creature, but what species didn't have their peculiarities, including humans?

Omar wagged his finger and informed Alex and his colleagues that camels could be finicky so handle them with care. With a light touch, Alex stroked the camel's neck, coarse fur that reminded him of the stubble on his own unshaved face.

When one of his acquaintances, Jeb, chuckled about his camel, Nathaniel, being just an animal, Omar stopped in midsentence, and with narrow eyes, he trudged over to Jeb and waved his hands at him.

"How would you feel if someone you didn't know pet you? These beauties have their own personalities and preferences. You insult me and them by suggesting otherwise."

Jeb's mouth gaped open, and he muttered, "Sorry."

With an "Humph," Omar got on his camel, shook his head, and curled his hand for the party to follow. He yelled, "Let's begin with the privilege of riding on Allah's gift."

For the next hour, Alex swayed with the camel, becoming

hypnotized by the majestic mammals roaming the sandy region. The guide described the various animals, and Alex relished the tidbits he offered. Until this excursion, he had never heard of the Arabian Oryx, a large antelope with long horns and white fur.

The guide stopped. "Shh. Let us watch these glorious Arabian Oryx, brought back from extinction."

Although Alex hydrated himself throughout the ride, when they finished the tour and reached their destination, his sandpapered throat beckoned for more water. As if reading his mind, a staff member approached him with an ice-cold bottle. After several gulps, he swung his legs off the camel and stood wobbling with every thigh muscle aching.

The guide approached him and chuckled. "You did good for your first time on a camel."

Alex nodded and lifted his eyebrows. "Believe it or not, I exercise every day, but I guess riding a camel challenges those parts of your body you forget about." He bent his knees and squatted twice.

"Ah, you can tell. Some people stumble around after their ride. Emma seems to like you. Pet her."

"You sure?"

"Yes, yes. I know Emma well and look at her. Calm and content. Just approach her and let her sniff your hand."

Alex glanced at the camel. Emma blinked her long black eyelashes at him.

He stepped closer. "Hey there, Emma." Raising his arm, he placed the back of his hand under the animal's moist nose, and she gurgled and sniffed.

"See." Omar clapped. "She has lowered her head. So go ahead."

Alex brushed his fingers across the side of her head and cooed. "Emma. Thank you for the amazing ride. Maybe someday, I'll come back with…"

Golden tresses curled their way into his mind. He shook his head hard, as if swatting the image away.

Omar cocked his head. "Did Emma spit at you?"

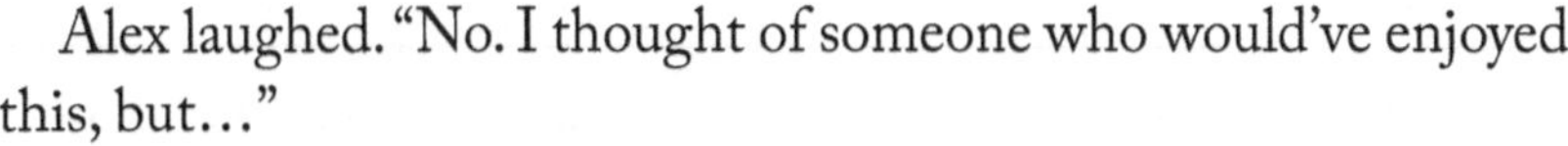

Alex laughed. "No. I thought of someone who would've enjoyed this, but…"

"Ah. A special lady?" Omar wiggled his eyebrows.

"Was."

"Will be again?"

"Not sure about that. We'll see."

Omar smirked. "She still occupies your thoughts."

"That obvious, huh?"

"If she becomes special again, you can bring her back for the camel beauty contest. I'm thinking of entering Emma."

"Whaaat?" Alex leaned back and jutted his chin.

"Yes. All over the Middle East, but…" Omar raised his index. "I will never subject Emma to cosmetic enhancements."

Alex's eyes widened. "Are you kidding?"

"No. I am not." Omar's words sculpted into sharp edges. "A few years ago, the Saudis booted forty camels from their pageant after their owners gave them Botox and other things, such as hormones, even elastic bands. The biggest crackdown in Saudi Arabia's contest history. Can you imagine?"

"Animal abuse." Alex knitted his eyebrows together and shook his head hard.

"Yes," Omar growled. "To do that to the voiceless. Never, ever, would I subject my babies to such cruelty."

"As an animal lover, I share your anger one hundred percent, but even if you're not crazy about animals, how can you support this kind of thing? Please tell me they didn't escape consequences for their actions."

"Banishment from future contests and…" Omar rubbed his thumb against his fingers. "Large fines."

"Good."

"Yes, the least they can do."

"What a story." Swirls of golden locks breezed around his mind.

Storyteller, I have one for you, if we see each other again and that's a big if.

Later that day, after a mid-afternoon, six-course lunch, Alex padded into his suite, tore off his sandy clothes, and soaked in the Jacuzzi for fifteen minutes. Delphina's face danced around him. Yes, he longed to view the next video, yet his unyielding self-control forced him to wait.

With some relief to his sore body, he entered the wet room, a doorless shower. Before twisting one faucet, Alex's gaze moved from top to bottom. A Herringbone tiled ceiling, a bench, brass fixtures, and a limestone floor.

Man. The Emiratis know how to court people.

He glided his index finger across the various settings. Ambient lighting, music, and various aromas. Regular, rain, or steam shower. The Hermes line promenaded across the oasis from shampoo to soap.

Her voice seeped into his mind.

Let me be, for the moment, Storyteller.

For the next twenty minutes, Alex drenched himself in luxury, grabbing a brush and pressing the bristles into his skin, as he scrubbed away the grime and sweat.

Tingling from the cleansed polish overtaking his frame, he inhaled the delicious eucalyptus aroma and switched the fixture to a cascading waterfall flowing over his body.

"Umm."

A golden figure swirled in his head.

Soon, Delphina. Soon.

After dressing in a light green polo shirt and tan khaki shorts, Alex padded over to the sitting area of his suite. His gaze circled the room, and he whistled again. The light from the late afternoon heightened the peach and gold colors, an enticing parfait. Another reminder of Delphina.

He plopped on the amethyst couch, brought his iPad to his lap, and extended his legs onto the ottoman. Rubbing his chin, he stared at the screen and jiggled his fingers for a moment. A jolt of anxiety shot through his chest, stinging his heart.

Calm down, pal. The worst has already happened. You've got this. Do what you always do.

Alex took a deep breath, rolled his head around, and rotated his shoulders. A moment later, the routine calmed his nerves, and he tapped on the red and white Gmail icon. As he scrolled through the emails, his finger halted at the familiar address with the large attachment. He stroked his chin again and clicked on the video.

Delphina sat with head high, hands lying beneath her chin, and flowing curls dangled from a loose bun.

Her background featured a colossal statue of a winged angel with a sword.

Tilting her head, Delphina's lips painted a smile. "Hello, Alex." She fluttered her eyelashes and swirled a curl as if waiting for a hello back.

Wow. Just seeing her image created an exhilarating spin for Alex. Anxiety wiped away, replaced by yearning.

Hold on, buddy. Let's see what she presents this time.

Delphina crossed her arms on the desk and glanced over her shoulder before turning her head back to the screen.

"Do you know who that sculpture represents, Alex?"

Stillness captured the moment as if she waited for his response.

"St. Michael, the Archangel, Delphina?"

"If you answered, St. Michael, you are correct."

She nodded. "I'm going to share with you about an event that occurred in January 2023. And as you can see, I'm doing it without trying to imitate another because this will be my last video."

Alex touched his chin again. Okay, Delphina.

"Last year, a thirty-two-year-old intoxicated man, Carlos Alonso, tried to rob a church in Monterrey, Mexico late at night. Jumping over a fence, he broke a glass door and stepped into the church."

She inhaled, pursed her lips, and narrowed her eyes. "And do you know what he took, Alexander? The statue of St. Michael."

She shook her head, and a handful of curls fell from the twisted tresses on top.

"But…" Delphina's index finger shot up, and she beamed, as a bronze blush crept along her cheeks, "as he tried to escape, Mr. Alonso tripped and fell on the mighty angel's sword."

The edge of Delphina's hand slashed across the side of her neck. "Yes, a serious lance near the jugular. He could've died, but God decided against it because someone saw him and called an ambulance. And thank God, no harm came to the statue."

Her eyes widened, and a mischievous grin darted across her face. "I imagine divine intervention may have played a role in the whole matter. Miracles happen, including…" a slow fade captured her lustrous smile, paling, and washing it away, "forgiveness and second chances."

Another hush breezed around Delphina, and her eyes filled. Plucking a tissue, she dabbed at the droplets sprinkling across her face.

Alex winced, and the remaining splinters in his heart throbbed.

Because of me, you, or us, Delphina?

A sniffle, a click, and St Michael's statue changed. Twisting her neck, Delphina raised her hands, with palms shifting toward the video behind her.

Folding his arms, Alex almost tipped over the iPad as he chuckled at the scene of a mother elephant and her calves displayed.

Yup. Even though I've become intrigued by camels, dogs and elephants tie for number one.

Delphina dipped her eyes and slanted her face. "Yes, Alexander, one of our favorites, the majestic animal we both love."

In a slow, deliberate motion, she lifted her head, and her eyes captivated him. "Alexander, we understand that these gentle giants have a high level of intelligence and strong attachments. And, as we've discussed…" her voice broke, and Alex's heart ached, "they can die from a-a broken—"

Trembling, she placed both hands over her heart. "He…" A muffled sound. "H-heart."

Tears rolled down her cheeks, and with each blink, a heavier flow. "So, Alexander, I expose my heart and soul to you, and this will be my last message."

Her eyes pierced the screen, grabbing his again, not saying another word for several seconds. Alex felt suffocated by the breathless silence.

"I know I made a terrible mistake, and you have every right not to respond to me." She curled her hand back, gesturing to the video. "But like our glorious friends, my heart will remain broken if you can't forgive me."

Her palms flattened toward the screen. "I'll survive. As you know, I've already endured trauma and betrayal, but this time—"

With hands knitted together, she shook her head. "This time, I'm responsible and must bear the consequences. So my dear Alexander, I bid you goodbye, and if I don't hear from you, Merry Christmas, and Happy New Year."

She blew a kiss, hugged herself, and flung her arms out. "To you."

The video halted.

Staring at the frozen image on his iPad for a moment, Alex rolled his fingers into a fist and tapped his mouth before closing the cover. He stood, sauntered to the window, and gazed at the late-afternoon sea.

A gentle melody of ebb and flow, soothing waves, invited dusk's arrival, as a drowsy sun yawned and drifted off to sleep.

Alex brought his hand toward his chin but released it before grazing his skin.

Time to let go of old habits, pal. That brief but hideous chapter ended long ago with a scribbled, "Finished Forever."

The corners of his mouth inched upward.

Delphina. You can't get her out of your mind. Right?

He sighed and glanced at his watch.

Time to dress for dinner. He trudged over to the armoire, carved with inlaid panels of Arabesque patterns.

Delphina, you've jumbled my thoughts and scattered them everywhere.

What do I need to do?

He shook his head, opened the doors, and rustled through his dress shirts.

Okay. You know the answer. But it will have to wait. Remember what you tell others. Focus, man, focus because the next few weeks will contain mounds of work—a good thing right now.

"My lovely son, I cannot wait to wrap my arms around you."

"Hey, Mom, in a few hours you will." Alex grinned during a FaceTime with his mother, Julia.

A youthful sixty with bobbed blonde hair, Julia sighed and crossed her palms over her heart. "The best Christmas present for me is having all three of my boys with me." She nodded. "And that includes your dad, who," she smirked, "acts like one of you while watching sports." She turned her head from side to side. "Shh. Don't tell him I said that."

Alex chuckled, raising his three fingers. "I'll quote my friend, Bart. Scout's honor."

His mother tipped her head back with a lilted laugh.

"Even though, Mom, I suspect dad knows."

She placed a palm on top of her other, leaned forward, and winked. "Yes, but we don't have to speak of it."

Alex smiled and then swiveled his body behind him. Folded clothes lay on top of the bed. "Got it, Mom, but if you want me to catch my flight, I need to get going."

"Hurry. Another Christmas in Paris." She blew him a kiss and signed off.

Paris at Christmas. Almost every year, they returned. Once, toward the end of the relationship, before he had enough, he invited Daphne.

What a performance! Kindness, generosity, and thoughtfulness on full display. As everyone raved about her to him, he wondered if he was wrong. But thank God, when they returned home, her usual behavior chipped away at his doubts.

Alex shook his head.

Last year, he and his family had an even better time, and it helped block out the residual.

What a blast!

He, his brother, and Dad joked around, ribbing their mother as the only woman. When it became too much and she said, "Okay, enough," they'd hug her, cooing her attributes and tolerance for her *boys*.

"Yes, all three of you."

His father winced and then embraced her. "Mother, my success started with my parents but sped up under you." He'd pluck a big smooch on her cheek. "Right boys?"

"Hear, hear."

As Alex folded his clothes and laid them into the suitcase, he imagined a carpet ride to Christmases Past in Paris.

Magical.

Lights twinkling everywhere as Paris attired itself in dazzle. No wonder it maintained its worthy title of the City of Light.

Staying in the Seventeenth Arrondissement made it easy to walk to so many sites.

The shops, restaurants, and other businesses lined the streets with extra sparkle, embellishing them for seasonal cheer.

Arriving two days before Christmas Eve, they'd stroll along Champs-Élysées, the most visited avenue in Paris. At Christmas, a glittering paradise. Each of its several hundred trees was lit right up to the Arc de Triomphe.

Along the way, the four of them would stop.

Beautiful reruns unfolded.

His mother would bring a hand to her mouth. "Oh my, I feel like I'm about to enter Cinderella's castle. You cannot describe this spectacle in words."

As they gazed at the majesty, his dad videoed them.

And he'd shift the iPhone camera to photos, snapping pics of him, Nick, and his mother.

Next, his mom took the phone from his dad and did the same.

With the final repeat, his father asked someone nearby to take a few photos of the four of them.

Then his dad would switch it to video.

While the accommodating stranger streamed, he and Nick would extend their arms, splay their fingers, and exaggerate a wide smile for a moment before linking in an embrace with their parents.

Another night, after a delicious dinner of French cuisine, they'd trudge closer to the lighted Eiffel Tower.

And on Christmas Eve, they'd attend Midnight Mass at Sacre Coeur in Montmartre.

Walking up the hill to the famous Basilica, Alex and his family commented on its beauty. The night sky, a velvet backdrop, provided the looming white domes with center stage. Before entering, Alex and his family would turn toward the panorama of Paris. A flickering rendezvous as it linked hands with the stars.

Once they entered the holy realm, Alex's gaze toured the interior. The stained-glass windows and the apse and golden mosaics filled Alex's soul with awe and an elevated respect for the divine. As the melodic Christmas hymns soared to the heavens, the glorious harmony enhanced his spiritual contemplation to greater depths.

Alex blinked and closed the book to Christmases Past.

Tonight? Another Christmas Paris, combined with elements of the past and a unique story of its own.

He glanced at his watch. Plenty of time, but why not get to the airport early?

Plodding to his dresser, he unzipped the garment bag and hung up his five suits. He unhooked it, laid it on the bed, and walked over to the drawers, opening and closing to ensure he packed everything.

Garbed in Dolce and Gabbana, black attire from jeans to cotton T-shirt, Alex sat on his bed and laced his Belvédère Chapo Hornback shoes. Jumping up, he grabbed his charcoal blazer. Fifteen more minutes before the butler, Abdul, would tap his door, enter with the bellman, and ensure that Alex had everything he needed for a safe journey from the hotel.

Scanning the room, he nodded.

Couldn't be more perfect except…

Don't go there.

Tresses breezed around like a swirling gust of golden leaves.

Alex grimaced, rubbed his face with his palms, and as he dropped his hands, he blinked.

The wind of long curls swished more.

Do I have to go put cold water on my face to banish you, Delphina?

Ping, ping.

Alex pulled out his iPhone from his blazer.

A text from his brother.

`Cool things happening soon.`

Alex thumbed a quick message back.

`Yeah. Looking forward to seeing everyone.`

About to place his phone back in the inside pocket, an email from Delphina sailed by his screen.

Oh, no. Alex tipped his head back, before returning his eyes to his device. The email blared across the screen, and he shook his head.

You think I can't resist you, huh?

For several seconds, Alex stroked his chin and stared at the email.

He tilted his head and gripped the phone, gaping at the bold subject line.

It teased him, cajoling him to open it.

Come on. I'm irresistible.

Okay, Storyteller for now, you win.

He clicked on the icon, and Delphina's email appeared in full, with the subject line stating, "A Merry Christmas Surprise."

Ugh.

He tightened his lips. Might as well get comfortable for the show.

Alex untied his shoes, kicked them to the side, and strode over to the high-back, cobalt-colored chair. He collapsed in the seat, tucked the rolled throw pillow behind his lower back, and rested his feet on the ottoman.

His hand hovered over the email before it wandered back to his chin, nestling in the webbing between thumb and index finger.

He rested the iPhone on his lap and thumbed his other hand on the rolled arm of the chair.

You're already whirling around my mind, and now you want to add to it.

Okay, Storyteller, what now?

Alex picked up the phone, clicked on the email, and pressed the video attachment.

Delphina appeared with the background of a European city. Florence?

With palms stacked on top of one another, Delphina, dressed in a fitted black, long-sleeved, high-buttoned dress, with coils cascading around her like strands of golden yarn, flashed a smile.

Waving, Delphina's voice sparked with energy. "Hello, Alexander. I changed my mind." A smile glittered across her face. "This really will be my last video. But I thought, Christmas is upon us, and I didn't hear from you, so I hope you at least consider my message, as a—a gift." With a lilted laugh, she twisted her neck and whisked her arm toward the image looming behind her.

Alex scanned the stone building. Italian Renaissance architecture, elegant and understated. The façade displayed enchanting windows decorated with grand cornices and artistic balconies.

A ruffle from her sleeve swayed in front of him. "Florence, which you may have guessed." Delphina rotated back to the screen and pitched forward.

She fluttered her eyes for a moment before they glimmered with moisture.

"You might ask why I chose Florence."

Delphina paused, as if waiting for him to respond.

Alex shut his eyes for a moment and shook his head.

Here we go again.

When he opened them, he stopped the video, grabbed a nearby book, planted it on the ottoman, and leaned the iPhone against it.

Sloping forward with elbows on his knees, Alexander breathed in the image, frozen in time.

Scheherazade, are you going to seduce me with another of your unusual stories?

A raspberry sputtered from his voice.

Stupid question.

His eyes shifted to his watch.

Okay. Time to unfreeze the golden statue and keep this show rolling.

Like a bungee cord, his index finger pressed the start button and sprang back, while he reclined inch by inch, as if moving through molasses.

Delphina laced her fingers, and the ruffles drooped along her wrists.

"This is the Palazzo Guidi in the center of Florence, now a celebrated landmark." Delphina lifted her hand, the ruffle rippling with her movement.

Sweeping her arm down her dress, she bent her head and raised her hands. "Which is the reason I'm wearing this dress." Her head popped back up, with her hands returned to a resting position on top of one another.

Alex raised his eyebrows. Unable to contain the foamy sensation brewing within him, the corners of his lips tugged up.

He nodded. Never saw you in such plain clothes, but it doesn't mar your beauty, Storyteller.

Delphina cocked her head. "I assume you know little, if anything, about the Palazzo Guidi."

Alex slumped in his seat.

No idea.

"Just in case you don't, the Palazzo Guidi became home to Elizabeth Barrett and Robert Browning. Sound familiar?"

Alex slanted his head back and forth.

English literature?

Delphina raised her index finger, and the ruffle flapped downward. "They were poets who fell in love and married in secret because her father opposed it."

"And?" Alex said aloud.

"When he found out," Delphina pursed her lips, "he disinherited his daughter." She shook her head. "Can you imagine?"

Alex lifted his palms.

I can't, but I'm not sure I care.

"You must wonder why I'm sharing this with you."

Alex furrowed his brow, letting one side of his mouth curl up.

I am, but based on your past videos, I'm sure you'll reveal.

Delphina cocked her head, and her eyes twinkled. "As they say, 'Good things come to those who wait,' but I want to tell you about the Palazzo, which I'd like to visit someday with—" Her eyes descended, and she paused for a moment.

Alex's brows knitted together.

Delphina's gaze climbed back to the screen. A shimmery glaze coated her eyes, accentuating the gold threading through them.

A sliver punctured his heart, spilling a drop of sorrow, and Alex's eyes pooled.

He pressed pause again, wiped his eyes with the back of his hand, then laced his fingers behind his head.

For several seconds, his gaze became unfocused.

Then he bounced up, clutched the phone, and paced back and forth.

Move, pal. It will help.

All right, Delphina. Let's get to the heart of the story.

Alex tapped the icon and started where he left off.

Delphina sniffled and fluttered her eyelashes. "The poets eloped." A smile peeked from her face like the sun winking through gray clouds. "And Elizabeth's cocker spaniel, Flush, went with them."

Trotting backwards to get in his reverse steps for the day, Alex

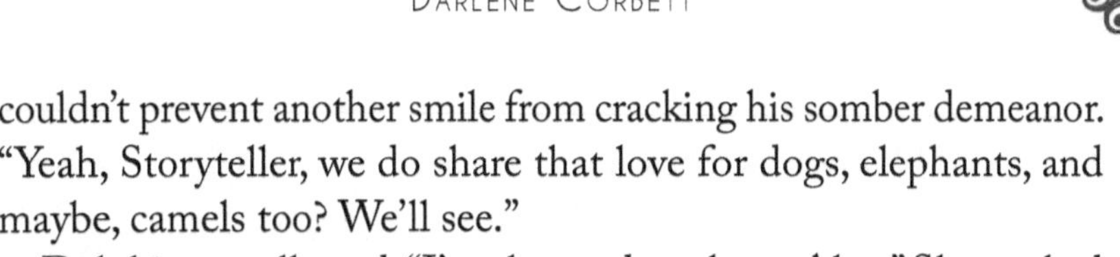

couldn't prevent another smile from cracking his somber demeanor. "Yeah, Storyteller, we do share that love for dogs, elephants, and maybe, camels too? We'll see."

Delphina swallowed. "I'm almost done here, Alex." She cocked her head, and a touch of mischief caressed her lips. "They stayed in Pisa before moving to the Palazzo. Their only child, Robert, nicknamed Pen, became their other love." She wrung her hands, and her smile faded. "Elizabeth died at age 56 in Robert's arms. He became bereft and couldn't bear to live there without his wife, so he took his son and left their Florence home. Years later, Pen purchased the Palazzo from the Guidi family and converted it into a museum, which people visit to this day."

A slow smile blossomed across Delphina's face like spreading petals awakened by the morning sun. "What's most important, Alexander, is that they loved each other." Her head dipped back, and she placed her hands over her heart.

Alex nodded, and a rush of sadness flowed through his body.

He paused the video, and his pace hastened as if someone raised a lever, pushing his body on a speed dial.

You know Delphina. It didn't have to go this way…

He meandered to the high-back chair and sank into it, and his hand found its way to his chin, stroking the old wound.

A wagging finger, hinting at forgiveness, popped into his mind.

I know. But can you blame me for hesitating?

Alex dropped his hand and studied the frozen screen.

Man, she better change the expression.

As he pressed the start button, Delphina arranged her hands into a prayer position. "Alex, I tell you this because Robert created a poem for her about love later in life, but I think it's pertinent to any time."

Delphina lips scrolled into a sparkling smile. "My dearest Alexander, I'm sending you a most glorious sentiment, and along with the other stories, I want this one to lodge deep into your soul. So please ready yourself." She waited a moment.

Alexander gulped as he pounded his chest, trying to halt the black and blue marks bruising his heart.

Delphina lifted her palms. "Grow old along with me. The best is yet to be. The last of life for which the first is made."

Tenderness glossed her eyes, and tears trickled down her cheeks like a gentle rain shower.

"Merry Christmas, Alexander." She blew him a kiss, and the video ended.

Alex gazed at the screen, pushing back tears with a cement shield.

He jumped up and grimaced.

Focus, pal, on getting out of here.

Grabbing his blazer, he slipped his iPhone into the inside pocket, sat back on the bed, and put his shoes on, lacing them tighter as he grit his teeth.

Standing up, his eyes promenaded around the opulent suite, with royal colors everywhere from oriental rugs, bed, chairs, sofa, and curtains.

Goodbye, Dubai. Maybe I'll return with someone. Or maybe not.

But for now? Paris, family, and Christmas.

Knock, knock.

"Coming, Abdul."

Chapter Twenty-Two

Delphina

Before every annual performance, Delphina opened her computer, moved the cursor, pressed the link to LisaMing.com. Clicking on the About tab, she leaned forward and re-read the genesis of *Heavenly Bodies*.

Elegant, sparkly font, highlighting the dedication to God and her parents, invited her to gobble the riveting tale written by Lisa.

Delphina bobbed her head, a smile frolicking across her face. Lisa, you're a natural storyteller, from website to stage.

The Beginning

In 2018, Lisa Ming's mother, Amy, had an idea.

When she approached her husband, Gordon, she expected him to remove his glasses, scoff, and stomp away with a one-word response: "preposterous."

But he didn't. Gordon lifted his eyebrows, cocked his head back and forth, and said, "Hmm." Stroking his chin, he sat in his favorite chair, a suede recliner, in front of the warm blaze he just stoked in their white brick fireplace. He sipped on his dry martini and curled his hand. "Tell me more."

"Our daughter discovered her faith again and wants to incorporate it into her work, but she needs our help. Here's what I think we should do."

Her mellifluous voice became more excited, and the words unfurled like a singer's notes reaching their highest peaks.

271

Her husband smiled. "Yes, my melodious wife. I like your plan."

Amy clapped, and her eyes filled. "Oh, Husband, I'm so pleased."

"Why would you think I'd see it differently?"

"Well, it's a financial risk."

"Wife, we've worked hard, and our financial success will not take a hit, even if this scheme of yours," he winked, "fails, but knowing Lisa, it won't. Her work ethic supersedes our sons'. Look at her schooling and her dance performance."

Amy nodded.

"We need to do this for her. If she believes God has beckoned her for something more, then we need to honor that."

"Yes, Husband. She's been so resistant to anything God-related, that I thought she was becoming a version of the younger, atheistic you."

"Wife, maybe she'll return to the teachings that converted me long ago, with your help, of course."

The next day, over FaceTime, Amy repeated every detail of her conversation with Gordon to her 21-year-old daughter. Lisa, training in the classical Chinese techniques, stared back at her mother with a gaping mouth.

Amy cocked her head. "Daughter?"

Lisa stood up and shook her fists like joyful maracas. "Tomorrow, I'll give my notice, pack my things, and fly back to Boston."

Two weeks later, she flew home and spent the next several weeks developing her plans. Soon, she scouted for talented dancers, lighting and sound technicians, and other stage assistants. Eighteen months later, Heavenly Souls debuted in Boston, and within a year, they traveled to other parts of the country.

Although her collaboration didn't reach the grand scale of her mentor's organization, its grandeur exceeded anything Lisa imagined.

I invite you to come see for yourself. And you'll learn more about the magical inspiration that came to me in a dream.

Delphina pitched back in her seat, closed her eyes, and brought

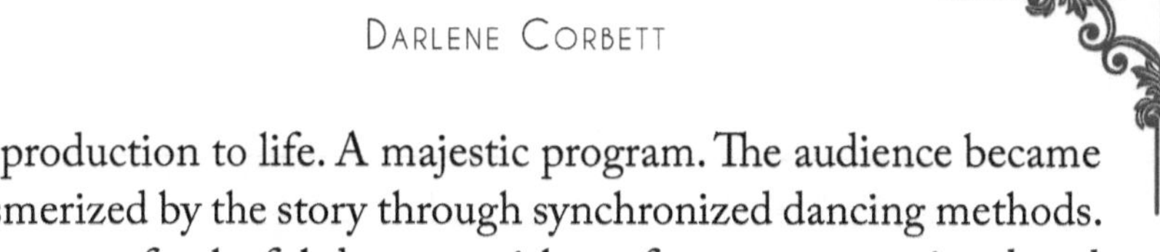

the production to life. A majestic program. The audience became mesmerized by the story through synchronized dancing methods.

Scenes of colorful dancers with perfect posture, twisted and turned their bodies, flipped with feet almost above the floor.

Oohs and *ahhs* echoed through the theater whenever a dancer surprised them with an extraordinary feat.

At the end of each performance, the crowd jumped up, clapped vigorously, and roared with a standing ovation. As Lisa sauntered out and waved, "Brava, brava," would echo through the chamber.

"Thank you. Thank you. And…" her gaze moved upward, blowing a kiss, "thank you."

Now, sitting next to her mother, Delphina immersed herself in the exquisite production.

Although turmoil ripped through her soul this year, she couldn't halt the thrill of the extravaganza from offering a temporary panacea.

Donned in shimmery garments, dancers swept their arms and spun around with elegant precision; water angels flowing and creating a luscious piece of art.

Her mother whispered in her ear. "Beautiful as usual, my love. I'm so glad Auntie gifted us with this again."

Delphina nodded. "Lisa's extravaganza exceeds beyond the imagination every year."

"Yes. Her creativity doesn't cease to amaze me, and she doesn't shy away from faith-based themes.

Since the birth of Lisa's creation and without interruption, Delphina's aunt gifted them tickets for Christmas.

The minute they became available, her Aunt Lydia purchased them. And two days later, she sent a bouquet of pastels wrapped around a unique card, displaying "Save The Date" in splendid *Scriptina* font.

During intermission, Lucia twisted and grabbed her coat from under her. "Delphina, help me with this."

"Why? Are you going somewhere?" Delphina took the left sleeve and looped her mother's arm through it. As Lucia tugged at it, she pulled her black leather gloves from her purse.

"Of course not. I'm just cold, aren't you?"

"No. The temperature feels right to me, but you're that cold?" She jutted her chin at the gloves.

"Listen. I'm older, and the chilliness creeps into my fingers more often. Remember your Sito's and my aunt's hands? They developed osteoarthritis in their fifties. Like this." Lucia pressed her left index finger further left.

"Well, it doesn't look like your hands have changed, but whatever."

Lucia jumped out of her seat.

"I'll be right back. Stay here and watch our bags."

Before Delphina uttered, "Okay," her mother trotted up the aisle, leaving her alone. As she waited, voices from the audience buzzed like bees around a hive. Her eyes met the beautiful booklet in front of her. Gliding her fingers along the satiny teal cover, she skimmed to the page that provided information about the next part of the program.

No. I'm not looking at my phone.

But her mind strayed from the page, prompting her to journey back to the last two weeks.

No word from Alexander.

Her nerves shredded like cheese on a grater.

She tried to avoid her mother, but Lucia would have none of it.

"My daughter. You don't know."

"Mama, I sent him heartfelt, and I mean *heartfelt*, videos that took me hours to develop."

"Yes, but…"

"No. Please don't but me—"

Lucia's smile crumbled, her lips shriveling like a scrunched piece of paper.

"Okay, Mama. I get it. You want me to remain optimistic, but the

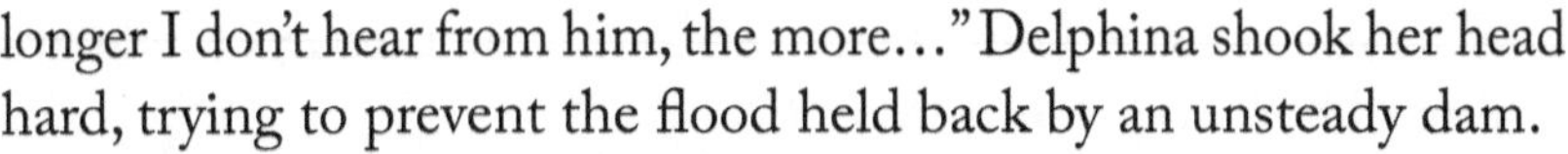

longer I don't hear from him, the more…" Delphina shook her head hard, trying to prevent the flood held back by an unsteady dam.

Lucia wrapped her arms around Delphina. "My daughter, be hopeful, as you tell your clients to write in their fresh stories."

Delphina nodded and breathed in her mother's signature aroma.

Stepping away from her, Lucia's six bangles clinked as she squeezed Delphina's shoulders. Her eyes glittered, and the corners of her mouth curved upward. "Now, my beautiful daughter, since we both have time off, we're going to have fun for the next couple weeks."

And a few days later, it began.

Every afternoon and evening, Lucia planned an event.

Sometimes Aunt Lydia joined them. Dinners at local restaurants. Visits to neighborhoods where glittering lights and icicles swathed the neighborhoods, creating a pearly enchantment.

One night, Lucia dragged Delphina to a Boston Grizzlies game. Lucia, an avid hockey fan, got seats in the Luxury Box from an online company with whom she advertised her services.

Delphina, less interested in hockey, sat inside, munching on chicken wings, ready to move on to the skewers of tenderloin and shrimp.

Chewing on a piece of salmon and hunkered next to her, Lucia said, "Isn't this fun?"

Delphina tilted her head back and forth. "I guess, but you know me. I prefer baseball."

"Yes, and I understand, but for me, baseball is too slow." Lucia wiggled her eyebrows and touched Delphina's knee. "Besides a certain handsome gentleman shares my passion."

About to respond, Delphina halted as cheering escaped from around the outer arena.

A man waved to the people inside the suite. "Come on. Fight. Let's check it out."

Everyone scurried out except for Delphina. Lucia peeked back inside. "Don't you want to watch?"

"Uh-uh. Some things haven't changed in five thousand years, and tonight I'm not in the mood to see bare-knuckle brawling."

Lucia jounced her head, raised her hands, and left.

Alex, also a lover of hockey, sparred with her about these testosterone-driven elites.

She leaned back and nibbled on a piece of shrimp.

A thirty-something-year-old man sauntered inside, picked up a plate, and added a skewer.

Tall, bald, and handsome, he smirked. "I'm full, but before I leave, will have one more."

Nibbling on her food, Delphina bobbed her head. "Yes. Delicious."

"Not interested in the fight?"

"No."

"Um, here alone?"

"No."

The man chuckled. "You're a woman of few words."

Delphina's lips kicked up. "I'm here with my mother."

As he stood, he tipped his head back, chewing on his skewer. Taking a napkin, he wiped his mouth. "Where's your boyfriend?"

She blinked. "He's in Dubai for work."

Screeching trickled into the suite.

"Yeahhhhhhhh!"

The man took another napkin, toweled his hands, and pulled out a card. "Well, pretty lady, before I leave, please take this if you and your lucky man become unattached."

His fingers touched hers, placing the business card in her hand. A bold, black, raised font splayed out. Sturdy like him.

Delphina's lips curved into a larger smile. "Pleased to meet you, Asher."

Nodding, he lowered his eyelids. "Please to meet you, um…"

A laugh crept out of her mouth. "Delphina."

"A beautiful name for a beautiful woman."

"You're most kind."

"Just expressing the truth." He pivoted and strolled out of the suite.

She stared at the card and sighed.

Asher Flaherty, CEO, Jupitina.

Not in the cards, Mr. Flaherty. Another place and time unless…

Oooh, wait. Hold on to it for Josie?

Alexander intruded into her thoughts, nodding.

Go away Alexander until I hear from you in real life. She coiled one of her curls to vanquish him from her mind.

Further eruptions from the fans made her refocus.

Her mother peeked her head inside. "Delphina, you're missing the fun…"

"Mama, tonight, not my thing."

Lucia blew a kiss. "Soon, more to come, but for now…" She whooped and went back out to the open arena.

And Lucia kept her word.

On another night, Delphina, dressed in a long-sleeved, fitted, red velvet dress with Stuart Weitzman heels, and her mother, wearing a white silk dress and jacket, joined their aunt at Symphony Hall for their Christmas program.

Sitting at one table in the Orchestra section, Delphina's heart jangled as the Boston Pops performed the traditional songs.

For a moment, Alex skidded into her thoughts, but her mother's fingers entwined with hers, which halted the ocean-eyed gentleman from invading her concentration.

"Delphina, your favorite."

And she became enraptured by the enticing song, "Twas the Night Before Christmas," bouncing and swaying as if she rode a sleigh.

Delphina understood her mother's motives. And could read her mind.

Draw a heavy magic marker line across her thoughts about Alexander. Involve her in as many activities as possible during the holiday season.

For most of the time, it worked. And following Mass on Christmas morning, Delphina joined her mother and Aunt Lydia for a trip to a mysterious destination, a gift from Lucia.

Riding along the Massachusetts Turnpike and heading west, Delphina sat in the backseat. Glancing at the snowy banks along the highway, a video of Alex streamed through her mind.

Lucia twirled her hand, and bangles clanged against each other, forcing Delphina to pause the reel.

"Let's celebrate Christmas." Lucia pressed the button on her radio, blaring familiar tunes.

"Not in the mood, Mama."

Her aunt, fifteen months older than her mother, turned around, and grabbed Delphina's hand. "Come on, Darling. Please."

Swinging Delphina's hand, her Aunt Lydia bobbed her head and sang.

"Okay, okay." Delphina smirked, snapped her fingers and shifted her body right to left.

Her uneven, high voice, mixed with her aunt's and mother's lower pitches, caused Delphina's bubbling laughter to pop and infect her mother and aunt.

As the car slowed down and exited the Mass. Pike, Delphina's insides rippled with excitement.

"Mama, you didn't."

"I did." Lucia glanced at her in the rearview mirror, and her aunt, who looked more like her mother's twin, winked at her.

"You conspirators, you." Delphina shook her head but allowed a smile to paint her face.

Passing through one of the small towns speckled along the mountainous region, Delphina's tension peeled away, replaced by a froth bathing her nerves.

An independent bookstore, gift shops, and an antique emporium framed by ice chunks shimmered like crystals performing with the sun.

Her eyes climbed the backdrop of the Berkshires, and she

grinned. "Oh my God. A glorious part of the Northeast that people often forget about."

"Yes. Look at the mountains." Lydia said.

Commanding and haughty, they hugged the surrounding area of western Massachusetts. Delphina imagined them waving hurry, causing a giggle to ricochet around her soul.

She rolled down the window, stretched her neck, and breathed in the crisp mountain air. A few snowflakes sprinkled the bridge of her nose, their coolness melting and tucking into her skin's warmth.

Lucia squealed. "Almost there."

Canyon Ranch. A hidden jewel.

A place for restoration and pampering. Wrapped in anonymity, the glitterati flocked to this Emerald City, where they indulged without recognition.

On Delphina's twenty-fourth birthday, she untied a teal bow, tore the silvery paper, and lifted the cover of a gold-colored box with a gasp.

Laying along a periwinkle velvet cushion, rested a card written in a *Hopeless* script. It stated: The Gift of Canyon Ranch. Her hand glided over the embossed calligraphy. Another present from her aunt, who penned the note with a swirl of sugary love and sprinkles of affection.

Delphina sniffed and brought the card close to her nose, inhaling the sprite aroma of eucalyptus.

Now, for the second time, Delphina joined her mother and aunt in a whirlwind of self-care. For three days, she immersed herself in educational classes, massages, and other wellness treatments.

The only blemish?

Lucia's determination to prevent her from any solitary interludes.

In the guest suite or the locker room, Lucia's sweet voice swirled around the room like a flowery fragrance. "Hi Delphina, ready for the next appointment?"

Delphina's body sagged for a moment.

She's beyond suffocating.

"Yesss, Mama. I'm all set."

"Just want to make sure."

Delphina escaped from her mother while having wellness treatments.

During a hot stone massage, Delphina closed her eyes as the therapist kneaded her back before placing smooth stones along her spine. Delphina sighed and forced words to flutter from her mouth. "So good."

Her skin and muscles tingled from the warmth permeating every inch of her body.

The sound of waves played in the background, inviting a pair of sea-color eyes to emerge.

Alex.

Delphina scrunched her eyelids.

But she couldn't banish him. His eyes grew more dominant, captivating her with long lashes and a dazzling display of shifting ocean shades.

The same thing happened while receiving the Hungarian scrub.

Not while the attendants exfoliated her body and not when they applied sea salt mixture, coating her with a healing cornucopia.

But once they brushed her with the oil, a radiance cocooned her, and a kiss from that lopsided smile threaded through her thoughts like a delicate silver filament.

She puckered her lips and mumbled, "Alex."

Those indulging experiences not only fortified her but provided time for herself and her yearnings.

By the end of the spa experience, the salve around Delphina's heart and soul shielded her from the claws of negativity.

Earlier today, the three of them departed from Canyon Ranch. Delphina's aunt drove so she and her mother could nap and freshen up for the evening. After arriving home, they hugged goodbye to Lydia, who lived in a condo down the street from her mother's. Eating a light dinner, they changed into the attire they had chosen before departing for the Spa.

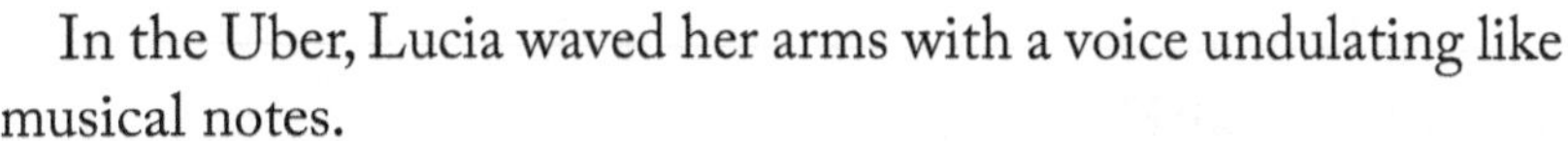

In the Uber, Lucia waved her arms with a voice undulating like musical notes.

Now sitting alone during the intermission, Delphina returned to the episode.

Her mother, the original storyteller, would relieve her, regaling others with stories, but tonight?

No. She wanted Delphina to entertain.

Something went beyond her typical modus operandi.

Did Mama think her daughter wouldn't notice?

It started in the Uber. Lucia pulled off her gloves, clapped her hands, and grabbed Delphina's wrists. "My darling daughter, to prepare for tonight, tell me the story of Lisa's inspiration."

Delphina smirked. "Okay, Mama, as usual, I'm giving my unique spin after reading her story fifty-million times, so if I forget anything, please jump in."

"Oh, I will, but you never miss a part when you tell the tale."

"Okay."

Lucia turned her head toward the driver. "Joaquin, am I pronouncing your name the right way?"

Delphina saw the man's eyes stare back through the rear-view mirror.

"Yes, Ma'am."

A squeak emitted from Lucia's seat as she bounced. "Well, Joaquin, you might enjoy this story, too, so listen."

Joaquin nodded. "Sure thing, Ma'am."

Delphina shook her head with a pluck of the lips. "Joaquin, please listen, but if you don't want to, no problem."

"I like stories. I hear many stories as I drive my customers to their destinations."

Lucia fluttered her eyelashes as her forehead almost touched Delphina's. "Everybody ready?"

Joaquin chortled, and Delphina raised her eyebrows, catching the depths of her mother's olivine eyes flecked with yellow. "Mama, who's everybody?"

Lucia's voice bubbled with froth, and she curled her hand with a swish. "You know what I mean."

"I know." Delphina blinked, and another smile bloomed across her face. "I'm just teasing you because, I don't know… you're beyond exuberant tonight."

Lucia bolted upward without releasing Delphina's wrists. "What do you mean? I'm being my authentic, excited self."

Delphina nodded.

"If you say so. I mean, you're always you, but it seems like, well, I don't know, embellished."

Lucia shifted in her seat again and lowered her eyes for a moment. "Ridiculous. When am I not elated about attending *Heavenly Souls?* Anyway, please begin."

No point arguing with her. "All right, even though it's written in the program, I'll do my best to add some dramatic effects, so here goes."

"In 2018, Lisa Ming, a professional dancer with a large organization celebrating traditional Chinese culture, experienced an epiphany, prompted by a recurring dream."

With eyes clasping Delphina's, Lucia bobbed her head up and down.

Delphina softened her tone so it rippled like silk. "Lisa's talent and diligence propelled her to splendid success as a principal dancer, one of the youngest in the troupe. But something troubled her. She couldn't put her finger on it. A heaviness began rolling over her, a leaden ball growing and pounding against her heart."

Lucia closed her eyes and nodded.

Delphina paused as her mother swayed, and her lips kicked up.

When Lucia's eyes snapped open, wispy words fluttered from her mouth. "I'm picturing the scene. My daughter, your storytelling abilities never cease to amaze me."

"Oh, Mama, it all comes from you." Delphina smiled widened.

"I quote from the song you used to sing, when I couldn't sleep. You are my inspiration."

Lucia clapped and touched Delphina's face. "No, no. You've gone far beyond me. Now please continue.'"

Delphina dipped her head and pressed her hand to her forehead. "Lisa asked herself: What can I do? How do I rid myself of this burden? I'll begin journaling and ask the universe to provide an answer.'"

"Joaquin, what do you think? Lucia asked.

The driver shrugged his shoulders. "Not sure, Ma'am, but the story's got me curious."

Lucia turned to Delphina and winked. "See."

Delphina grinned. "Whatever you say, Mama."

Lucia curled her fingers at her. "Okay. No more interruptions. Continue."

"The universe didn't provide the answer. She'd examine the stars and ask, 'Why aren't you helping me?' They'd flicker, appearing to say, 'What do you want from us? We're here because of something greater than the universe.'"

Delphina shook her head back and forth.

"God, right?" Joaquin squealed.

"Yes, Joaquin, but wait until you hear the rest."

"Got it."

Delphina's voice became undulated from a whisper to a crescendo. "Now, even though Lisa's family baptized her and raised her Christian, she wandered away from God, like many in her generation. But one night—"

Lucia's hands drummed on the seat. *Thud-thud.*

"Lisa couldn't sleep. The heaviness spread to her soul, swallowing any glimmer of lightness." Delphina paused for a moment.

"She flipped back and forth, sat up, and took a sip of water from the cup on her nightstand. Out of nowhere, words scribbled along her sleepy mind: *Through God, all things are possible.*"

Lucia hugged herself. "Oh, my goodness. I'm getting the chills."

A whisper of a smile breezed across Delphina's lips. "Bringing her hands to her mouth, Lisa gasped, bounced out of bed, and looked out the window. The stars, twinkled, as if saying, 'Yes.' Wondering if she should turn back to an invisible God, Lisa kneeled, recited a prayer, and asked for inspiration."

Lucia's eyes widened, and the outside cars and trucks zipping by them, beeping and screeching, had no effect on Delphina's concentration.

Lucia clapped her hands, and mischief danced in her eyes. "And Joaquin, wait until you hear what happened next!"

Joaquin grunted, and Delphina glanced in the rearview mirror, capturing his crinkling eyes.

Delphina's smile expanded, and she pitched forward, opening her palms. "Lisa plopped into bed, folded her arms, and stared at the ceiling before somnolence invited her to drift off to sleep." Delphina's voice became wispy. "A deep, deep sleep where dreams slipped under the imagination's door."

"Yes." Lucia's fists shook up and down, jingling her bangles like a tambourine.

She loved her mother's zest when she shared her tales.

Her mother. Her Maestra.

No wonder she became a storyteller. Blame it on the mother. A smile flowered on her face, and she emitted a giggle.

"What's so funny?" Lucia's hands went to her hips, and with a smirk, she cocked her head.

"Oh, Mama. I thought about how you've mesmerized me with your stories for as long as I can remember, and I hope my abilities become half as good as yours."

"What do you mean?" Lucia's eyes narrowed, and she seized her daughter's wrists again. "You're far superior to me in all ways."

Delphina's eyes pooled. "Oh, Mama. You have a loving mother's bias."

Lucia shook her head. "No. Right, Joaquin?"

"I dunno, Ma'am, but if you say so."

With a sigh, Delphina's lips curved. "Okay. You win, so let me tell the rest of the story."

"I'll stay quiet until the end." Lucia's thumb and index finger zipped across her lips with a slight jangle from her bracelets.

Delphina's gaze became unfocused for a moment. "Let me think. Oh, yes, so she had a dream. It started with celestial beings circling around, dancing and looping, in an arrangement unlike any other Lisa ever saw. After the angels pulled away, a brilliant light appeared. Lisa had experienced nothing like it. A voice spoke, '*Through Him all things are possible.*' Just like the message that popped in her mind before going to sleep."

Delphina raised her arms.

"Ma'am, not to interrupt, but you have a knack for a good yarn."

She jotted a smile at the eyes, darting back and forth in the rear-view mirror.

Delphina leaned back and waved her arms up in the air. "The light retreated, the dancers returned with another unique display, before disappearing into a multi-colored pastel cloud. Lisa's eyes flashed open, and she bounced up, placing her feet on the floor, and turning her head to the window, catching the sun make its morning debut."

Lucia's hands steepled onto her chin as her green eyes sparkled, and gold strands waltzed through them.

My mother. I could give her a boring monologue, and she'd still view me as the best she's ever heard.

Turning her palms up again, Delphina's lips breezed into a smile. "So, what happened? Lisa opened her journal and wrote for an hour. Later that night, about to go to sleep, she brought her hands together and offered a promise. 'God, most high, if you lend me your talent, I'll sprinkle the earth with thanks through dance.' She fell asleep, and the dream exhibited the angel troupe performing another unusual dance. This continued for another three nights. On the last morning, Lisa called her mother, Amy, and shared everything that happened."

Lucia rubbed her hands together. "Yes, and the family supported her decision to develop *Heavenly Souls*. Correct?"

"Yes, correct. They agreed to help her even though everyone knew the risk, especially because of the religious sprinklings. But Lisa refused to do it any other way."

Her mother's head bobbed up and down.

"It took courage on her part. Don't you agree, Mama?"

Lucia blinked and nodded.

A pleasant hush danced into the vehicle even as the outside beeping and traffic grew louder. Delphina took a deep breath.

Wow. Telling the story helps me put aside some of my sadness.

"Darling?" Lucia's voice swirled through the quiet. "How about sharing Lisa's revelation about Christianity in China during the beginning centuries, A.D."

"You want me to retell that part again?"

"Yes, and…" Lucia raised her eyebrows, leaned forward, and said, "I think Joaquin might find this piece of information interesting. What do you think, Joaquin? Would you like to hear more?"

"Sure. Never thought about it."

Delphina puckered her lips. "Lisa added this in her introduction, to educate people about some of the earlier times where Christianity laid its footprint into China."

Joaquin's head shifted back and forth. "Keep going, 'cause I dunno any of this."

"Lisa's new embrace of Christianity prompted her to do some research, and she discovered that in the Xi'an Stele Forest rested an astounding, nine-foot artifact, referred to as the Luminous Faith, erected on January 7, 781 in the Tang imperial capital, now modern day Xi'an."

Joaquin's eyebrows knitted together. "Hmm."

Lucia's fingers curled on the middle section of the front seat. "You're liking this?"

"Ma'am, I'm learning something, and you're right. Your daughter has a way with words."

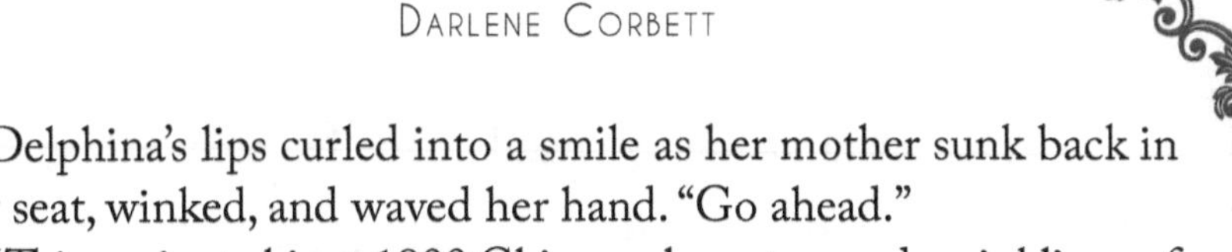

Delphina's lips curled into a smile as her mother sunk back in her seat, winked, and waved her hand. "Go ahead."

"This ancient object, 1900 Chinese characters and sprinklings of Syriac text, celebrated the first arrival of Christians in China who brought with them the 'luminous faith.' Yes, the Syriac text revealed *Allaha* and *Msbiba*, translated into English, God and Christ."

"Knew none of this," Joaquin said.

"Most people don't, which is the reason Lisa devoted one scene around this and explained it in her program."

"You never hear much about religion in modern China. So, what happened?"

"The emperor allowed Christian communities to thrive, but it changed in 845 with an emperor who extinguished all religions except Confucianism and Taoism."

"And that was that?" Joaquin's words trickled into the backseat.

"Based on Lisa's research, no. Jesuits arrived in the sixteenth century, and many people became Christians, both Catholic and Protestant. We hear little about it now, but like traditional Chinese dance, religion continues to exist in present-day China."

"And, Joaquin, we are going to see Lisa's celebration of Chinese classical dance displaying themes of Christianity." Lucia said.

"I think my wife would love it. She's a believer. I'm, 'meh,' but I go to church with her, anyway."

Delphina smiled at the eyes staring straight ahead. "Oh, Joaquin, once you go, you'll never want to miss because she changes it every year."

"And, Joaquin, maybe you'll become inspired."

Joaquin chuckled. "We'll see."

Lucia shifted her gaze to Delphina. "Like my daughter and me, whether it elevates your faith, Lisa's production will mesmerize you."

Delphina's eyes waltzed with her mother's. "Yes, and it takes an amazing dancer and choreographer like Lisa Ming to bring a production to such heights."

Lucia squeezed Delphina's hands. "She has storytelling skills like you."

"Mama, no comparison to Lisa's talent."

"*Humph.* That's according to you. On a smaller scale, you're just as grand." Lucia wagged her finger at Delphina. "Remember, you use yours for healing."

The lights began blinking, and Delphina fluttered her eyelashes, extinguishing her daydream.

Where is my mother?

She had turned on her phone for a few minutes to scroll through her emails. About to power it down, a text appeared from her mother.

> *Talking to a distraught client. I'll watch the rest from the back.*

Delphina shook her head. Even though her mother exclaimed she no longer performed psychotherapy duties in her role as matchmaker, Delphina knew better. Once a therapist, always a therapist.

She placed her phone back in her purse, leaned back, and sighed.

For the second half, Delphina's soul blazed.

More lustrous costumes with vibrant colors of rose, blue, and teal swirled around like a kaleidoscope. Old China's layered history mingled with Christian narratives.

Finely tuned dancers leaped, twisted, and danced in harmony as the apostles preached the good word.

Delphina's heart soared. She shook her head, clasped her hands, and the corners of her lips tilted up. She glanced at the empty aisle seat.

Oh Mama, I hope you aren't missing any of this.

Soon she became a dancer within the story, like reading an engrossing novel. Her jumpy nerves about her mother's whereabouts faded into the background.

Graceful movements, a flowing, gentle waterfall, erased the

passage of time. The bright light seared the stage as the conversion of Saul to the Apostle Paul dominated.

With the last act unfolding, someone rustled their coat and plopped into Lucia's seat. Delphina tilted her head. The individual placed their left, black-gloved hand on the armrest.

By the size of the appendage, a man or a bigger woman sat next to her. Delphina's eyes dipped to the side. A heavy black coat-like cape resembled her mother's, but more masculine. The leather boots laced tight revealed enormous feet. A familiar musky scent wafted to her nose.

Very male and Alexander-like.

Don't go there, Delphina.

The individual leaned closer to the left side of the seat, and Delphina scooted as close to the left side of hers.

A raspy voice whispered, "Did you know that classical Chinese dance aligns with the human body movements. And…" A gravelly voice whispered. "It leads to less extreme strain than ballet?"

Delphina turned her body and stared at the man. A wide-brimmed, inky-colored hat sloped over his face. He stroked a pencil-thin, black mustache.

Who does this guy think he is? Some kind of Zorro?

His head tipped toward her again. "And did you know about some travelers introducing Christianity in the early centuries of A.D.?"

She refused to look at him. "Sir, I'm trying to watch this, and you're sitting in… oh, forget it."

Delphina crossed her legs tight and hugged the left side of her seat even more.

The finale. Stunning.

Hope and renewal gleamed as the dancers looped their arms and swept around the Apostle Paul.

Sparkles and shimmering light caused *oohs* and *ahs*.

At the end, a thundering applause echoed through the chamber. Delphina sprang out of her seat, joining everyone else for a standing ovation.

Clapping her hands, Delphina tilted her head upward to a standing Zorro, now mustache-less. He dipped his head down, and a familiar lopsided smile painted his face. Delphina's eyes widened, and although words became trapped in her throat, her heart leaped.

Alexander brought his index finger to his lips, *shh*, before shifting his eyes back to the stage.

To stop trembling, Delphina kept her hands close together. Clapping with a light touch, she swallowed.

Am I hallucinating?

With a gaping mouth, she shifted her head like a marionette pulled by strings.

He tipped his hat and grinned. "You're not the only one, Storyteller, who can act out a tale." He wiggled his eyebrows.

Delphina giggled. "Okay, Zorro."

"And I did my homework about *Heavenly Bodies.*"

A million stars rained on Delphina's very being, as she took in the presence of Alex.

His voice trickled into her ear. "And, speaking of Zorro. Did you know Zorro was super intelligent and compassionate with a strong moral compass?"

Delphina's eyes pooled. With her gaze pushed forward, she shook her head.

"And he needs someone like him. Wouldn't you say?"

She turned toward him and nodded.

The applause dwindled, and chatter filled the vacuum. People began shuffling out of their seats.

Alexander sat down and grabbed Delphina's arm. "Sit with me for a moment, please." He removed his gloves and his hat, combing his fingers through his silver-streaked locks.

Delphina's body shivered as she sat in her seat. Trying to open the trapdoor, to allow more words, she shook her head. "I, uh, I need to let my…"

"Don't you worry about Lucia." Alex brought his face close to hers. "She knows all about it."

Delphina twisted her body to look back. Peeking through the crowd, she spotted her mother, beaming and waving at her.

She pivoted back in her seat and shook her head. "I feel like I'm in a dream."

"No dream, Taibhseach." Alex grasped her fingers. He released her hand and wiggled his fingers to the inside of his coat. "Ah." Keeping his hand hidden, his eyes grazed hers for a moment. He sighed. "Now, time to get serious. Please close your eyes."

Delphina skimmed the crowd for a moment and noticed a few people pointing at them.

Alex followed her gaze, and his knuckles brushed her cheek. "Let them stare."

"They think you're going to abduct me or something like that."

"Maybe I am, but right now…" Alex's eyes danced with hers. "Close those gorgeous eyes of yours."

Delphina's eyelids drifted down. The sounds changed. Through the talk of the moving crowd, a seat flipped up, and footsteps trekked toward them.

Shh. Talk dwindled. A few peeps. Then nothing.

A hand tapped her knee. "Open your eyes, Taibhseach."

Her heart thumped, and her eyelashes fluttered as if she awakened from a long slumber like Sleeping Beauty.

She opened her eyes to his, soft and caressing. Stooping in front of her, his face came so close to hers, she could see her reflection in sea-blue gems of wonder. For a moment, she turned her head, noticing a crowd around them.

"Look at me only." Alex touched her chin and laughed.

"Okay."

His fingers entwined hers, brought them to his face, pressing his lips to her wrist. She felt intoxicated, as if injected with a love potion.

Releasing her hand, he pulled from his coat a familiar aqua box, snapped it open, and plucked out a Marquis-style diamond ring. He kneeled, and with the band between his thumb and index finger, he stroked her cheek with his other hand.

"Delphina, my beautiful storyteller, my Taibhseach, will you marry me?"

"Yes, yes, yes."

He slipped the sparkling jewel on her finger. Tears flooded her eyes. Bouncing out of her seat, Delphina tumbled into his arms onto the floor toward the seat in front of them. She kissed his cheeks and breathed in his earthy scent until she found his lips. As their mouths came together, she savored the taste of Alex, a mix of peppermint and manliness.

"Yay!"

Delphina looked up, glanced back at Alex, as her mother stepped closer with tears streaming down her face. Clapping, whistling, and shouting came from the observers surrounding them. Soon the applause became louder and reverberated throughout the theater.

"Here I come to give you the biggest hug I can muster." Lucia's voice meandered closer.

Delphina turned to see her mother skipping down the stairs, and Alex stood up and took Delphina's hand to lift her.

Lucia entered the row and embraced them. "Oooh." She shifted and clutched Delphina. "My darling daughter. I'm so ecstatic."

Delphina narrowed her eyes and smirked. "Hmmm, Mama. I'd say you knew something about this?"

Lucia cocked her head toward Alex and brought her thumb and index finger together. "Maybe, a little."

She put her arms around them again, tucked her head down, and sobbed.

Delphina raised her head and found Alex's soft gaze sweeping over her.

The corners of her mouth tilted up, and staring at her beloved, her heart did the same.

Forgiveness and a second chance at love.

Did she deserve it?

As Alex caressed her eyes with his, no need to answer yes.

Chapter Twenty-Three

Six Months Later…
Alex

Alex tried not to inhale too much of the smoky scent, spouting from the swinging censer. He had experienced nothing like this until today, and his partaking in the sacred ceremony would remain his first and most memorable. As the incense swirled around them, he visualized a scene from Arabian Nights.

Yup, pal, nothing will ever hold a candle to this. Not only because of its novelty, but because of its royalty. A Holy Palace. One of many.

He looked up, and his eyes roamed over the ceiling. Gold and red dominated, with elaborate frescoes and mosaics. Saints and religious images displayed the influence of the Byzantine style of the Eastern Christian Church.

His laced fingers tightened around long silky ones, poking through a satiny, meshed covering. A squeeze, like a plush hug, rewarded him.

Trying not to cough from the powerful smoke, Alex sniffed before shifting his gaze to Delphina.

The matching crown to his sat on her chignon—a simple but sparkling headpiece.

Capturing her amber eyes that watered and gleamed like smoky topazes, his mouth embellished a smile to prevent his own waterworks from bursting forth.

As they circled the table with a Cross and the Gospel for the second time, Alex's heart soared to another level, as if he flew on eagle's wings.

Man, I knew nothing about this until Delphina. We exchanged rings and held hands. Then the Priest placed the crowns on our heads, and we sipped the wine. Now the Dance of Isaiah.

On Valentine's Day, at an intimate dinner in a small Italian restaurant in the North End, Alex sat with Delphina by the window, hands entwined. The unique eatery, around for fifty years, offered small, separate rooms, for privacy and romance. Hearts dangled from the ceiling of the dark but cozy atmosphere. An elegant marble fireplace held a comfortable blaze, and crackling logs spit intermittent embers to make its presence known.

Keeping his eyes on Delphina's face, Alex's lips dipped into the smooth skin of her hand and laid a sweeping kiss on it.

She closed her eyes for a moment. "Hmm."

Releasing their hands, electric sparks shot through Alex, and he smirked. "Coming attractions, my Scheherazade."

Delphina cocked her head, and her lips formed a subtle, enigmatic smile. Wispy words sprang from her throat with a scintillating tinge. "I can't wait."

With eyes locked on hers, Alex gulped on his wine, and she did the same.

He placed his goblet on the checkered tablecloth and dug into his Veal Scallopini. "Delicious. How about yours?"

Delphina raised her finger and nodded. Wiping her mouth, she placed the fork down. "Yes. One of the best Shrimp Scampi I ever tasted."

Alex cut his food, and about to take another bite, his eyes shifted to Delphina. With her hands in her lap, she gazed at her food and blinked.

"Everything okay, Taibhseach?"

She lifted her head and clasped her hands beneath her chin. "I want to ask you something, but I'm not sure," she tilted her head back and forth, "how you'll feel about it?"

Taking another sip of wine and placing it down, he laced his hands, then lifted his palms. "You know me by now. I'm open, within reason."

Delphina bobbed her head and inhaled. "Okay. You know how both of us want to have a traditional ceremony for our wedding?"

"Yup." Alex said, lacing his fingers again. "Are you still in agreement with that?"

Delphina knitted her eyebrows together. "Oh, you kidding? Of course. I don't want to follow that new trend of a barn wedding."

"Hey, now that you say it, I've heard a few buddies of mine say they're getting married in a barn with a J.P. for the day."

Delphina shrugged and lifted her eyebrows. "To each their own, but never for me. Nor my friends or my clients, but their friends. They're hearing no religious affiliation from church to officiating."

He grabbed her fingers again. "Call us old-fashioned."

"Because we are." They said at the same time.

Alex smiled at her, and sparkles coated in tenderness spiraled through his body. Releasing her fingers, Alex swallowed and folded his hands under his chin. "Now that we see how simpatico we are, tell me your idea, Storyteller."

Delphina giggled. "I must get used to the pseudonyms you have for me. Taibhseach, Storyteller, Sheherazade."

"The three fit you, depending on my mood, but while I finish my meal, I'll listen to your proposition."

Sealing her palms together, Delphina's eyes sparkled. "I think you might like the idea because we're traditionalists, and what could be more traditional than a Lebanese Christian wedding ceremony?"

Alex nodded, and his lips flirted with a smile. "Hmm. A Christian Scheherazade and now a Middle Eastern wedding ceremony. Who knew?"

Delphina tipped her head back, and a frothy laugh burbled from her throat. "Yes, and we don't know the accuracy of Scheherazade except her universal storytelling ability. Regarding Roman and Eastern Catholicism, the doctrine doesn't differ, but in the wedding ceremony, it's beyond magnificent, like having a frosted cake but with lots of piping."

The server, Victor, ambled over. "Sir and Miss, are you finished?"

Alex lifted his palm toward Delphina.

Delphina looked at her almost-empty plate. "Yes. Thank you, Victor. Beyond full."

"I guess it's a yes for both of us, Victor. As you can see…" Alex nudged his chin at the few scrapings left on his plate. "Delicious."

The bearded young man smiled at Alex, removed their plates and silverware onto the tray, and stood for a moment.

"Dessert? Coffee?"

Alex's eyes found Delphina's. "My lady?"

"How about something we can split?"

"Sounds good. What do you recommend tonight, Victor?"

"The ricotta cake seems popular."

"That and coffee for both of us."

Victor moved away from the table, and with his chin in his hand, Alex said, "Okay. No more interruptions, I hope."

Delphina beamed. "Let me tell you what happens. There are four parts, with the first being the *Betrothal Ceremony,* where we exchange rings, which isn't so different from a regular Catholic Church wedding. The same with the next step where we have the *Joining of Hands* section, where we join hands to symbolize our union."

Delphina's eyes widened. "So far, what do you think?"

"Yeah. Sounds good. I haven't been to many traditional weddings, but so far, this doesn't seem so different."

Her eyes lit up. "Wait. You haven't heard the best parts, which are also the unique."

Alex's heart warmed again as a dazzling ribbon surrounded it.

She electrifies me.

He nodded with a half-smile.

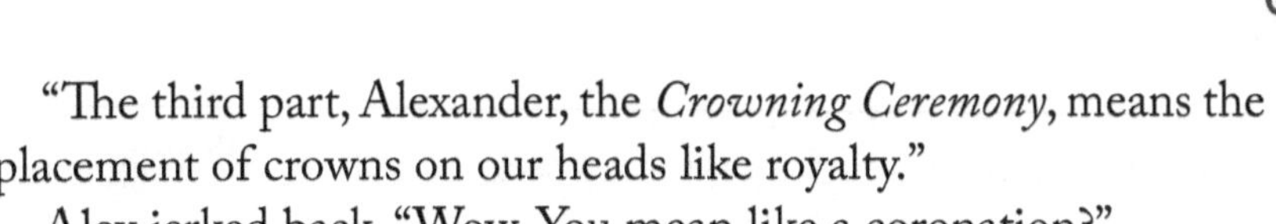

"The third part, Alexander, the *Crowning Ceremony*, means the placement of crowns on our heads like royalty."

Alex jerked back. "Wow. You mean like a coronation?"

Delphina smirked. "Not quite, but you feel like royalty." She tapped the table. "Let me finish."

Victor returned with two plates of sliced ricotta cake, a coffee pot, and cups. As he poured the steaming coffee into each cup, he asked, "Any cream or sugar?"

"No, thank you, Victor. We're all set."

Victor bowed and moved away.

As Alex lifted his cup, he nodded. "Whenever you're ready, Storyteller."

Delphina nibbled on a small piece of cake. "Hmm. Delicious." She took a sip of coffee, dabbed her mouth with her napkin, and laced her fingers. "Next, the *Sipping Blessed Wine* ritual, where we drink from the same goblet, and finally, the best part." Delphina balled her hands into fists and shook them up and down.

Alex rested his chin on the other hand, and his eyes grasped hers. "Storyteller, you continue to amaze me."

"Oh, Alexander, you know, the same here, but I must finish, or I'll fall into your eyes of ocean blue."

Alex nodded. "I'd love that, but for now, I'll eat while you talk."

Delphina grabbed his free hand for a moment. "Good. During the *Dance of Isaiah*, we hold hands and follow the Priest around a table three times."

"Still wearing the crowns?"

"Yes."

"This sounds romantic and sacred all in one. Traditional. Beautiful. But a couple of questions. First, what are the origins, which I assume involves the prophet, Isaiah?"

"Yes. Because Isaiah prophesied a Virgin would give birth to our Savior, thus, a special dance named in honor and celebration of him."

Alex nodded as he chewed on a bite of his cake.

"What's your second question?"

He lifted his index finger, took a swig of coffee, and rested the cup back on the saucer. "What's the meaning of walking around a table three times?"

"It symbolizes our first steps as a couple in the eyes of God, with the circular procession meaning eternity and lifelong commitment."

Alex's mouth dropped open for a moment.

Delphina shifted her face and peered at him. "What?"

He lifted his hands. "Wow, and knowing me, why would you think I wouldn't like it?"

Delphina flattened her palms on the table, thumbed her fingers, and her downward gaze became unfocused. A curl of stillness unfurled between them.

Give her a moment, Pal.

Her eyes tiptoed back to his and cracked words dripped from her throat. "Full transparency?"

Alex's chest crunched as if a reptile chomped on it, and his fingers drifted toward his scarred chin.

It must be about her ex.

Delphina blinked. "You look upset."

Alex dropped his hand, leaned forward, and threaded his fingers. "Not at you, but I know what you're going to say."

She nodded. "Yes. Jude."

The reptile took another bite. "Well. As you know, I'm not Jude."

Shaking her head, tears floated again in Delphina's eyes. "I know." She pounced on her napkin and dabbed her cheeks. "It's just that…" She swallowed. "Sometimes the old habits burrow through the strongest wall of trust."

The corners of his mouth couldn't resist their upward swing. "I understand." He grasped her hand. "Please tell me, so we can put the past to rest."

Delphina continued touching her eyes. "Well, I considered myself an independent thinker, but Jude had a way of convincinge me to follow his decisions." She sniffled and released her hand from his. "Grant you, he loved my taste and didn't control me around money, but…" Delphina leaned forward. "If he felt strong, he'd stroke my cheek, and say something like, 'Babe, come on. Look how much I've put aside for you,' with a lascivious grin or a wiggle of the eyebrows."

Squinting his eyes, Alex asked, "Do you mean what I think you mean?"

She closed her eyes for a split second and nodded. "Yes. You'd think I deprived him of food and water."

"So, he didn't understand restraint?"

"Oh, he did, but every so often, he'd stomp away from me. 'You don't know, Delphina….' Like I didn't have the same urges."

A fire ignited inside Alex, and he gritted his teeth. "As a healthy male with the same drive, this guy made it all about him."

Delphina took a deep breath. "Yes. I wasn't conceding, but he convinced me to go along with things which he couched as being in our best interests." She pursed her lips. "And although I'm feisty and held my stance on intimacy, I tolerated his domination on other things." Her gaze became unfocused. "I viewed it as—flexibility." She shook her head and reached for his hand again.

Threading her fingers with his, Alex brought them to his lips. "Listen, Taibhseach, you're not the only one. I told you about Daphne, almost marrying her because I thought the same thing. I'd often get frustrated but would wrestle with myself and decide to let it go."

She tilted her head, and her fingers tightened with his.

Another moment of quiet spilled into the space between them, with comfortable chatter, laughter and clanging from other tables surrounding but not permeating their entwined hush.

"Wha'cha thinking about, Storyteller?"

Squeezing their connected fingers, lacing their fates as one, Delphina calligraphed a dazzling smile. "I'm thinking about how alike we are. Easy-going, but not to the point of being push-overs."

"Yes. In the long run, we held onto our true selves." Alex's chest, now simmering from the blaze, remained a toasty warmth like an evening cup of hot cocoa.

Inhaling with a smile on her face, Delphina dropped her chin into her other hand. "I never thought I could be so comfortable with anyone like I am with you."

He raised his eyebrows. "Same here, Storyteller, and you know what? For a long time, I remained naïve, thinking most couples lived like that, based on my parents' marriage. Not perfect but good."

Delphina shook her head. "Well, even though my dad died, I watched some of my friends' parents, and they seemed comfortable with one another. But you don't always know. As I grew older, I realized the pretty picture didn't always reveal the truth lurking underneath. And as a therapist and now storyteller, I've heard from my millennial clients how their parents acted like they had a flawless marriage which wasn't always the case."

"Yeah. When I got to high school and then college, some of my new buds told me their parents were getting a divorce or had split earlier in their lives. I realized not everyone had a marriage like my parents." He lifted his eyebrows. "Let's be more like our parents. Authentic and communicative."

Delphina bent forward. "Alexander, my Taibhseach, we will."

"Have I ever told you I love the way you say my name?"

Moving her head from side to side, Delphina's other hand found their interlaced ones. Her fingers stroked their unity.

"All the time."

Alex's eyes became hooded, and a languid *shh* wisped through the room.

Man, this amazing woman. All mine, and soon, one in mind, body, and soul.

She fluttered her eyelashes. "My turn. What are you thinking about, Alexander?"

His gaze descended to their hands as he moved them back and forth, as if riding on a swing together.

Alex blinked and looked at her again. "I'm thinking about how lucky I am, and about our ability to talk about things. I hope that continues."

Delphina swallowed. "Alexander, I believe it will, and that you forgave…"

"Stop, Delphina. No more. You deserve me." Alex's lips teased a smile. "And if we have a fight, and I'm in the right, you'll have to woo me back with a story."

She giggled. "Deal. And you know what?" She released her other hand and raised theirs.

He shimmied their joined hands. "What?"

"If you're in the wrong, I expect you to share a story or two."

Her face glowed from the nearby fire, and he softened his lips. "I second the deal."

The incense tickled his nose, causing him to return to the present.

They finished the third circle and waited as the Priest gave a final blessing. "In the name of the Father, Son, and the Holy Spirit."

His eyes ascended to the balcony, where the musicians readied themselves to weave their magic.

A pianist swept her hands across the piano, signaling the final hymn, the Great Doxology. Chimes jingled, and the fingers of the harpist glided across the strings, like an offering to heaven.

Alex kissed Delphina's cheek, lifted his arm, and she looped hers through his. As they stepped down the aisle, with ribbons of white and purple flowing from the ends of the pews, Alex waved at his parents. His mother's tears streamed down her face, and his father curled his arm around her shoulder, winking at Alex.

Lights flashed, while clapping and hoots came from both sides. His eyes found Bart's, who raised his thumb and yelled, "Well done, Boy Scout." As Alex moved along, he could see in the corner of his eye, Bart bringing his fingers to his mouth. A piercing whistle traipsed behind him.

He and Delphina had discussed the number of attendants at

their wedding. As he thought, she wanted less than most and decided on a Maid of Honor only.

Fine with him. And no surprise to anyone that he chose his only brother and best friend, Nick.

Delphina struggled with whom to pick. Her two close friends were from different areas of her life. Instead of hurting anyone's feelings, she decided on her aunt, who resisted at first because she viewed herself as too old. But at the coaxing of Delphina and Lucia, Lydia said yes.

Like Lucia, Lydia had a unique beauty about her. He never understood why she didn't marry, or the reason Lucia chose not to remarry. Luck maybe? Who knew, but they still had lots of life in them, so maybe someday.

Right now, though, he focused on his bride and this special day.

Hands reached out and brushed across his jacket sleeve, injecting him with a potion of loving wishes.

Alex turned his head to his wife, and she squeezed his arm, sparkling like a flawless diamond.

Swinging her bouquet of white roses, purple delphiniums, and callas, a tinge of vanilla from the lilies breezed across Alex's nose, forever reminding him of his delicious bride. Delphina's eyes onto his, and in a sing-song voice, she said, "We did it, Alex."

A warm, frothy flow seeped through every cell in his body, and an expansive smile elaborated the joy deep within his soul. "We did, my Storyteller, we did."

Delphina

How did her mother manage this feat?

Delphina's head tipped back, gazing at the various crystal elephants, dogs, and camels dangling from the ceiling.

Her eyes shifted, scrutinizing the rest of the room.

Walled, floor to ceiling windows with periwinkle curtains tied back with crystal bows. An invitation to the outside scene of peachy and rosy dusk.

Her eyes descended to the heart-shaped tables clothed in pastels of pink, aqua, and yellow silk. Curving white metallic legs held everything together. Guests dressed in black-tie attire chatted away, finishing their meals of filet mignon or grilled salmon.

Centerpieces with flower arrangements of orchids, lavender roses, yellow peonies, and calla lilies, nestled within crystal elephants, dogs, or camels, crowned the table displays.

Servers wove in between, balancing trays carrying coffee and a variety of exotic cupcakes, including Pina Colada, Strawberry Daiquiri, and Cookie Dough.

Her gaze dipped down to the whitewashed hardwood floors peeking out between hand-knotted Oriental rugs of different sizes and delicate colors.

The harpist from the ceremony and a cellist strummed strings of soft music to the melodies of Mozart and Chopin. A different pianist from earlier joined them. Her fingers deftly breezed across the keys, reminding everyone that subtle notes whisper and serenade even in the background.

The Beautiful. A boutique hotel like no other.

The logo: Come and experience *The Beautiful.* You'll leave feeling just as beautiful.

A new hotel, taking on the persona of Cinderella's castle, huddled high on a hill, north of Boston. Overlooking the ocean, the place became wealthy New Englanders' sought-after venue for wedding receptions. Lucky for Lucia that one of her clients, ecstatic with her matchmaking services, offered his connections with the owners. And blocked out this Friday in July.

Delphina's lips curved up as she thought about her mother's determination to give her the best. She sighed.

"What'cha thinking about Storyteller?"

Delphina turned her head, moved her face closer, and stared into the ocean-colored eyes, luring her to dive into them.

"How I'm living a fairytale come…"

The guests became louder, and forks ticked glasses.

Clink, clink, clink.

"Kiss, come on, you two."

"Umm. Let's give them a show."

Delphina's heart pranced. "Let's." She leaned into him, his lips locked with hers, and their arms looped together, an infinity symbol of eternal love.

Unsealing their lips in slow motion, Alex rubbed his nose along hers before caressing her cheek. A tingle pulsated through her body.

Cheers and whoops crammed the room.

Delphina shifted her gaze from her husband and blew a kiss at the lively attendees.

Alex stood and bowed, his hand resting on his belly. Delphina's eyes crawled up her husband's torso and reached his profile, as her soul soared like the highest notes from a violinist's strings. His dancing eyes found hers, and extending his arms, he directed his upward palms toward her.

Whistles screeched through the room with more thundering applause.

Delphina's fingers laced with Alex's as he pulled her up, and rising, she pinched both sides of her wedding gown and curtsied.

As they stood, Delphina's eyes skidded across the smiling faces and landed on Josie, her bestie from graduate school and fellow Christian yogi. Next to her sat her old bestie from childhood. Reunion. Who thought it could happen?

Her mind flipped the pages to earlier this year.

New Year's Eve morning, a knock at her townhouse. Delphina peeked at her Ring app. A UPS signatory truck sat outside with a worker dressed in the symbolic brown uniform pacing back and forth.

Delphina opened the door to a young, lanky, pony-haired man.

"Miss, I need a signature."

"Sure." Delphina took the proffered pen and scribbled her name. He handed her a UPS express envelope and stepped away.

"Thank you. Happy New Year."

The worker turned around and smirked. "You too, miss. My shift ends at three. Party time." And he jogged toward the truck.

As Delphina closed the door, she studied the express package, tore off the top, and pulled out another envelope, edged with blotted colors of turquoise, purple, and rose.

A floral aroma wafted from it and seeped deep into her olfactory glands.

Tanya.

Her familiar cursive dominated the front.

Delphina's name sprawled across the center with a line.

For a moment, she stared at it, before plodding over to her desk. She sat down on her high-back ergonomic chair, retrieved the elongated letter opener, a gift from a client, and slit the top of the envelope.

She pulled out the stationery, shut her eyes for a moment, and opened the creased letter that revealed the same majestic colors.

Dear Delphina,

Where do I begin?

You've been in my thoughts forever, and so many times, I wanted to reach out and tell you how much I wronged you. My cousin, I realized, was as narcissistic as your ex, and about six months after terminating our friendship, I distanced myself from her. I love my aunt and didn't want to cause my mother pain or interfere in their close relationship, but my mother confided in me she understood Margo's self-centeredness and saw me suffering from the loss of our connection.

Until now, I couldn't write. On Christmas, I prayed and concluded: What do I have to lose, so here I am.

I don't know if you'll ever forgive me, but just know, I'll never find a bestie like you.

No matter what happens, Delphina, know that I'm rooting for you and hope you have found true love. You deserve it.
Love always your past BFF,
Tanya

A sugary lightness spread through every fiber of her being. Delphina grabbed her phone and texted her right away.

```
Got your letter. Thank you. Let's
get together.
```

Within seconds, her phone pinged. And that became another new beginning. Another second chance.

Alex squeezed her hand, she returned to the present. Sitting down, his lips brushed hers again.

A few more people shouted, "Yeah!"

Alex cocked an eyebrow at her and turned to the crowd. "Enjoy, but that's it for now. The rest? Between me and my gorgeous bride."

A few moans.

Delphina tilted her head back, and laughter bubbled from her throat.

"So, you never finished telling me about what's happening within your beautiful head."

Delphina exaggerated a pout. "What about the rest of me?" She touched her knotted pearl and silver diadem headpiece. Then her fingerless, gloved hands swept down her cream-colored, chiffon sleeveless gown, accented with motif lace, and mother-of-pearl buttons down the middle of her torso, matching those gliding down her back.

Alex leaned forward and whispered, "Are you kidding, Taibhseach? Haven't I told you? And wait until later."

Rising again, his fingers clasped the champagne flute. "Esteemed guests, may I have your attention?"

Delphina looked up, and Alex's eyes caressed hers before turning his gaze.

The chatter and clatter simmered down, and a warm hush enveloped the room, as the attendees stared back.

"I don't want to overdo it, but I can't help myself."

Chuckles reverberated.

A familiar voice shouted, "Hey, Boy Scout, it's your day. Why not?"

Alex jutted his chin to Bart and saluted. "Thanks, Boy Scout."

He glanced at Delphina and winked.

"So, most of you know, my bride tells stories, and doesn't each of us have a story?"

Nods. Yeses. Smiles.

Delphina nestled her chin in her hand, the froth bubbling throughout her cells. Her eyes skimmed Alexander, taking in the silvery streaks woven within his darker gray mane. His monochromatic attire, a slate-colored tux, vest, and shirt topped with a bowtie embroidered with elephants heightened his arresting looks.

How lucky am I?

What a class act. The real thing. And not too shabby on the eyes.

"If you don't know, and I won't get into the specifics, my bride's ability to spin a wonderful tale bewitched me to the point of no return."

Alex reached for her hand. "So, my suggestion to all of you: Regale each other with stories. Share them with your children." He dipped his head toward her again, brushed his eyes across hers, and returned his gaze to the guests. "Add a touch of humor, and you will mesmerize them forever. Stories embed in our brain cells, right?"

Heads nodded. A few hollered, "Yes."

Delphina's gaze sailed over the crowd and landed on her mother. Lucia wore a fitted crimson sleeveless silk gown, with a matching ascot fascinator over her long, silver hair. Bracelets jingled on one hand as she waved to Delphina, while her other hand dabbed at tear-stained cheeks.

"Now, I'd like to make a toast." He pivoted toward Delphina.

"To my bride. A storyteller like no other. A beauty inside and out." Swiveling back to his guests, he raised his flute.

A blanket of shimmery joy swathed her. She hugged her arms and lifted her head toward Alex. When he glanced back at her, their eyes latched for a moment, a magnetic pull melding them into one.

The guests lifted their glasses and said, "Hear, hear." They sipped in unison and applauded again. Alex sat back down.

Delphina inclined her head, and her breath grazed his ear, immersing herself in his musky scent. "You're mine now. Every bit of you."

His lopsided smile sprawled across his face, enhancing the sparkle of his sea-colored eyes, like sunlight waltzing on the crests of ocean waves.

Delphina shifted her gaze. The small ensemble of musicians departed, drifting out of the room without making a peep, opposite from the booming arrival of the Middle Eastern Band.

An olive-skinned, white-haired gentleman, dressed in a black tux, stood adjusting the microphone as the other men set up their instruments. He placed his fingers on the grille of the capsule.

Thump, thump.

Everyone stopped.

"I see I got your attention," said the man with a thick accent.

He bowed. "Amir, here, at your service." Pivoting, he swept his hands toward the five other musicians. "In a moment, I'll introduce my talented brothers and the unique instruments they play, but first…" Amir swung his arms open wide. "Keific."

Lucia stood and clapped, "Keific, Amir. Everyone, Keific means how are you?"

Spinning around, she said, "If you haven't experienced the exhilaration of a Middle Eastern band, you're in for a treat." She blew a kiss at Amir.

He slanted his head to her. "Thank you, beautiful Lucia. Now, let me introduce my talented partners in music before I describe my instrument, the Oud."

Amir waved his arm. "First, Emile, who will give a taste of the Ney."

Emile, a bearded gentleman of about fifty, waved. He lifted a long, thin wooden flute-like instrument, tilted it, and brought it to his lips.

For several seconds, a breezy, mystical *whoosh* echoed throughout the room. As the pitch became higher, it created a siren-like lamentation.

Delphina glanced at Alexander. Rubbing his chin, he turned and grabbed her hand. She shut her eyes, taking in the haunting music emitted from the modern version of a very ancient instrument.

Doum, Tak, Jingle, Jingle

Delphina's eyes popped open. A man danced along the front of the band, creating intricate steps, shaking his tambourine-type instrument, and twirling. The guests clapped to the rhythm of his movement. A younger version of Amir, the dark-haired man's eyes snapped, and his rosebud lips blossomed into a wide smile as he bowed.

"Our baby brother, Michel." Amir chuckled into the microphone. "He likes to give you a taste of the evening's delight. And his instrument…" Amir rolled his tongue, "the Riq."

Amir pivoted toward the band and pointed to a mustached man, similar in age, tapping on a drum.

Thrum, thrum, thrum.

"My twin, Elie, creating magic on the Darbuka," Amir boomed. The man beat harder on the instrument for several seconds, before standing, whirling his hand, and bowing.

As Amir continued introducing two of his other brothers and their devices, Delphina's gaze shifted toward a single figure making his way toward Alexander's parents. His father stood, shook his hand, and grasped his other arm. The gentleman, a tall, broad-shouldered man, with steel-gray hair threaded with white streaks, bent down and kissed Alex's mother's cheek.

"Who's that, Taibhseach?"

Alex turned his head away from the violinist, whose bow, gliding across his instrument, released high notes like the splendor erupting from a soprano's ascending voice.

"Mr. Peter LaFlamme. Do you know who he is?"

Delphina pursed her lips. "Hmm. Sounds familiar but not sure why?"

Alex nudged his head toward Lucia. "I bet Lucia would know." He returned his eyes to hers. "Now, any ideas?"

"Hockey?"

"You got it."

A tuxedo-clad Peter LaFlamme bounded toward them. Glorious greenish-hazel eyes dominated his face, and his crown of iron-gray hair grazed the back of his collar. A wide mouth blossomed into a smile of pearly-whites, and the magnificent mark of a cleft chin, added to a painted, almost perfect symmetry.

Alex bolted out of his seat and bent forward. Peter put his arms out. "Alex, so glad I could make it." As his arms surrounded her husband, his dark chartreuse eyes, crinkling with a smile, found hers. He released Alex, and his eyes danced at both.

"Please introduce me to your stunning bride."

"Peter, meet my beautiful Delphina."

Peter bowed, took her hand, and kissed the top. "My pleasure."

Delphina remained in her seat. "Thank you for coming, Peter."

"I wouldn't have missed it for the world, but a delayed flight interrupted my promptness. I couldn't wait for the ceremony, which someone told me involved crowns."

Delphina nodded. "Yes, a traditional ritual for Syrian Orthodox and Eastern-rite Catholics."

Peter shook his head, and his smile collapsed from his face. "So annoyed I missed it. Years ago, I attended a ceremony with my former wife and witnessed the grandeur of such a display. It seared in my mind."

"Hey, Peter, not the same, but we'll invite you over to see the recording, once the videographer edits it."

"Great."

Peter pivoted his body toward the guests and the band. "Wow. You also bought a Middle Eastern band. Great." His gaze skidded over the crowd and reached Lucia, lingering for several seconds.

"Looks like a lively group."

As if reading her mind, with Peter's eyes glued to Lucia, Alex slanted his face toward hers. "Yes, Delphina's mother, the striking woman in red, created this fairytale for us."

Without turning back, Peter nodded. "Quite the magical show." He spun around. "Should I assume she has a Middle Eastern background?"

For a moment, Delphina's heart ached. Her mother sacrificed so much for her.

"Yes. Middle Eastern blood comes from both my parents. My mother is Syrian, and my father, from what little we know, Iranian."

Why stop? Let him know more about Mama.

"My father came to the United States on a business trip and fell in love with my mother. They eloped, and before I came into the world, he vanished on a visit to Iran. My mother did everything she could to gather information about his disappearance but received no cooperation from the Iranian government."

Delphina gulped. "My father's presence surrounds us. Some might see it as a fantasy." She glanced at Alex and grabbed his hand. "But I don't."

Peter cleared his throat. "Well, from everything I've heard, your mother raised a remarkable woman."

Warmth puckered throughout her insides like cookies rising on a baking sheet.

"My mother loves…"

Amir strummed the Oud, signaling the musicians to join him.

"Come, everyone and dance the Dabke."

"I love this dance. If you don't mind…" Peter said, moving toward the dance floor.

"Of course not, Peter. We're right behind you."

Alex laced his fingers with Delphina's. "Shall we?"

She brought their hands to her cheek. "Yes, you'll now get another taste of Middle Eastern culture."

As they stood, Alex leaned into Delphina, brushing his lips across her ear. "Hey, what happened with you sharing so much about your mother with Peter?"

Delphina tilted her head. "My love, you and I couldn't miss Peter's focus on my mother. I want good for her, so maybe someone could melt her icy resistance." She wiggled her eyebrows at him. "Like an ex-hockey player taking his stick and cracking it?"

As they strode to the dance floor, Alex nodded and chuckled. "Good one, storyteller. I've never talked much about Peter, but he's an amazing guy who's endured some painful tumbles himself." Alex lifted his brows. "And not exclusive to the ice. Will tell you more later, but I thought you said Lucia wants nothing to do with dating."

Delphina grinned. "For years, when I brought it up, she'd say, 'Shush, you. I found love long ago. Taking care of you and helping others remain my purpose in this life.' But now she sees I've found love with the best of the best…"

"Ah, Taibhseach…" He shook his head. "Not sure about that, but I'll give it my best. How about that?"

Delphina tossed her head back and laughed. "Me too, but getting back to my mother, maybe she'll open herself to the possibilities. You know. The very thing she advocates for others. A second chance at love?"

Alex and Delphina stepped into the circle. "If anyone could change her mind, Peter's the man. A total straight-shooter, generous, and believer that his talent came from God with lots of arduous work to augment it."

The band's musicians played their instruments in a tapestry of woven synchronicity. Guests linked hands, snaking their way around the room in rhythmic harmony, stomping their feet every few beats.

Lucia and Lydia shouted, "Yalla, Yalla, Yalla." Others echoed them, pleasure splashing across their faces. Some chanted "Ah. Aiwa." As the enchantment swirled through the room, many of her mother's friends yelled. "Heey, Heey, Heey."

Alex squeezed Delphina's hand. "What a blast, Storyteller. A tradition we'll share with our children."

Delphina's ecstasy barometer rose off the charts. "Yes." As she allowed rainbow colors to flow within her, her eyes skimmed the guests, and she caught Peter dancing across from her, his gaze focused on Lucia.

Delphina bent forward to see her mother a few places down from her right. Laughing and stomping her feet, Lucia twirled toward the center of the circle. Her satin gown, a shimmering rainfall of crimson liquid, lifted and twirled, revealing a subtle front slit.

Lucia raised her arms, clicked finger cymbals on her thumbs and middle fingers, twirled, and rotated her hips.

Releasing Alex's hand, Delphina clapped, and hooted. The guests stopped and did the same. More cheers. "Yalla, Yalla."

She leaned into Alex, laughing.

Click, click, click.

Lucia's finger movements harmonized with her steps.

As she whirled one way and winked at Delphina, Peter meandered towards her, causing Lucia to freeze for a moment before resuming her steps. With arms up, she circled around Peter, whose athletic prowess permeated his dancing abilities. The oud, violin, rig, and the qanun laced together, embroidered an even more sumptuous tapestry of music.

Catching her mother's eye, Delphina winked. Lucia's eyebrows lifted, before twisting again and breezing along with the unexpected partner.

Delphina took a deep breath. Second chances. Her love, Alex, and her best friend, Tanya.

Will God extend that to her mother? How about her aunt? Her eyes lifted, and she offered a silent prayer of thanks and hope for her happiness to extend to Lucia and Lydia.

"What's going on in that pretty head of yours, Storyteller?" Alex asked, his voice tiptoeing into her ear.

Delphina lifted her head, and with her eyes dipping into his ocean waves, she sighed.

No words formed, unable to describe the resplendence gushing through her. Delphina's lips curled up, and she shook her head. Alex nodded and wrapped his arms around her.

A cocoon for the moment, but soon, two butterflies joined, flapping their wings and navigating the topsy-turvy world of life, for the rest of their lives.

What an amazing story they'll write. And the title?

The Book of Us.

Darlene Corbett

Darlene Corbett views herself as a lifelong learner, a pursuer of excellence, a work-in-progress, and a seeker-of-the-truth. For over thirty years, as a licensed therapist, she has helped people get unstuck.

Darlene began putting her thoughts on paper in 2011 and hasn't stopped. Her blogs can be found on such sites as Sixty and Me, BizCatalyst360, and at DarleneCorbett.com. These articles set the stage for her first book, *Stop Depriving The World of You*, published by Sound Wisdom.

Throughout her career, adjectives used to describe Darlene include, animated and effervescent, which tends to contradict the common perception of a psychotherapist.

Darlene lives in central Massachusetts with her beloved Shih Tzu, Churchill.

Mesmerize is her second novel.

Thank you to my editor extraordinaire, Shanda Perkins, and Maestro Publisher, Mike Parker. You're the best. I'm so grateful God led me to you.

WordCrafts Press

A Song I Heard the Ocean Song
by Laura Mansfield

Land that I Love
by Gail Kittleson

Paint Me Fearless
by Hallie Lee

This Isn't Shakespeare
by Stephanie Cardel

You've Got It, Baby!
by Mike Carmichael

www.WordCrafts.net